Collected Stories of Gwyn Jones

Collected Stories
of
Gwyn Jones

~

UNIVERSITY OF WALES PRESS
CARDIFF
1998

British Library Cataloguing-in-Publication Data.
A catalogue record for this book is available from the British Library.

ISBN 0-7083-1457-0

**Published with the financial support of
the Arts Council of Wales and the Rhys Davies Trust**

Typeset at the University of Wales Press
Printed in Great Britain by Gwasg Dinefwr, Llandybïe

Contents

Introduction (from *Selected Short Stories*, 1974)   1

From *The Buttercup Field* (1945)

The Pit   7
The Buttercup Field   28
A Man after God's Own Heart   38
All We Like Sheep   44
Kittens   50
Shacki Thomas   58
Ora Pro Boscis   65
The Dreamers   73
A Night at Galon-Uchaf   82
Gwydion Mathrafal   91
The Passionate People   101
Their Bonds are Loosed from Above   111
Take Us the Little Foxes   120

From *The Still Waters* (1948)

The Green Island   131
The Still Waters   188
Bad Blood   194
Shining Morn   198
A White Birthday   202
Four in a Valley   207
The Prisoners   214
Down in the Forest Something Stirred   237
Guto Fewel   247
Goronwy's House of Gold   258

From *Shepherd's Hey* (1953)

Shepherd's Hey	268
The Brute Creation	299
Old Age	307
Copy	317
All on a Summer's Day	328
Two Women	337
A Death on Sistersland	363

Publishers' note

The spelling and punctuation conventions used in the original printed versions have largely been maintained but have been standardized within this volume.

Introduction
(from *Selected Short Stories*, 1974)

~

EVERYTHING an author writes is part of an autobiography, by his own hand taken down, and may be used in evidence against him. But which autobiography? For in the nature of things he has two, just as he has two lives, one factual, the other fictive, the first communicable to his public (assuming he has one), the confined circle of his acquaintance, or his private audience of one, the second a very withdrawn affair indeed, not fully intelligible even to himself. His factual, or external, record of verifiable events and dated publications does not take us very far, for if we expect birth, without which he is nothing, and death, with which he is nothing, verifiable events are not all that important in an author's work. It is his transformations, even deformations, of events, situations, persons, which are important. Whether what he writes about ever happened, to himself or another, matters only if he chooses to make it matter, and then only so long as his reader can be made to believe over an appropriate period of time that it could likewise happen to him. In a context of the creative arts truth is hard to define, and fact not much better. Apart from an ability to read, the main requirement for the acceptance and enjoyment of so fantastic a commodity as narrative fiction is faith.

This applies to its writer too. When William Blake at the age of four saw God put his head in at the window, he had an experience which even agnostics must envy. Lesser men have humbler illusions; but two childhood memories of my own, of being lost on a mountain at the age of two, and of being caught in the reverberations of a pit explosion at the age of six, though in large measure self-engendered and in their details fictitious, have seemed part of my life's truth ever since. The desolate overtones of the one fortify my belief that men and women are congenitally loseable and self-destructive, so that from time to time they lodge themselves in narrowing tunnels of doubt, fear, and aloneness, from which in life they must be rescued, though in fiction they

1

may press to the dead end. The sombre burden of the other has helped keep me on a particular course of human sympathies, and in story-telling gave me fixations on darkness underground as an ultimate horror, and fire anywhere as our most fearsome destroyer. Also, both memories are rooted in my natal soil, and pre-figure those pastoral-industrial or pastoral-paradisal settings in which my stories have always chosen to locate themselves.

These compulsive imaginings, only tenuously linked to fact, and necessarily re-shaping and transcending it, do not, if we are lucky, cease with our childhood. We could not be authors, artists of any kind, if they did. They are part of that fictive life which is more important to the author as author than the daily recitative of trains caught, opportunities missed, and the rise and fall of a bank-balance. I am speaking, need I say, of imaginings of a longer haul and deeper reach than the transient day-dreams that make men groan and dogs whimper. Powerful fictions, if they move us, and noble feignings, if they free us, once we trust to them, and sustain them, and augment them, will prove decisive influences on our thought and feeling, and so on what as creators we are and do.

The fictive like the factual life finds room for more mundane items than the presages and afterglows of imagination and memory. Every writer of fiction is by definition a born thief, and proud of it, his eyes and ears agape on acquisition. One reads that even so assured and prolific a short-story writer as Maupassant had a standing tariff for anyone who would give, lend, or sell him an anecdote or theme. To illustrate great things by small, my 'Ora Pro Boscis' started life as someone else's yarn, orally delivered, about a deservedly much-decayed South Wales county family. I supplied the noses and the law. 'All We Like Sheep' was vouched for as true by the friend who told it me, and since I would put nothing past those impassioned and gesticulating music-masters who control the ocean-swells and avalanches of three-valley chapel *Messiahs*, I believed him, and still do. 'Guto Fewel' was a present from the poet Huw Menai, an enigmatic reminiscence of how a young married woman in the Rhondda, entirely respectable and a friend of the family, dropped her many-petalled calyx of camphorized petticoats over his darkling infant head, for reasons never stated. He thought it bad for the boy but good for the poet. I judged it would have destroyed me, and in the hope, maybe, that it yet might, he made me free of it. I add that poor wasted Guto is not to be confused in any detail with the sparse ascetic Huw, and that the rest of the story is invention.

But what do we mean by invention? Certainly not a digging down into unknown, unused, virgin seams of story, for there aren't any. Years ago, in Greenland, which ought to be far enough off, heaven knows, for some discreet, unobservable literary light-fingering, I heard the story of a storm-beset hunter forced to take shelter alongside the altar of a deserted chapel. The first night he was joined there by a he-bear, and shot it, gladly. The second night he was joined by a she-bear, and shot it, troubledly. The third night he was joined by a young bear, their offspring. I cried out, 'No. Don't go on!' and left the hut, to my friends' consternation. Surely I didn't carry my declared aversion to the needless destruction of life to this length! Nor did I. But the whole story – *my* whole story – had burst open in my chest. Chapel, altar, Father, Mother, Son, Man the Destroyer – myth, legend, wondertale – the human and the brute creation – never, I thought, was there a story so made for me. The fate of the third bear, that of the hunter, these I must work out in my own way. That same evening a kindly young Dane offered me a paperback, saying, 'Perhaps you would like to read it by yourself?' Alas, I should have known all along that it would be in print, for the unanswerable authority which assures us that to every thing there is a season, and a time to every purpose under the heaven, does so only after informing us that there is nothing new under the sun, and no novelty on the face of the earth.

In any case, those bears were not for me. The fictive life has its limits. I doubt that I could ever think myself into a bear or a hunter of bears. To write about something you have to identify with it, and you can't identify with what you don't know. Probably it is this knowledge and identification which constitutes an author's truth, so it is important for him to realize where they will most readily be found. With most there is no problem. It is a miracle that men write at all, but granted that they do, the growing-ground of their fictions is easily discoverable. Literature exists in a context, not a vacuum, and that context tends to be the scene of our nurture. In every act of creation, physical, mental, or spiritual, whatever else we do, we explore and extend ourselves according to our perceptions and powers. Genius has its private boundaries and the capacity to break through them, and literature has never lacked far-questers and exotics, but for the most part, what men are, what they know, what they feel, grows from a place or region. This can be provincial (in the literal not pejorative sense), metropolitan, or in respect of some nations national. For me, it seems unnecessary to add, this means Wales, and therein South Wales, and still more narrowly the mining valleys of Gwent and Glamorgan on the one hand, and the thirty-mile central arc of Cardigan Bay and its hinterland on the other.

Regionalism of this high and honourable definition has a status as estimable as any other form of writing, and has been a main feature of the European and American literary tradition. For his region – it can be as small as Eire, Calabria, or Berlin, or huge as the Deep South of America – the regional writer will feel an inescapable though not necessarily an exclusive attachment. He will understand its people, as no outsider will ever understand them, and be driven to act out that understanding in words: their character, personality and traditions, patterns of behaviour and impulses to action; what they believe in, their hopes and fears, bonds and severances; their relationship to each other, to the landscape around them, and the creatures they share it with. He will be closely instructed in what Hardy calls 'the seasons in their moods, morning and evening, night and noon, winds in their different tempers, trees, waters and mists, shades and silences, and the voices of inanimate things.' Of all this he will say, 'This, these, are what I have!' If his gifts are modest but genuine, his following will be small but appreciative; if he is a Hardy, Joyce, or Faulkner, by virtue of what his region has given him he will be heard with reverence throughout the world.

This is not intended as an inflated claim for regionalism, which doesn't need it anyway. It means no more than that an author's subject matter chooses him just as much as he chooses it; and that many authors find a particular compulsion and virtue in the subject matter of that region of earth they believe to be uniquely theirs. There is no question of being dictated to by your region. You can always produce a South Wales mining valley of your own – so long as you were born in one. River, railway, road on their thin ledges, snaky chains of houses, the dramatic alternation of pit and ferny hillside, the people as they are, and still more as they were – for inevitably as you seek to produce or invent you find yourself reproducing and re-ordering the reality you know, the suddenly remembered dawn voices of men, a joyous neighing of strike-freed pit-ponies kicking at the river, the dragging crack of iron-shod boots as the men on afternoons tramp homeward for supper. Equally, you can always produce your own West Wales cwm – provided you've lived there a decade or two: the narrow roadway, gorsebloom headland, drift of sheep on the hillside inland, soft blue slumber of the summer sea, noontide swoon of islands. And animals – no need to invent those. Or the people, recurrent Adam on the green land, silent, watchful, enduring, carrying you and me and the whole world on his back; and the recurrent woman, Lilith or strong Eve, blackberry-haired, foxglove-tongued, sleek in her smooth black dress as a seal in water. No need to invent those either. Recall, let them move, and they live. Not necessarily as they did, or do; but as they might, and as you and their fates would now have them.

With this we reach the highest privilege of the fictive life. The writer of stories can play God to his creation. How we can prove intellectually or by ratiocination that there is a moral order in the world, that the universe has significance, and life a meaning, I don't know. Yet most of us start off with these assumptions or struggle to acquire them, if only because their denial is so bleak and deathly. How happy then the writer of fiction, that he can impose order and pattern, law and sanction, meaning and significance, on the private creation which circumstance forever tempts him to make public. Remembering always that God makes mistakes, that Eden was marred, and that Adam and Eve and Pinch-Me show the wounds of that marring.

GWYN JONES

The Pit

~

A KERMAN came by the pits just after eight o'clock. There were four of them, and near each a high bank of rock discarded from the ore. These were now thinly grown with silver birches, feathered with young ferns, starred with saxifrage and wild strawberry flowers. The stones were about a foot to eighteen inches wide and thick, many of them embedded in livid moss, and those lying loose nearer the pit edge handsomely weathered. The first pit and the fourth coming from Coed-y-Mister had, said the countryside, been sunk in Roman times to meet the level running in under the hill at the Ystrad, and had been worked off and on through fifteen hundred years. The two middle ones had been cut through the rock by Lewis Tywern the ironmaster in Chartist times, had made him a wealthy miser, and had been abandoned as it grew difficult and expensive to fetch the ore out by basket from the pits or by tram through the level. Around two pits, one Roman, one Lewis Tywern's, there still hung from rotten posts the last rust-riddled strands of wires; the other two were open to the hillside, twenty yards from the disused path. In this path, which led from the Roman Steps to the ruined farmhouse of Coed-y-Mister, there were still visible beautifully smoothed stones grooved by the wire that had pulled the full trams to the shoots above the Ystrad. Because there was no fencing, occasionally a sheep went over and, once only, a dog. The largest pit of all, the one Akerman had visited three or four times, had claimed a child, but that was in the days when it was still being worked.

He went to the edge. From the curtain of trees opposite he heard the complaining of birds at his presence, and smiled. The pit was roughly circular, some eighty feet across. For three parts of its round it went steeply over smooth bluffs of ruddy stone mottled with moss, very warm looking in the apricot coloured light. In four places a tree went out from where its roots knitted frantically into a crevice, and there were tufts of greenery twenty or thirty feet

7

down. On the fourth side there was a convex slope covered with last year's leaves, and then a drop to a ledge that he could just distinguish in the brown darkness which always filled the shaft. Carefully he stretched himself on the grass and worked forward till his face was clear of obstruction. Nothing to see. For as the setting sun slipped from the brow of the hill, it cast solid-seeming shadows into its heart.

Then he shouted. He had barely times to hear his voice die feebly in the pit when with a frantic squawking a flock of jackdaws broke raggedly from the trees where they had been watching him and made uneven flight over the chasm. They wheeled and came back to the trees, but half of them, uneasy still, went off a second time with a loud clapping of wings and much jabber. Getting to his feet, Akerman shouted again just as they settled, whereon out they poured in full flock like a devil's chorus screaming across the pit, so that a ewe with two lambs to Akerman's right ran off all huddled. They swarmed up over his head, cursing and jeering, with a hundred insults telling him to take himself off. 'All right,' he called to them; 'but I'll be back to-morrow. I'm going down that pit.' He grinned, reading meanings into their cries. A reprobate with a hanging feather banked within a yard of his face. 'Don't worry,' he said, 'I'm going.' The last he heard of them as he set off towards the steps was a tetchy interchange of suspicion and one commanding squall. Hang-Feather was making a speech.

The Roman Steps led from the mouth of the level at the Ystrad to the ancient earthwork at Castell Coch. Much of it above the point where he joined the way was grass-grown, but in places he could see the series of wide flat steps at the sharper ascents, and there were ten-yard stretches of curbing on the model of the Roman roads he had seen in southern Italy. No chariots could have come this way, though; the iron ore must have been slave-carried in baskets. 'Seen a bit of misery in its time,' he reckoned, wagging his head.

He reached Castell Coch in twenty minutes. The stone house in which he was staying had been built within the earthwork itself. Castell Coch: Red Castle – in the evening one saw why it bore its name. The sun was just sinking behind Moel Wen. Here on the hill top the light was a lovely soft gold, and the stone outcrop seemed flushed with blood under a tough skin. And what a view! To the west he could see the debouchment of three valleys into the open Vale, and far away the oak trees of Coed Duon went in slow successive folds into fairyland. Behind him, when he turned towards the Ystrad, he found the brown dusk stretched up the hillside to the home meadow, but Cader Emrys wore a purple robe and a crown of light. Then, even as he looked, in a minute, the giant drew a dark hood over his head, and the sun left him.

As he stood there, Mrs Bendle came from the house and crossed to the well. She looked towards the red and yellow streamers above Moel Wen and saw him on the mound. He went down to her, telling himself not to hurry.

He hesitated. 'Bendle in?'

She had been treating him this way for a fortnight. 'By the fire. He's a terror for being kept warm, is Tom. Winter and summer, day and night.'

'Bed and board?' he asked, watching her. She was a fine, sly-faced woman, smooth and supple. Her throat was like milk, her hair raven-black. Akerman's age. As high as his mouth.

'If you say so, sir.' Her eyes flashed at him, her mouth drooped humorously, then she had turned to the well again.

'In his place I should want as much,' he challenged.

'As much, sir?'

'Cherishing at bed – and board.' He leaned over the well beside her. 'And don't keep calling me "sir".'

'But I ought to. It is proper.'

'I call you Jane, don't I?'

'Sometimes' – she smothered a laugh – 'when my husband can't hear you.'

He knew he was colouring, but as the bucket came up he reached for the handle, his grip locked upon hers. 'What I ought to do with you – '

'You'll tip the bucket!'

'Never mind about the bucket. There's plenty of water where that came from.' Setting his left hand to the bucket he caressed her soft round forearm with his right. 'Why didn't you come this afternoon?'

'Why should I – sir?'

'Because you promised you would.'

She pushed his hand away. 'Oh, no, I didn't!'

'Oh, yes, you did! But never mind now. Will you come to-morrow?' He had forgotten about the pit.

They were walking towards the house. She looked down at her feet. 'It's my day for mam and dad to-morrow.' She smiled sideways. 'And what would Tom say?'

He scowled, knowing himself a fool. 'Tom will say nothing – if he knows nothing.'

'It's bad you want me to be, I know. And tell my husband lies!'

He could have struck the slut. But she had pushed at the door, calling out: 'Tom, here's Mr Akerman,' and he could do nothing but follow her inside with the bucket of water. 'Put it in the bosh. There's good of you, sir.'

Bendle said nothing. He was of middle height, very broad, indeed fattish, none too well shaven. Forty years old. He wore a shepherd's jacket, earthy looking trousers stuffed into short leggings, and heavy boots. His red hair was fizzed out at the sides, but the top of his head was quite bald. He was reading a three days' old newspaper, though whether he got anything from it in so bad a light Akerman couldn't say.

'Turns chilly on top here when the sun goes,' Akerman suggested, putting his hands towards the small fire.

'It's too late in the year for fires. They make more work,' said Mrs Bendle, as she went into the scullery.

Akerman had picked up the poker. 'Someone has to make them, I suppose.'

Bendle put down his paper. 'It's women makes the fire and fools play with it.' He got up boorishly and clumped into the scullery after his wife.

Later, they had supper. Akerman's meal would have satisfied the former holders of the earthwork: brown bread, cheese, lettuce and an onion, a pint of milk. The other two drank tea. Only one part of the conversation mattered to Akerman. Mrs Bendle was leaving at half-past seven in the morning to catch the train at Maes-yr-haf, four miles away. She did not know whether she would be back at eight or ten o'clock. Bendle could expect her when she came. First, and foolishly, Akerman thought of slipping out at dawn and waiting for her on the Steps; then he looked at Bendle. What he had said about fools playing with fire. Cutting the rind from his cheese, he thought of Bendle in a rage. Heavy shoulders, thick neck like this rind, bull head, shag eyebrows, he could see his powerful jaws going like machines. Awkward to handle if he came at you. He looked full at Mrs Bendle. No cause for rage – yet.

The two men smoked while Mrs Bendle washed up outside. Akerman offered his pouch: 'Good stuff,' he said. 'Try some.'

'Try some more, you mean.'

'You said that, not me.' He watched him press the tobacco down with a stumpy finger. 'I may go down one of Lewis Tywern's pits to-morrow. The big one.'

Bendle looked up. 'Why?'

'Curiosity. And habit. I've done a lot of cave work. I like it.'

'You won't find much to interest you.'

'What if I don't? Could you come with me?'

He shook his head. 'Got something better to do with my time.' He fell to puffing steadily.

'You've got a rope in the – ' he pointed ' – the shed there?'

'Ay. I got a rope.'

'Long enough, is it?'

'Ay. Plenty of rope.' He looked into the bowl. 'I'll give it you.'

In the scullery outside his wife began to sing a Welsh lullaby. Akerman leaned back in his chair, listening and thinking. There was no savour to his pipe. He felt the strong beat of his heart; heard it too. Even her voice had a sly laugh in it; the lullaby was tender and caressing. He knew nothing of the Welsh words but found himself nodding as Bendle with half-shut eyes beat time to her singing with his pipe. 'Sing it again, 'merch i,' he called to her when she finished; 'Sing it again.' She did so and Bendle hunched to the fire. 'When I was a crwt of a boy, no heavier than a bag of nails,' he said at the end, 'I remember my grannie singing that to my sister who died.' He began knocking out his pipe against the square palm of his hand, and blew as he stood up. 'I must see to that cow before I go to bed. There was a mistake for you.' He lit a lantern. 'Ten minutes I'll be.' He had hardly gone from the room with a pan of hot water when his wife came inside.

'It's in her belly, poor creature.'

'What is?'

She laughed. 'Her calf, what d'you think?' She began to rake out the fire, rounding out her hips as she bent in front of him. 'It makes you wonder, don't it?'

'What does?'

'Oh, nothing. Hasn't it been a nice day?'

'It might have been.'

She stepped away from him. 'It is so nice in the woods at night, lying among the flowers, looking up at the moon.'

So fierce a vision possessed him at her words that he had to stand up. 'I'm willing to try it,' he said, dry-mouthed.

'Only there's no moon!'

'There will be, in an hour. Will you come?'

'What a question – sir! Whatever would my husband say? Oh no, I couldn't do a thing like that, could I?'

'Listen!' He came quickly around the table and moved between her and the scullery door. 'Before he comes back – '

'We mustn't forget that he will come back, must we, sir?'

'And if you call me *sir* once again, I'll do something I'm wanting to do, at once, husband or no husband. Understand?' He thought she would have dared him, but warily she nodded, half-smiling, and rubbed the flats of her fingers across the table top. 'Come here,' he ordered.

'Why then?'

'Because I don't like you always dodging away from me. Come here!'

Slowly she came a little nearer. 'Yes?'

'What time are you coming back to-morrow night?'

She glanced, he thought uneasily, at the door. 'Why?'

'Because I'm going to meet you. And bring you home.'

'You can't do that,' she said. 'If I come by the eight train at Maes-yr-Haf I shall walk with the Trefach folk as far as the Ystrad.' She looked towards the door.

'Then I'll wait at the mouth of the level. And help you up the Roman Steps.'

'You mustn't talk such things. If my husband came in and heard you – '

'Who cares?' Her mouth, her throat affected him almost to drunkenness. 'Give me a kiss!'

'No, no!'

Before she could draw back he had her by the shoulders. Their lips met, hers full and wet and soft, his dry and harsh and bruising. For one moment she clung to him hotly, kissing and taking kisses, and then she broke roughly away. 'No, no!' It was then they heard the scrape of a bucket on the scullery floor. Without a word, hands to hair, she was through the door that led to the stairs. Akerman, a wave of cold dousing the flame in his veins, turned to the table and was fiddling with the lamp when Bendle came in. 'Giving a bit of trouble,' he said steadily.

'Your fault, was it?'

Akerman stared at him. 'Possibly it was.'

'It's best to leave well alone. Where's the wife?'

'Gone to bed, I think.' He patted at a yawn. 'Not a bad idea, either.'

'No.'

'How's the patient?'

'She'll manage.'

'Then I think I'll have a glass of water and away to go.'

In the scullery, pouring water from the jug kept on the drainer, Akerman noticed a strange thing. Part of the plaster had broken away over the bosh that morning and the bit of shaving glass that hung there had been set at an angle against the rack. He saw that it reflected the living-room mirror, and what could be seen in the living-room mirror was the table edge where he and Mrs Bendle had kissed. He managed one gulp of water and poured the rest down the sink, but when he came back into the living-room, Bendle had gone upstairs.

After a minute he followed him, holding his candle well aloft to illuminate every corner of the stairs and landing.

When he came downstairs in the morning, it was to find Bendle about to leave the house and his wife long on the way to Maes-yr-Haf. His breakfast was set ready on the table, the kettle steamed on the oil stove in the scullery. 'Good,' he said, and smacked his hands together.

Bendle dawdled. 'You serious about the pit?'

'I am.'

'I'd advise you not.' He used last night's phrase. 'Leave well alone, that's best.'

He seemed troubled. Akerman's anxiety about the scullery mirror grew less. 'Don't worry. But I'll borrow your lantern, shall I? I know all there's to know about caves and pits. No nerves to bother me. Start to worry when I don't get back.'

'Ah,' said Bendle. He pulled at his legging, frowned, then straightened up. 'And what time?'

Akerman poured out his tea. 'I may go off for the whole day. Expect me when you see me.'

'Like my wife, then?' Before Akerman could reply he had gone out, but at once reappeared. 'Don't say I haven't warned you.' With that he went for good and Akerman finished his breakfast and had a smoke before going to the shed for the rope. It was very strong, and there was plenty of it. Plenty of rope! He screwed up his eyes, remembering Bendle's phrase, remembering other phrases of his. He sat on the back door bench for some time, wondering. Mrs

Bendle was a slut and a cheat; so far he had made a fool of himself to no purpose. What was wrong with himself tramping four miles to Maes-yr-Haf and catching a train for a long way off from Wales? But his vanity was against it, and his desire. If he met her to-night at the mouth of the level, he'd fetch her to account before they reached Castell Coch. Then, to-morrow he would be off – not another day here – and so let her know what he thought the worth of her. Nice in the woods, looking up at the moon. He felt again her lips against his, the soft weight of her breasts, her loins under his hands. He would not go away before to-morrow.

He found and opened the lantern. The stub of candle was tilted right over, so he set it straight and went into the house for a better supply. He knew where everything was kept and slipped two candles into his jacket pocket. Then, thinking facetiously and yet with a hint of panic: 'I can always eat candles!' he stuffed several more alongside them. He made sure that he had matches, his own beam torch, his penknife and odds and ends. He put half a loaf and a piece of cheese in his knapsack, and a flask two parts full of whisky. By this time he was growing out of taste with his venture and again sat on the bench out of the sun, wondering.

He'd feel a damned fool if he didn't go. 'Worse be one than feel one,' he said aloud. Alone as he was, he said other things aloud too, about Mrs Bendle, perversely pleased with himself for doing this. He stood up. He would go just a little way down. No one could say he was afraid.

In twenty minutes he was at the iron pits. It was little more than ten o'clock. 'Hullo there!' he called, and the jackdaws dashed from the trees to revile him. While they swooped and swore, he worked out where the level would meet the pit shaft – somewhat to the left of the slope over the first ledge. Best have a look from there, but first he pitched a stone half-way across the crater. Pang! it came off a distant ledge; then pang! again but fainter, and at last a noise like breath sucked in between the teeth as it met water. Five hundred feet? Six? More? And how far down to the level?

With all the care in the world he passed his rope twice around a tree trunk as thick as his own body, growing near the brink, and the knotted it securely to a second tree six feet away. Slowly he paid it out into the pit. 'Here goes,' he said finally, and began his descent. With only his face above ground level, he hung awhile, staring around. He felt a hundred eyes on him. Climb back up, climb back up!

His feet made untidy tub-like holes in the leaf-laden slope, and then he went down the short drop to the first ledge. It was cooler here, but there was light enough for him to do without his torch. He stood for half a minute, his hand gripping a stout iron bar sunk into the rock, and looked up at the smooth penny of blue sky above him. Nothing would be more natural than that a face should peer over at him. But there was nothing – not even a jackdaw flying across the chasm. He now looked down, but had to wait till the glare left his eyes before he could see much. He fancied the opposite wall slanted towards him as it went further down. 'Hm,' he began, and ended – 'Jane Bendle!' though she had not been present to his mind when he began to speak. 'Well – ' He gave his rope a turn around the iron bar, after dragging at it with all his might, and went over on the next stage. He had his torch tied to his button-hole with cord. At once he saw that his own wall was falling away from him and that the shaft was growing narrower. He was glad he had given the rope a turn around the bar; it made him swing that much less. Even so, he would be glad to reach the second ledge. Down another twenty feet, thirty feet, forty, sixty – when would it – ah!

The wall of the pit, which had fallen right away from him, suddenly became a wide, flat terrace, on which he landed clumsily, striking his left hip and skinning the knuckles of his right hand. A flash of light rather than an oath went through his head, and then he was moving cautiously towards the back of the shelf. He was not surprised to find right behind a small level stoutly timbered off. This must be a heading driven from the main road to the Ystrad. The rope secured, he lit his lantern.

There was little to see. The rock was bare as a shin-bone, and as dry. There were many boulders, though none of them, so far as he could judge, had fallen from the roof. From the level he could not even see daylight, and from the front edge of the platform the opening was a thin gash of white. Cloud going over, he judged it, and sat down, frowning into the darkness. He had done enough. He had had enough. He felt very cold, and cursed lumpishly.

Then something happened. He heard a rushing from above, stones and earth began to whang down the pit, the lantern went out as he snatched it up, there was a vicious rustle within a yard of him, and he was knocked a dozen feet as the rope went cracking under his knees. There was a loud groaning of timber from behind him, then silence, except for the clear, plangent notes of the last small stones falling.

For a minute he lay in the darkness, afraid to move lest he go over the edge. He endured a full paralysis of horror before he began to tremble and found his voice. 'What is it?' he asked huskily. 'What happened? Who is there?' With shaking fingers he struck a match, but it went out with the flare, and he failed three times before remembering his torch. It was still on the cord. 'Pray God – ' he stammered, and clicked the button. The first thing he saw was his rope running *flat* and two-fold along the floor, and at sight of it he trembled so violently he could not direct the beam. He began to whimper, then to cry, and then he was shouting and choking and beating his fists on the rock under him. He did this for some time before the sounds brought him to his senses and he lay quiet, he did not know how long, in darkness.

Gradually he found courage. 'No good crying,' he said calmly. 'Light the lantern and see. That's the thing.'

He did this. His rope was still fast to the balk, but it had fallen from above and both ends were downwards from the platform. His lantern and knapsack were safe. A bubble of hysteria rose from his stomach to his throat, but he fought it and won. 'What – ?' he asked, 'what – ?'

He went to the entrance to the level. Could he get out that way? He flashed his torch along the timbers, sickened by their size and preservation. He looked inside. The walls so far as he could see were dry, the roof solid, the floor unlittered. The slow travelling light picked out some figures inside the gate, and he steadied it to read: 60ft. He looked at this till it was imprinted on his eyeballs.
$\downarrow$

What could be sixty feet down? 'The main level,' he said excitedly. He walked to the edge of the platform. Where his rope went over he saw two artificially-made grooves about eighteen inches apart, and a foot back two holes drilled in the rock. Lying flat, he thrust his head as far out as he dared, his torch flashed downwards. In half a minute he rose to his feet, grunting. He had picked out the top of an iron ladder about twenty feet down. Once only he looked up to the top of the shaft, put his broken knuckles to his mouth and sucked them, and then, having satisfied himself that the rope would hold, lowered himself downwards. He went very slowly, and soon found the ladder. From here progress was easy, and even before he expected it he was on the next ledge. Landing, he gave his rope a tug. No Bendle this time to – but he felt that same bubbling of hysteria at the thought, and to drive it away began to talk about the pit in a loud, determined voice. There were lengths of rail here, very rusted like the ladders, pieces of timber, and the clean and frightening skeleton of a sheep. And at the back he found the mouth of the level.

It had been gated off like the smaller one above. As above, his torch went flashing inside. It was seven or eight feet high at the entrance. 'I've got to try it,' he said. He had grown very confident and so practical-minded that he pulled a contemptuous face at the notion that he throw a stone into the water at the bottom. 'Something else in hand,' he said severely. 'Get on with it, not mess about.' He carried a short length of rail back to the timbered level, tested and pushed and probed. It would be easy. He inserted the rail between the timbers and, using it as a lever, managed to force one of the horizontal pieces off the nails. He could now enter the level – if he wished to. Facing a grim moment, he began to sing: 'When the fields are white with daisies I'll be there.' I'll be there, Mrs Bendle! But behind all this went images he dared not outface: of himself lost in the level, cut off by a fall of rock, coming out to another pit, plunged into bottomless water, poisoned by bad air, falling and breaking a leg, hunted by Something the black level might contain. So he sang to cheer himself, as he had whistled when a boy on a lonely country road, to keep away this Something.

What was the time? He looked at his watch. It was a quarter past eleven. He had been down the pit more than an hour.

And now came a second noise from above. First a hissing, then a smash, then a heavier one, and as he crouched to the ground he saw a large, shapeless, whirling body go from the darkness of air to the darkness of water. He had just time to hear the chink and patter of tinier missiles before it struck bottom. The noise of the splash came up in rapidly overtaken waves, as though the water itself was washing upwards from shelf to shelf, tearing the air into gouts, sucking and buffeting like rollers trapped in a gulf. It subsided abruptly, leaving him battered with noise in a painful silence. Raising the lantern he saw a small piece of dark material on the edge of the platform and went towards it. It was his face flannel.

Bendle! The thought he had forced from his mind came back so strongly that he gasped like a swimmer taken with cramp. Bendle had followed him, Bendle had untied the rope, Bendle had gone back home and removed every trace of him, Bendle would tell his wife he had gone away that day. Bendle, Bendle, Bendle! He could see him standing above the leaf-deep slope, his bull neck thrust forward, heavy jaws clenched, listening so intently. He leapt up. 'Bendle!' he shouted, 'Bendle, Bendle – for God's sake, Bendle!' His voice clattered about the shaft, boomed back into his lungs, suffocating him. 'I never touched her, Bendle! I never! I never!' To be up there in the sunshine, under God's blue sky! To be free, free! 'I'll go away! I'll do anything! Kill me after, only help me out! Bendle, for Christ's sake, help me out!' He was dancing with terror and hope. 'Bendle! Oh Bendle!' He choked with sobs, his chest split in two. 'Oh, oh, oh!'

Through the echoes of his shouting came a roaring from the shaft. A boulder tore down a yard from where he stood, a second smashed itself on the ledge above, the iron ladder clanged under a mighty impact. A multiplied crashing and rumbling filled his ears with the noise of an avalanche. Snatching at the lantern, he ran back to the level and climbed through the timbers, the bombardment growing madder each moment. From inside, the lantern threw gigantic bars of yellow light through the gating, and through these bars boulders and splinters hurtled incessantly. Rocks a foot or more square rebounded from the walls of the shaft, shot from its irregular declivities, playing hell's own tattoo before they thrashed into the water below. Some of them burst like bombs on his own ledge, spraying the sides with shrapnel, lumps of stone singing through the air and thudding against the heavy timber framework which protected him. Something went past him with a sigh, to rattle down the stone tunnel; from below an ocean of watery echoes lashed up at him; and through it all he could hear the tremendous sonorous song of metal struck like a harp. He dared not look out, and what he saw as he pressed himself to the floor and joist was Bendle, in bright day, throwing down the cube-shaped blocks of waste till the shaft reverberated as under a hammer.

The uproar continued for ten minutes, great stones cascading all the while to destruction. On the ledge outside nothing would have saved him. Whether Bendle had calculated as much he did not know, but he himself judged that most of the stones, rolled rather than thrown down the leafy slope, would leap away to strike the far wall level with the first ledge and thence smash off, whole or in jagged pieces, to fall sheer to the ledge he had descended

18

from, or, just missing that, to the one behind which he now cowered. At least twenty such crashed within as many feet of him, the last of them bounding, hardly splintered, against the rock face left of his head.

The silence when it came was shocking. His ears went on humming and roaring, and there was a muffled bludgeon beating bad time inside his head. At last he left his shelter. The ledge was screed with rubbish, the timbers sconched, the skeleton hit to pieces. 'All right, Bendle,' he whispered, actually fearful lest Bendle should hear him. 'All right.'

He went back into the level and trimmed a new piece of candle. Thank God he had plenty of candle! His hearing became normal again, his head cleared. He had, he reckoned, the third of a mile to go and with a convulsive effort of mind brought himself to start. He must forget everything else except the will to save himself. 'When the fields are white with daisies – ' he began, but bit the words off as the roar of falling boulders was renewed behind him. This time he smiled grimly. 'Fool,' he said, 'wasting his time.' If he got out soon, to go quickly back through the woods, surprise Bendle as he levered up his ammunition, push the fool over the edge to go bump, bump, bump to the bottom! And Mrs Bendle – He laughed out loud. Trust him!

He was a fool to laugh in a level. A noise might set up tremors, those tremors strong enough to fetch the roof in. He looked up, very grave now. The height had decreased to little more than five feet already. As he lifted the lantern against the face of the stone, his foot kicked against something, so that he stumbled heavily. He panted, had to set his hand against the cold wall, for there were tramlines running ahead of him. 'Oh!' he cried. 'Oh!'

Then the roof come down to four feet six, so that he went clumsily doubled. The sides were cut clean and plumb, the floor was flat and worn. The air was fresh and there was a slight draught on his face. Here and there, just as in a coal mine or a railway tunnel, were manholes let into the sides, big enough for a man to shelter in. 'In less than a hour,' he said exultantly, 'in less than a hour I'll be out.' That cold air was coming straight from the Ystrad, and he had covered a hundred yards already! Almost as he spoke the tunnel went half right, and on the left he saw the opening of a subsidiary shaft running up and away in the direction he had come from. The level of the second ledge he judged it, and was puzzled by a buzzing in his ears. This grew louder with each step he took, and after twenty yards and a sharp turn became a dull rushing noise shaken intermittently like a pulse. Twenty more and the rock throbbed with it, the gush of a pent-up river seeking low level seeming to push the air faster along the tunnel. It was on his right, no great distance away, the heavy baritone of fast-moving water. It grew colder, the sound a thunderous bass, and then he saw it. Through a fault in the rock a band of black water stretched foamless and unspilling. He had the fancy that if he advanced his fingers it would break them off like pencils. It had the might of a hundred times the flow in sunlight, this unflurried electric stream sucked into blackness. Alarmed, he hurried away.

After another hundred yards, the roof for a long stretch not more than three feet six, he came into a lofty hall. It went so high that his lantern did nothing to illuminate it, and even his torch could not find the centre of the dome. It was some fifty yards across, and circular, save for a huge bulge on his right. From a floor that grew increasingly irregular towards the rim there reared tremendous rounded bastions, so symmetrical that they gave the impression of being tooled by men. The light of the lantern fell softly from their brown masses as Akerman moved slowly around. A pantheon given to silence and emptiness, his footfalls the first in fifty years. He tried to imagine it aglow with lamps in its working days, when men no bigger than he trundled the heavy trams of ore and sent the only noises of an aeon around the vast hollows of its ceiling. 'We don't know we are alive,' he said wonderingly.

It was now, as he came back to the rails and found the other end of the tunnel, that he grew afraid. Bending to enter it he gasped, for he had imagined some huge, shapeless Being of the Hall behind him. He turned, shuddering, and snarled when he found nothing. 'Fool!' he grated, and bent again, and once more had to turn, the hair all alive on his neck. In these black antres who knew what might dwell? Shoulder demons, hunters from behind. 'Nonsense,' he said, 'Nonsense!' Men had worked here, crawling about like bees in a hive. Why, look! there was the haft of a mandril. He caught it up, a weapon, rubbed it against his face, careless of the dirt. 'Come on!' he said hoarsely, staring about him. 'You or Bendle – come on!'

But nothing came. The fist-blows of his heart slackened. 'All right,' he said, 'all right.'

Then, in the mouth of the level, a new panic brought him up stock-still. How did he know he was right? Were there other exits from the hall, with rails? Had he taken the right one for the Ystrad? Had he even gone the whole way round and was now retracing his steps towards the pit? This was a hundred times worse than terrors of the dark. Was the air still blowing against his face? With frightful vividness he thought of the piled-up hillside above him. Four hundred feet of unbroken rock under which to creep and creep till your lantern gave out and you were part of the dark for ever. The whole weight of it rested on his shoulders, compressed his chest so that he could not breathe. He drew his hand across his forehead, caved forward, caught at the wall for support. Breathe slowly, he told himself, breathe slowly! He must go back to the hall, work around it to the other mouth of the level and go on until he heard the waterfall. That would settle one doubt. Then he must return to the hall and come around it in the other direction, and if he found no other exit there was nothing to worry about. If there were other exits – He threw the weight from his back and set off.

He had no fear of a Being of the Hall as he went back, after leaving the mandril haft at the mouth of the level. He came to an opening which he recognized as that he had left and, sure enough, after going some way along it, he heard the roar of the river. Back he came to the hall and around it, to his left this time. 'There you are,' he said, when he found the mandril haft; 'what did I tell you?' He was a fool to have doubted that the air still blew on his face. He went on.

There was an odd feeling in the middle of his body, as though a tennis ball had been stuffed under the V of the breastbone. 'Because I'm doubled up,' he thought and said, but it was growing bigger and harder. It took him half an hour again to recognize that he was hungry – this where a runnel of clear water was squeezed from under the rock and went gently along with him. He took out the bread and cheese and the flask of whisky, all of which he had forgotten. After eating, he took a couple of mouthfuls of spirit and felt warm and confident. He was glad the little stream was going his way. It showed he was going downhill, towards the Ystrad. For several minutes after drinking he sat there in a golden tent of light, resting. His watch said half-past two, and at first he could not believe it. He had been down the pit four and a quarter hours.

After attending to his lantern he started off once more. He must be more than half-way. At the slowest reckoning he would be at the Ystrad by four o'clock. And then? It would be barred, he knew that, perhaps locked and double bolted, but once he saw the light of day he'd have no fears. At the worst, he had only to wait until eight o'clock, when Mrs Bendle would come that way from Maes-yr-Haf.

Mrs Bendle! Head bent, going sideways under the low roof, he thought of her till her naked body glowed before him in the darkness, white as bone. So nice in the woods at night, lying among the flowers, looking up at the moon. 'All right,' he said, 'all right.' He would be quits with Bendle then. He hissed, changing hands on the lantern, surprised to find himself alone as the vision of her milk-and-raven nakedness faded from in front of him.

Without warning the runnel squeezed back under the right-hand wall. Was he going up a slight incline? Still, there could be only the one way, so he kept on unworried. Easy going, plain sailing, nothing to it. So he thought elatedly, and only superstition prevented him saying so aloud. To match his mood, the floor dipped again on the sharpest gradient he had so far found. His breathing grew deeper and more laboured. Surely this was the last stretch towards the Ystrad. Any moment now he'd see daylight. All right, Bendle. All right, Mrs Bendle. He heard himself panting and forced himself to walk slower.

In less than a minute the tramlines divided at a full set of points and led off at an angle of thirty degrees into two levels of equal size. For a moment he stood gaping, and then examined them carefully. There was nothing to tell him which was the right one. He had his first sensation of panic since leaving the great hall. Left or right? He made a futile attempt to assess the compass, and then felt the need of sitting down. In a very deep voice, which he did not recognize as his own, he began to assure himself that it did not matter which road he took, as both must lead to the same opening. It was now half-past three.

Finally he decided to go right, ridiculously equating left with wrong. After twenty yards there was a new forking off – in impossible directions, so it seemed to Akerman. He retraced his steps and made a sally down the left-hand tunnel. This ran true for forty yards and then, as he was congratulating himself, branched into two. He was very worried now, and had to get a grip on himself before deciding to take the right-hand turn. But in less than five minutes he came to a fall of rock and knew a year would be no better to him there than a day. Without delay he went back into the road to the left. Soon he was climbing again, steeply, and the rails had come to an end. He went on for a couple of hundred yards, twice bearing right, before deciding this would not bring him to the Ystrad. Once more he must go back and take great care with his turnings. But ten minutes later he came unexpectedly into a bigger level with tramlines. This both frightened and comforted him: frightened him because clearly he had failed to keep his bearings, comforted him because the main level to the Ystrad must be tram-bearing. Nor had he any idea whether to go left or right along this roadway. Fatalistically he went right, but before long discovered that he was going back along the level that had brought him so straight-forwardly from the pit, so in a cold sweat he turned yet again and after half an hour found himself at the same main fork. He looked at his watch. It was a quarter to five. He had been down the pit six and a half hours.

He was very tired. He sat down and took a drink from his flask. It did him good, for the flutters of panic seemed always to come from his stomach. 'Work it out,' he said: 'Let's work it out.' Evidently he must go to the right, unless the roadway blocked by the fall was the proper way to the Ystrad. In that case – he resisted the temptation to drink again, saw to the lantern and, with his teeth chattering slightly, began to walk. At the parting from which he had already returned once, he decided to go left. He knew that freedom must lie within a hundred yards, perhaps a hundred feet, if only he could get to it. But he covered at least the greater distance before coming into a round rock chamber with a fourfold set of points and three other galleries leading from it. He felt certain as death that one of these was the way he wanted, and that this was a clearing house near the Ystrad end of the level. 'Which one then?' he asked, and noticed how shrill his voice was. 'Why don't they put directions?' One gallery looked exactly like the others, and all were menacing. Then, leaving this small chamber, he had exactly the feeling that had terrified him in the great hall: that some blacker shape in the darkness stretched out hands after him. 'Don't!' he cried; 'Don't', and stood stiff and trembling and telling himself not to be a fool. But he had given the darkness life and a power of listening – listening to his footsteps, listening to his words, listening to the horrors that tightened around his heart. 'Don't!' he said a third time, his head on one side, and went blundering down a gallery. In ten minutes he was facing a dead end.

He had just resolution enough to follow the rails back to the rock chamber. From time to time he said in a broken voice: 'Must get out. Appointment with Mrs Bendle. Must get out.' He went blundering down the next gallery, began to make little runs, bumped against the sides. His forehead was bleeding. 'Must get out!' he said, giddy and staggering.

He stood staring stupidly. There was a great yellow lake in front of him, and by holding up the lantern he could not see to the end of it. At his feet the rails dipped gently into it, and so shallow was the water that they travelled several yards before disappearing. 'Got to go on,' he muttered; and then: 'No, got to go back. Yellow water'; and went stumbling away. He was talking all the time now: about getting out, Mrs Bendle, the tramlines, the Being who was Darkness. Several times he nearly fell, and his clothes were badly torn. 'Like a rat,' he sobbed, 'like a rat!' At the rock chamber he ran to the third gallery and went into it headlong. At once he fell sprawling, knocking the wind from his body, and the lantern was jolted from his hand and went out. Strangely, this restored some measure of self-control, and after scrambling for the lantern and lighting it, he sat still for several minutes. It was twenty past six. He was quite certain that if he were not out before darkness fell on the hill, he would not get out at all. This was not because by that time his candles would be at an end, but from the operation of a time limit he had sub-consciously come to accept. 'Must move,' he told himself, and at once was in the rock chamber. 'Ah!' He went back into the gallery, walking quickly and at length dazedly. Surely he had been walking like this since he was born! The world above, the sunshine, the rain, the white clouds, these were all dreams of his. All creation centred in his head. But the birds, the little birds that flew and sang – . He began to sob, terrible dry-throated sobs, and then to howl like a dog.

He was at the yellow lake again. He looked at it and ran away. When he came to the rock chamber he entered another gallery at random and ran forward crying all once more he reached the yellow lake. Back he went the third time, and back he came to it. He ran crouching and fell often, and always found and lit the lantern. Several of its panels were now smashed, and its light was much dimmer. Sometimes he was mounting endless stairs, sometimes running from shadows that gambolled noiselessly behind him; sometimes he was tiny as a pinhead, sometimes swollen to the tight verges of the tunnel. Sometimes he saw Mrs Bendle – not the delicious vision of her nakedness, but an elongated, swirling, slimy body, with green cheese-mould for hair, her breast wet and rotten, the eyes like cockles. Even when he could not see the face, he knew it was Mrs Bendle, no other, who waited for him now at this corner, now around that. And wherever he ran, whatever he did, always he came back to the yellow lake.

The sounds he made were now part of the mine. They clashed about him, endlessly repeated, challenging him to cry and howl and whimper. No recognizable word came from him, yet he was never silent. And so long as one throb of strength was in him he would go on running, running, running.

Then the yellow of the lake, the yellow of the lantern swung up in a blinding, golden flame as he struck his forehead full on the rock, and for a long time he knew nothing.

At last he stirred, and in time sat up. There was a clashing of knives in his head; he felt cold as a toad. Through the dullness of his brain regret that he still lived cut like a razor. All his pains seized him together, and he could not light the lantern without crying out. His torch and knapsack were gone; he was down to his last piece of candle. The gentle light fell on the yellow lake, and, sickened, he turned away, resting the lantern on his naked legs, hoping to warm them. Soon he leaned back against the rock, his head nodding, and saw to his left two tiny green points of light. They moved, and he came to know it was a rat watching him. This was the first living thing he had seen since he descended the pit, and he felt a great love for it, and wanted to stroke it and nurse it. But as he moved the lantern it dodged past him into the water, and he saw it swimming ahead in line with the tramrails. His mouth fell open, his eyes glared under the bloody eyebrows, he shook like a mammet. He got up and walked into the yellow lake he had fled from so often. He went very slowly, drawing his foot along the inside of the rail not to miss the way. Now the water was to his knees, now to his thighs, now it set clamps on his belly; but he went on, lifting the lantern higher. Slowly the water rose to his chest. He could not have been colder in a coffin of lead. The roof was slanting steadily towards the water, the floor fell as steadily beneath his feet. The water now came above his armpits. Soon the roof was six inches from his head, the water to his neck; then it was three inches and he had to tilt the lantern. He made six strides in an eternity, and the roof rubbed his hair and the water touched his chin. For one unforgettable fraction of time he saw around him the yellow ochre and a slight swirl as of something swimming ahead, then the lantern went out and he let it fall from his fingers. The water now lapped his mouth, and he tilted his head back so that his nose and forehead scraped along the top. One stride – two – three – the water jolting into his eyes before the roof lifted miraculously from his face. Three strides each a century long, and his mouth was clear. His foot struck the tramline. To his shoulders, his chest, his waist, his knees, his ankles the bitter line sank, and he was slishing forward, his hands before his face lest he dash it against rock again. He fell on his hands and knees to follow the rails and crept on to dry ground, shivering so hard that from time to time he could not proceed. He moved forward with appalling slowness, and it was fifteen minutes later he came to a turn and saw a weak diffusion of light ahead. His tongue came out to lick his lips, but he was now past emotion and continued to crawl. It was not for twenty minutes that he looked up again and saw ahead of him a dull beam of light reddening the rock. He blinked and went on crawling and did not lift his head until he himself was part of that beam. He looked with curiosity at what he did not know were his hands, felt pleased and amused at them. The Ystrad entrance to the level was not ten yards away, and he went crawling towards it. Quite properly there was room for him to squeeze himself past a block of stone, fallen from where it pinned a stout paling, so through he squeezed, leaving half his jacket behind him. For a minute or two he sat playing with the dust, and then with animal patience dragged himself on all fours into the road. He looked up, and then down, and was not surprised to see Mrs Bendle coming up the road from Maes-yr-Haf.

Bendle was with her. For their part they saw something half human flopping along the ground towards them. It was three-parts naked and unutterably filthy. The hair was grey, the face indistinguishable for blood, the hands raw. It had a voice, too, and squeaked as they came up with it: 'I came. I said I'd come.' Then it looked up at the man, 'He did it,' it cried. 'He made me like this!' It collapsed, sobbing, its face in the dust.

There was a long silence left to two thrushes over the level. Mrs Bendle looked at the thing at her feet, then at her husband. 'We never – . We never – .' Her voice guttered out, and she panted for breath. In Bendle's forehead a thick red cord pulsed, and he clenched his right fist. He dropped on his knees. 'No,' said the broken mouth, 'oh, no!' But Bendle's fist unclenched, his thick hand stroked the bloody hair. 'Don't be afraid,' he whispered. 'I won't hurt you, machgen'i.' Very gently he caught Akerman up in his arms. Then he rose, his burden to his chest, and after one strange glance at his wife set off for the Roman Steps and the house at Castell Coch. She, her face grey and rat-like, her fingers pinching at the buttons of her bodice, followed slowly behind, and it was so they disappeared, all three, into the quiet woods.

The Buttercup Field

~

It was too hot.

Far too hot. Gwilliam went slowly down the narrow path, regretful he had left the cold flagged inn. Once only he looked at the sun. White transparent flame licked at his eyes and then patterns of black circles dripped before him. He blinked, his eyes wet, and the black circles changed to white suns revolving in blackness. He shook his head, muttered, and forced his vision to the bright buff dust of the cracking pathway, the glinting green of coarse hedgerow grasses and through the high climbing hawthorn and hazel the intermittent flashing of the buttercup field.

But it was too hot. He was a fool to be out of doors. Back at the Rock and Fountain there were stone floors, fresh-wiped tables, cold beer; here in the blaze he could feel a thin spray of sweat pumped incessantly through his pores, and his shirt clung to his back like a snake. The brim of his hat was sore on his forehead.

The sun was still short of the zenith. Its rays poured fluently over a gasping world; its brightness was a barrier endlessly interposed between field and stream, flower and leaf, between Gwilliam and the fretwork shadows of the beech trees. The low line of the southern hills was clear and yet infinitely distant, fringed near Tan-y-Bwlch with a delicate massing of birch and mountain ash, gently declining on the left into the unseen valley of the Rhanon. To the north the high bare mound of Mynydd Mawr leaned away into mid-air, the lumps of his lofty barrows as distant in space as time. It seemed to Gwilliam that if he shouted in that loaded air, his voice would stop a yard from his lips. And he felt unbelievably alone.

Then he heard a swishing fainter than birds' wings over a lawn. He was almost at the gate and paused to listen. The silence was alive with the thousand thin voices of a summer's day: the humming, buzzing, zooming of insects, dry rubbings of sheathed bodies against grass and bare earth, quiet patterings in the hedges,

28

the marvellously sustained vibration of seen and unseen living things. Then he heard the noise again and knew what it was – the death whisper of grass as it meets the scythe.

He checked at the gate. The buttercup field poured like cloth of gold to the hidden boundary stream, swept smooth and unbroken to left and right in half a mile of flowers, taking the noontide air with the yellow radiance of angels' wings in old manuscripts. The brightness made him unsteady. He had to narrow his eyes, tighten his jaws, for the whole world gleamed like the forehead of a god.

It was then he looked close right and saw the old man. He was dressed in funeral black, most old-fashioned. His hat had a low crown and a wide stiff brim; there were big flat lapels to his coat, which was cut square and long; his trousers were full at the ends and dropped stiffly to his glittering shoes – shoes with bright brass eyelets. Though it was later Gwilliam noticed the eyelets.

He was bending away from Gwilliam, and with a small sickle had cut a straight and narrow swathe some fifty feet long. The buttercups had collapsed like slain infantrymen, and those nearest Gwilliam were already screwing up their petals as the sun sucked the last sap from their stalks. He must have finished his row, for as Gwilliam watched he straightened his back, took off his hat for a moment, replaced it, swung the sickle from one hand to the other, and was setting off again at right angles to his former line when he discovered there was a watcher.

Gwilliam had the impression he was stupified to see anyone there. He rubbed the back of his left hand across his cheek, and shifted the sickle uncertainly. The sun poured blackly from the turning blade. Then he looked, as though in wonder, at his handiwork.

To make the best of it, Gwilliam opened the gate and went towards him, his feet tearing great gulfs in the spread flowers.

'You are looking for something?' he asked, and glanced from the sickle to its spoils, from the flowers to the old man's face. It was a strong, handsome, wilful face, with a hook nose, eyes deep as midwinter, white hair under the brim of his hat, and a stiff three-inch beard under the excessive curves of the mouth. There were blackish clefts in his tough-folded cheeks. Seventy, thought Gwilliam, or more. Not less.

'Maybe I am looking for yesterday,' he returned slowly, jerking his chin forward, studying Gwilliam, who felt foolish and snubbed.

'I'm sorry. I made a mistake, I see.' He turned away brusquely.

'No mistake,' said the old man; and as Gwilliam halted, embarrassed: 'I said nothing less than truth.'

His voice was mellow but powerful, his words like rich red earth translated into sound.

Gwilliam felt the hot hand of the sun against his left side. His heart was throbbing with a slow but mighty motion. It was crazy to be standing full in the sun like this, yet his sudden sharpness lay near his conscience.

'Gold is easy enough to find here,' he suggested, gesturing around at the buttercup field; 'but that is not always as precious as yesterday.'

The old man brought down the point of the sickle thoughtfully and cautiously against his heavy toecap. 'My yesterday *is* a golden one.' For a moment they stood silent. 'I am looking for a gold finger-ring.'

'Then let me help,' said Gwilliam. He shook his head at the flowers crushed by their feet. 'Just where?'

The other still held the sickle against his toe-cap. 'Where?' He pointed to the drying swathe he had cut. 'That was the back wall of the house.'

Gwilliam frowned, puckered his eyes for the sun and puzzlement. The old man's face moved, but was far from a smile. 'You do not understand. You cannot understand. But I am telling you – the house stood there. Tŷ'r Blodau Melyn, the Buttercup House, as this field is Cae'r Blodau Melyn, the Buttercup Field.' He looked over towards Mynydd Mawr. 'But it is of no concern.'

'You mean – a house stood here?'

'A house, yes. That was the back wall.' Gwilliam saw play in the muscles of his face. 'But it is of no concern. Mae Tŷ'r Blodau Melyn wedi mynd. The Buttercup House is gone.'

The words of his own language fell from him sombre and poignant, like stones into Gwilliam's hot brain. 'Tell me – ' he began, but – 'Listen,' said the old man. 'Listen!' The urgency of his tone made Gwilliam strain for some noise around them, but he heard nothing save the gush of his own blood, and, once, the dry black voice of a crow, till the old man spoke again.

'You never heard tell of Ann Morgan of Llanfair. Lovely Ann Morgan was what the whole world called her. You never heard tell of her? Fifty years ago it would be, now.'

'She lived in the house that stood here?'

'Where we are standing now. But I forgot. You are a stranger. You could know nothing.' Gwilliam saw the sweat jerk down his cheeks.

'Tell me about it,' he said.

'Tell you about what?'

'Tell me about Ann Morgan and the house and the gold ring. There is a story?'

He nodded, looking to the sickle. 'A story,' he repeated. 'I have not forgotten it. Nor,' he almost whispered, 'lovely Ann Morgan.'

Then, like the pouring of water from a jug he began. Gwilliam wanted to move towards the shade of the beech trees, for the sun had now reached the top of his climb and hurled his beams from behind Tan-y-Bwlch as though to burn and kill, but the old man was staring past him as he talked, he could not catch his eye, and so must stand in the trembling air, whilst honey-heavy bees made their broken flight from flower to flower, and the pollen fell in yellow dust about the brass eyelets of the old man's boots.

'Ann Morgan was the daughter of Gwynfor and Jane Morgan, who lived in this house as Gwynfor's parents and grandparents had done. She was their only child, and would take all they had to leave, which was much. So without her beauty she would not have lacked for a husband – and she was lovelier than the falls of the Teifi at Cenarth.

'There was a man living at the stone house beyond Llanfair Bridge who fell in love with her. Fell in love with her early, when she was 10 and he 12 years old. His father was blacksmith to the parish, and shoed horses, repaired waggons, and kept tools as sharp as this sickle. So far as he and the world could judge she too fell in love with him, but later, when she was 17 or more, and he full man. The parents on both sides were against them: hers because Eos y Fron was poor and a wild young man besides, his because they resented Gwynfor Morgan's notion of his daughter being too good for the son of a blacksmith. Eos y Fron! The Nightingale of the Fron was the name the people of the county put on him, for he sang lovelier than the thrush in April. From Llanaber to Cwmfelyn, from Maenan to the valley of the Rhanon, there wasn't a man to open his lips when Eos came into the company. Had he been born a prince a thousand years ago, we should read how he drew the stars out of heaven with the silver wires of his songs.

'Yet his voice was his danger. There was always open house and free drink for Eos y Fron. That was why he ran wild when very young, and wilder when old enough to know better.

'It was his voice that won Ann Morgan's heart. Jane, her mother, died in the winter of one year and Gwynfor in the spring of the next. The suitors were thicker than these flowers: a man to a buttercup in June, and twice as many in July, and all with a house, a trade, a flock of sheep, or a bag of golden sovereigns. And all, so they said, willing to take Ann Morgan in her shift. Though her house and her money, they admitted, would come handy. But one night Eos y Fron came down the narrow path, just as you came to-day, and so to her window, standing ankle deep in flowers. The drink was in him, maybe, but he sang that night to justify his name – and he sang many nights after. No need to be surprised the dog was not set on him. It was a time of full moon, and the field in its light a pale paradise. The quick hour was too beautiful for earth.

'A fortnight later he met her one evening on the road to the quarry. They stopped and talked, and he saw her home. The same night next week he saw her again, and often after that, and by bragging, flashing his white teeth, and by singing quietly the songs of the countryside, he made her fall in love with him for all the world to see. He went to work like a slave at the harvest, hoarded his wages though his fellows laughed at him, and before November was out she was wearing his gold finger-ring. They were to be married at midsummer.

'Eos y Fron gave up his pot companions. He accepted no more invitations to houses and taverns, but stayed at Llanfair in his father's house and learned all he could of his father's trade. It dumbfounded the village that a girl could so change a man, and there were plenty to bring up the old proverb: 'Once a lover, twice a child.' But he did not care. For lovely Ann Morgan he would have done all things under the sun save one, and that one – give up Ann Morgan.

'Before the turn of the year he was oftentimes at Tŷ'r Blodau Melyn. Sometimes the old servant was there in the room with them, sometimes it was his own mother who went with him, for though he had smutted his own reputation twice or thrice he would have burned in hell before a bad word came on Ann Morgan.'

For the first time his eyes found Gwilliam's. They frightened him. The old man swallowed, nodded several times with harsh movements of his head, and for a moment seemed to arrange his thoughts in order.

'Lovely Ann Morgan!' he said. 'A lovely name for the loveliest woman who ever set foot in the fields of Ceredigion.'

'You knew her well?' Gwilliam asked, knowing his question a foolish one.

'I knew her well. But the tale is of Ann Morgan and Eos y Fron, and John Pritchard the bard of Llanbedr. You must hear the rest of it now.' For Gwilliam had put his hand to his forehead. 'Listen! For three months Eos y Fron found himself in God's pocket, and then, four days after Christmas, John Pritchard came to Llanfair. He was a relative of Jane Morgan, Ann's mother. As was to be expected, he called at Tŷ'r Blodau Melyn. As was to be expected, he fell in love there. No one out of childhood would blame him for that.'

'But if he knew she was engaged to be married to Eos y Fron?'

The old man stared. 'If you were John Pritchard – if Eos y Fron had been John Pritchard – it would have gone the same. I tell you, no man in this world could see her as she was that winter at Tŷ'r Blodau Melyn without throwing the world at her feet.' He looked from the field to the horizon. 'There is nothing in Wales to-day that can give you a notion of Ann Morgan's loveliness.'

'But what did Eos y Fron do?' asked Gwilliam.

'He knew at once. Within an hour. From the way he looked, the way he talked. And John Pritchard knew that he knew, and he cared not a buttercup for all his knowing. He was a bard, as I said, from Llanbedr, and if Eos had the nightingale's voice, John Pritchard had the language of heaven. In a full room, you'd see as many men cry at a poem of his as at a song of Eos y Fron's – and more men laughed when he changed his tune. They reckoned at Llanbedr that John Pritchard knew the metres better than Lewis Tywern's brindle bitch her pups, and if he recited to the weasels he could lead them from the burrows.

'He set himself to win Ann Morgan. Eos y Fron had to work in the daytime, and it was then John Pritchard did his courting. He sat with her for long hours, and from his lips came words finer than Taliesin's. He could talk like the little waves on the shore at Tresaith, with a music that lapped into your soul; his poems imprisoned the mountain brook; and when he wished his voice was serene as meadows under snow.

'Soon Eos y Fron knew he was losing Ann Morgan. Not that for months she did not keep face with him, but that is one knowledge native to all lovers. In March there were bitter scenes between them. He struck John Pritchard, who did not strike back. One night he struck Ann Morgan. And for that may God hate him through all eternity!

'That was the end. He did not see her for a long while. I have said that he was a wild young man until the last autumn, but now he seemed mad in his wickedness. He went back to the drinking, was out mornings with the mountain fighters, grew foul mouthed enough to disgust the foulest, and in less than two months was packed from the house by his father, old Dafydd Glo. This was a heavy blow to his mother, but he made it heavier by cursing both parents as a man would not curse the dog that bit him and swearing he'd burn the smithy over their heads when next he set foot in Llanfair. That night he went to Tŷ'r Blodau Melyn with a short iron bar in his hand, and when they refused to open the door, smashed in the biggest window frame and would have done who knows what damage inside had not the labourers run up from the village and bound him. For a month he was in gaol in Cardigan, and then came out to terrify all who met him.' The old man looked square at Gwilliam. 'He was a brute, and he lived like a brute. It would be better had he died like one, then.'

'I thought – ' Gwilliam began. He was dizzy with the glare. The buttercups seemed to his aching eyes a pool of metal from the ovens, a-flicker, cruel.

'Do not think,' said the other. 'Listen! John Pritchard stayed on at Llanfair. He went oftener to Tŷ'r Blodau Melyn now. He was a man reckoned handsome, much my height, and had grown a beard as a young man. He was a kind man – the whole world would grant him that. And he loved Ann Morgan as much as man can love woman. No one can tell, but it might well be that between his love and that of Eos y Fron there was no more than a pinhead. But while his rival was giddy and fierce-tempered, even savage in the end, John Pritchard was kind and gentle and yet impassioned. So with time Ann Morgan did not forget Eos y Fron but was glad she had been saved from him. For his name was now filth throughout the countryside.'

The sickle had slipped to the ground. The old man stood there like a black statue, grotesquely still in the blaze of afternoon. To the heat he now seemed indifferent. Even the sweat had dried off his cleft cheeks. The square-cut coat set off his stooping shoulders, as though they were carved from wood. His brow was shaded, but a shaft of yellow light lit the dryness of his lips.

'John Pritchard and Ann Morgan were married on the twelfth day of June.' Gwilliam lifted his head at the date. 'As it might be – yesterday. They were married at the chapel in Llanfair. There was a great to-do in the village, and a feast all day at Tŷ'r Blodau Melyn. They walked back to the house in the buttercup field, all flaming with flowers as you see it now, men and women, boys and girls, two by two, and John Jones's fiddle to keep their feet and hearts in tune. The guests stayed on late, as they still do in these parts – later by far than John Pritchard wanted them to. For if Ann Morgan had been lovely before, that day she was enough to give eternity for.

'It was eight o'clock when the last guest arrived. It was Eos y Fron, not too drunk. If John Pritchard had killed him then as he crossed the threshold from the buttercup field – . But inside he came, and for a while was civil. Most there were afraid of him, the women all. He took the colour from Ann Morgan's cheeks, which before carried such red as Peredur's maiden, like drops of blood on snow. She was Ann Pritchard now, but who would ever think of her as that? Lovely Ann Morgan!'

He fell silent, and Gwilliam, his head a-throb, the hot blood shaken through his bursting veins, was silent with him.

'He came at eight o'clock. Soon after the guests began to take their leave, but he settled himself into the ingle and went hard at the drinking. Some who were there dropped a hint, some were blunt, but Eos y Fron stayed on. At last the only folk there were John Pritchard and Ann Morgan, Eos y Fron and Abel Penry the mason and his wife, who did not wish to leave the three of them alone. Then Abel said outright that they must all be going, and shook Eos y Fron by the shoulder, but he dashed his head aside and said angrily he'd go in his own time. Abel then made it plain they would be going together – and Abel was craggy as his trade and not a long-suffering man. It was when he found himself slowly levered upright by Abel that Eos y Fron told why he was there. He wanted his ring back. This amazed John Pritchard, for Ann Morgan had seen no reason to tell him that the ring now caught below her knuckle was the other's gift. But he was a reasonable man; he pointed out that the ring could not be buttered off that night, but that it should be sawed off the next morning. This calmness of his maddened Eos y Fron, who swore she'd not go into the same bed as John Pritchard wearing his ring. He'd see the pair of them in hell flames first. He raved, but as he grew grosser than the sty Abel stuck him so hard on the mouth that the teeth cut through his lips and from nose to chin he was a mess of blood. Then he went, and what he said at going was known only to himself.'

The old man, still as a stone watched his listener. 'There is little left to tell. Not long after midnight a fire broke out in Tŷ'r Blodau Melyn. It burned with a terrible fierceness, as though it fed on oil and fats and bone-dry wood.' His voice came deeper from his chest. 'John Pritchard and Ann Morgan were trapped in their room at the back of the house. They found the shutters of their window barred from outside, though they had left them open, and John Pritchard lacked strength to burst them apart till the flames spurted up the wall to help him. By that time the clothes were burnt off his body.' He pointed with the sickle, which he had picked up. 'The back wall was here; the window here. The buttercups grew to the very stone. He fell through it, still alive, but the yellow fire took Ann Morgan. All her loveliness went out like a moth's wings in flame.' His hard fingers ripped the rigidity from his face. 'Lovely Ann Morgan!' he sobbed, and crouched into the buttercup field.

The angry sunshine ribbed his black coat with yellow. Sickly Gwilliam saw how the buttercups threw their pale reflection on the mirror of his polished boots. He swayed a little, hearing him from the ground, brokenly. 'They found John Pritchard that night and took him to a house in the village. It was late morning when they found Ann Morgan. Neither John Pritchard's nor Eos y Fron's ring went into the coffin with her. A beam had crashed on to her left side, and the dust of her hand and arm lies somewhere in this patch of earth. Where I seek my yesterday.'

An age passed for Gwilliam while he did no more than swallow drily. The he moved nearer, set a hand to the old man's shoulder, to raise him. 'Mr Pritchard – '

'Pritchard! You fool, you fool!' cried Eos y Fron, and his hand sought the sickle. 'John Pritchard died that day, good riddance to him! What was his loss to mine? Fool!' He glared up at Gwilliam. 'And what if I did it?' His voice was cut off, his mouth gaped. 'Listen!'

In his eyes Gwilliam saw the chasms of hell. He stumbled backwards, and as his head rocked the buttercup field flashed into living flame. It tilted, flaring past the horizon, licking the mountain tops, filling the sky with masses of unbearable yellow. Then to his unbelieving ears came the hoarse crackling of fire, the snap and splinter and fluttering roar of a conflagration, and through it, for one moment of agony, the screaming of a woman in terror and pain. He shut his eyes, clasped his hands over his ears, and fell backwards to the ground as red-hot pain welted his cheek. Then, his eyes open, his hands from his ears, he saw Eos y Fron with his sickle and heard his dry cracked laughter. He stepped nearer for a second blow, but Gwilliam lost his faintness under peril, and lightheadedly ran for the gate. Into the overgrown path he went, running like a maniac from the sun, hearing a maniac's shouting behind him, and feeling the drip of blood from his jaw to his chest.

His footsteps were set to a tune, and the tune went: 'Eos y Fron is looking for his ring.' But his heart pumped blood to a different rhythm, and the rhythm was: 'Lovely Ann Morgan!'

A Man after God's Own Heart

~

ICAME to the pub just as I was feeling too fagged to go any further. The Seven Maidens – did you ever hear a nicer name for a pub? It lies about eight miles the other side of Pensarn, and it's worth the walk. Clean. Fresh sawdust, fresh beer, tobacco smoke not yet stale – it had all the mellow sustenance that makes clean pubs and clean stables such lovely nosefuls for thoughtful men. Mind, it's very lonely all around there. If you dropped dead on the road, you'd not get the pennies on your eyes for a week or more. But the Seven Maidens is the hub of a six or seven mile wheel, and of an evening by paths, green roads, and hedgerows, its customers come to their decent pleasure.

I booked a room there for the night, and took it easy for a while, and vaselined my feet, and knocked a sprig down with the round handle of the poker in my room. It was about eight o'clock when I went downstairs: blinds drawn, paraffin lamp alight, good fire going, the haze of fine fellowship blue-grey to the ceiling. There were four or five farmy sort of men round the skittle board at the one end, and perhaps three or four others away from them playing darts and arguing about the score. In Welsh, of course, so I gave them good night in *yr hen iaith* and went to the fireside.

But for one man I had it to myself. I nodded to him as I sat down, and made the usual remark about a good fire. However – and here the story really starts – he just fixed his eyes on mine, dropped them, and said nothing.

'Have a drink?' I asked him, and at that he looked up. The landlord brought it, looking more than a shade interested, I thought. A rusty, genteel-gone-shabby sort of fellow, my new acquaintance was, dressed in a darkish suit, very much worn, and a cheap felt hat on the bench near him. A dog-without-a-tail look about him. Unmistakably no countryman. 'Iechyd da!' said I, and took a swig – after all I *had* been walking and was still thirsty – whereon he nodded and swigged too. We were properly intro-

38

duced, I thought. But not quite. It must have been five minutes before he opened his mouth. 'King David,' he said. Just that. In English.

'King David,' I repeated.

'King David,' said he, and looked into his pint. 'A man after God's own heart.'

'That's right,' I agreed. 'He was.'

I felt sure it was the first time in a long while for anyone to agree with him about King David. 'You think that?' he asked.

'I do. He was a man after God's own heart. We are told so.'

'Yes,' he said, 'We are.'

We fell silent.

'You think that?' he asked suddenly. 'In spite of everything? That he was *that*?'

'I do,' I said again. 'The Good Book tells us so.'

He nodded, and I nodded, I drank, and so did he. We warmed one to the other, and after we had drunk some more I persuaded him to come up to my room. I thought at the time that everybody there, landlord, wife, and customers, behind their elaborate ignoring of us were keen enough to know what was going on, but there were no questions, not a hint even, before I left next day. He smoked a lot of cigarettes, I remember. Mine, all of them. But I got his story out of him.

His name was Reedy. He was born in Cardiff, near the Hayes. My job makes me something of a phonetician, and I had gone a good way towards placing him before he told me this. His father was a watchmaker, and he became a watchmaker himself. I gathered that Reedy the elder left him a twofold inheritance: a failing trade and a more than wholesome fear of God and the Devil. He was at pains to tell me he had always been a chapelgoer and for many years a steward, and I could imagine him very well with his eyes fixed always on the works of a watch or on the preacher for the day. Physically he wasn't much of it: medium height, no particular colouring, snaggle-toothed, yet not displeasing. After the old man died he lived all on his own, except for a woman who came in three times a week to clean through. At first there was a bare living, but when he found himself dipping into his bit of capital he knew he had to make a change or go under, so at last he advertised for a married couple to take the rooms over his shop. Eight shillings a week would make all the difference, and he had it worked out that he could have his dinner with them and maybe get the shop scrubbed out as part of the bargain – though when it came to the push, he hadn't the nerve to ask this last. Within a week he got his couple, a Mr and Mrs Evans. At this time Reedy was forty-six. The Evanses were in the early thirties. The husband was a porter for a firm somewhere near, and, on Reedy's showing, a decent, hard-working man.

Mrs Evans? – It took him just over a month to fall in love with her.

I am sure I was not the first he told this story to. Nor shall I be the last. At times evidently it gets too much for him, and tell he must.

Soon he could think of nothing but Polly Evans all day long, usually with the deepest misery – so much so that when she ironed his collars he hated putting them on and soiling them. He was a keen chapelgoer, but now he was losing grip fast. He had a conscience that was always nagging him, but it made no difference. During the tenth week he went upstairs one day when Evans was out, knocked at their living-room door, and she let him in. For a time they sat talking, but he started to make those absurd answers of a man whose mind is elsewhere, till after a bit she asked him if he felt bad, and out it came. He babbled and cried and fell at her feet and kissed her shoes, and when she forced him to stand up he clung to her frantically, feeling that if he let go the world would fall away from under him and he go down into the echoing emptiness of hell. When she didn't push him away, he was unbearably happy and unhappy at the same time. He was as near fifty as forty, remember. And he asked her to go away with him.

Naturally she refused, and he was honest enough to tell me how relieved he was when she answered No. But it couldn't rest there. After what he had done he was ashamed to pass the time of day with Evans. He was afraid of him, too, but Polly evidently knew when to keep her mouth shut. It was a fortnight later before there was a development. Evans had been put on some late job that kept him out till twelve each night, and now Reedy, resolved to put all to hazard, called Polly into the shop after closing time. Once again he fell on his knees before her, begging her to take pity on him or he'd throw himself into the dock and end it all.

I hold no brief for Reedy. I hold no brief for Polly. Her decision, and their intended action, are none of my business. But this is where we come to King David, if only indirectly. For at this moment God came between him and Polly.

So he said. There are other explanations. But the fact is that he did not – could not – touch Polly, who must have been very puzzled by it all. What had suddenly become so complicated for him surely appeared simple to her. But she did not get annoyed, or feel slighted, or persuade herself she had been made to look a fool. She took life as it came – and she was a good sort. And dullish.

With this, things took a new turn. First and least important, he found business better for the next few weeks. A reward for virtue, maybe. I say least important, because he was past caring about the business now. He had a mind above watches and his pew stayed empty on Sundays. God had come between this man and woman, but He could not prevent him thinking of her with an intolerable desire. Day in, day out, it racked him now, and there was always this Presence between them. His health was poorer. He lost much sleep. How Polly acted during those weeks he did not tell me, but I imagine her as eating heartily and singing as she worked, and from time to time shaking her head when she thought back. 'But not with a married woman,' he told me, with a quite painful sincerity despite his inconsistency. 'There was something held me back from that. Not common adultery. But if only she was free!'

If only she were free! For a time the idea was just a feebly unpleasant rankling way back of his mind, and then one day it bit into him like a ferret into a rat's brain, with a dry and bitter crunching. For a time he was thinking how convenient it would be if Evans fell ill or if the chances of his employment brought him to a painless, instantaneous end. Lifting crates and dodging among trucks – the thing was not impossible. I think he would have regarded this as a lifting of the ban, a sign that he could go straight ahead and marry the widow. Anyhow, the suggestions were in the air if the Almighty cared to adopt them. But Evans was healthy and took good care of himself, and so it was that Reedy's brain spawned strange and frightening speculations.

Then events moved rapidly. Evans, as I said, was working nights. Polly had gone to the second house of a variety show, probably at short notice, for her husband could have known nothing of it. Reedy was indoors alone. He sat there brooding and pitying himself till at last he felt he must get out for a walk or go crazy. So he locked up and maundered miserably the length of the embankment, feeling lower and lower, and looking at the shining water and the not-so-shining mud, until he set off for home again. He told me, but I don't believe him, that a Voice inside urged him to go back. Anyhow, voice or no voice, he got back to find Reedy's burning like a pot of fat.

You will have noticed that Reedy had a turn for melodrama; and now, while the brigade did its best and the neighbours crowded so spectacular a fireside, he tells me he wept.

Then Evans arrived. He saw him running from a van that had given him a lift, and as though it had to be, Evans saw him too. I didn't get much of a picture of Evans from Reedy: it was all Polly when it wasn't himself. 'Where is she?' he cried. 'Inside,' sobbed Reedy, and Evans, poor devil, rushed for the house and was inside before the firemen could catch him. They found him at the head of the stairs, later. He had tried to hide his face at the end. Death had not been merciful. But dreadfully thorough.

'It was Providence,' said Reedy. 'Right or wrong, it was Providence.' In a way it was. Certainly the situation was changed. Polly was free. He tried not to think of it like that until a respectful period had gone by, but he couldn't very well help himself. I think he suffered remorse, but not so long as he made out – decidedly not longer than the respectful period. He harped on that Voice, rather. Sending him back just then, in time for Evans. I did not hint that there might be voices other than the One that had worried him off Polly.

At the end of the respectful period he asked her to marry him, and she agreed. By this time he had a job assembling watches at a mass manufactory, and she was back at the cinema where she had worked when single. They could not altogether avoid publicity, but chose a registry office for the ceremony. 'I couldn't have faced out a big do,' he confessed. There was a honeymoon at Bournemouth. One more sentence and an explanation tell everything. The marriage was never consummated. God, he explained, still stood between them.

They had to part, need I say? There must be a clean sweep, and for that he must leave Cardiff. According to him, he gave her more than half of all he had, and then he moved about a bit before settling outside Pensarn. He kept a little general shop there, and next day I had a look at it from outside, but I did not see him anywhere. I had been thinking about Evans too, and frankly, I did not wish to see him. He was lost to the world there, and that was what he wanted.

Of course, he was only in part King David. They both sent Uriah to his death, that they might enjoy the man's wife. The resemblance ends there, except that they both had to pay heavily. God's curse was on them both, Reedy explained many times. But he had one comfort with it all.

King David was his stand-by. He thought, you see, that there was hope for him who got nothing from his sin, and that unpremeditated, if he who begat Solomon on Bathsheba was yet a man after God's own heart.

All We Like Sheep

~

A MAN and his dog were working sheep on the hillside behind
Siloh. This was a famous place for sheepdog trials, a dry
rough-tufted terrain on a big bald mountain between two coal
valleys. From where he stood he could look east and west to two
black and glittering rivers, smudged with tip-strewn villages and
steamy pit-heads, and beyond these to the ferny flanks of the next
rows of hills. It was a still afternoon, and curtains of smoke clung
to the chimney pots so far beneath him, hazing the long jerky
chains of houses. To the north a progression of humps and ravines
carried him fifteen miles to the claws of the Beacons, and south he
saw all the valleys of western Monmouthshire crawl like veins on
an old man's hands to the coast plain and steely strip of estuary.
There was a time when he had farmed Brynllan, near the valley
bottom, but that was a long time ago. He now kept sheep and a
few milkers on the crofting at Brynhir. His name was Cadno.

He was a tall clean-shaven man of seventy, with a perverse and
bitter face, though now he looked pleased enough, even excited.
He spoke mildly to his dog, a sly upland mongrel whose tongue
streamed scarlet from his blackish jaws, but the dog, though he
stirred his tail and grovelled, kept his distance. This was their
relationship: obedience and just treatment – neither asked for
more. For a long time back Cadno had been content here on the
mountain; something in the unyielding land dowelled with his
own temper. Stooping, he picked up a jag of stone, worn at the
base but with a wounding edge still. He nodded several times. He
was like that stone, he knew it. The dog watched him, warily.

In another half an hour he would be on the other side of Siloh
wall, at a funeral. Gwion Lewis's funeral. They had been great
friends once, Gwion and he. It was proper he should go to his
funeral. Though whether Gwion would have gone to his – he
dropped the stone – ay, he'd have gone, only too true! But he
hadn't lasted, had Gwion; he had no rocky core to him. The old

man looked around. The emptiness, the cold, the winds and the barrenness would have broken him. A weakling at heart – you could tell it by his wish to be brought home to Capel Siloh. All that money too –

He had decided to join the funeral on the hillside. He chuckled maliciously. It would be a surprise for some.

All We, like Sheep! A pity Gwion couldn't know – . He spoke again to the dog, his voice edged, so that the brute flattened his ears and shivered slightly before crawling to heel. In one place the cemetery wall had slid outwards and the gap been plugged with armfuls of gorse, but these too had recently been dragged aside and there was nothing now to stop man or sheep from walking in among the graves. Almost immediately inside the gap he came upon Gwion's open grave with a coffer of fresh-turned earth beside it. Stepping closer, he stared into it, his lips projecting a little, his eyes hollowing under pressure of his brows. He nodded, as he had nodded at the stone, with a solid yet humorous satisfaction. So this would be the last of Gwion! Apart – his eyes changed, subtly, unpleasantly – apart from his story. He saw Gwion at that moment as he had seen him fifty years ago: short and thickset, with a wedge-shaped head and brief blunt nose, and those black and pool-like woman's eyes under the blue-black sweeping eyebrows. A great one after the girls he'd been, with those eyes of his, a great one for courting – he grunted – a great one for not getting caught. They were the musician in him, too – those eyes – not only the sweet singer, but they showed his feeling for music, his passion for lovely sound, his dream of power. What a conductor he would have made! All the great names, Caradog, Penderyn, Llew Rhondda, he'd have beaten them all had he lasted. Suddenly it seemed to the old man standing by the grave that the days of their youth had been all song and happiness, with choirs in every village and orchestras the length of each valley. He began to shake with rage. 'You know, God!' he cried menacingly; 'You know!' The hair rose on the dog's neck, his quarters trembled.

But he must be going. He kicked once, clumsily, at the heaped-up earth and watched a few handfuls trickle into the grave, then he crossed the graveyard, past the chapel, went through the gate and so downhill. In a few minutes he could see the funeral climbing towards him, so he stepped in to the hedge, the dog obsequious behind him, and as the hearse went by removed his hat with a gallant flowing gesture. Everyone seemed surprised to see him. As though he'd be anywhere else that day for twenty pounds! He contorted his mouth to hide a grin, and seemed to those watching to struggle with a deep and painful emotion. But just as the last of the walkers reached him the procession squeaked to a halt. The road was now too steep and rough for wheels, and from here they must carry. Six strong men (he knew the story), a guinea for each of them, would carry old Gwion to the chapel, where the minister (he grinned again, hiding his jaws with his hat – three guineas left for *him*) would laud to high heaven a man he'd never known but who had religion enough to leave a bequest to Siloh. As though God cared a rap for their coloured glass and gewgaws! It was all vanity.

Gwion's brother-in-law had got down from the first coach. As chief mourner he was fat with self-importance; unction oozed from him like the richness of good sage cheese; he stood to gain a tidy penny and was filled with a vague and well-controlled benevolence. In view of them all he advanced on Cadno, like a plump and splayfoot pigeon approaching a hawk, his hand outstretched, his mouth wet. 'It's the heart, friend,' he cried, for all to hear. 'We feel it *here*.' He tapped his left breast. 'It was good of you to come, Cadno! It was *good* of you.' For some of his words he appeared to plunge into a bog of emphasis and pull them sucking forth. He turned his face to the hearse, from which the coffin was being hauled. 'He would have *appreciated* it, Cadno. After all these years – poor Gwion! You were such friends – *su-uch* friends!'

Cadno nodded, his eyes searching the past. 'It's all vanity,' he said roughly. 'We learn that much.' Disquieted, the brother-in-law moved away, still smiling with his skin. Several of the mourners greeted Cadno, one or two offered a handshake which he accepted brusquely. They needn't expect honey and wine from him. Yet they had been on his side at the beginning of the trouble: summer friends and sunshine neighbours, all of them. He started to walk uphill behind the coffin, watching the brother-in-law at the minister's ear, telling the tale no doubt, the furtive glance behind. Was he telling the truth – how Gwion had robbed him, stolen his sheep? Or twisting it all to Gwion's side? He felt hard as a stone towards them all. Ay, Gwion boy, they were against you then who now come lickspitting along behind; urging him to make a court case of it, groaning at a sheepstealer's wickedness. To think of it was to marvel how soon trust turned to treachery, friendship to hate. How soon folk forgot and forgave. But not he, Cadno! He was hard – ay, he gloried in it. Like a rock to friend or foe – and Gwion chose to trick him over the sheep, steal from him. The dismissal of his case in court had hurt him at first, but it made no difference in the end. Everyone knew the truth, knew Gwion a thief. He had bided his time; his chance, he knew, would come.

All We, like Sheep! He nodded sardonically at the coffin. The hand of God made manifest. At the green gate he spoke to his dog who slipped away to the grass verge. Gwion boy! God and Cadno had been too much for him. It was Gwion himself, three months before the trouble, who made the choice. Truly the Lord foresaw and guided all. Taking his seat at the back of the chapel he thought with approval of the sure and cruel humour of God.

Cadno reflected. For two wretched sheep! He had been less hard in those days. If Gwion's need was so great he would have given him the sheep. At least (he forced himself to the truth) he would have given him credit. He could have asked, anyway.

The hymn was finished, the minister was into his address. Cadno shut his ears to it. He shut his eyes too, that he might not see the quirking curiosity directed his way, and was carried back to the old brick concert hall that night forty-odd years ago, to the packed benches, the solid arch of the choir, the harmonium to the left, the violins and double bass, to Gwion's lifted shoulders, his weaving arms. To Handel's *Messiah*. Gwion's choice! Ay, ay, there were grand singers in the valley those days, nothing like them now. But they sang badly that night. Did they know? At least, did they suspect? 'Worthy is the Lamb' – a ticklish chorus for a sheep-stealer to conduct; 'He shall feed His flock like a shepherd' – even the dullest would sense it, surely; 'Behold the Lamb of God' – and 'All we like sheep are gone astray.' He remembered and thrilled to the dangerous exhilaration of those waiting hours. He guessed God Himself must have smiled and wagged His great head at so deadly a stratagem. For when they reached 'All we like sheep' from scattered seats in the building came a tremulous, mocking 'baa-aa!' He could still see Gwion's frightened start, the droop of his baton, could hear the 'sh-sh-sh' of the shocked audience, the voices of those brave enough to sing on; but that devilish baa-ing was too much for them, they blundered into silence, shuffled their feet, rustled their copies, turned gaping to their neighbour. And all the time the bleating continued, 'baa-aa, baa-aa,' till Gwion after one feeble gesture to his choir hurried from the rostrum. A week later he had left the valley.

Opening his eyes, Cadno smiled sourly. That was forty-odd years ago. He could admit it now: if Gwion had lost, so had he. Cadno Brynllan to Cadno Brynhir, that was the measure of his loss. Those fields by the river, the gay frisians with their dripping teats, the fat soft sheep – for the stony uplands, the three Welsh blacks, the springy sweet-fleshed ewes. No matter! He looked at the mourners, naming them to himself. Ay, the same ones, bitch-driven by their women, the ones who'd set against him for taking that justice the law denied. In a year he had lost his milk round, odd things happened at market, he had bad luck too. They began to say he was mean: why couldn't he let a couple of sheep be missing without all that vindictiveness? What if the poor man did steal them? You had only to think of Jacob and Laban and the half-peeled rods to know that kind of thing had always gone on, in the most respectable families too. And they said that to interrupt the *Messiah* was sacrilege, the bleating a blasphemy. Little they knew of the God they so freely flattered and cajoled, that grim Ironist who had taken His laugh at Cadno too! – Not that Cadno held this against Him. They understood each other very well, God and Cadno.

He heard the minister speak of forgiveness. The greater the offence, thus he heard him, the more merit in forgiveness. What after all was man's forgiveness compared with the Infinite Mercy of God? Cadno bent his head, lest he be seen to smile. Infinite Mercy a sheeptod! Justice not Mercy was what God had promised. They were deceiving themselves fatally, these apostles of Mercy, these milk-thinners, these shortweight counter-jumpers, thse Dai Smallcoals from the pits. Had they forgotten that dismal horde who departed past the left hand of the Almighty into the Everlasting Pit? *Everlasting* – that was the strong word. Not for a day, a year, not even an age – but for ever! That was God's way. That was Cadno's way. These people before him, they were afraid of the Book. Afraid to know that hard and subtle God Cadno had found on the mountain. He heard, as he expected to hear, the preacher speak of Gwion's life after he left the valley, how he had toiled and moiled and prospered in his chosen field of endeavour, and how, when his immortal part took wing for heaven, his clay sought confusion in the clay of his fathers. But the preacher said nothing of Cadno forced to leave the honeyed lands of Brynllan: all Gwion, Gwion, Gwion, you'd think he was a saint, a cherub, a deacon in Siloh. But God is not mocked, thought Cadno.

He was glad when they were on their way to the open grave. The dog had been watching for him through the gate. Some signal no one else saw – he slipped inside, his nose to Cadno's knee. Cadno felt a moment at hand he had waited for almost a lifetime. He watched with relish the smooth lowering of the coffin, and it was then he flicked lightly at the dog's head. He was away through the gap in a flash.

The brother-in-law approached him, holding the minister's arm. 'In the *heart*, friend,' he said; 'it's *there* we feel it. Forget and forgive' – he raised his podgy hands – 'forgive and forget. We are all members of a *Whole*, Cadno.'

Cadno sneered: 'You mean, a Pit.'

The minister flinched, one or two changed feet among them, and the brother-in-law dropped his hands. He was hurt; he had behaved so well; he would have protested; but at that moment two terrified sheep burst through the gap in the wall, a sly and furious mongrel at their heels. The first swerved under the feet of the mourners, scattering them, the second fell into the grave and its hoofs beat a frantic tattoo on the coffin lid. 'Baa-aa,' they cried, 'baa-aa!'

The mourners surged and stammered, growled then grew still. But Cadno, his face taut, had turned from them to seek approval skywards. Suddenly they saw his jaws loosen in a smug and ugly grin.

'All We, like Sheep!' he cried, in a great prophet-voice.

And knowing their deed blest, man and dog turned for the gap and the farm at Brynhir.

Kittens

~

SHE wasn't waiting at the corner. He halted at the edge of the pavement, peering anxiously to and fro, and then saw her white glove beckon from shadow. He crossed over, his relief still tinged with uneasiness, touched the brim of his hat. 'Hullo,' he said, 'hullo, Glenys.' She was shorter than he, just the loving height, between slender and thin. Her mouth and eyes blotched her face viola-fashion, the smooth contours of her cheeks fell through a shallow curve to a slightly blunted chin, the nose was pretty, straight-bridged, and in harmony with the chin, a little squared at the nostrils. The nicest face in the world, for someone else's sweetheart. Her costume was dark, black it looked to him, she had a silver-fox stole loosely on her shoulders, her blouse like her gloves was white – he could see it gleaming, and the big buttons with the flower pattern on them – his eyes kept returning to them. That she was older than he pleased and flattered him, as he was pleased and flattered by her make-up, her clothes, her style, by all that made her different from the girls and women of the village. She belonged to a setting of advertisements, shop windows, motor cars, men dressed like bank managers, and this flattered him most of all. And yet, he thought, I'm here with her. Of all the men about here I'm the one. The one she chose.

'Been waiting, Morri?' Her voice too was different; a voice with class. His tongue felt fat and loose when he began to talk.

No, no, he said. Not he. Only a minute, anyway. 'Had to call in the Institute,' he told her, watching her face. 'See the team for Saturday, you know.'

'You'll be playing?'

'Got to.' It wasn't a pressing question, but it gave him something to say as he took her arm. 'Shove um right off the field without me. Strength in the back row to lock um, see.'

'Oh, I know. And you are terribly strong, Morri, aren't you?'

'Oh I donno. Average, about.'

She looked up into his face as they passed the hanging light where the mountain road starts its climb. He was a haulier from the Red Vein, hardly more than twenty, well-clamped and supple. Between the temples his face was white and broad, but it narrowed downwards like an axe-head; his hair was black and oiled; she saw his jaw glistening from too close a shave. His eyelashes were longer and softer than her own, his eyes like black fur. She smiled, approving him.

As he smiled back she squeezed his arm into the soft of her side. 'More than average, Morri. Why, just feel this arm!'

'Ah,' he said, and halted. He grinned, rather sheepishly. 'Feel that, Glenys.' He guided her hand to his biceps, flexing slowly and powerfully, till her fingers were clipped between his fore and upper arm. 'Try and get away, uh?'

But with admiration and a squeal she failed. He dilated with mastery and pride and moved his shoulders happily inside his coat. 'What a strong arm!' she praised, and moved gently and as it were by accident, so that the arm was behind her back and crooked about her waist. As they walked on, up the sunken road, her head was against his shoulder, and his nostrils snuffed the dry exciting smell of her hair and the fox stole. Soon they were past the quarry, and without a word said left the road and leaned for a while on the fence that led to Bryn-Eithin. Below them, swung in an arc, they could see the lights of three villages, and linking these the road and railway spattered with red and yellow. Down in the valley bottom were the smudged lamps of the Red Vein collieries, those in the sidings winking and blinking as the trucks were shunted into long clanking lines. All this din of wheels and brakes and line-points came to them thin and silvered across a hillside of gorse and fern, as much a part of the place as the yelp of a dog from Bryn-Eithin or an owl hooting from the Penllwyn wood. Over against them, in the next valley, the Cwrt Mawr steelworks troubled the dark, and suddenly they saw a vast red surging behind the clouds as fire died upwards from the jaws of the ovens. As the darkness thickened again, 'Look,' she said, and pointed to the way they had come, the unlit tunnel of the sunken road.

'What, Glenys?'

'It's horrid!' She turned quickly to face the trembling sky over Cwrt Mawr. 'All that dark – and the quiet – and the things there may be in it – '

But to him the dark was friendly. 'You wouldn't do underground, Glenys.'

'No,' she said grimly. 'I wouldn't.' She pressed against him.

He fell silent, for a moment oppressed by things he couldn't understand. This down she had on the valley, which seemed so good to him – . But there, she was different – that was the fine thing about her. He drew her to him, holding her clumsily, his hands moving irresolutely over her back as though afraid of crushing her.

'I'm glad I met you, Morri. I couldn't have stuck it out here after Cardiff if I hadn't.' She pulled at his lapel. 'It's the one thing I'm sorry about, going – '

'To-night, Glenys?'

'I've got to. I must catch the twelve-ten down. You know how it is.'

He broke in. 'I've brought it, Glenys.'

'I'm terribly ashamed, Morri, taking it. It's awful for a girl to have to do. And if dad knew – '

'He don't have to. Nobody don't.'

'You're a lovely boy, Morri.'

'That's all right, Glenys. You'd better – ' He released her, fumbled in his pocket for his wallet. There was a thin sheaf of notes in it, held by elastic, which he handed over without counting.

'I'll pay it back, every penny. And the other.'

'That's all right,' he said again, dry-mouthed, watching her put it safe in her handbag. 'Glad I had it, Glenys.'

'As soon as I saw you I knew you were the real man around here. There was something as soon as I set eyes on you. I knew.'

'No,' he muttered, 'I'm not much really. Haulier, you know. Not a bad job, mind – still – '

She began to tell him how fine he was, how generous, and again how strong. Her stole, heavy with scent, brushed his underjaw, and with it he could smell the untamed animal odour of the fur itself. 'I've got to go, Morri – you can see that – with dad the way he is. He doesn't understand me. He never has. No one ever did about here. I know how they talk. They think it wicked for a girl to look nice and want something better than the Gelli.' She checked on her mistake, but he had noticed nothing. 'He'd kill me if he knew I'd taken money from a man – from you, Morri. You won't tell, will you?'

'No,' he said, 'no.'

'And you'll come down and see me?'

'Regular, Glenys – often as I can.'

'Any time you want to, Morri. If you don't forget me. You may, Morri. These other girls about here' – her voice changed, began to throb through him, ' – you must be awful with them, I'm sure, a boy like you. Aren't you?'

He was torn between truth and vanity. 'It's you, Glenys,' he blurted, 'it's you are the one.' And he spoke truth. Her looks, her clothes, her maturity struck at something in him deeper than vanity. She was music to him, and singing, and poetry.

She took his face in her hands and kissed him. 'Nice Morri!' But her mind was still full of the money he had given her. 'I'll be on my feet in a couple of months, easy. I'll have a nice little flat, I expect. Nothing'll ever be too good for you with me, Morri.' Her thin fingers stroked his hair. 'You're a real man, Morris – the only one around here. You're different – anyone can see that.'

'Glenys,' he said, 'Glenys!'

His voice, his face, his hands were to her pages read and known. Centred in her brain was the icy spiral of calculation, but this did not stop her growing excited, confused, sentimental.

'Glenys!' he cried hoarsely.

'No, dear,' she whispered, trying to break from him. 'Please, Morri!' Then her nails tore his wrist with the violence of fire. 'Morri, you mustn't!'

'Why not, Glenys? Damn it all – '

'Because you lent me the money? Let me go, will you!' She struggled from him, her handbag falling to the ground. 'I didn't think you'd do a thing like that. If I've been nice to you it wasn't because of the money.' He bent, humiliated and tormented, but she was before him, straightening again, making show to unclip her bag. 'You'd better take it back, if that's the way you feel about me.'

'No,' he said ashamedly, 'I wouldn't take it. Glenys – don't be angry. I didn't mean anything, honest I didn't.' He drew her to him again, patted her shoulder, abasing himself, yet with it all feeling cheated and desperate. 'Don't be angry, there's a girl. I didn't mean anything, honest now.' She was so weak compared with him, her bones like pipestems under the silky flesh, that his desire suddenly melted into compassion. 'So small,' he said, 'so little, mun. I donno my own strength. I'd do anything for you, Glenys, honest I would.'

'And I'd do anything for you, Morri, so long as you didn't think it was because of the money. You're the dearest boy I ever met.

Hold me again, Morri. Hold me closer! And kiss me, to show – '
But he was glum, baffled, half-hearted, his arms were slack and
heavy. She pressed her lips to his, at first acting a part, but soon
taking fire from his brute strength. 'If it wasn't that you thought it
because of the money,' she prompted. 'Please say it, Morri.'

The thought troubled him. Had it been the money?

'Please say it, Morri.'

'It wasn't the money,' he said, and hid his face in her hair.

'Because I'd be common then, wouldn't I? If you're a nice girl,
it's very hard – but I should have known with you, Morri.' Honour
satisfied, her handbag safe, she encouraged his caresses; above
them the sky trembled and glowed, and he saw the white of her
skin flush with rose. Something in her expression shocked him
even in the flood-tide of passion, but she spoke. 'Look, Morri, you
see – I'll do anything to make you happy!'

It was a little after eleven when he reached home. His brother was
not yet off the afternoon shift. His aunt, who looked after the two
of them, had set his supper alongside his brother's under a clean
teacloth, and was still darning by the fire. She was a dry-tongued,
cold-faced collier's widow. He was slightly afraid of her. But tonight he greeted her off-hand, for after all her day was over, then
wetted the tea from the kettle on the hob, and sat to table.
Straightway the black-and-white by his aunt's side came over to
claw at his leg, and he lifted her up. 'Goh,' he breathed, 'like little
toy bones!' He could feel them no thicker than pipestems under
the silky fur. At the thought his eyes glowed, and his aunt,
watching, saw his lips move.

'Been drinkin'?' she asked sharply.

'No.'

She twitched at her wool. 'Been mashin' then?' The edging of
contempt offended him, but he wasn't braced for anger. Instead,
his eyes lit up again under their long black lashes. 'And who's the
lucky lady?' she asked. His silence irritated her. 'Or is it a secret?
P'raps I could make a guess.' Ostentatiously he yawned, but she
struck off a name on her little finger. 'It wouldn't be Gwen
Vaughan now, would it?'

'Her?' He smoothed his thighs, good-humouredly. 'Chair-legs!'

'No, no it wouldn't be Gwen – and of course she's sweet on that
Thomas boy. Now would it be Mildred Lewis, I wonder?'

He yawned again. 'She's waiting for the whistle, I don't doubt.'

'Ay, but is it your whistle, Morri?' She was a cunning woman who made her approaches by indirection. She now struck down a third finger. 'Or it might be Mrs Colonel James's daughter from the Mansion who's waiting for the whistle. P'raps you went for a ride to-night in the Colonel's Rolls Royce, was it, Morri?'

'Ah, cut it out!'

'No, somehow I don't think it was Miss Colonel James. Then there's – ' her voice cut like glass, ' – it wouldn't be that fly piece of Hugh Bowen's, I suppose?'

'No harm in s'posin'.'

'You fool, Morri!'

'Think so?' Again his eyes glowed, his hands opened and clenched and then lay open.

'What sort of good is she to you – a piece like that? All high heels and a bit of fur round her neck – and scent! Her old man out of work these ten years and more – I'd like to know where she gets things from.'

'Then why the hell don't you ask her?' he flashed.

'I don't have to.' He looked up, startled. 'There've been trade over that counter since Eve's day. And there's no need for language.'

For a moment he looked like flying into a rage. Instead: 'What's a hell or two among friends?' he said roughly, and flung his collar and tie to the sideboard behind him. He felt clawings at his trouser leg, and was relieved to be able to swing the kitten up to his shoulder. *Mm-mm-mmrr-mmrr-mmrr*, she went, and bit gingerly at his ear. Her fragility moved him to an ecstasy of strength and protection. As her fur brushed his underjaw and he could smell the queer animal smell, he breathed hard; his eyes smouldered. They know, he thought, they know the ones they like; they know the real men.

'Old enough to be your mother,' said his aunt.

He jumped up, shouting. 'For Christ's sake will you keep your tongue off her!' She stood up to brazen it out, but for the first time in her life was afraid of him. 'You've got your old man's temper,' she said slowly; 'and look what that done for him. I thought you had more sense.' She sat down again, began to put away her darning. His hands unclenched, his jaws slackened. 'All right,' he said unsteadily. 'All right then. Only shut your mouth.'

His aunt was nodding her disgust when they heard the scrape of boots on the bailey and the double stroke of the latch. His brother Mog came in, black-faced, red-lipped, and with whitey rings under his eyes. He was a brisk-moving man, and just now his coaldust lent him the lugubrious mask of a nigger minstrel. He dropped his cap inside the fireguard. 'Ay, ay,' he said cheerfully.

'I'm off to bed,' said his aunt. 'Everything's ready on the table.'

'Okeydoke.'

At the passage she turned, defiantly. 'And you might try to put some sense into this brother of yours.'

Mog grimaced. 'Uh-uh?' He started to eat, and supped tea noisily. He was six years older than his brother. 'Whass the fuss?'

'Nothing,' said Morri. He picked up the kitten. It might as well come out this way as any other. 'She been on to me, the old fool – '

'Oi, oi!' Mog was shocked.

'Gabbling. Been on to me 'bout girls. As though I'd give a brass tack for any girl 'bout here.' His tongue ran inevitably to the one name. 'Talking 'bout Glenys Bowen – you know.'

Mog stopped chewing, his mouth overful. 'You haven't – '

He stroked the kitten. He could feel rage rising in him again. By god, they had only to say –

'I'm askin' you!'

'No,' he said sullenly. Something in Mog's tone made him strengthen the lie. 'Catch me!'

Mog reached for his mug. 'Okeydoke.'

'Anyhow – why?'

'Heard to-night from whassisname up Top Row – Dai Jinkins – that's him – she've took best part of ten quid from that butty of his – that left-handed feller, whassisname.'

His hard fingers closed like gates around the kitten. She squealed and her claws ripped his wrist. 'More fool you,' said Mog, as Morri watched a pinhead of blood fill the deep end of each scratch. Under the scratches he saw other abrasions and one long pale weal running back to his cuff. Well –

'And thass not all. Poor flamer!' Mog's nigger minstrel eyes rolled and then rested on the big black Bible on the sideboard. 'She's the Scarlet Woman on the White Horse, and the Sixth Plague that plagued Egypt. Boyo, she's the Fire that Burns.'

'Meaning?'

His lips were nearing the scratches when Mog's answer sickened him. He drew his wrist away. 'So you been lucky, Morri.'

'Ay,' he said after a moment, 'I been lucky.'

Mog stared over his shoulder. 'Sure?'

'I said, didn't I!'

'Okeydoke, da iawn!' He watched Mog untie his thongs and shake the grit from under his knees. So this has happened to me, he was thinking; no one can do anything for me, and to-night she'll go to Cardiff and that'll be the end. He saw Mog glance at him again, uneasily, and hated his brother. He was glad when he went upstairs for his bath. For a while he sat on, looking at his wrist. When at last he knew what he must do it was a quarter to twelve. She would be catching the train at the Gelli: he would join her at the Red Vein halt. He didn't move till he felt the kitten clawing at his leg.

When Mog came downstairs after bathing he found the room empty and the door ajar. He was worried, but closed the door, sat down, and lit a fag-end. He was at the end of his smoke when he noticed the kitten under the table. He picked her up, but she was dead. Blood and froth were about her mouth and nostrils, her bones yielded everywhere under his hands.

'Morri?' he whispered. 'For Christ's sake, Morri!'

He hurried to the door and stood listening, watching. He could hear the wagons being shunted into the Red Vein sidings, and the sky filled with blood as they fed the ovens at Cwrt Mawr. 'Where are you, our kid?'

He tugged on his boots and was crossing the bailey when he heard the twelve-ten for Cardiff pull out of the halt. Soon it passed him, slithering on the down gradient. It whistled, one long shrill blast, and slid into the Penllwyn tunnel.

The whistle hung on the air like a shriek. 'Oh, Morri,' he cried softly, 'where are you? Where are you, our kid?'

Shacki Thomas

~

SHACKI THOMAS was fifty-two, shortish, and bandy from working underground. Unemployment was straitening his means but could do nothing with his legs. But play the white man, he would say – though I'm bandy, I'm straight. It was his one witticism, and he was not using it so frequently now that his missis was in hospital.

He was going to see her this afternoon. He gave a two-handed pluck at his white silk muffler, a tug at the broken nose of his tweed cap, and so went out the back way to the street slanting sharply from High Street to the river. The houses were part soft stone, part yellow brick, and grimy; the roadway between them was decorated with dogs and children and three new-painted lamp-posts, and each parlour window showed a china flower-pot nesting an aspidistra or rock fern. He passed his own window, and saw that the fern was doing famous, though he'd forgotten to water it since Gwenny – oh, Gwenny, Gwenny, he was saying, if only you was home in our house again!

Twenty yards in front he saw Jinkins the Oil and hurried to catch him up. Owbe, they said.

''Orse gets more human every day,' said Jinkins from the cart, and to forget his troubles Shacki made a long speech, addressing the horse's hindquarters:

'Some horses is marvellous. Pony I used to know underground, see – you never seen nothing like that pony at the end of a shift. Used to rip down the road, mun, if there'd a-been anything in the way he'd a-hit his brains out ten times over. Intelligent, Mr Jinkins? You never seen nothing like him!'

As they approached the railway bridge, the two-ten to Cwmcawl went whitely over. The horse raised his head.

'Now, now, you old fool,' cried Jinkins. 'It's under you got to go, not over.' He turned to Shacki and apologised for the dumb creature. ''Orse do get more human every day, see.'

58

But Shacki couldn't laugh. It was Gwenny, Gwenny, if only you was home with me, my gel; and fear was gnawing him, wormlike.

Turning away beyond the bridge into High Street, he found the old sweats around the cenotaph. For a minute or two he would take his place in the congregation. A lady angel spread her wings over them, but her eyes were fixed on the floor of the Griffin opposite. GWELL ANGAU NA CHYWILYDD said the inscription. 'Better death than dishonour'; and as Shacki arrived, the conversation was of death. 'I once hear tell,' said Ianto Evans, 'about a farmer in the Vale who quarrelled summut shocking with his daughter after his old woman died. Well, p'raps she gave him arsenic – I donno nothing 'bout that – but he went off at last, and they stuck him in the deep hole and went back to hear the will. Lawyer chap, all chops and whiskers like a balled tomcat, he reads it out, and everything in the safe goes to Mary Anne and the other stuff to his sister. So they has a look at the safe, and what's inside it? Sweet fanny adams, boys, that's what.' By pointing a finger at him, Ianto brought Shacki into his audience. ' "And what'll you do with the safe, my pretty?" asks the sister – like sugar on lemon, so I hear. Mary Anne thinks a bit and then brings it out very slow. "If it wasn't for my poor old mam as is in heaven," she says, "I'd stick it up over the old tike for a tombstone".' He scratched his big nose. 'What's think of that, uh?'

His brother Ivor picked his teeth. 'Funny things do happen at funerals. I once heard tell about a chap as travelled from Wrexham to the Rhondda to spit into another chap's grave.'

'Might a-brought the flowers up,' said Ianto.

'No, not this chap's spit wouldn't.'

'I mean, there's spit and spit,' said Tommy Sayce. 'I mean, f'rinstance – .' A moist starfish splashed on the dust, and he changed the subject. 'How's the missis, Shacki?'

Shacki looked from Ivor to the lady angel, but she was intent on the Griffin. 'Thass what I going to see, chaps. Fine I do hope, ay.'

They all hoped so, and confessed as much. But they were all fools, and the worm fear was at Shacki's heart like a maggot in a swede. 'I got to go this afternoon, see,' he said, hoping for a chorus of reassurance and brave words, but – 'I remember' – Tommy Sayce took up the tale – 'when little Sammy Jones had his leg took off at the hip. "How do a chap with only one peg on him get about, doctor?" he asks old Dr Combes. "Why, mun," doctor tells him, "we'll get you a nice wooden leg, Sammy." "Ay, but will I be safe with him, doctor?" asks Sammy. "Safe? Good God, mun, you'll be timber right to the face!" Thass what doctor told him.'

'Ah, they'm marvellous places, them hospitals,' Shacki assured them, to assure himself at the same time. 'Look at the good they do do.'

'Ay, and look at the good they don't do! Didn't they let Johnny James's mam out 'cos she had cancer and they was too dull to cure it? And Johnny thinking she was better – the devils!'

The worm went ahead with his tunnelling. 'I carn stop, anyway,' said Shacki, and low-spiritedly he left them to their talk. Not fifty yards away he cursed them bitterly. Death, death, death, cancer, cancer, cancer – by God, he'd like to see that big-nosed bastard Ianto Evans on his back there, and that brother of his, and Tommy Sayce, and every other knackerpant as hadn't more feeling than a tram of rippings. From the bend of the street he looked back and saw the lady angel's head and benedictory right arm and cursed her too, the scut of hell, the flat-faced sow she was! Nobody have pain, or everybody – that was the thing. He cleared his throat savagely and spat into the gutter as though between the eyes of the world. Self-pity for his loneliness brought too big a lump to his throat before he could curse again, and then once more it was all Gwenny fach, oh, Gwenny fach; he'd like to tear the sky in pieces to get her home again. If only she was better, if only she was home, he'd do the washing, he'd blacklead the grate, he'd scrub through every day, he'd water that fern the minute he got back – he was shaking his head in disgust. Ay, he was a fine one, he was.

Then he went into the greengrocer's, where the air smelled so much a pound.

'Nice bunch of chrysanths,' he was offered, but they were white and he rejected them. 'I ain't enamelled of them white ones. Something with a bit of colour, look.'

He bought a bunch of flowers and three fresh eggs for a shilling and fivepence, and carried them as carefully as one-tenth his dole deserved to the Red Lion bus stop. Soon the bus came, chocolate and white, with chromium fittings. He found the conductor struggling with a small table brought on by a hill farm-woman at the Deri. 'Watch my eggs, butty,' he begged, and stood on the step till at last they fixed it in the gangway, where it lay on its back with its legs up in the air like a live thing gone dead. Through the back window Shacki saw a youngster running after the bus. 'Oi, mate – '

'Behind time,' said the conductor hotly. 'This here blasted table – '

He came for his fare and to mutter to Shacki. 'I never had this woman on board yet she hadn't a table or a hantimacassar or a chest in drawers or a frail of pickled onions or summut. Moving by instalments I reckon she is, or doing a moonlight flit. Iss a 'ell of a life this!'

As the bus went on up the valley, Shacki made a gloomy attempt to put in proper order what he had to tell Gwenny. The house was going on fine, he himself was feeling in the pink, there was a new baby at number five, he'd watered the fern – and he must tell her summut cheerful. Like what Jinkins said to the horse, and this here conductor chap – proper devil-may-care this conductor, you could see that with half an eye. Near Pensarn he saw lime on the bulging fields, like salt on a fat woman's lap. The grass under it looked the colour of a sick dog's nose. He saw farming as a thin-lined circle. If you hadn't the grass, you couldn't feed the beasts; if you couldn't feed the beasts, you didn't get manure; if you didn't get manure, you had to buy fertiliser – which brought you back to grass. All flesh is grass, he heard the preacher say, and all the goodliness thereof is as the flower of the field. The grass withereth, the flower fadeth – duw, duw, what a thought! It made a fellow think, indeed now it did. Yesterday a kid, to-day a man of fifty, to-morrow they're buying you eight pound ten's worth of elm with brass handles. Oh, death, death, death, and in life pain and trouble – away, away, the wall of his belly trembled with the trembling of the bus, and the worm drove a roadway through his heart.

At Pensarn a girl stood at the bus stop and said: 'Did a young man leave a message for me at the Red Lion?'

'Yes, my dear,' said the conductor. 'He told me special you was to let me give you a nice kiss.'

'Cheeky flamer!' said the hill farm-woman, but the girl looked down in the mouth, and Shacki felt sorry for her. He explained that a young man had run after the bus at the Red Lion. Ay, he did rather fancy he was a fairish sort of chap 'bout as big as the conductor, so – 'It must a-been Harry,' the girl concluded. 'Thank you,' said Shacki, as though she had done him a favour. Indeed, she had, for he could talk about this to Gwenny.

Later a collier got on. 'Where you been then?' the conductor asked. 'Why you so dirty, mun?'

'I been picking you a bag of nuts.' He took the conductor's measurements, aggressively. 'Monkey nuts,' he added. He did not enter the bus and sit down, but stood on the step for his twopenny ride. 'We got to draw the line somewhere,' the conductor pointed out.

Shacki was cheered by the undoubted circumstance that all the wit of the Goytre Valley was being poured out for his and Gwenny's benefit. What Jinkins said about the horse now. And this about the nuts – . And that gel at Pensarn! What funny chaps there was about if you only came to think of it. He began to think hard, hoping for a witticism of his own, a personal offering for Gwenny. She had heard the bandy-straight one before, just once or twice or fifty times or a hundred, or maybe oftener than that. Something new was wanted. A fellow like this conductor, of course, he could turn them off like lightning. Here he was, looking at the flowers. Shacki waited for his sally. They were his flowers, weren't they? Diawl, anything said about um was as good as his, too.

'I likes a nice lily, myself,' said the conductor.

'You look more you'd like a nice pansy,' said the collier. He grinned, the slaver glistening on his red gums, and winked at the hill farm-woman. 'Cheeky flamer!' she called him.

'You askin' for a fight? 'Cos if you are – '

'Sorry, can't stop now.' Still grinning, he narrowed his coaly eyes. 'But any time you want me, butty, I'm Jack Powell, Mutton Tump. That's me – Jack Powell.' He prepared to drop off, and the conductor kept his finger on the bell, hoping to fetch him a cropper. 'Oh no, you don't, butty!' They heard his nailed boots braking on the road and then through the back window saw him fall away behind them, his knees jerking very fast. 'I'll be up here Sunday,' threatened the conductor, but Shacki didn't believe him. He'd lay two-to-one Jack Powell any day, and was glad a collier could lick a bus conductor.

'Don't forget to stop at the hospital,' he said by way of reminder, and the conductor, as though to recover face, told a tale about the patient who wouldn't take a black draught unless the sister took one too. To please him, Shacki smiled grimly and wagged his head and said what chaps there was about, but he now thought less highly of the humorist, and as they came nearer the stopping place he could feel that same old disturbance, just as though he wanted to go out the back. Bump, bump, bump, the driver must be doing it deliberate, but try to forget, for he might be going to hear good news. She might even be coming home. He grovelled. Home, like Johnny James's mother, hopeless case, cancer of the womb – not that for you, Gwenny fach, he prayed, and Ianto Evans, for speaking of it, he thrust into the devil's baking oven. Bump, bump, bump, if he didn't get off this bus soon he'd be all turned up, only too sure. He felt rotten in the belly, and the worm turned a new heading in his heart.

He alighted.

Inside the hall, he found from the clock that as usual he was five minutes too early for the women's ward. 'Would you like to see anyone in the men's ward?' He thought he would, if only to pass the time. So down the corridor he went, for it was a tiny hospital, run on the pennies of colliers like himself. The men's ward had a wireless set, and the patients were a lively lot. Bill Williams the Cwm borrowed Shacki's flowers. 'Oi, Nurse,' he shouted, 'ow'll I look with a bunch of these on my chest?'

It was the sporty probationer. 'Like a big fat pig with a happle in his mouth,' she suggested.

'There's a fine bloody thing to say, Nurse! Don't I look better'n a pig, boys?'

'Ay,' said Shacki, thinking of the flowers of the field. 'You looks like a lily in the mouth of 'ell.'

Bill started to laugh, and the other men started to laugh, and, seeing this, Shacki became quite convulsed at his second witticism. The blue small coal pitting his face grew less noticeable as his scars grew redder. It was a laugh to do a man's heart good, and it came down on that tunnelling worm like a hob-nailed boot. 'You'll have matron along,' the probationer warned them.

Then Shacki took his flowers from Bill, and grinning all over his face went back through the corridor to the entrance hall. He'd make his lovely gel laugh an' all! He felt fine now, he did, and everything was going to be all right. He knew it. Tell her he'd cleaned the house, and about the baby at number five, and about Jinkins and the collier and the girl and the conductor and Bill Williams the Cwm and him – it'd be better than a circus for Gwenny.

Into the women's ward. Nod here, nod there, straight across to Gwenny with all the news between his teeth and his tongue. Then he swore under his breath. Matron was standing by Gwenny's bed, looking like a change of pillowcases. She was so clean and stiff and starched and grand that he felt small and mean and shabby before her, and frightened, and something of a fool. Respectfully, he greeted her even before he greeted his wife, and when she returned his good day, thanked her.

'We've got good news for you, Mr Thomas. You'll be able to have Mrs Thomas home very soon now.'

'Oh,' he said. He was looking down at Gwenny's white smile. A murderous hate and rage against all living things filled his heart, and he would have had no one free of suffering. 'Cos she's better?'

'Of course. Why else?'

He put the eggs down carefully, and the flowers. Then he fell on his knees at the bedside. 'My gel!' he cried out hoarsely. 'Oh, my lovely gel!' With her right hand she touched his hair. 'There, there, little Shacki bach! Don't take on, look!'

'You are upsetting the patient,' the pillowcase said severely, 'and you are disturbing the ward. I shall have to ask you to go outside.'

It was a quarter of a minute before he got to his feet, and then he was ashamed to look anyone in the face. He snuffled a bit and rubbed under his eyes. 'All right, matron,' he managed to say. 'You can send for the pleece, if you like. I'm that happy, mun!'

He saw his old Gwenny looking an absolute picture there in bed, and thought these would be her last tears, and such happy ones. And with the thought he looked proudly around, and could tell that no one in the ward thought him an old softy. He didn't hate anyone any longer. He was all love, and gave old Gwenny a kiss as bold as brass before he walked outside. He knew they'd let him in again soon.

Ora Pro Boscis

~

FOR Sir Rhodri Plas Mawr it was the best of Friday mornings. Not because the sun was shining and the wind blowing, not because Bessi the Blaen had the evening before littered four healthy puppies, not even because he owned all he saw. He caressed his vast nose and said 'Ah!' He was happy and excited both, like a dog rolling on a dead mouse. It was court day.

He'd show 'em! By jumping george, he'd show 'em! Lot of thieves picking over his land, huh. The rabbits they'd got away with would load a gambo, and the birds – his face lost its smile – his lovely birds – it was worse than murder. His lovely shiny-breasted birds tied up in sacks, and all to pack a poacher's belly. 'Worse than murder!' he grunted.

'Yessir,' said the maid, clearing his breakfast tray.

His mouth opened, but he shut it again without a word. In the shadow of Sir Rhodri's nose it looked like a lead mine under Snowdon. Not that the nose was uncomely. For a man twice his size it would be perfection. It had line and rhythm and character, and when he blew it it had tone. And though ashamed of it as a lad, as a man he was not dissatisfied. It marked him out in a crowd, gave folk something to remember him by, and he thought it patrician. Not a collier's nose, he used to tell himself, and others; not a grocer's nose, and they didn't grow that way on dustmen or duns. A virile organ, he had been assured.

'Well?' he asked the girl.

'Mr Bevan is downstairs to see you, sir.'

'Couldn't you say so at once? Tell him fifteen minutes.' He wanted a word with Bevan. Right enough to point out that his place on the bench was best left empty – after all, he hadn't sat a dozen times in as many years, just now and again when for the look of the thing he paid a visit to Plas Mawr – and justice was justice, neither for rent nor rape, quite right. But Bevan's hints that he'd better stay away altogether – He blew his nose, hard, and those below remembered the Last Trump.

'Morning, Bevan.'

'Morning, Sir Rhodri.' A poor little squit of a fellow, Bevan, no more to him than a row of spring cabbage.

'Sorry to keep you waiting. Lovely morning, Bevan. And a great occasion.'

'As you say, Sir Rhodri.'

'I hope the Bench will make this a lesson to the whole neighbourhood. This – what's the chap's name?'

'Thomas Thomas.'

'Thomas Thomas – ah!'

'They call him Tomos Tynypwll round here,' said Bevan. 'I doubt if there's many know his right name. And some call him Tom Bugle.'

'Musical, is he? A real taffy, eh?' And Sir Rhodri recited:

Tomos was a Welshman, Tomos was a thief,
Tomos came to my house and stole better than a leg of beef, blast him!

He laughed and rubbed his hands together. 'Well, so long as they get it right on the charge sheet, eh? – Thomas Thomas or Tomos Tynypwll, no odds. He needs a lesson, Bevan, and all these pinchers and poachers. We must be firm with this bugler who bugles my birds.'

He was disappointed that the agent, usually so sharp, missed his joke. 'We'll be that all right. We'd better not show too fierce, though. Just let the law take its course, Sir Rhodri.'

'Who said anything else? Justice, that's what we want. That's what we'll get.' Sir Rhodri warmed up. 'If I was a vindictive sort of chap I'd be sitting on the bench this morning, not among the public. But I've always been a man to uphold the constitution and appearances. In my position, Bevan, I must set an example. These labour chaps, you know – .'

Bevan agreed this was very handsome of Sir Rhodri. 'And since you feel that way about it, Sir Rhodri, I really believe it might be better – '

'Well?'

'To be frank, Sir Rhodri, that if you decided to stay away even from the body of the court – '

Sir Rhodri shook his nose, and the rest of his head swung with it. 'Nonsense, Bevan! Damned nonsense! My rabbits, aren't they?

And my birds. Wara teg, Bevan: fair play's a jewel, as they say. If I haven't a right to be present, who the devil has?'

Bevan admitted his right. 'But I still think it might be better. I wish you would, Sir Rhodri.'

'Now look here, Bevan – ' Sir Rhodri grew red and hot, like a hollow radish. 'I don't know what's going on behind my back with some of you.' He waved Bevan's mouth shut. 'First there's you, pretending to save me trouble; then there's that fat-lugged sergeant telling me I needn't bother to be present; then there's old Powey; and now there's you again. I'm a patient man, but I'm getting angry. Know the word, Bevan? Angry – See!'

Bevan saw and said he saw, but that didn't save him now. Sir Rhodri rolled him out like a dollop of dough, north-south and east by west, and when at last he thumped him back to shape it was only to a rough likeness. '*See*, Bevan?'

'I can only say I acted for the best.'

'All right then.'

'And I think you'll be sorry, Sir Rhodri.'

'You'll be sorry unless you shut up,' said Sir Rhodri, shoving his snout forward.

Yet the thought stuck with him as he drove the two of them a mile and a half to town. Sorry, indeed. Tomos Tynypwll might be sorry and anyone else he gave the rough end of his tongue to, but he, Sir Rhodri, the big shot around here – why, he owned the place. He'd show 'em!

Yet when he met the local justices behind the court-room they lacked hwyl. No question of it, they were sick as dogs to see him. Not even sherry brought them together – Bristol Milk at fourteen bob a bottle. And it was galling the way they stared at his nose when they thought he wasn't looking. It wasn't as though they'd never set eyes on it before. And that chap Bevan – the look on his face. Pious. Smug. Bit of a martyr. Sir Rhodri was becoming most uncomfortable. Perhaps they thought he meant to bully them, give justice a squeeze, like an orange, like a – chrrm! Like a parlourmaid, he was going to say, but that was levity. He sought to cleanse their hearts of doubt. He cared less than a tick's elbow for the rabbits, he assured them, never touched the things, no fat on their ribs, but a principle was at stake. Property. Ah, property! Where should we be without it?

Where would you be without it? thought the magistrates, for a moment forgetting his nose.

Time to get a move on, thank heaven! Sir Rhodri, to show his high-mindedness, did not take the seat reserved for him, but sat like an ordinary chap on an ordinary form. His appearance was bound to make a stir, but he thought the public rather pleased than resentful that he had shown up. Bit of feudal feeling left still, thank God, despite the bolshies. Not that he saw anything to grin about.

The preliminaries were quickly over. 'Call Thomas Thomas.'

The crowd (it was now he noticed what a big crowd it was) rustled, hummed, and sat back. Two johnnies in mufflers sitting in front turned to stare at the great man, but this was one of the penalties of greatness and he looked through them.

'Thomas Thomas!'

Tomos Tynypwll went into the dock, and Sir Rhodri gaped.

He was dress in corduroy trousers, yorked under the knees, a green velveteen waistcoat of his granddad's time, a red and white neckerchief, and a railwayman's jacket. He was bland as a blown-up pig's bladder, yet gay as a gander in May. He looked the sort of chap who'd take dandelions to a harvest home and touch the parson for a pint on the strength of it. There was a happy murmuring along the wooden seats, and Sir Rhodri wasn't sure whether he had gone blue, grey, or cheese-green. The height and build, the shape of the sconce – and that nose! Doubting there were two such in Wales, he foolishly felt for his own.

Tomos greeted a friend in court, one of the mufflered johnnies, and was sternly reproved, whereat he ducked his head, and his case was begun. For a time Sir Rhodri heard nothing of it: disbelief, humiliation, and rage beat about his skull. Not that this mattered much: he knew the evidence pretty well. Jenkins the keeper and Police Constable Ponty Jones would testify that they had seen the defendant on enclosed land at a suspicious time, that they had given unsuccessful chase, that two newly-dead rabbits had been found in a shed at the defendant's home. The case was cast-iron and stone-doddle. A ticket for Botany Bay in the old days.

He was thinking: How little we know our fathers!

'Then how do you account for the two rabbits found in your shed?' he heard Gracegirdle ask from the bench.

'Thass easy.' Tomos hoicked his thumb at the keeper. 'He put um there.'

Gracegirdle did his imitation of Silvanus Williams of Pontygwyndy, K.C. 'Quite so, Thomas Thomas. You have proof of this – er – allegation?' But Tomos was muttering at Jenkins the keeper, and he had to repeat the question, without irony this time.

'Proof? Three bags full, mun. There's a feller – he told this feller he'd put rabbits in my shed one day, Jinkins did.'

'Why, you flamer!' cried Jenkins, but was roughly silenced. 'Order in court,' said Tomos reproachfully.

'One moment, Thomas Thomas. Who told whom, and what?' Tomos goggled at him. 'I mean, who told someone else about putting rabbits in your shed. This is an extremely serious allegation – charge – I hope you realize that?'

'Seven years hard,' said Tomos. 'For Jinkins, your worship.'

Gracegirdle waved this away. 'Please, Mr Thomas. You say the keeper told someone he would put rabbits in your shed. Very well – whom did he tell?'

'My sister Blodwen's oldest girl's young man's uncle, your worship.'

'Yours sister Blodwen's youngest – '

'Oldest, your worship!'

The Clerk whispered in Gracegirdle's ear. 'Yes, yes, I was coming to that. Can you produce this – er – distant witness, Mr Thomas? This distant relative, I might almost call him.'

Tomos winked at the men in mufflers who squirmed till their corduroys purred like cats. 'On'y in a wooden box, your worship. He's wedi pobi, gone aloft, drawed his wages.' He raised his hand. 'As the hymn says – '

'Never mind what the hymn says! This is a court of law, sir, not a gymanfa ganu!' Tomos was heard to mutter something about the singing at Beulah. It was at this point that Sir Rhodri allowed his eye to be caught by the man on the stand. Smiling, Tomos stroked his nose. Sir Rhodri looked away.

'I'm trying – ' began Gracegirdle, then altered his sentence. 'I'm trying to help you.' He smothered Tomos's attempt to thank him. 'What was the name of this witness you mention as deceased? As dead!' he bellowed, before the defendant's eyebrows got half way to the ceiling.

'I called him Davy,' Tomos admitted. He pointed to the men in mufflers. 'These boys knew him well, poor feller.'

'So you called him Davy?' Gracegirdle was doing Silvanus Williams again, but Plas Mawr is a long way from Pontygwyndy. 'And what did your sister Blodwen's oldest daughter's young man call him, pray?' He snatched the word from Tomos's mouth. 'Besides uncle, I mean?'

'He called him Flannel Belly, your worship.'

'I must warn you – '

' 'Cos he used to wear a bellyband from September till May, your worship.'

There was tittering in court. 'Quite a long bellyband,' said Gracegirdle, to fetch the laugh over to his side of the hedge. The Clerk was whispering. 'Yes, yes, I was coming to that. This Davy Flannel – was it he or the keeper who told you about the rabbits?' The Clerk whispered again. 'I know, I know. This Davy, then, told you, and Jenkins told him – so you say.' Tomos nodded. 'Now what precisely did he say? The exact words, please!'

'He told him he'd put rabbits in my shed.'

'But my good fellow – the exact words! He didn't use the third person, I imagine?'

'No,' said Tomos. Gracegirdle felt he was getting near the bone at last. 'There wasn't no third person.' People were putting their hands over their mouths, shuffling on their seats. 'Except me.'

The magistrate dropped to second gear. 'I mean, did the speaker say, for example, "I intend to put rabbits in the shed of Tomos Tynypwll"?'

'No.' Sir Rhodri saw Gracegirdle thanking God for a monosyllable. 'He didn't mention you at all. Jinkins may be a mochyn, your worship, but he's not such a mochyn as to bring the Bench into it.'

The keeper struggled to his feet, but Ponty pressed him down again. As for Gracegirdle, he looked both hot and faint, but saved his face by threatening to clear the court. 'Silence! I must have silence!' He felt everyone was laughing at him, but how the devil could he do other than he was doing? And the Clerk was whispering in his ear. 'I know,' he snapped. 'I was coming to that.' He looked sideways at his fellow magistrates, and didn't like what he saw of Mrs Evans the Farm.

'Now, Tomos,' he began quietly, 'I've given you a lot of rope, and I shan't give any more. You understand? I want a straight answer to a straight question. You were seen inside the Plas grounds on the night in question. Do you deny that after the evidence we have heard?'

'Not guilty,' said Tomos, after some thought.

'Yes, or no, do you deny it?'

'Deny what?' Tomos smiled at a friend in court, and was fiercely rebuked. 'No,' he said.

'You don't deny it?'

'I mean No, I wasn't there.'

Gracegirdle was breathing very hard now. 'You have heard two independent witnesses testify they saw you there, yet you deny it.' He almost pleaded with the scallywag before him. 'I want to help you. Have you an alibi?'

Tomos's face cleared. 'No,' he said gratefully, 'but I gets backache awful in wet weather. Them old alibis!'

There was laughter in court and Tomos looked well pleased. Sir Rhodri coughed four or five times, blew his horn, and kept his big red face in his white handkerchief as long as he decently could. If only the joke wasn't partly on him! So thinking, he frowned unconvincingly at the mufflers, who nudged each other and stared him out. 'Another interruption and I'll clear the court,' snarled Gracegirdle. Then: Justice, he thought finely, justice and Hywel Dda, let me do justice. 'I meant,' he said, 'have you anyone to testify that you were in some other place at nine-thirty Tuesday night the twenty-third of June?' He thought it best to repeat his question, so that this big-nosed imbecile could take it in. And Lord, he prayed, give me strength this day! But Tomos was so long a-pondering that he had to ask it a third time, sharply.

'Mistaken identity,' said Tomos then.

'You know what that means?'

'Someone 'bout here the spit image of me, your worship.' He winked at the mufflered johnnies. 'Like Mrs Davies the Deri's new baby the spit image of Jinkins.'

No wonder Gracegirdle lost his temper. 'You – you,' he began, while the horrified Clerk rushed to his side. 'Who the devil could be mistaken for you, you – you – '

It was Tomos's moment. One of the mufflered johnnies made a noise like a hen, Gracegirdle clapped his hand to his forehead, and Sir Rhodri felt his stomach turn its toes out, as the defendant turned at leisure towards the crowded seats. For a half-second he stood nodding, and then took his nose between fingers and thumb. 'As it might be Sir Rhodri himself, your worship,' he said respectfully, but loudly.

The hen became a crazy farmyard, then laughter enveloped the room. This was what they'd been waiting for, the dole-drawers, the mouchers, the rabbit-snatchers – to see old Privilege up at the Plas with a stoat on the end of his nozzle. Uncollared colliers hooted at royalties, blackcoats at dividends, even the godly had their snigger. There was comment so crapulous from the mufflered johnnies

71

that, on the bench, Mrs Evans' bonnet shot the length of its elastic. The uproar grew, the gavel rapped noiselessly through it, Gracegirdle was on his feet and shaking his fist at Tomos, whose hand, as it kept to his nose, extended its fingers in an old-fashioned and unmistakably derisive way towards him. Then officers began to clear the court, and Sir Rhodri, though they passed him by, went outside too. Well, he'd been made to look a fine fool. Sooner he cleared out of the place the better. But he couldn't clear out of the story – he knew that. They'd be telling of noses in a hundred years around Plas Mawr. He glowered after his agent, but Bevan was keeping out of harm's way. He scribbled a note on a sheet of paper and handed it to a constable.

He was still there, in the little hall, when Bevan came up behind him, 'Case dismissed, Sir Rhodri,' he said nervously.

'I want to see that chap Tomos!'

Bevan fluttered his wings. 'D'you think it wise, Sir Rhodri?'

'Who are you to judge?'

They had not far to go to find him. He was mouching down the corridor with the mufflered johnnies. 'Hey, you!' But Sir Rhodri's summons struck even himself as the wrong one. 'Mr Thomas, could I have a word with you?' 'Go ahead, you,' said Tomos graciously. Sir Rhodri groped for words.

'I've always fancied one of they cigars,' said Tomos, eyeing Sir Rhodri's waistcoat pocket. 'And these boys here.'

Sir Rhodri lived up to his nose. 'Here, take the lot.' They were pleased, and said so. They've got me on a string, he thought, but had lost his vexation. After all, if the old dad – 'There's just one question, Mr Thomas, if these gentlemen would perhaps be good enough to drink my health over the way there – ' He nodded for Bevan to go with them. 'Just one question, Mr Thomas, if you don't mind.'

'Not at all. Ask you, boyo. Got a match?'

Sir Rhodri handed over a boxful. 'Keep them. What I wanted to ask, Mr Thomas – you wouldn't remember, perhaps, but did your mother ever go to work up at the Plas?'

He saw something in his brother's eyes he couldn't put a name to. He felt pretty shabby, did Sir Rhodri then. 'No, not my mam. But my dad was always about the house. That would be before you were born, I fancy.' He smiled and blew smoke all over the place, including Sir Rhodri. 'Biggest nose in Wales, my old dad.'

Sir Rhodri dropped his bowler.

The Dreamers

~

IT WAS in the poet's month of May that Rhisiart Rhisiarts of Pont-y-Bwbach dreamt a strange and beautiful dream. He dreamt that he was walking towards Capel-y-Mynydd with a woman at his side. She was tall as his mouth, lithe as a lily, and smelled sweeter than mint after rain. She hung on his arm like a sunlit cloud as they went towards and into the chapel, which was filled with folk of a substance less than flesh but more than shadow, and where they were married by a minister who looked like Merlin and talked like Lloyd George. The ceremony over, they left the chapel, which had somehow silently emptied itself, and walked back through the fields to Rhisiart's house in the valley. A harp sounded from heaven, a brook sang penillion-fashion beside them, and white trefoil filled the footprints of the lady. Rhisiart's heart trembled with fear and joy, his head was thronged with poems of a splendour unknown, his rough hand cradled the lily-fingers of his bride. They reached the little book-strewn house at last, still with no word between them, and then, as Rhisiart bore her in his arms over the threshold of their room, the dream ended and he awoke in grief and loss and longing.

Now to appreciate the strangeness of this dream we must remember that Rhisiart was forty and a solitary, that in his day he had passed very high in the college and ever since had been reading a thousand years back. All such are strange beings, and Rhisiart was stranger than most. His particular and private strangeness was that he was frightened of womenfolk, though to hear him talk you'd never have suspected this – but it is a main misery of our natures that ignorance breeds fear, and of women he was uncommonly ignorant. He hadn't so much as kissed one in fifteen years, and then it was his third-cousin on a Whitsun treat – a deed to be held against no man, surely. Yet he was a great scholar, and could tell you the colour of Vivien's eyes or what size shoes Rhiannon wore. It is likely that no man since Lancelot was more intimate with Gwenhwyfar, and what he didn't know about Olwen, Kulhwch didn't know either. But of sweethearts, none; and of loving, not an hour.

Not that he hated or despised women, or would ever be cruel to them. If they were six or seven hundred years old he could easily be brought to cherish them – and at forty the forest is far from mid-winter and the sap still rising. But he covered uncertainty with severity, spoke from unease with a dry tongue, and his fondlings were reserved for the smooth sides of old folios. He had even written a poem or two on the subject, in strict metre, though so far he had kept these strictly to himself.

But his dream shook the lessons of a lifetime. For the rest of the night he sought vainly to sleep and seize the happiness so brusquely denied him. It was a sad Rhisiart who came downstairs in the morning. As he cut his bread and butter and steeped the tea, for the first time he resented the quiet of his homely mornings; his window was cut from the sun by the mountain beyond, and a grey dull light banished the apricot glow of his dreaming. The fire mouldered and smouldered, what had been a welcome profusion of litter looked worse than a broken crow's nest, and before finishing breakfast he tipped tea on his copy of Llywarch Hen.

He couldn't settle to work. Thoughts he could not regulate drove him out-of-doors. It was hours later, on the mountain side, that he came to a decision. He had been miserable and puzzled, but all along with more sense than to tell himself it was only a dream and didn't matter. Dreams mattered tremendously, and when they held out prospects so enchanting wouldn't he be duller than dull to ignore them? For five thousand years men had believed in dreams, and there were the Bible and the Mabinogion to prove it. He closed his eyes to think.

He had it! He turned and went striding over the springy grass, past the crumbling stone walls, alongside the brown brook to his house. 'Guidance!' he cried, 'Guidance!' First he cleared half the table with fierce shovelling movements of his hands, and then lifted from his top shelf a mighty canvas-backed volume of the Triads. From this granary of native wisdom, he was sure, a grain would emerge to foul or fatten him. Closing his eyes tightly he opened the leaves at random, and at random set his finger on the right-hand page. What would it say? Ha! THREE THINGS I LOVE TO SEE: HONEY ON MY BREAD; THE FACE OF THE WOMAN I LOVE; AND A ROPE

ROUND THE NECK OF AN ENGLISHMAN. He swung his glasses and cogitated, for this, while not decisive, was certainly suggestive: Rhisiart loved honey better than a bee, and had no great fondness for the English. (Hadn't they hanged an ancestor of his in 1437, and all for stealing a yellow mare?) He would try again. Ha! THREE THINGS WITHOUT WHICH A MAN IS NO MAN: A STAFF IN HIS HAND; MONEY IN HIS PURSE; AND A WIFE IN HIS BED.

His doubts lasted no longer than you'd take to count twelve twelves. Then he read the triad through a second time with his glasses on and slammed the volume shut.

'So be it!' he said – and was surprised at the depth of his voice – 'I will find myself a wife!'

It was a moment of exhilaration and he viewed without flinching the tea-stain on Llywarch Hen. What a future was opening before him! He felt himself one with seekers for the Grail. Somewhere she waited, that exquisite half-seen lady of the night, and ahead lay the tremulous drama of acquaintance, courtship, and consummation. He drew a meal together, hurriedly consumed it. There was no time to lose. 'A wife,' he cried, 'a wife of my own!' With staff in hand, purse in pocket, and the door on the latch, he set briskly off.

The weather kept fine for him, and he travelled with the sun, south then west through Monmouthshire. That day he walked from Pont-y-Bwbach to Brynmawr and saw not a woman to remind him of his bride: they were too tall, too short, too fat, too thin, had a broken tooth or a shrill voice, or maybe a pimple on the nose. But though all Wales were the casket, he'd walk and seek and find. The second night he slept at Tredegar, and next day walked ten miles down one valley and eleven miles up the next to sleep in Rhymney. The fourth day he walked twenty-five miles and slept in Cefn; the fifth night he was in Aberdare, where it was wet and Sunday; and the sixth at Pontypridd, where he felt himself as far from paradise as ever. He now moped and drooped till the landlord feared for his reckoning and a commercial traveller asked him what was on his mind.

'I am looking for a woman,' replied Rhisiart sadly.

'Try Cardiff,' said his comforter. 'You'll find all you want there.'

Rhisiart thanked him for his interest and decided he would, and next morning in good time set off by road. He was afraid that if he used train or bus he might miss his destiny, for the Triads, unlike the Book of Job, say nothing of either. Well, he foot-slogged it through Treforest and past the bottom of Nantgarw, had a drink of water at Taff's Well and another at Tongwynlais; the sun climbed higher, the breeze sank, it was front lawns and flowers all the way to the Cross Inn. He was in Park Place when most people have their lunch, and had his, frugally, on a bench in the Park. Before him was a spectacle that swelled him with assurance of triumph: palaces of silvered stone and the long curtain wall of the Castle, promenaded by peacocks and out-topped by a shattered keep. The sky was pale blue and drifted with almost motionless white cloud; around his head swam the odour of wallflowers and tulips; buses trumpeted and tramcars clanged in the mellow distance. It was a scene where Branwen in brocade or Bercilak's lady in cloth of gold would be more in keeping than city fathers in bowler hats and vestrymen's striped trousers.

With the thought he dusted the crumbs to the sparrows and stood up. He went into town by Kingsway and moved through the crowds, his nose to the wind. He looked at many, and many looked at him. He was a tall man with a cat-head, hair like bull's wool the day after the fair, and rag-mat eyebrows. His nose was beaked, his cheekbones high, his ears like meat-hooks, only thicker. He wore a corduroy waistcoat, his heel-tips clanked, and he'd left the crease of his trousers somewhere this side of Brynmawr. Some thought him an artist, others didn't know what to think, and to certain fussy ones he looked the kind to gobble little girls up. How picturesque! they said; or How odd! or How horrid! – according to group and fancy. But Rhisiart, staring about him, clenching his staff, striking off sparks, had no thought for this: he was too dazzled by a revelation of female loveliness. This was all around him: from magnificent, languishing ladies who spoke with plums in their mouths down to brisk little working girls, their faces rich with youth and mirth, he saw dozens, scores, hundreds, of dear, delightful, alluring, tantalising creatures, any and each one the worthy object of a lifetime's love and cherishing. Why, he exulted, there isn't one of them I wouldn't –

He stopped dead, upsetting the traffic. Any and each one – but to choose – he had to choose. What a problem! A fine firm-built amazon in tweeds and criss-cross brogues banged into him from behind; he staggered against a poppet in a fur cape, tripped, reeled, and fetched up against two dainty darlings whose waists cried out for an arm to encircle them. Must a man starve in the midst of plenty? Must he?

It was now, as he gauchely caught at his crumpled hat, mumbling and bumbling for pardon, that he saw go smoothly past a figure that roused in him the tenderest recollection. She was tall as his mouth and lithe as a lily, and at first her face was hidden. Now or never – silence was damnation. He gulped.

'I beg your pardon,' he began timidly.

She had a delicate enamelled face that reminded Rhisiart of a cowslip or a sunlit cloud at evening.

'I have been wondering – '

She offered him sixpence.

'No. It's a mistake. It's because I had a dream six nights ago – '

She had thought him wild-looking but civil, but now she feared a savage. Clipping her bag to, she stepped back.

'I wanted to ask you – please!' cried Rhisiart.

'Well?' It was a voice of such beauty and finality that Rhisiart thought of the name-plate on a coffin.

'I had a dream six nights ago. I thought I got married, only I woke up too soon. To a woman like you. So I thought perhaps – '

Her face matched the velvet peony on her jacket. 'Really! In broad daylight too!'

'I'm sorry,' said Rhisiart miserably.

'Is he annoying you?' asked a burly brute in a green pullover. 'If so – ' He was privet to Rhisiart's gorse, a thick-head hero eager for fame. He folded his fist, and Rhisiart took the weight of his staff, in case.

'I made a mistake,' he said humbly. 'I ask your pardon. But,' he added, 'it was no ordinary dream.'

They hurried away from the tanglewood madman, the hero outwardly solicitous and inwardly congratulating himself, holding her elbow in the genteelest fashion, but Rhisiart slunk like a dog into a side street. He thought it dismal he should fail, and after a while returned to the crowds, waited on inspiration, and tried again, but Beauty lacked Bounty, and a threat to call a policeman sent him scuttling to cover. A third time he ventured out but this time chose a timid one. Marriage is one thing, but prison for the most part another, and he was thinking it wise though ignoble to catch the first train for Pont-y-Bwbach when coming along the pavement towards him he noticed a tall, slim, and most potently attired young woman. She wore a flowered frock and a cartwheel hat, her shoes glittered in the sun, her gloves and bag were white, her bangles of coral, and in all ways she looked better than poppies in corn. Soon she was close enough for him to see that her lips were scarlet, her hair like gold, and her eyes changed from red to green as the words came out of his mouth.

'I beg your pardon,' he began, and she stopped. For him, Rhisiart, she stopped! 'I had a dream six nights ago – '

'That was nice, honey,' said the girl. 'Tell me about it.'

He did. That she should listen was joy; that she smiled was pure heaven. Words flowed to his tongue. He developed quite a hwyl.

'And it ended at the top of the stairs?'

He said Yes with his hands.

'Well, fancy that!' She laughed. 'That's where mine begin.' He was still working this out when she asked him: 'Would you know her again, to speak to?'

He knew, he told her warmly, that she was lovely enough to be queen to all men from Wye to Towy.

'That's a pretty tall order. Would she be like enough me, d'you think?' She laughed again, taking his arm. 'Shall we be going?'

'To Pont-y-Bwbach?'

'No fear!' Rhisiart grew anxious. Something had gone wrong, possibly her spelling. 'How about to where you left off, honey?'

'But there's been a mistake,' he said agitatedly. 'You don't understand.'

'Of course I do,' she laughed. 'We're only young once, that's what I say.'

'It's not a laughing matter. My whole future depends on it. I'm looking for my wife.'

Her eyes changed back through yellow to red, her knuckles tightened over her bag, and her lips went twice as thin. When he tried to explain further, she told him lots he didn't like hearing, and called him what he knew he wasn't. Wife indeed! Between these two bus stops? Didn't he believe in live and let live?

She moved off handsomely but in a hurry, and the next minute a policeman was tapping Rhisiart's arm. 'Where you from?' he asked coldly, and listened. 'And what you think you're up to?' Rhisiart could tell he didn't believe him. 'Fine old scandal this'll be for Pont-y-Bwbach,' said the bobby angrily. He scratched the small of his back and then the back of his head. 'But there, I'm a Monmouth-shire man myself, and we've got to stick together, I s'pose. There's a train for home in twenty minutes, and you better be on it. Get me?'

Rhisiart got him, dead centre, and had breath left over for thanks. He'd had his bellyful of dreaming. At Newport he had time to visit a bookshop, and before he reached Pont-y-Bwbach was translating Juvenal's Sixth Satire – the One on Women – into Welsh.

'Hear about Pugh the Bryn?' the porter asked him. He was quite a stranger after six days' absence.

'What about him?'

'Buried this morning at Capel-y-Mynydd. That's life for you,' said the porter.

'On the contrary!' Rhisiart gave up his ticket, thoughtfully. His head was full of his reading: no doubt she'd poisoned him or got her paramour to push him under a cart. Women!

'Pneumonia,' said the porter. 'Galloping.'

Rhisiart laughed sourly. Maybe! The world was easily deceived still. Poor fools of men! But Pugh was a neighbour, and he'd better call before nightfall. Then a new thought filled his head. Mrs Pugh's estate and his own were not too dissimilar. She had buried a husband that day, and he a wife. It was a quaint idea and he played with it all the way to the Bryn. His boots were black and his collar six-days-dirty, so he was dressed for the part all right. Not far from the Bryn he met Jeremiah Jenkins and gave him good-night. 'And it is a good night,' said Jeremiah. 'But a sad affair?' Rhisiart suggested. Jeremiah's thoughts seemed elsewhere, for he nodded and said it might have been worse. With that they parted. He had been best man at Pugh's wedding, had Jeremiah, and Rhisiart judged him stupid with grief.

With his new-opened eyes he saw surprisedly what a fine piece Mrs Pugh was. Thirty-eight years old and never a child of her body, and the whitest neck, past question, in all Monmouthshire. Maybe the tears had made her eyes gleam, but gleam they did most disturbingly. Her mourning blouse was relieved by a gold locket, and her stockings were silk, not wool. Looks more like a bride than a widow, thought Rhisiart harshly.

He took a glass of port out of respect, and because he'd been walking and was dry it went down so fast he had to have another. He never drank, and after the second glass was much surprised to hear the china dogs barking on the mantelpiece.

'But it's all in the stars,' said Mrs Pugh. 'And it all comes through to us, if only we know how.'

'Maybe.' Rhisiart was not committing himself.

'Now you are a man with schooling, Mr Rhisiarts – '

A little here and there, true.

'And you know more than most of us.'

He sipped his port. 'I wouldn't say that, Mrs Pugh.'

Well there, if she insisted! 'And you keep a still tongue in your head. So I'll tell you, and ask your advice.'

He hadn't meant to beam, but he could tell by the feel of his face that he was – for the first time in years – at a woman. Such sense, such deference, such a white neck!

'I am a great one for dreaming, Mr Rhisiarts. Pugh told me, poor feller, it's because I eat a good supper, but it makes no difference if I go to bed as empty as a kettledrum. If there are dreams to be had, I'll have them. I dreamt that Pugh would cross over, Mr Rhisiarts – a week before the very day, I dreamt it. Do you believe in dreams, Mr Rhisiarts bach?'

'I do,' he said earnestly, 'I do. You interest me strangely, Mrs Pugh.'

'And it came true.' She took out two handkerchiefs and chose the one with lace on it. 'I'm only a poor widow, Mr Rhisiarts bach.'

He groaned. 'Poor little woman, poor little woman!'

'And that's not all I dreamt. And this is what I wanted to ask you about – for no one has more feeling for a man with schooling than I have, Mr Rhisiarts – I dreamt I got married again double quick.' His eyes grew big as tea-pots. 'Was that a wicked dream, Mr Rhisiarts bach?'

'It came from heaven, Mrs Pugh.' In his left-hand pocket his fingers touched the libeller of women and recoiled as from a snake. 'I too have dreams. What dreams!'

'I don't know what people will say – '

'Pah!' He shot his port to the pit of his stomach. 'That for them!'

'I always knew you were a man with schooling,' said the widow.

'And dreams,' said Rhisiart; 'dr-r-r-reams, Mrs Pugh! I thank God in the highest, Mrs Pugh, and I thank God in the lowest, for that lovely dream. We should always follow our dreams. You dream and I dream – everybody dreams. And what did Dyvynwal Moelmud himself say of dreams? He said: Better a good dream than a bad awakening – that's what he said, Mrs Pugh, and he one of the three National Pillars of the Island of Britain – one of the three Beneficent Sovereigns of the Cymry.'

'There's lovely you talk,' said the widow.

Rhisiart leaned forward and caught her hand. 'Mrs Pugh, little woman, look – couldn't we – couldn't you and I – ?'

'I'm quite frightened of you, Mr Rhisiarts. A poor widow like me all on her own in the house – I couldn't even call out for help if you was to – '

'I mean, get married,' said Rhisiart.

'Oh good lord enow!' she cried. 'And I might have too, only Jeremiah asked me on the way back from chapel to-day.' For a moment she looked as dashed as he; then she brightened and nipped his leg playfully. 'Never mind, Mr Rhisiarts bach. You shall be my third, never fear.'

'No,' he cried, 'No!' and reached for his staff. He looked so funny standing there that the widow Pugh laughed till her fat shook.

'Women!' cried Rhisiart.

A Night at Galon-Uchaf

~

TWO MEN were climbing a hillside by a gorse-bound path. It was evening in late October, the sheep pressed to the mountain wall, and a red wind blew from the east.

'Gwynt coch Amwythig,' said the first man. 'The red wind of Shrewsbury.'

'Gwynt traed y meirw,' said the second. 'The wind of the dead men's feet.'

They were bards, Gurnos of Galon-Uchaf and his nephew Madoc, from Trefente, coming from market in the next valley but one. Gurnos was a man of fifty or more, tall and lolling, with a long, red, mild, clean and unwhiskered face, and a forehead running a good way back over the top of his skull. He was a famous belly-dog, this Gurnos, and a middling poet. He had the second sight, too, and would sometimes take the evil eye off a neighbour and sometimes put it on, and in his youth he had cured men of wavering and many a maid of malaise. His mother's name was Creiddylad; of his dad she told how he walked over the mountain one day with a bag in his hand and an owl on his shoulder, as it might be a man-midwife or Gwynn ab Nudd himself the fairy king. Certain it was that Gurnos lived on next to no work, though his farm was sharp as a hawk's beak, and he alone of men to-day had the secret of the honey-hearted mead. His nephew Madoc was in the mid-twenties, a lean and flashing man with the metres at his finger-ends and a heart of flame. He had married a red-haired girl from Glamorgan ten days before, and they were here at Gurnos's farm for a fortnight. He was eager to be home, and they walked fast, with the wind behind them. There were friends and neighbours, too; they were behind their time. On the crest, where the white grass poured flat, they paused ten heart-beats, sucked the gale, pointed to the valley they had left, and then dropped gladly under the mountain rampart. Above them the wind clutched and staggered, then sprang for the Bwlch and the pass to the sea.

'Gwynt ffroen yr ych,' said Madoc. 'The wind of the ox's nostrils.'

Caught without a counter, Gurnos waved his hand at the rigid hills and flurried sky. Below them, a third of a mile down the slope, they could see the buildings of Galon-Uchaf, low, blunted, and shadow-smudged. Near the farm a tipless arrow-head of ragged bank funnelled the wind past the cowsheds, and a six-foot wall of untrimmed stone, daggled with pink wash, flung it outwards from the living quarters. The roof was humped with turf and rough as a boar's back, and stripped lilac trees creaked and rubbed by the front door. As they came near, two men were approaching from the other side, so they waited for them, gave them greeting. They were Lew Watkins and Mordecai Jones from Llangua, in the coal valleys, dressed in black with bowler hats. As the door opened they removed these hats and palmed their bald heads gravely.

Day had now almost died from the sky, but westwards over the Bwlch was a thin sour belt of sun-starved light frayed with a pylon, a cairn, and three side-spilled oak trees. 'Man, too, goeth down like a bilious sun,' said Lew, pointing. 'Ay,' said Mordecai, 'but on the Great Day as surely the grave shall spew him up again.'

Gurnos laughed from his feet up, and Lew, and Mordecai coughed from a stiff chest, but Madoc was already through the door. 'Gwen,' he was shouting, 'I'm back! Gwen, I'm back!' Gwen blushed, and everyone started to laugh, for from his voice it seemed he'd been away weeks, not hours. 'I was the same, just the same,' said a leather-headed man from a corner. 'When I was your age I couldn't give my missus time to take her hands out of the flour.' 'No,' she agreed, 'but now I could bake cake for all Cardigan.' The leather-headed man's name was Evans. On Sundays he was a great one to cry out 'Glory be,' or 'Halleluiah,' or 'Walk with me, Jesus,' during the sermon, but all times else he was salt on a fox's tail: therefore, on Sundays he was known as Evans Halleluiah, and on weekdays as Evans Tally-ho. Now when his wife groused at him he first cleared his throat, then thought better of it and scowled ferociously at two russet-coloured thirtyish men in corduroys who squatted broad-bottomed on three-legged stools, nudging each other and squirming with delight. They were the brothers Wat and Tal from Pwll-hobi, cowmen and dog-breeders. They spent so much of their time with animals that they had no art to converse with men. Under each of their stools lay a slant-eyed foxy corgi bitch, and to hide their joy and spare the leather-headed man's feelings they now bent inwards over them, communing with grunts, gasps, barks and whistles.

I'll not be like that, thought Madoc, furious and foolish both. But he read the message of Gwen's wide eyes, her joyous kindly smile, then he smiled too. He stood for a moment, wordless, his hands outstretched, like a ship's carved figurehead straining to the sea. In that moment an incomprehensible experience was shared by all the company, for as they watched these proud and splendid lovers they achieved an extension, an independence, of time and place. They knew themselves still at Galon-Uchaf, felt the full pressure of their chairbacks, yet the walls had fled outwards to mountain and sea; they still saw the yellow of fire and lamp, but they inhabited simultaneously a timeless and unlocalised world. With all this a wantonness warmed along the blood, a fast-borne sweetness into heart and brain, so that they lived again old kisses and caresses, drew from memory or wove from dead desire the velvet loveliness of summer nights and courting days and fondling under the trees. Their breath came slow and deep, the light from their eyes was at once languorous and sparkling, their nostrils sniffed the bitterness of broken fern or the green sweetness of bruised grass. Then Gurnos laughed. Madoc had seized Gwen's hands. The others sat back in an after-calmness of emotion as genial as it was puzzling and rare. Only the boys from Pwll-hobi nodded as though they knew what had happened, while the two golden bitches whimpered a little and licked the heels of their masters' boots.

The one of the company who took longest to find herself again was the widow Simon from Isa'ndre, down the slope. She had been married off too young to a farmer too old, who, like David before him, wanted a Shunamite to cwtch him up in bed and keep his back warm. Like David, too, he was a religious old fellow, and could tell tales of every wicked wench from Aholibah to Jezebel. He'd spent so many evenings reciting Leviticus to his rib, that she came to feel if she so much as looked at an empty pair of breeches Satan's claw was on her. He was pretty cracked the last year or two, and took the trouble to have a five-foot likeness made of himself in knotty oak, which by day did sentry-go in the parlour and by night in their bedroom. She was thus so constantly under his eye, so cowed by his surveillance, that when at last he reached for heaven she dared not disregard his final order still to take old Simon to bed with her, so there she lived at Isa'ndre with an oak-tree husband, and she a round, dark woman with heavy hips and cheeks like a neat's tongue. Watching young lovers turn from the road, the sparrows in spring, or the farm bull in his pride, she would tell herself life was but a licked-out honey-pot – and turn to catch a leer on Simon's riven chaps. She couldn't come even to Gurnos's without him, and this very evening the old tyrant, freed from brown paper wrappings, waited for her upstairs at Galon-Uchaf. But a minute or two back she had felt a laceration of heart as ecstatic as it was agonising, and Mordecai's hatchet-face, till then unknown, had swung into her thoughts and hovered there like a seagull in a headwind.

Soon they were at the eating and drinking. Gurnos brought in an armful of rich and ruddy bottles, and the Pwll-hobi boys fired off the corks. They ate where they sat, with Gurnos and Madoc and Gwen to serve them. The men drank from two-handled tankards, the women were weaker vessels, but the boys from Pwll-hobi swung each on a bottleneck like hedgehogs on a full udder. Lew and Mordecai had been to a funeral that afternoon and had a tale to tell. They'd been burying Amos the Rhiw, and they all knew what six wicked sons he had – and one virtuous daughter. For a wonder all the sons had turned up for the occasion – 'Or no wonder at all,' cried Lew, 'for weren't they to read the old man's will before carrying him from the house? Well, there was the old man in his coffin, and there were the six sons, big men they were, hard and strong, two from the pits, two from the sea, and two from gaol – and there was the daughter. A nice piece, too, the daughter. And there was the lawyer. And there was Mordecai and me.' The boys from Pwll-hobi nudged each other, their mouths had fallen open. 'So they read the will. Not a penny to the sons, my lovelies, but the house and the furniture and the money in the long black stocking all to the nice daughter.' He kept them waiting, on some speculation of his own. 'But they were wicked boys, those boys the Rhiw. They felt the old man was laughing at them, so what did they do, those boys the Rhiw? They took the old man out of the coffin and gave him a damn good hiding before putting him back – that's what they did, those wicked boys the Rhiw.'

Gwen shuddered, Gurnos laughed, belly and all, and the boys from Pwll-hobi hugged their knees with delight. 'They'd had to buy black, mind,' Mordecai reminded them. 'You got to be fair.'

Nothing would do after supper but that Gwen should sing to them. And so she did – an old song of love and longing that pleased them well in their fat and idle state. Then Tally-ho's wife played on the harp till all sight and notion of a well-fed, plumpish matron fell from the mind, and their eyes filled with tears for the pain and passion and thwarted glory of man. It was while they sat silent and glum after this that Gurnos, to ease their spirits, brought in the true metheglin that only he could brew. It shone with the perfect gold of headland gorse, and as the cork came out the corgis drooled and dribbled on the pitched floor. Lew slapped his bald crown like a man despairing of a profitless youth, Wat and Tal knuckled spit from the corners of their mouths, they all breathed in hard as Gurnos tilted his jar and splashed the bright celestial liquor into two rows of glasses. Gurnos gave a toast: 'The man with the owl!' – and silently they drank. It at once seemed to Madoc that flowers would spring up wherever Gwen walked, and Lew knew himself as good as married to Amos the Rhiw's daughter, the house, the furniture, and the money in the long black stocking. Tally-ho's wife dreamt she was harping to the archangels, and to the boys from Pwll-hobi it appeared past all doubt that their next litter would contain a white-boot gorse-blossom corgi with a coal-fox face and devil's eyebrows. For Gwen it was a moment she would never forget till her grandchildren put pennies on her eyes and her soul slipped naked and old through the broken pane – for as she drank she felt life in her womb, the very image of Madoc sunk in her loins. She looked up at him, her lips parted, her eyes so happy that Gurnos couldn't steady his hand as he watched her; then he glanced away to the widow Simon, saw her eyes foxily on Mordecai, herself so busied in mind that her glass had tilted and a trickle of liquid light ran to splash fragrantly on the tiny round floor-stones. He moved forward, jar in hand, servant and host, cosseting them, till late into the night they rose unskilfully on loose-hinged knees and made their way bedwards.

It was hours later when Madoc woke by the side of his red-haired wife. The clouds had streamed free of the moon, and he saw a ladder of light falling from window-bars to bed-end. It was very still and very beautiful. He listened, but the wind had blown itself out to sea, and for a time all he could hear was Gwen's quiet breathing and the whispering of floorboards and rafters. He turned slowly, his arm over Gwen. Thus it was, he thought, to be happy. Almost against his will at first, words were falling into his brain like moonlit raindrops, little runnels of verse were forming there, filtering down, strengthening each other. He lost all run of time, poised on the edge of sleep and poetry.

It was then he heard the knocking at the door – a quiet and patient knocking. It came again, and he withdrew his arm to lie on his back staring up at the ceiling. He thought it odd that no one was stirring. He looked at Gwen. A thick soft rope of hair lay against her cheek, he could see her eyelashes fine and long, she made a slight kissing movement of her lips. As the knocking came again he grimaced. Where was Gurnos? The Pwll-hobi boys?

A minute later he was on his way downstairs. The folk here – were they drunk? Or shamming sleep? He saw the whole household, lying awake in the moonlight, some with a gnome's eye to the ceiling, ass-ears astrain, each man waiting on his fellow's effort. He saw them in distorting mirrors, colloped like bloodhounds, with whiplash noses, bulging brows and rubber mouths, their knees upstuck, askew – he could have shouted or laughed aloud at this fantastic pageantry.

When he opened the door there was no one there. He felt the air blench on his legs and shoulders, as though frost had come with the calm. For a moment he stood rubbing his chin, then with a complete faith in things as they were he went silently upstairs to Gwen. She was awake and waiting. Cold as a trout he slid into her embrace, his mouth muffled in her untied hair. Heat crept, then pounded through his limbs, and they were swept through a great tempest to the slow-running harbour of sleep.

Mordecai, too, had heard the knocking. He, too, went quietly downstairs, marvelling that no one else was astir. Lew slept heavily, ballooning his lips and snorting into his blanket like a stallion in a feed-rack. But Mordecai was with the wakers, his thoughts on the widow Simon and the farm at Isa'ndre. He had a touch of stone-dust on the lungs, had Mordecai – a present, no charge at all, from the deep seam at Llangua Number Two. He'd seen other men, known them well, who'd started with a touch – their chests walled up, their pipes choked with it, you'd think they'd had a concrete mixer at work inside them. He'd heard them cough and gasp and spit their way into the grave. But up on the hills here, away from it all – A fine woman, too, the widow, without a grey hair, and a bosom round as a turnip – Here was Lew as good as fixed – duw alive, a fellow had to look out for himself, and especially if his lungs were quilting with stone-dust.

At the second knocking he went downstairs in his long flannel nightshirt and his boots in his right hand. Like Madoc, he found no one, but unlike Madoc he noticed a ladder leaning against a bedroom sill at the end of the house. No one could call him nosy, but he thought he'd better see what was doing, so with tingling soles he climbed to the sill. By the clothes lying over a chair he could tell it was the widow Simon's room; further in he counted two heads on the bolster. It looked the end of a dream all right. Well, he thought grimly, I'll see who the flamer is, anyway; so he lifted the window with hardly a squeak, bottomed himself inside, and with thoughts halfway to murder tip-toed to the bedside. He would do something terrible, he knew it – something mad and violent. Then he noticed two strange things. The first was an uncrumpled width of pillow and eiderdown between the sleepers, the second was the unnatural stillness of one of them. The widow – what a lovely breather she was! sweet as a cow! – she was all right, but the other – 'nuffern i! he gasped, it's been too much for him; he's with the angels! His rage rivelled back. Cautiously he felt for Simon's noggin. Some odd sensation in his fingertips – he bent closer.

To say that Mordecai had mastered or even grasped the situation would be to exaggerate, but he wasn't born in Llangua for nothing. He now put his boots at the foot of the bed, withdrew old Simon with a hand of silk and slipped hopefully into his place. For ten minutes he lay there and thawed, and then, as the widow stirred and sighed, he put his arms around her. For her part the widow woke from confused dreams and warm imaginings. She was sick, sick, sick of living with a lump of wood, of sleeping with cold feet when there were men like this Mordecai about. She hoped for a miracle. She got one.

'Did a little girl, then!' crooned Mordecai, folding her to him. Everything that happened afterwards happened very naturally.

The third to hear the knocking was Evans Tally-ho. He had been dreaming how he was on a red carthorse, eighteen hands high, wall-eyed and barrel-bellied, chasing a fox the other side of the mountain. Once or twice the fox changed into the minister at Capel-y-Mynydd, and he, the horse and the minister would stop to shout 'Halleluiah! Halleluiah!' before beginning the chase anew. But later there was a change, and the fox kept turning into Mrs Tally-ho, and try as he would he couldn't catch up with her. You'd think it money for mud to catch a fox with a harp under its arm, even on a barrel-bellied carthorse; but that's where you'd be wrong, he couldn't. This at last made him downright depressed, for he had the notion that if he could only catch up with her all sorts of exciting and delightful things would follow. So on the whole he welcomed the knocking that fetched him back to sense and sent him noiselessly downstairs. He had time before starting to see how smooth and girlish Mrs Tally-ho looked in sleep. Downstairs, like the others, he found no one, but was encouraged by the quiet and the moonlight to make a circumference of the house. He noticed the ladder, but gave it no second thought till, on his return to the door, he found it locked behind him. The boys from Pwll-hobi! Hadn't they been running him the whole evening? Well, he'd show them a new trick before he was through. No one seemed to be using the ladder, so he carried it off and set it against his own window. Stooping, he gathered a handful of gravel, the very bell and clappers of country sweethearts, and flung it against the pane. At once his heart began to bang like a drum. Iesu Mawr! he thought (for his oaths were always very respectable), I haven't done this since I went to Mair's the night before she took me for good or bad, for better or worse, for ever and ever, amen. His own words beat up against him. I couldn't wait, I couldn't wait in those days. His legs were cold, but his heart was hot. He threw more gravel, and more still before the window opened. 'It's me,' he called hoarsely. 'It's me, Mair!' She looked down suspiciously as he started to climb then a delicious trepidation, twelve years in press, set her trembling. She helped him over the window-ledge. 'Arr!' he cried, 'why a lot of old talk? I wouldn't swop you, cariad, for all the women in the White Book!' Even in her exultation she thought this too good to last, but she wasn't the woman to fall over Tuesday looking for Wednesday, and joyfully she closed the window.

They were all on the late side in the morning. But all well pleased with themselves. First, Lew announced his decision to marry Amos the Rhiw's one virtuous daughter. He'd been thinking it over, he said, and what with those six wicked brothers the girl and the gold needed caring for, and he was the man for the job. He was jovial and confident. Hadn't he seen the light in a dream? The Lord always looked after his own. He departed at half-past nine to tell the lucky lady, the smuggish Tally-ho's at his tail, but no

Mordecai. Mordecai was to see the widow Simon back to Isa'ndre. 'We thought we'd be getting married in a week or two,' said Mordecai, rather red on the neck. The widow smiled sleekly into the V of her blouse throughout the surprise and congratulations, and the little golden bitches ran to lick her hands.

After breakfast the folk from Galon-Uchaf were to walk with them part of the way. They were at the end of the first field when Gurnos asked whether they had forgotten something. Mordecai was shaking his head when he saw the widow's lips move. 'And me a monkey!' he cried, light breaking hot and bright.

In two minutes he was back at the house. A big sharp hatchet caught his eye outside the door – it might almost have been left there for a purpose.

Some way off they all looked back. By the time Mordecai had caught them up a thick blue shaft of wood smoke clambered skywards over Galon-Uchaf. Then, as they watched, it snapped and hurtled towards them at the first blast of the reviving gale.

'Gwynt coch Amwythig,' said Madoc. 'The red wind of Shrewsbury.'

'But it's blue!' cried Gwen.

'Red or blue,' said the widow seriously, 'it's an ill wind that blows nobody good.'

But the last word, like the first, lay with the bards:

'Gwynt traed y meirw,' said Gurnos slily. 'The wind of the dead men's feet.'

Sniffing the breeze, the widow slowly nodded. Meantime, Mordecai had lifted his hat. He was always one to show respect, was Mordecai.

Gwydion Mathrafal

~

GWYDION MATHRAFAL was a man with a great love and a long quest. His love was for Wales and a Welshman here and there; his quest was for the grave of King Arthur. Ever since his twentieth birthday he'd been loving and looking, and if others held it more profitable to look for gold or sway or love in the laps of young women, Gwydion wasn't the one to argue with them. To every man, he would say, his own madness. But in his search for truth he had found little save the lie of the land, and at the summit of his years won only a one-man school under the shoulder of Plynlymon. He had also, against his better judgement, got himself married, and fifty weeks in the year lived with his bent-nosed, beetle-backed wife who nagged him, and her sister, an untrodden, drab-feathered hen for ever cackling of the black hawk Death who swoops from above. Sometimes a dark serpent of revolt would coil through the furtive currents of his blood, but the fangs never quite struck home, and he would endure them a winter and summer longer.

The most remarkable thing about Gwydion's ideas for the future was that they were more remarkable than his notions of the past. 'I will restore his crown to Arthur!' vowed Gwydion.

'When you find him,' jeered his listeners, whereat Gwydion would nod seven or eight times, drag a wide snort up his hairy nostrils, and walk off with his eyes turned up and his palms spread down.

For some years back he had been spending his unchained summer fortnights at Castell Môr. Here, out of sound of the sea, a rock clambers three hundred giddy feet, a rock the colour of beech bark and dull-glossed as vellum, grained and polished through a thousand generations by the blue waves now so far withdrawn that you couldn't see their pouring from the highest point of the castle. On the other, the inland side, the slope was slower though still steep, a series of grassy bastions humping up towards the last blank face of stone. Right on top of the rock was a ruin of no great size but an incomparable splendour. The rains had fretted and the winds rubbed it, moss had crept there and bushes knotted, the myriad mouths of rodent time had mumbled it into the bluff itself, and a million birds mortared its foundations. Slender mountain ash clouded it further, and in the grassy court a stub-oak leaned north-east. Its loneliness was prodigious; its element air. The most desperate effort of Gwydion's imagination had never garrisoned it with men or shadows; his deepest researches filled not a year of its history. Yet of one thing he was sure: it was a ruin before the Normans set steel shoe over the Border. To what, then, was it a monument? And to whom? He had had his disappointments in the past, from Carn Cavall to Cader Idris, but this time he knew.

He had a long memory, had Gwydion. After seven hundred years he still felt bitter towards Geoffrey of Monmouth for spreading that yarn about Avalon and the sleeping Arthur. But there, weren't all Monmouthshire men liars? And didn't the Black Book say:

> *A grave for Mark, a grave for Gwythur,*
> *A grave for Gwgawn of the Ruddy Sword,*
> *But a mystery is the grave of Arthur?*

So these last summers, the minute he could pack his bent-nosed wife off to her auntie in Flintshire, it was to Castell Môr he took himself. He was a swarthy man and very hairy except on the head; he wore pebble glasses with bent steel rims, and a shirt of red flannel to match the whites of his eyes. His mouth was on the big side, and his lips loose, and it might almost be said of Gwydion as was said of Gwefyl son of Gwestad, that on the day he was sad one of his lips dropped to his navel and the other turned up like a cap on his head. He was rheumaticky too, and if he rose or sat too briskly his joints would crackle like squibs on bonfire night. Otherwise he was just like the rest of us, except for his long arms and short legs. He never wore a hat, and his forehead soared like a knowledge-stuffed eagle from the nest of his eyebrows. Every time he came to Castell Môr he used to take lodging with a man named Ianto at a sludgy farm not far from the rock. He was like a walking cowpad, this Ianto, come wind or weather, wet or dry; but his wife Megan was a happy stirring lass who never said die to any dirt but her husband's. Once a week Ianto would get crying drunk in

Pengwern, the market town, but his little cob Fairy always brought him safe home with the groceries. Gwydion looked forward to these Monday booze-ups, for it was only when he was under the influence that Ianto took the slightest interest in King Arthur. He would then listen for hours, his eyes like glass-alleys, and at last sing 'Calon Lân' before lurching off to bed. But always by morning he had forgotten every word Gwydion told him.

One day in August Gwydion set off from Ianto's farm with a hunch that the day would be in some way a famous one. It was almost twelve months since last he climbed the wondrous rock or sat against the slanting oak. White cloud-balls hung from the blue of heaven, sunshine dripped from the bent stems of his glasses, and his blunt legs bore him through a world reborn from a cataclysm of light. Near him the fields sparkled like shallow emeralds, the high bastions were a cool seaweed-green. He passed a row of split stakes all ochre and scarlet, and saw stones glinting like frost or baring broad veins of biscuit and brown. The whitish ruins and the rock top had receded upwards and outwards from earth, more cloud and light than stone. He stood still a moment, clutching the whiskery lobes of his ears, and Ianto's sheep stood with him, white woolly hummocks. 'The world's great mystery,' he muttered to them, 'the grave of Arthur!' He felt, but did not look, smooth and bland as a milk-bottle.

At the foot of the eastern slope, in the shade of a crusty oak, he was surprised to find Ianto's cob and handcart. He thought he had gone to Pengwern as usual, for it was market day. He gave the cob a piece of cheese rind and started his climb. Puffs of breeze cooled his back and he could see them slipping through the blue under-grass ahead of him. But what was Ianto doing here?

The climb seemed longer than usual, and with every step he left not only earth but reality behind. Had he passed a hairy caterpillar going his way, he would have greeted him as Welshman and brother. He put his hand to his head when at last he reached the stone face, and found it wet. Black shadows chilled the hot white steps, and he could hear his knees crackle as he hoisted them high and still higher; he was glad to press his hands against the solid stone of the gateway, and in a bit of a daze passed through to the green court. He expected to find Ianto there, and wouldn't have been dumbfounded to find Arthur keeping him company. What he didn't expect to find was a young man in green tweed bloomers eating lettuce and cheese under his, under Arthur's, oak tree. He had an insolent, well-bred way with him, this young man, and was doing his best to grow a moustache.

'Aha,' cried the young man, spotting Gwydion, 'enter an aboriginal!' He studied him for six long seconds. 'Drawn from its lair by the smell of cheese.' He held out a tit-bit.

Now, no man had less liking than Gwydion for the English, and one day he hoped to write a marvellous book which would send them all scurrying back across the Dyke, and perhaps over the North Sea. He also held firm by the Levitican text which declares it an abomination for man to wear the garments of woman. So he looked the young man over from his miscarried moustache to his baggy bottom and shook his head, grimly.

'You do well,' said the stranger, 'for toast cheese has already cost you heaven.' At this point Ianto entered the court, and he waved him over to Gwydion to form an audience. 'You look doubtful. I will enlighten you.' He sat upright, his finger-tips precisely together. 'Once upon a time – need I say it was a long time ago? – a small number of Welshmen entered heaven. But such is your race, they quickly showed themselves unworthy of it. They sang about the streets at night, they smelt vilely of leeks, and between them invented the bicycle that they might the more speedily undo their angel sweethearts.' Gwydion blinked. 'Whereupon the Lord sent for Satan and offered him the lot. But Satan was too spry. Not he, he said; hell was hot enough already. But he felt sorry for the Lord and tipped him off how he might at least throw his tormentors into outer darkness. So the Lord, after consulting all the saints save Taffy, one day made a great toasting of cheese outside the Pearly Gates. The wind was in the right direction, the odour was wafted throughout heaven, and when they smelled it all the Welshmen left the mischief they were at and ran headlong through the gates. And when the last one was outside, the Lord said to Peter, "Okay Peter," the gates swung to, and since that day not a Welshman has been permitted to enter heaven.'

But Gwydion was shaking his head. 'I know the story,' he said curtly, 'but you have it wrong. For the honour of Wales I will set you right.' He motioned to Ianto, to show him there was nothing to fear. 'Once upon a time – need I say it was a long time ago? – a small number of Welshmen entered hell. They were rather a rough lot, English-speaking, from the South. Within a week or two they had Y Diawl absolutely beaten – and he knew it. He was losing weight fast, and hair, and the curl was out of his tail, so he went to the Lord with his troubles. He had some splendid tenors from Llanelly, he told the Lord, if he'd care to – But no, the Lord said he wouldn't. There were some rugger men from the Rhondda, to say nothing of the referees – if the celestial pack needed strengthening, and there were rumours that it did – But no, the Lord was firm about folk from the Rhondda. "But I'll tell you what you can do, Diawl bach," he went on, and told him about the toasted cheese. "Only don't let on to St David, will you?" said the Lord. Well, Y Diawl promised, and when the wind was in the right direction he toasted cheese outside the gates. The Welshmen – English-speaking, mind – were up to all kinds of ructions when they smelled it, but they didn't let the brimstone grow under their feet. They were off the floor of the Bottomless Pit before you could shout *Caws Pobi!* the gates crashed to behind them, and since that day not a Welshman has gone to hell.'

'I never heard a lovelier story,' said Ianto, and threw a sliver of dry mud from his breeches.

The young man nodded pity and approval. 'Your story shows all the sensitiveness of an inferior race. We English wouldn't turn a hair at losing heaven. After all, we have our Empire. As sure,' he added, 'as my name is Martin Dolorous.'

Gwydion felt the blood in his neck. A long-toothed lettuce-eater in green bloomers tell him he was inferior! Without as much hair on his lip as would make a keepsake! Yet after a fashion he felt himself host in his own country and blanketed his passion.

'Where is your art?' asked Dolorous; 'your science? Your great men?' He watched the light skim off Gwydion's glasses. 'Where is your King Alfred?'

'Hywel Dda,' gasped Gwydion.

'Shakespeare?'

'Dafydd ap Gwilym!'

'Your Drake?'

'Prince Madoc,' cried Gwydion, 'the discover of America.'

'Never heard of him. You must mean Columbus. Where's your Queen Elizabeth?'

'She was a Welshwoman.'

Said Dolorous: 'So's my Aunt Fanny!'

'Not she!' shouted Gwydion. 'You are English to the seat of your bloomers. Your silly bloomers,' he added. 'Possibly your Aunt Fanny's bloomers!'

'Anybody but a mountain goat,' said Dolorous, 'would know these are plus-fours.'

'Plush fours? We don't call that plush in Wales. We call it tweed, I can tell you.' He saw Ianto grinning, and began to grin himself, showing his big dog teeth. For the honour of Wales! 'You say your names is Dolorous?'

'And proud of it! Yours, I expect, is Shinkins?'

Gwydion guffawed. 'We speak in Wales of the Three Dolorous Blows. You are the First Dolorous Fly-blow.'

'Silver changed hands,' said Dolorous calmly, 'the night of your begetting.'

Gwydion roared with laughter and beat his fists against the sides of his knees. National pride, joyous rage, and a touch of the sun lifted him into the realm of heroes.

'Probably a threepenny bit.' Dolorous was developing his theme. 'Your mother was drunk at the time – and who shall blame her?'

For the most part men will lightly endure to be called the thing they are not. Gwydion's laughter grew and grew, and he could see Ianto's eye fixed hopefully on him for a come-back. 'There are three things much like the other,' he announced, 'an old blind horse playing the harp with his hoofs, a pig in a silk dress, and a love-child prating of hire.'

'Dewch!' cried Ianto, thinking this came from the Bible, 'you can't beat the Old Book, can you?'

'Or was it monkey-nuts?' asked Dolorous, unpleasantly calculating the length of Gwydion's arms and the breadth of his nostrils.

A brief silence fell between them. 'If we cannot be gentlemen – ' began Gwydion. 'But there, the pigling to the sow's teat and the swine to his grunting.'

'Better a pig than an ape,' cried Dolorous.

Gwydion removed his glasses. His eyes flashed red battle. 'An ape?'

'A Welsh baboon!'

Gwydion handed his glasses to Ianto. 'A baboon?'

'A Cambrian anthropoid!'

'An anthropoid.' Gwydion knew the first round at hand. The blood of his raiding ancestors flushed his bald head, his joints cracked defiance, he smacked his kidney lips. 'A *Welsh* ape?' asked Gwydion, that it might be justifiable homicide.

'A Welsh ape,' Dolorous agreed, showing braver than he felt. He snatched up a sandwich for defence.

Then Gwydion took off his coat and they all saw red, for the scarlet flags of his shirt-sleeves flamed before him. 'Dear Jesus,' prayed Ianto ecstatically, 'let there be violence this day!'

'Here, on the grave of Arthur – ' began Gwydion.

'He's a myth,' bawled Dolorous, scared but reckless. Then he wished he hadn't.

'A myth!' Gwydion jumped in the air with rage. He looked for a weapon, but found none. 'I will graze the Red Dragon on the green field of your bloomers! I will print on your lying Saxon heart six hundred and thirty-four Stanzas of the Graves! And finally, I will hold you under water till the bubbles rise!' He would have continued, but Dolorous flung a sandwich and hit him in the mouth. With a war-cry he leapt forward, and Dolorous turned and fled his simian onset. Over the sward they dashed swifter than leopards, but Gwydion cut him from the gateway and he doubled to the western rampart. Here Gwydion's fingers hooked air an inch too late as he whizzed round a block of fallen masonry, and by the time he recovered Dolorous was five feet above him and ready to kick. But Gwydion was now in his oils; he beat his chest and started to climb. He took a clout on the forehead before getting within claw distance, and then Dolorous ran thirty perilous yards with much dexterity, neatly dropped back into the court, and was comfortably ahead at the gateway. Something had already gone wrong with Gwydion's wind and he quickly gave up the chase, but Ianto could hear the vanquished heels of Dolorous skidding on the steep stone steps. He stood there with Gwydion, who was puffing like the Llangwyryfon express, watching him bound to safety, and then to their delight Dolorous missed his footing, slipped and slithered, and finally bumped to a halt against an outcrop of white rock. For a full minute he lay there stunned. 'The wide hosts of England,' panted Gwydion, 'lie with the light in their eyes.' Then they saw him get to his feet, shake his fist at the castle, and walk off with a limp. Ianto slowly peeled a piece of cowdung from his legging; this he threw down the slope, and then explained excitedly and with praise for Gwydion how he had brought the enemy sight-seeing from the White Hart at Pengwern; and thereafter Gwydion, his breath once more his own, talked long of valour, his quest, and the dear land of Wales.

'But who is this Arthur with you?' Ianto asked him at last. This sober Ianto.

With the sun on his back Gwydion told him: the greatest king of the Cymry.

'And dead he is with you?'

'Dead he is. And what a day that was for Wales, little Ianto!' Gwydion's long arms made mute appeal to heaven, but not for long. 'The darkest hour the Cymry ever knew! Ah, little Ianto, if Arthur had his deserts it's wearing black we'd be this minute, and there'd be mourning bands round the neck of the Dragon.'

He was enjoying himself and went on like this a good while before they parted, Ianto to find Fairy and do the shopping at Pengwern, Gwydion to chase the Dolorous Beast round and round the slanting oak.

It was late into the evening when Gwydion and Megan heard the rattle of wheels and the stepping of the little cob. They turned out at once to help Ianto and the groceries indoors. Then Gwydion took the horse round to the stable and saw to him for the night. As he came back past the parlour window he heard Ianto even more tearful than usual.

'What are you crying for, Ianto?' she was asking him.

'What a day for Wales, our Megan! And you here at Castell Môr the long hours through, and not a breath of it in your pretty ears. Boo-hoo!'

'What is the news then, Ianto? It's frighten me you will unless you tell.'

'The darkest hour we Cymry every knew! It's a black night-shirt for me to-night, Megan, for I'll never be the same man again. We've lost our best friend, Megan – the only friend of Wales. The king is dead – King Arthur! Boo-hoo-hoo!'

'Oh,' he heard Megan say, '*him*! Here, lift your leg, Ianto, and I'll tug your other boot off.' He heard the sound of a fall.

His hand on the latch, he looked up. The stars were prancing in heaven; the happy hour lay ahead.

'Now your slippers,' said Megan. 'While you are on the floor, take them out, good boy, from down in under by there.'

'I will wear my slippers,' Ianto granted, 'but all night through I will cry tears for King Arthur.'

And now, for the second time that day, Gwydion felt a memorable event at hand. The conviction of it grew in him like love or hunger or hope. His hand fell from the latch and he turned through the yard and into the fields. He walked in a daze, his eyes on Castell Môr. A flying-buttress of mist had risen to the rock from the brook on the right, and as he came nearer he could see this mist compress and thicken till it hung like a bridge from the upper to the lower world. He wiped his glasses, but it went on changing. The underside stayed pale and tenuous, merging through moonlight into air, but rapidly its higher limits were defined as an opaque arch dependent from the castle to a vast meadow starred with cowpads. It began to change colour, rose and sulphur-yellow and dusky blues and greens gleamed on the white causeway; it now looked palpable as snow or salt or chalk. Again he stood among Ianto's sheep, clutching the lobes of his ears; again he muttered: 'The world's great mystery!' He felt wondrously enlarged, as though he'd need wireless to get in touch with his feet. Humble yet exalted, he awaited a miracle. For a while he saw only streamers of mist, pale flags and pennoncels; then he could see how a company rode out from Castell Môr, silken lords of the olden time and all the queens of the world, lovely as seashells. And at their head, on a white stallion with a scarlet saddle-cloth and jewelled peytrel, rode Arthur. They came gaily over the bridge to the starred meadow, pied dogs capering about them, and cantered away to the brow. He heard the blowing of a horn.

They were hardly out of sight when he ran madly after them. His arms waved, his head jolted, his knees cracked prodigiously. Then he fell and lost his pebble glasses. It took him a long time to find them, and when at last he reached the brow the fields were empty and the horn was still. He turned to the castle and the bridge had vanished.

When soon afterwards he reached home he found Ianto by the fireside, all huddled and fuddled. His lips had formed a round red chimney-pot, through which his breath blew fuff-fuff-fuff. Suddenly he opened a wet eye and began to tell Gwydion about Wales's great loss. 'You can't trust those old Baptists,' he concluded hoarsely. 'The King must be buried in Siloh, by Mr Evans.'

'The King,' cried Gwydion, 'must be crowned in London! By all their Holy Highnesses!'

Ianto gave one shocked hiccup. He squinted horribly and raised a finger as though to tap his nose. Then his head slipped and he snored. Nodding, Gwydion appointed him Keeper of the Royal Beeves, with a castle in Taprobane.

Then Gwydion blundered upstairs.

Sir Gwydion fell into bed.

The Lord Gwydion kissed Arthur's sword in a dream, and the green stars paled in the east.

The Passionate People

~

'WHY, sir,' says Quaint in Vanbrugh's *Aesop*, 'I'm a Herald by nature; my mother was a Welshwoman.' But if not only one's mother, but one's grandmother, and that grandmother's grandmother be Welshwomen – what then? For so it is with me. Whether all my grand-dads are of so pure a strain I don't know. We have had side-slips, why deny it? blots and by-blows. I stand in some degree of consanguinity to everybody in Henllys parish, from Sir Rhodri up at Plas Mawr to black-faced Molly of the Bryn who lives in tally with a mole-catcher. And I am ashamed of neither. Nor is Molly of me.

I mention Molly because she is the living image of my ancestress Mary Ellis, who was born here in Henllys in 1723. I have her picture before me at this moment, enclosed in a heart-shaped locket, the work of Edward Harris of Nantgarw, an enameller of note in his day. *Ætat suæ 17*, says the inscription on the back. Sweet seventeen, indeed. Raven hair, sidelong eyes, rosy lips, teeth like milk – a little stylised, clearly, but on Molly's showing a lovely girl. Molly is older, of course – she was all of twenty-seven when she left Tom Merry for the mole-catcher (she must have been, she was twenty-four if a day when she left me for Tom Merry) – but I see Mary Ellis not only in her face but in her body too: the high round bust and supple waist, the smooth hips and sliding carriage she shares with so many women of my native parish. The Ellises were farmers at Berllangron, and comfortably off.

Of Seth Parry I have no portrait. The *Star of Gwent* for March 28, 1744, calls him handsome, and there is evidence that he wore a gold earring, a neat and fine one, in his left ear – partly from vanity, partly as a specific against poor sight. He didn't at this time wear spectacles, and this too was vanity.

Of Caradoc Edwards I have neither portrait nor account. The *Star of Gwent* is content to call him a very passionate man.

Record of their disaster begins in the *Star of Gwent* for January 9, 1744. The compiler of this hardly remembered news-sheet was Josiah Richards of St Woollos, of whom his second son's memoir tells us he was once offered a pipeful of tobacco by Joseph Addison – glory enough for a Monmouthshire newsmonger. His notice is brief and clear, and to that extent Addisonian.

> RURAL TRAGEDY. It is now confirmed that Seth Parry of Henllys is held in Usk Gaol on a charge of manslaughter. The dead man is Caradoc Edwards, a wheel-wright of St Teilo's, Henllys. Parry has been committed to the next assizes.

By the 13th of the month Richards knows a little more.

> HENLLYS TRAGEDY. Seth Parry is committed to the March Assizes on a charge of murdering Caradoc Edwards, wheelwright of St Teilo's, Henllys. The body of Edwards was found in the woods near his home on New Year's Day. It is freely asserted that in the dead man's right hand was a gold earring known to be the constant ornament of Seth Parry. The affair is rousing much feeling at Henllys, where, thanks to the precepts of the local gentry and clergy, such instances of human depravity are comparatively rare.

I have read Richards' last sentence many a time, with an increased liking for that *comparatively*. It was a brutal age, we must remember. And Henllys, then, if not now, had a reputation to lose.

Richards now held his peace till March. Brooks overflowed, bullocks changed hands, there is a witty paragraph on Welsh help (by way of convicts) to the sugar trade, but of Seth Parry in gaol and Caradoc Edwards in his grave, nothing. And nothing of my ancestress Mary Ellis. The Assizes were held at Monmouth town, as was customary, and Richards waited till their end. I expect a fair number went over from Henllys to hear Seth Parry receive sentence. The facts were simple: Seth Parry killed Caradoc Edwards and killed him for Mary Ellis's sake. What the *Star of Gwent* had to say of Caradoc Edwards was true of all three of them – they were very passionate creatures. Listen to Seth on trial for his life:

> *Mr Justice Mason*: It is probable, fellow, that you have already spoken too much. But I should be sorry to deny the Court's hearing to a

creature standing in mortal jeopardy. I ask then, do you urge the privilege of self-defence?

Seth Parry: I urge nothing. I slew him like the dog he was. As I would slay him a hundred times had he a hundred lives to lose.

Mr Justice Mason: This is the language of criminal rage. If you persist –

Seth Parry: And may he burn in hell, the rotten dog! It will be my comfort there to see him writhing.

This was a comfort he might count on being not long denied. The reason for his high behaviour becomes clear from another piece of evidence.

Mr Justice Mason: Repeat the words spoken by the Prisoner at the Bar on that occasion.

Henry Marsh, inn-keeper: The Prisoner was in my best room on the night after Boxing Night, and said there in my hearing and that of John Harcombe, Matthew Penry, and –

Mr Justice Mason: They will have opportunity to testify. Speak for yourself, fellow.

Henry Marsh: I beg your Lordship's pardon, my Lord. The Prisoner said he had known for a long time that Caradoc Edwards was licking his chops for Mary Ellis of Berllangron, and swore he'd cut the heart out of him unless he gave over.

Mr Justice Mason: And he accompanied these words by a gesture of some kind?

Henry Marsh: He drew a clasp-knife, at which we were all much affrighted.

There now came an interruption from the Prisoner, who shouted that he had killed Edwards with his hands, man to man. He was none of your Italian stab-in-the backs. He fought clean, like an Englishman (*sic* Welshman!). But his Lordship had no mind to listen to rant and threatened to have him removed from the Bar unless he bore himself more seemly. Then came the examination of John Ellis, father of Mary Ellis.

Mr Justice Mason: When did the Prisoner first approach you in the matter of your daughter?

John Ellis: It would be three years ago.

Mr Justice Mason: Why did you refuse him?

John Ellis: Because he is a fierce and headstrong young man, who would bring her pain and sorrow – as he has done, damn him!

Mr Justice Mason: Watch your tongue, fellow! You will answer in form. In my Court even a murderer may expect proper treatment. Even a murderer, I say.

John Ellis: I am sorry, my Lord.

Mr Justice Mason: And well may you be. What was the Prisoner's reply to your refusal?

John Ellis: He swore that if he did not have her, no one should.

Mr Justice Mason: Go on, man. You are holding something from me.

John Ellis: He said he would be the death of any man who came near her. I laughed at this, but he cursed me and said he'd do it with his bare hands.

Mr Justice Mason: And what does your daughter think of this?

John Ellis: My Lord, she says she loves him.

And so, for the first time, we meet my ancestress. She must have been in court, though not called. Otherwise it would be hard to account for Seth's speech after sentence had gone against him.

Seth Parry: My Lord, and Gentlemen of the Jury. I have had fair trial and make no complaint. I slew Caradoc Edwards as, given the same circumstances, I would slay any man in this court. I gave my word and I kept it. And I give my word now: No other man shall have and enjoy Mary Ellis. Had she been given me when I asked for her, none of this misery had arisen, and for that I curse her father. For Caradoc Edwards I have no regret. He was a meddling fool, and would take no warning. And remember – it is not within the power of this court to part me from Mary Ellis.

The court thought differently and he was sentenced to hang at Newport. And early in June, hanged he was. The *Star of Gwent* made much of the occasion, and I am sorry I cannot quote Richards in full. He had fallen from the grace of his Addisonian days, and when he might be reading Pope (who in two months' time would be dead as Caradoc Edwards) had evidently been wasting his time with the *Seasons*. Otherwise, how account for the opening sentences hereunder?

The melancholy tale is now concluded, and the woods of St Teilo's sleep their wonted sleep. As the years roll out their vari-coloured pageant, they will know again the scarlet and yellow of autumn, but never again, we trust, this springtide yellow of jealousy or the scarlet of shed blood. On Tuesday morning Seth Parry was hanged at

Newport for the murder of Caradoc Edwards, wheelwright of St Teilo's. 'There is no art to read the mind's construction in the face.' This was a man of candid and handsome appearance, agile, quickwitted, young. I saw him at the Bar of Justice, heard his shouts and curses, and still I admit a nobility in his carriage, though touched with Cambrian wildness. But the awful Precepts that guide to Joy and Prosperity had been lacking from his youth, and in his miserable fate we observe the lamentable effects of *Atheism* and *Free principles* . . .

We are not a little ashamed to relate of any daughter of Gwent that she could so ignore public admonition and her conscience as to be present at the last ceremonies of a malefactor. But Mary Ellis, for whom murder was done, attended at Newport on Tuesday and saw the execution of her wretched paramour. He refused all spiritual consolation and instead of prayers shouted out: 'Remember me, Mary Ellis.' The body, as is customary, will be available for anatomical curiosity, and it may thus be said of Parry, as of other rascals, that in death he was more useful than in life . . .

Remember me, Mary Ellis! An admonition pathetic, sinister, or absurd, according to taste and anticipation. But here, perhaps, I had best proceed by way of digression. The clothes and pockets of a hanged man were at this time (and much later) the hangman's prerogative. The body might be disposed of in different ways. Richards was mistaken in thinking that it was usually 'available for anatomical curiosity.' It was the easiest thing in the world for friends or relatives to get hold of it for decent burial. Students of the period will recall how the celebrated highwayman, Du Vall, the pink of purse-cutters in his day, lay twenty-four hours in state after his execution, in linen worked by duchesses and other admirers. Sometimes relatives or friends went one better than recovering the dead body: they received it alive. Money had to pass, of course, and resolution be shown. This was the case with the highwayman Mansard in 1716 (he was hanged a second time in 1719); Thomas Judd survived hanging at Manchester five years later; there were three cases from Newgate alone between 1730 and 1740; the tradition holds at Carlisle, Edinburgh, Lincoln, Derby, Bristol and Winchester. To this list we may now add Newport – surely a great satisfaction to local patriots and antiquaries. Seth Parry was cut down while still alive, and his body stripped and passed back under the scaffold where friends were waiting to receive it. They had brandy, hot blankets and a surgeon – and a cart. Off went the coffin on another cart, loaded with a proper balk of timber, and off went Seth Parry to life and freedom. *Remember me, Mary Ellis!* The words take on a new meaning, become matter-of-fact. For it was Mary Ellis who saw to this strange rescue. Mary Ellis and a younger brother of Seth Parry – that James Parry who afterwards built the mill below Lleweney weir. As for the surgeon, there was a medical etiquette even then, and he did nothing to advertise his best case.

Before nightfall Seth Parry, no doubt with a very stiff neck, was on board the *Ojibway* in Newport roads, Mary Ellis was back at Berllangron facing her father, and the two brothers of Caradoc Edwards were standing treat to anyone in Newport who'd drink to hell fire for the hanged man. I gather this last from the Court records now preserved in the Public Library: 'June 14. Geraint Edwards, for being drunk and breaking windows, June 9, fined 6s. 8d. Gwilym Edwards, the same.' There were smaller fines for four sympathisers. So everybody, one way or another, had cause for thankfulness.

By the way, watch this Geraint Edwards, elder brother of Caradoc. We shall meet with him again.

It was two years later, in the summer of 1746, that Mary Ellis robbed her father of a fair sum of money and disappeared. He made no attempt to trace her. He didn't encourage conversation. He kept hard at work. Local talk was that he was glad to get rid of her, that she had run off to London, that she'd soon be on the streets, in gaol, in America. No one had a good word to say for her. Yet one or two had come courting, despite past history and Seth Parry's bravado, for she had looks, youth, the promise of consuming passion, and money behind her: occasionally a handful of gravel spattered her window, and an enterprising boy bach set foot to ladder (Henllys is famous for its boys bach, even to-day), but it was risk to no purpose or gain. No kisses, no fondling, no courting in bed – nothing to set against the dogs and smallshot – they soon gave over. One night two or three wags, far gone on the Cross Foxes beer, sneaked into the yard and shouted under her window: 'Remember me, Mary Ellis!' What did she think? What did she feel? I often study that pretty portrait – imagine her older now, the rondeur and the bloom of her cheek contracted more than a shade, the mouth now sensitive to pain as well as joy, the lovely eyes drained of the candour, the ingenuousness of girlhood. I tempt myself to think of Mary Ellis, sitting up in bed, her hair about her shoulders, knuckles to mouth, listening to those rough shouts, hardly recovered from the heart-breaking confusion of such an awakening. I could wish to rush out upon those drunken louts, batter them into the mud and dung, stamp on their faces, kick them senseless for the senseless suffering they caused her. Such hate and championship I feel – and I a degenerate law-abiding fellow who hardly know the inside of a Monmouthshire gaol – western Monmouthshire, anyway.

But it was the boys bach of Henllys who were given something to remember when Mary Ellis left Berllangron that July. She was seen in Newport the next day, accompanied by a man with a hat drawn well down whom I suspect to be James Parry. Beyond that, not a word, for six years.

Her return was in mid-August, 1752. She was now twenty-nine years old. Her father (if fact outdoes fiction in strangeness, why not in banality too – if you find this banal?) was dying when she reached home. She had come because of James Parry, who years before had seen her off to Bristol, for a purpose soon to become clear, and had now gone to John Ellis on his sick-bed and asked him whether he wished to see his daughter again.

No one will be surprised that after his first stupefaction Ellis cried that he would, and that of all things under God's grey heaven his daughter was still dearest to him. Nor need we doubt Mary Ellis's motives in returning. She got the farm, true enough, but nothing in her story suggests she ever set profit above her affections. We have it on James Parry's testimony (believe me, the family has a good literary record) that Ellis knew great and poignant happiness those last days – 'such as brought tears to my eyes to behold,' are his words. It was his particular task to make grief lighter for Mary, who oftentimes in company with him alone bitterly reproached herself for long neglect and past cruelty. Her first outburst after her father's death was 'such as does violence to our mortal frame and might not long be sustained. It will be better for her when her husband comes.'

For Mary Ellis was now married – had been married six years and had two little sons. The husband reached Berllangron before winter, they tried to sell, but failed. In a matter of months they had fitted into the farm like fingers into a glove, and their sory might well have ended here in comfort, calm, and obscurity.

But for Geraint Edwards.

Mr Carey (her marriage had made sad work of May Ellis's pretty name) was a handsome trim-made man a few yars older

than his wife. He wore spectacles with strong hooks to them, and
there was a white scar on the lobe of his left ear. Just such a scar as
Seth Parry would have where Caradoc Edwards in his death-
struggle tore out the earring. There came a time when this scar
was very present to Geraint's mind. Just when, no one knows. It
was Geraint's misfortune that as a young man he had been taken
up by local sportsmen and matched against the best the
neighbouring counties had to offer. He handed out some good
hidings, and took some, till his fight with Tom Brewer of
Gloucester. He was game all right was Geraint – too game – he
kept on his feet till Tom had broken him for life. As a toe-to-toe
fighter he was now useless, though dangerous enough mauling
and brawling. Never very bright, he was now addleheaded yet
cunning, dim-thinking yet tenacious of an idea, when he had one.

He was, says James Parry, 'an ugly dog.' A well-worn phrase,
this, for many readers, but James Parry had read less then they. To
him the words conveyed an exact and vivid image.

Whether Mary Ellis grew suspicious of this brutish man is hard
to say. But there is evidence a-plenty that she spoke bitterly of him
as a drunkard, a wastrel, a disgrace to Henllys. Geraint, however,
was not sensitive to dispraise, and was biding his time. As for Seth
Parry (not to make a mystery where none exists), he reacted to
suspicion by threatening to horsewhip Geraint if he found him on
his land. Also, as though life had taught him nothing, he fitted a
new gold earring into his left ear, where it looked none too
ornamental against the white rip-scar. All his days he had worked
hard to disaster, and now it was at hand.

His death, like his hanging, took place at Newport. The
symmetry is truth's making, not mine. The old proverb says those
born to hand need fear no drowning. Seth illustrates the converse
of this. He was born to drown.

In the early autumn of 1755 he made a journey to Bristol to
attend to matters concerning his former residence there, and
went, as might be expected, by boat from Newport. He was back
in Newport on the Wednesday, on the word of many who saw him
well pleased with himself. He took a bed for the night at the
Trelegar Arms, had a meal, and later went for an outing through
the little town. There had been heavy auctions in Newport that
day. Welsh-speaking folk from the countryside swarmed in the
streets, the inns foamed beer. Amongst the roisterers was Geraint
Edwards, always glad of drink and excitement. Whether he was

there to meet Seth we shall never know, but the odds are against it. But somewhere or other he set eyes on him, and from then on the one thought filled his head. I don't suppose he thought in any clear way of killing Seth; we can dismiss the notion that he regarded himself as the instrument of a long-delaying justice; but he meant to come face to face with his enemy and in his dull way he must have savoured a long-lost sensation of power and purpose. He could *make the man pay.* The only known remark of his that evening that can be dated after his catching sight of Seth was learnt from a gipsy acquaintance who caught at him in High Street. He first stared, she said, then pushed her away, muttering words of this nature – that *he could make him pay.* Soon afterwards he was seen going towards the bridge, a dangerous structure on tall and muddy piles. He was brought out of the river two days later. No one saw Seth again, dead or alive.

One man's guess is as good as another's. But for completeness' sake I must mention the diary kept by Josiah Richards' son, also of St Woollos. Under the date September 2, 1755, after recording the recovery of the body from the Usk, he makes this entry: 'The men who brought the body ashore are honester than their kind. I talked with them this afternoon. There was a broken pipe in the pocket of the jacket, and tight-clutched in the dead man's hand a gold earring. I was able to examine this last. It was not of wire, but presented at its extremity a flat surface, and on this may be read, in neat lettering, *Remember me, Mary Ellis.*' Thomas Richards then recalls the scene at the hanging of Seth Parry in 1744, and wonders what cause Mary Ellis should have to remember this other dead man. Some days later he knew. He paid a visit to Berllangron, taking the ring with him (he doesn't say how he acquired it). He reproaches himself for clumsiness. His news, he writes, stunned her: she couldn't weep, couldn't speak even for some minutes. He describes the extraordinary pallor which accompanied her dumbness. 'She is a woman much above her way of life,' he admits, 'her air is elegant and superior, she plays the housewife diligently and with authority, if one may judge by the order and cleanliness which surround her . . . She is more handsome than might properly be looked for in her station. He would be no unlucky man who might engage her attention at some more propitious time.' A Latin quotation is the end of it for Thomas.

It would be well if I too could end on so well-bred a note. Mary Ellis lived on to the end of the century, and when an old woman, talked somewhat of her affairs to her sons. One of these entered the army and was killed by the accidental explosion of a cannon, the second busied himself about the farm. The third, born six months after his father's death, had a narrow red birth-mark on the lobe of his left ear. He lived a long time and had seventeen children, which would savour more of diligence than passion, had they all been born in wedlock. Only six of them were, though. He had the unluckiest kiss of any man in Monmouthshire, and the red birth-mark still works out on the unlikeliest ears. I'm rather proud of mine, but it's different for the chairman of the petty sessions, I can see that.

I was telling this story in the Cross Foxes last Saturday when a fellow named Geraint Edwards hit me in the eye. 'I never did like the Ellis part of this parish,' he said. Naturally I let him have it. I'm sorry for the landlord, and I'm sorry about the policeman, but no one named Edwards can hit me in the eye and think that's the end of it.

My unclaimed (and unclaiming) cousin on the bench will send Geraint to gaol, that's one thing. It will be my comfort there to see him writhing.

Their Bonds are Loosed from Above

~

And Jael went out to meet Sisera, and said unto him, Turn in, my lord, turn in to me; fear not. And when he had turned in unto her, into the tent, she covered him with a mantle.

And he said unto her, Give me, I pray thee, a little water to drink, for I am thirsty. And she opened a bottle of milk, and gave him drink, and covered him.

Then Jael Heber's wife took a nail of the tent, and took an hammer in her hand, and went softly unto him, and smote the nail into his temples, and fastened it into the ground: for he was fast asleep and weary. So he died.

Blessed above women shall Jael the wife of Heber the Kenite be, blessed shall she be above women in the tent.

YOU wouldn't think there was anything in the fourth and fifth chapters of Judges to give a woman named Manod a bad turn, and she living in a fine house next door to a Methodist chapel. But that's where you'd be wrong. It gave her a turn all right. One Monday morning.

The house was in Eglwys Street, and its name was Brynhyfryd. You never saw a nicer house of its kind, with a coloured glass panel in the front door, a piano, and a big oak dresser from Flintshire blue as the sky with willow-pattern china, and on the window table in the parlour a well-dusted Bible with gold clasps. You never saw a nicer widow either, of her kind: clean and respectable, threepence in the plate every Sunday, and none of your fly ones dangling a line for anything in navy trousers. A widow who kept to herself, and could keep to herself, for what with the insurance of Manod, deceased, she had more than her leg to fill an old stocking with. He was a peculiar fellow, that Manod – you never knew quite where you were with him. He had ways. And what a soaker! It couldn't last, everyone knew that – after. Here to-day and gone to-morrow, and a last big bottle of brandy gone with him. Well, here's our wreath. It wasn't as though we didn't warn him.

No one in Eglwys Street will forget Sunday the 24th. Three hundred planes over, the wireless said. They rough-ploughed the city and sowed it with glass. No night for sleeping. The very dead shuddered in the ground.

Yet, like many another, Mrs Manod came down that Monday morning with more curiosity and exhilaration than dread. Nothing had fallen too near, not a window was out at Brynhyfryd. Yet there was something different about the house, she felt it at once, something – she could not say. She lit a fire in the kitchen, had her breakfast. It was towards nine o'clock, as she drew back the curtains in the parlour, that she noticed the Bible open on the table in the window.

She would have shut it without thinking, and only later felt surprise, had she not noticed a number of ugly brown smudges on the right-hand page. This vexed her, for the Bible was a great treasure, and the less meddling with it the better. She bent forward to examine the smudges and could not help reading a few words. Among them were *nail* and *hammer*.

Mrs Manod felt herself in the midst of a silence that stretched past earth to the tingling stars. Yet it was silence audible, vibrating on the ear like telephone wires on a mountain, in a high wind. She had, too, a sensation that everything save the Bible was receding from her on all sides, as though titanic springs had contracted outside our mortal dimension. But the Bible, its leaves humped up at her like two unbroken waves of the sea, displayed in glittering black letters the tale of Jael and Sisera, not word by word but verses, chapters, simultaneously. Then she grew aware of the pulsing of her blood, the jump of her heart. There was a smell from the smudges that sickened her.

But Mrs Manod was a brave and strong-nerved woman. For some minutes, she stood gripping the table, then she took out her handkerchief, flicked at the smudges and their dusting of red earth, shut the Bible with a heavy slapping of leaves, pressed the gold studs home, and walked back to the kitchen.

Ten minutes later she re-entered the parlour. The Bible was shut and flat, the window secure, everything was very tidy. She went back upstairs, put on her coat and hat, and went out, locking the door after her. The buses were running and she set about such shopping as she could.

Talk, talk, talk. Everybody talking – friends, strangers, even old enemies talking. She heard a woman – no one could help hearing her: 'Not a thing damaged, look, not a window, not a cup, not a blade of grass on the lawn. But the cuckoo in the cuckoo-clock, he started at eight this morning and went on cucking eight hundred and forty-four times. Our Harry counted him. Not even soot down the chimney, but that cuckoo he cucked eight hundred and forty-four times, like our Harry counted. "Spring in the air," I said to Harry, but "Spring a leak," said Harry to me. Something we've come to, I tell you!'

Mrs Manod nodded, though the conversation was already racing past her. There was an explanation for everything, if only you could think of it. 'I had a book blown open on the table,' she said, loudly, to anyone who cared to listen. 'The window was shut, but the book was blown open. A big Bible, with gold clasps on it, blown open.' She said nothing about the smudges.

'That's right,' said the woman who had spoken first. 'Proper pagans, them Nazzies. They'd go for a Bible like St Patrick for a snake. There's that cuckoo-clock of our Harry's – it cucked eight hundred and forty-four times, like I was telling this lady only this minute – '

'A big Bible, with gold clasps,' Mrs Manod repeated. 'Blown wide open. The window was shut all the time.'

She was steady as a rock now, and stayed steady. In the afternoon she was asked to help with meals for the bombed-out, at the chapel next door, and was hard at work till nightfall. She was taking off her apron, fagged-out, when behind her a voice said: 'They hit the cemetery too. Mind, they aren't spreading the news up there.' There was a harsh laugh. 'Better them than us.' The first voice continued: 'One or two made a move last night who might have been expected to stay put for ever.' Someone else said 'Sh-sh-sh,' the talk ended feebly, as though they had noticed her and remembered Manod, deceased.

Inside her own door, Mrs Manod hesitated and then went to the parlour. The Bible was shut and flat, the curtains drawn, everything was very tidy. She thought once to look again at the smudges, but instead hurried upstairs, locking her door, forcing a chair-back under the knob for safety, fastening the windows. When after many hours she fell asleep, the night-light was left burning.

It was still burning when she awoke from nightmare. There was a bustling noise under her window, at the front door. She saw the clock on the chair at her bedside. Eight-fifteen. She rushed from bed, tore at the curtains, tore at the catch. 'Wait!' she cried to the milkman leaving her gate. 'Wait, I want to pay you!' 'But it was only – ' 'No, wait!' she cried again. 'Don't go!' He looked up, groped for his book. 'Righto.' He began to whistle, a cheerful jiggy tune that helped her into her dressing-gown, to the switch on the landing. But no light came, and she had to pass the parlour door in the dark. 'It's not the money,' she said at the front door, blessed daylight flooding the passage. 'I had a bad night. I thought I heard something. I was afraid to go down. And I couldn't get a light – I wanted you to look. It's all dark from the black-out. I've been afraid, I think I must have been.' He was a big fat fellow, with a bloodhound's face and red hands, and put his book into his pocket. 'The electricity's off all through town,' he told her. 'It's the bombs.' He stepped past her, doubling his left fist into his right palm. 'For your sake and his, I hope he ain't here.' He looked back and saw the postman passing the gate. 'Oi! Might be a burglar in the house. Keep an eye on the front.' The postman was a small man, a local preacher, Mrs Manod had heard him next door many a time. 'Then God have mercy on him, a sinner.' 'Amen,' said the milkman, nursing his fist.

But there was nothing there. The milkman went right through twice, pulling every curtain back, at Mrs Manod's request looking into cupboards and wardrobes, and coming a bit red-faced from under the bed. 'Not a sign,' he said. 'Anything seem to be missing?'

'Not a thing, not a thing!'

'That's a bad lock,' said the milkman, in the scullery. 'You could think you'd locked that, and every other time it would have slipped right round to open again. Look.' He twisted. But Mrs Manod wanted to be on her own. She had her bag in her hand by this time. 'Not at all,' said the milkman, telling a shilling from a halfpenny by the feel of the rim. 'A pleasure. Any time at all!'

The postman was still there, frowning. 'If we can't help a fellow christian without taking – ' he began. 'But there, I can put it in the collection.'

The door closed behind them. Mrs Manod stood for a moment holding her heart. Otherwise it would jump right out of her body. Then she pushed at the parlour door. The Bible was shut and clasped, the china shone, everything was very tidy.

The flat cover of the Bible was the loveliest sight she had ever seen. A fine broad cover of boards overlaid with black leather, blind-tooled, with a gold shield in the centre, the edges like yellow silk. And flat.

But was it quite flat? Was it? Or was there a ruffling of the gilt edge? a mere nail-breadth of white against the gold? And were these flattened crumbs of earth from the milkman's boots? O merciful Jesus, were they?

Mrs Manod cupped her hands over her mouth. Then, resolutely, she crossed to the window table, unclasped the Bible, lifted it open. Again she had the sensation of a world speeding away from her through the tightening of titanic springs beyond any edge that thought could reach to; again there was envelopment by a strung silence through which hummed the tension of taut wires. The Bible had opened at Judges, at a page brownstained and crumpled, and embedded in the twenty-first verse of the fourth chapter was a sharp, slender, headless nail.

Then Jael Heber's wife took a nail of the tent, and took an hammer in her hand, and went softly unto him, and smote the nail into his temples, and fastened it into the ground: for he was fast asleep and weary. So he died.

Mrs Manod stood there by the table for a very long time. She could feel the heavy gush of blood from her heart, and even the damp and chill that slowly crept upwards from her feet; but she had no power of motion, nor any means of purposeful thought. There was horror all round her, but it could not break in one bound through the stupefaction which blanketed her reason. She was roused at last by a growing awareness of a smell so foul she could not endure it, and went blunderingly to the kitchen, where she was sick.

For a long time afterwards she sat by the kitchen fire, watching the orange flames clamber through the sticks and coal. She rubbed her hands together, thrust her shins almost against the bars, and once she got up hurriedly to lock the door leading to the passage. She was piecing things together. She had never lacked nerve, had Mrs Manod. There had been a time, indeed, at a crisis of her life, when she had shown a hardly credible courage and strength. She was thinking back to it, now.

An hour later and she had joined a small group of women outside the cemetery gates. These were locked, and a well-spoken, patient official was assuring one caller after another that there had been a slight disturbance, it was true, that no one could be allowed inside just for the present, but that everything was in hand and by to-morrow he didn't doubt, etc., etc. There was no need for distress: the authorities would take care of everything with promptitude, efficiency, and reverence. But Mrs Manod wasn't satisfied. In Eglwys Street lived an employee of the parks and cemeteries authority, who looked none too easy when she knocked at his door after tea. Well, all he could say was – his words added up to nothing. What part of the cemetery? Well, there, Mrs Manod, you really must excuse him from answering a question like that. He hedged, raised his hands, shook his head, but Mrs Manod got her answer from his wife's pitying yet gloating eyes. All would be as it was to-morrow, though. She startled him at that, grabbing his arm. To-morrow? He was certain? He'd swear it on the Bible.

'There's a woman for you,' he told his wife, when Mrs Manod had gone. 'There's devotion! And all for a chap as killed himself with a bottle of brandy. Paralytic, as the saying goes. He was a rum sort of chap, too, something about him, you never quite knew where you'd got him or not.' He put his feet inside the fender. 'I'll smack him down good and hard to-morrow, too true I will.' He told his wife stories that made her back crawl. 'It's a secret, mind. Not a word! I'll have that bottle of beer now, Emmie, I think.'

Mrs Manod had a busy evening. First she cleaned the parlour. The bits of earth she threw into the kitchen fire, remarking their colour; the carpet had a good stiff brushing; the nail (it was rather like a very long gramophone needle) she put into an envelope in her pocket; the Bible was shut and dusted. When she had finished, everything was very tidy. She also took the bolt from the coal-house door and rescrewed it in the scullery, and she saw to the catches of all the windows. It pays to be careful of one's bit of property. And she felt better when she was doing something.

Before she could go to bed the raid of the 26th started. It lasted till long after midnight. There were explosions between her and the cemetery at which she smiled grimly. In time, bombs fell nearer Eglwys Street and the doors and windows rattled in their frames. This worried her, and from worry she came near panic. If they were blown in what was to stop anyone – she had almost said *anything* – entering? She thrust sticks into the kitchen fire, threw on more coal, lit a second night-light. In a quiet fraction of time she heard the crackle of her slates as shrapnel fell. Surely no one would be tempted from cover on a night like this? A mobile gun had run to the end of the street; it began firing raggedly, so that the house shuddered, her saucepans jingled, and the toasting-fork alongside the chimney fell frighteningly into the steel fender. This dreadful gun, punctuating the uproar, was worst of all to bear. Her bowels leapt at its crack and whine; she waited through its silence in agony.

Suddenly, terror drove out terror. The din was at its worst when she saw the knob of the scullery door turn. She got stiffly to her feet, her head jerking forward. The knob was twisted sharply, then furiously, but the bolt held. For a moment it rested, then turned slowly and powerfully left, right, left, right, but the bolt was heavy and the screws long, and nothing happened. It rested again: the knob itself like a tiny round baffled face. Mrs Manod grinned. She'd always been too clever for him. Too clever for everyone.

She was still grinning at the knob when there came a knocking at the front door. She stopped then, her eyes going from scullery to hall-passage. The knocking came again, more loudly. She wavered. It might be *him*, but it might be a warden, a fire-fighter, a gunner, a first-aid worker. Carrying a night-light she went swiftly upstairs to her own front room, saw that there were matches handy, blew out the light, and opened her window an inch or two. 'Who's there?' She strained her eyes downwards. Over most of the street there was a pale blue light pronged with orange and red, but the chapel fell blackly across Brynhyfryd. 'Who's there?'

The gun at the corner sent all other noise rocketing outward. It was in her heart to slam the window, draw the curtains and have light, but instead she pushed it up further and leaned her shoulders out. 'Answer!' she cried. 'Who's there?' An unspeakable savour of corruption reached her nostrils. 'Go back,' she cried; 'Go back where you belong!' She began to laugh. 'The door is locked, and you can't get in. I've always been too clever for you.'

Knock, knock, knock, 'Go back,' she shouted; 'Go back where I put you. You've only got to-night. And the door's locked and bolted.' She screamed with laughter.

Then Mrs Manod saw a sight few may see and live. Huge fountains of fire spouted from the railway station to Eglwys Street, each with a roar that shook her head like a doll's. The hollow air sucked her forward, the window sprayed like hail into the street, stunned and bleeding she saw where the dark had been a tattered human beating at the knocker below. She fell back into the bedroom as the house opposite reared like a huge red horse; there was a thudding followed by a lurch, and then a long grinding and crackling. The floor, she found, had tilted under her. Through a hole in the wall opposite she could see flames blowing like washing in a wind, and as she huddled herself together the corner of her room slid out into the roadway. Two thoughts came to her mind. The first – and she had never been more serious – was: Well, the government will have to pay for this! The second was: Nothing in the street below could survive that explosion. She nodded to herself. Nothing.

She must move, though. There were flames behind her, she could tell, as well as over the street. She got to her feet, painfully. She had never lacked nerve, had Mrs Manod.

But at the head of the splintered stairs she stopped, and for all the fire around her her blood grew cold and slow as ice. Something was coming upstairs to her, something on all fours, tattered and scorched, with great labour and application. 'Don't!' she cried. 'O merciful Jesus, don't!' It didn't raise its head at her outcry, but slowly dragged its knee one step higher. At each movement it appeared to overcome some more than mortal dislocation. And past the clean and acrid smells of smoke and red destruction there came the odour of its decay.

Yet its slowness was deceptive. How quickly it came near! She ran back to the bedroom, but the door was out of plumb, she couldn't fasten it, and hurried panting to where the wall fell to the street. But the flames – she could not face them. Through all the uproar of the night she heard a rubbing and shuffling at the door and saw it open. What entered was shrouded in charred linen, but part of the head was exposed, and part of the arms. Her jaw yammered like a dog's at the foul bone, the blue-black of rottenness, the horror of the skull. It turned in her direction at once, moving on wrists and knees, the fingers hooked ahead, purposeful and informed. The nail! The nail! She snatched the envelope from her pocket, flung it between the hands. It stopped, the fingers groped and found. Thank god! she thought, thank god! It would leave her now.

The left knee crept forward, the left hand thrust for her foot. For the first time it lifted its face, and Mrs Manod threw herself shrieking into the street.

Mortal time had almost ceased for Mrs Manod. She had but one flicker of sight and thought to come. When her eyes opened it was to see something like a filthy whitish caterpillar crawling head-first down the broken brickwork towards her.

They were as good as their word at the cemetery. Everything was very tidy there the next day. But the man from Eglwys Street swore an oath. 'Where's this one been?' he asked. His companion thought for a second. 'Hell and back, by the look of him.' The man from Eglwys Street bent and considered. 'By god!' he said.

He went away, but soon returned. Manod, deceased, was giving him something to think about. 'Leave him be a while, that's the orders. His wife was killed last night. She'd have given him the apples of her eyes, that woman would. I wish I had one like her.' He bent his back again. 'See that?' He scraped with his fingernail where you or I wouldn't. 'Stuck in the side of his head. You could still play the Dead March in *Saul* with it.'

'What are we leaving him for?' grumbled the other. 'Adding to our work!'

'That woman pined for him,' said the man from Eglwys Street. 'Only last night she was asking and bothering. Before she got hers. They can be buried together now, in the one grave. Dear, dear, I think that nice,' said the man from Eglwys Street.

Take Us the Little Foxes

~

IT WAS in the Horse's Head one afternoon, when he should be
cleaning ditches, that Dewi Lloyd heard tell of the little foxes.
He was a queer old twist was Dewi, and getting queerer every day.
There were even those to mutter that if he got much worse – but
there – what else could be expected of the Llanvihangel Lloyds?
Think of Morri, his brother that was, who kept a ferret under his
shirt when the policeman was looking, and on gentlemen's
premises when he wasn't: if he hadn't been killed with the Welch
at Givenchy, he'd have run into real trouble would Morri. Then
there was Moy, so nosy and mean that at last he had himself
buried under the front lintel just to keep an eye on his flighty
widow. Drunks going home to Hirwaun – 'You can't trick me, you
saucy faggot!' they'd hear the ghostly whisper – and Evans the
Vestry using the kitchen window every time he cuddled her.

Dewi came squirming into the Horse's Head this afternoon, just
as the talk grew high-minded. 'Ain't it in the Bible?' cried Billy
Stop-tap, degenerate son of nine-pint men and skittle kings. 'Ain't
it in the Holy Book?' He raised his glass. 'One's medicine, two's
comfort, and three, dear brethren, three's the fiery pit. A-ah!' He
wiped his whiskers. 'That's why I always has four, to be on the safe
side.'

'It's marvellous,' said Lew Lewis, Pantbach garage.
'Everything's in the Bible, mun.' Hearing them speak of the Bible,
Dewi removed his hat. 'When Elijah went to heaven in the fiery
chariot – wasn't that the first aeroplane?'

'And the water turned into wine.' This was the landlord,
bringing Billy's fourth. 'There's a fine text!'

'And don't it say, "Take us the foxes, the little foxes"?' broke in
Davies the keeper from Lluest. There was applause for his
learning. 'Ay, it's all there, boys, if only we look for it.' He
borrowed a light, found Dewi's eye upon him. 'Must have been
chaps like me even in them old days.' The thought warmed him,

he sat there savouring both beer and biblical repute, and cast forward to a future of paradisal polecats. Meantime Dewi admired his shiny leggings so openly and sincerely that he just had to stand him one from the wood.

'I hear tell,' said Billy, 'how you dug out three little uns at the Gelli yesterday.'

'Three little what?' asked Lew.

'Three little red fellers – babby foxes.'

Dewi's glass was to his lips, he could even feel the froth of it, but he had to set it down untasted. 'Cubbubs?' he stammered.

The keeper held his hands out. 'That length.'

Dewi's hands came out too, as though levered from behind.

'That length?' He closed his left eye, drew his head back for exactitude of study, while the talk turned elsewhere. 'What you doing to do with um?' he asked suddenly.

'With what?'

'Little red fellers.'

The keeper spat, dead-centre. ''Stroy um. To-morrow.'

The talk swung away again. Dewi looked into his glass, liked what he saw there, and took a good pull. 'Where you got um?' he asked presently.

'Got what?'

'Little red fellers.'

'In the empty pigsty up the house.'

Dewi rubbed his neck. 'Is their mama dead?'

'Too true she's dead.' Davies stood up, smoothing down his knees, scattering ta-tas and see-you-agains. As he started off home he found Dewi sidling along with him in a desultory, mongrel-like way. A spade glittered on his shoulder like a diamond on a dunghill, and he oozed country smells and crafty innocence. 'Going my way?' asked Davies suspiciously. 'Righto,' replied Dewi, as though accepting an invitation. He was a hobgobliney sort of chap to look at, with round eyes and a scrag of beard. They were almost at Lluest when the expected happened. 'Could I have a look at um, Mr Davies mister?' Davies nodded, disgustedly, and then shook his head as excitement made Dewi stumble and change step.

Round they went to the back of the big house, past the flower beds and through the kitchen garden. The sties were under the wall to the right. 'Dampo, dampo!' cried Dewi, and hissed, seeing three wickedly-pretty heads a-cock at the scrape of their boots, three brushes you could lather your chin with. 'Like little corgis,' said Dewi. Davies straightened his back and Dewi flattered him with imitation; deliberately they filled their pipes and took a puff or two, Davies very much the great man – as though he owned all the pigs and people in Llanvihangel. The air was still as sleep, their smoke thinned into the mirror of the sky, and Davies held forth with weight and wisdom on one important topic after another; but Dewi, nodding often and copying his every action, was really chasing game of his own, and when at last Davies heard the whistle blow for time, he stuck his face out towards the sty, saying: 'How about one of them for me, Mr Davies mister?' As an afterthought, he added – 'There's a lovely man!'

Davies clicked his teeth – four pound ten's worth of 'em, from the best dentist in Croes-y-Ceiliog. 'You're daft, Dewi. What 'ud a man do with a little fox, 'cept destroy him?'

'They never done no harm yet,' Dewi wheedled. 'On'y one, Mr Davies, lovely man.'

'I know you,' cried Davies. 'Didn't I give you that ferret – and look what happened!' He saw Dewi's lips a-bubble with excuses, but silenced him. 'I ain't like you, Dewi – I got a position to keep up, and I got my duty to do. Anyway, you'd have nowhere to keep him.'

'Get a kennel,' cried Dewi. 'Keep him on a lead, like a good boy, see Mr Davies – lovely man!' With the last two words he dribbled visible respect and affection.

'I said No! And I'm going to have my tea.' Dewi stood starting at the pigsty. 'I said I'm going to have my tea. You clear off now, d'you hear?'

'Righto,' said Dewi, standing his ground.

A quarter of an hour later he was knocking at Myfanwy Price's down on the Duffryn road. He had something under his coat, and his looks spelled conspirator in Welsh or English. He was chuckling as she opened to him, a chuckle she'd heard before.

'What's it this time?' she scolded. 'Weasels, hedgehogs, or is it a camel or a helephant from Hinja you want me to bother with?'

'Not a camel, Myfanwy.' He shuffled his feet, grinning, all soft soap and simplicity. 'On'y a little fox.'

'Fox? My god a'mighty!'

'On'y a little un, girl alive!'

'Don't you bring no old fox in here, Dewi Lloyd. I'll screech the place down first.'

'But it's a little un, Myfanwy,' he pleaded, while his right arm pumped eloquence. 'Look – this length. Just a twti little red feller – and don't it say in the Bible' – he touched his hat – ' "Take in the little foxes, for as you do take in others, surely shalt thou be took in yourself"? And no one would know he was about even – 'specially if he had the lend of that kennel out the back.'

'Kennel! My old dog 'ud turn in his grave.'

'Old Twm? Duw, Myfanwy, I didn't think he'd mind.'

Myfanwy shook her apron. 'There's no fox comes in here and that's final. Tie him up and come and eat some food, there's a good boy now.'

'I ain't hungry,' said Dewi, on his dignity.

'Then come in and smoke your pipe.'

'I ain't thirsty neither.'

'Then go to the devil,' said Myfanwy Price, 'and all foxes go with you!' He might have changed his mind about the food, but she gave him no chance: by the time his nose twitched twice he was the wrong side of the latch. So he made a few bubbles with his mouth, scratched under Major Downing's cast-off fishing hat, and then peeped under his coat at his treasure. He was there all right. 'There's a boy,' he crooned, 'little fox, look – llwynog bach!' As happy as daddy, he set off for his one-up-one-down cottage past the Duffryn cross-roads.

There and then began the strange adventure, the idyll, of the roadman and the little fox. It was no secret. Davies knew, Myfanwy knew, and soon the sucking babes of Llanvihangel knew that crackpot Dewi had a llwynog bach. When he returned from divvy-digging in the coal valleys Major Downing of Lluest knew – and had a terse word for Davies as a consequence. Yet for many weeks no one really saw the fox. Somewhere on his wanderings Dewi had found a monstrous lock and key, he now set a bar across his door, and to his own amazement locked up when he went a-field. To questions he replied evasively or not at all, grinning sheepishly the while, and his eyes restless as mice on a window sill. The little fox? 'Righto,' he said. 'What did he feed him on?' 'Righto.' Was it true they shared the same bed? He grinned, mumbling chinwards, getting himself out of reach in a way that would be rudeness in a taut-witted man.

Then Lew Lewis came to the Horse's Head with a weird story. He'd been driving back from Hendre late, by moonlight, and whom should he see on the Duffryn hillside but Dewi Lloyd, and the little fox with him. 'On a lead – and I'm telling no lie!' Next night Davies saw them from behind the stone wall. They were coming head on when llwynog bach must have scented him, for he dragged on his cord, well-down by the stern, and after a brief exchange of civilities Dewi yielded and they headed back up the mountain. Soon it came to Dewi's ears that he'd been spied on, that there was no need for secrecy, and during the summer it was no unusual sight to see him walking to work with llwynog bach on a string at his heels. Arrived at his pitch he would tie him to a tree trunk or post, and proceed with his business of roadman. When he felt like it he would break off for a chat, talking seriously to llwynog bach about how rich Major Downing, Lluest, was and how kind Mr Davies, who'd butchered his baby brother and sister. For the first couple of months llwynog bach was uneasy; he'd curl himself into his brush, but be up quivering at a cycle bell or distant bark, and if he heard a hen squawk or a duck go quack, tapes of spittle would hang from his chops to the ground. But time and Dewi worked wonders. In August he put all on one throw, and in the moonlight took away the lead from the fox's neck, who first scouted round, not exuberantly like a dog, but with a furtive, dubious joy, and then was lost in the shadows of the hedge. Dewi felt he was going to cry – 'Don't go, little llwynog bach, don't go away and leave me, mun' – then he stopped trembling and whistled the twisty little tune Morri had taught him before he passed out with the Welch at Givenchy. He was clinging frightenedly to the last note but one when a piece of shadow slipped forward on the right of him, and the next second he was rubbing the rakish head, kissing the cold nose: 'Llwynog bach, oh llwynog bach,' he babbled, 'I knew you wouldn't leave me, see.' A perilous joy went knife-like to his heart, with shaking fingers he slipped the cord on, touched his hat to the Man in the Moon, and hurried home. Llwynog bach had a rabbit for his supper that night, and where it came from was nobody's business.

It was somebody's business, though, when two fowls vanished from behind the Red Lion. The disappearance of a Sunday joint or two was first thought the work of a tramp, but tramps don't eat a goose raw – and the remains of a goose raw were soon to hand. The local Force called on Dewi, as one man, and spoke its suspicions, Myfanwy shouted rudely after him on the Duffryn road, and Davies, his ears stinging, hunted him out with an oath-strewn warning. Dewi was vague and ingratiating, again he called

Davies a lovely man and counted the bobby's nice buttons. Llwynog bach, he protested, was the best little boy in Wales, but he was worried when they left. For llwynog bach now went for walks alone, and his ways were the immemorial ways of his kind. There was blood on his tongue and blood in his belly, and he'd taste it till the end of his days.

That this wouldn't be long delayed was the common faith of Llanvihangel. Those who hadn't lost anything were sorry for Dewi. As if a daft chap like him hadn't enough to go on with! Kind-hearts wagged their heads, passing their glasses up, said 'Ah, well,' before going on with the day's business. Anyway, the owner of Lluest was the man – let him get on with it. And get on with it he did.

There was no false pride about Major Downing. No side, either. So long as a feller knew his place and kept to it, that was all he asked. He called on Dewi one evening at his cottage, with a double-barrelled gun and a double-barrelled plan concerning llwynog bach. Davies was with him. 'I don't knock,' said Davies, so in they went.

Dewi was seated by a small fire backed with turf, and opposite him, his coat a-gleam, lay llwynog bach. As they entered he rose and slunk to the corner behind his master, into half-darkness, ears erect, muzzle forward, pulsing with terror. Dewi rose in alarm, his eyes licking faster than flame from master to man.

'There he is, sir,' said Davies unnecessarily.

'I'm sorry, Lloyd,' said the Major. 'But I hope you'll see reason. Your fox has been killing fowls again. I'm afraid he's got to go.' He saw the poverty of the room, the rough ladder to the loft, and felt this gave Dewi an unfair advantage. But get it over, that's the thing. No messing. 'If I can get you a dog – ' He wished the feller would hold his eye for a second on end. 'In any case, it's my duty – in fact, I should really be bringing a summons against you now. Now listen, Lloyd – I've got a gun outside – ' Dewi had begun to chew spittle with fright. 'If you'll let Davies bring him outside, it can all be over in a second. Well?'

Dewi shot one of his quivering glances back to the fox, who lifted his head. 'Wicked man,' he said. 'No.'

For the shortest moment of time it came into the Major's head to act vigorously and talk afterwards, but God bless my soul, he thought, I'm a beak not a bandit. And maybe his regard for property withheld him, or, better still, an awareness that to kill a man's friend and walk off after a five-bob tip would not be quickly off his conscience. 'I see. Can I sit down?' he asked.

'No,' said Dewi. 'Go away.'

The scandalized Davies started forward, but the Major checked him. 'Now listen, Lloyd. Either we shoot him to-night or a policeman will come here with a warrant and take him away. If he were mine, I'd rather know what happened to him. I'd rather see him get a quick, clean death while he knows nothing about it.'

'He know now,' said Dewi. And it looked as though he did. Llwynog bach was panting loudly, he had given up looking at his enemies. He had eyes for Dewi only. He worked his way forward on his belly, his face a startling blend of cunning and trust, till at last his head pressed against Dewi's leg, and then as Dewi bent he nuzzled his nose into his fingers. 'Well, I'll be damned,' said Davies. 'If he don't talk English!'

'He's mine,' said Dewi frothily. 'You go.'

The Major looked from fox to Dewi. 'All right,' he said, and switched the attack. 'We don't shoot him – I hope. But you can't keep him,' he hurried on. 'You'll have to turn him out on the mountain.' He saw this hadn't sunk in, and tried to explain. He offered good advice, the unblinkable truth, began to feel paternal. 'I'll send a car along to-morrow evening, we'll set him free up by Creigiau, and he can go and take his chance.' He was getting on like a rat in a sack when he noticed the fox. He had stopped panting, occasionally he twitched his nose this side or that, with a sly contemptuous grin into the fire. Knows a damn sight too much, he told himself – as Davies said, must talk English. He pushed out of mind the entirely fantastic picture the idea conjured up, and caught a swift revelatory leer from llwynog bach. Too damn knowing, too damn knowing by far. He was struggling against dreams, it seemed to him, or nightmares: the half-daft roadman, his eye slithering, the sly, observing beast – 'That's all,' he said brutally. 'Take it or leave it. To-morrow, at five. Or I'll put a two-two into him. Come on, Davies.' Half-way through the door, he saw the fox bare his gums, watching him with hate. 'Would you!' he snarled back.

To-morrow came and the car with it, the Major himself at the wheel. He had insisted on Davies bringing a gun – nobody was going to get last laugh at the Major, no-by-God-sir! Davies felt bitterly about this, but a job's a job these days. He was to keep Dewi company in the back seat, and couldn't have been more embarrassed with Big Bertha on his knees. The fox (what a dandy he was – with an old-gold gleam to him!) showed terror at the car, but when Dewi hauled on the string in he jumped, and away they went. For a mile or two Dewi seemed almost paralysed, but then, though his hand never shifted from the fox's neck, he recovered enough to stare fascinated at the driving wheel and gear-change, and once Davies had to hold his coat-tails as he leaned over the front seat to see the miracle work. He sat back, gaping, but when next Davies caught his eye it was all misty and mazed. Eight miles out they dismounted, there was a sentence from the Major and two from Davies, a mumbling command from Dewi, and they started to climb the springy bank. The skyline was two hundred feet up, and they were puffing hard when they made it – all except llwynog bach, now released, and keeping just ahead of them by stealthy spurts. The Major sat on a tump and took out his pipe. 'Now, Lloyd,' he snapped, 'drive the damn thing away.' He filled his lungs, once was enough, with mountain air. Damn nuisance. Might be embarrassing, but all for the best really. Hoped the chap wouldn't cry. Damn nuisance, chaps crying. Even cracked chaps. *Especially* cracked chaps. Get it over, that's the thing. No messing. 'Come on, Lloyd!'

Davies coughed and looked at his boots as Dewi began to come on. It took the Major somewhat longer to realize that they were acting the kind of farce which strips the living skin from its players. The more Dewi waved his arms – the more grotesquely, the more desperately – the more convinced grew llwynog bach that sport was afoot. He leapt playfully from side to side, made little rushes to nip at Dewi's trousers, and once spun head over heels. This terrified Dewi, who knew he must send him packing or see him shot. He now grabbed him by the scruff to drag him, but this suited llwynog bach very nicely, and he scratched his neck vigorously on Dewi's forearm. Even when the grip tightened till he yelped, to show that no offence was taken where none was meant he fawned and flattered his master. Dewi's mouth began to make little bubbles, his hat fell off, and squire and keeper felt their necks a-crawl as he looked in their direction and then, horribly, kicked llwynog bach in the head. Davies flinched, and 'For God's sake!' cried the Major, for Dewi was running after the fox, kicking at him, the victim slow to take the hint. He was shouting and slobbering, half in Welsh, and the Major put his pipe away. In Dewi he had vision enough to see himself, his family, all humanity – naked of pretence, stripped of the solemn plausibilities – and he didn't think much of the view. 'We can't have it!' he cried shrilly.

Davies, stop him!' They caught at Dewi's arms, held him, but he went on sobbing and cursing the fox, to drive him farther off.

'Call him back, man!' shouted Downing, his stomach cold. 'Call him back. Keep the blasted fox, if you must!'

But Dewi could think only of death for llwynog bach. The brute was now thirty yards off, watching them over his shoulder, no surprise on his face, but a devilish contempt. When the Major called to him, he stood alert for a moment or two, and then trotted slowly away. They released Dewi's arms, who at once snatched up a stone and threw it. It went near, but missed. And now, while Dewi sobbed and cursed and fumbled on the ground for missiles, and the other two stood sick and humiliated, the fox set off at an easy run towards the crest of the next slope. Every thirty or forty yards he stopped and looked back at them, delicately and with apparent calm. The last time he halted was right on the brow, and it seemed to both Davies and the Major that he nodded slowly at them, as though at last he had their measure. Then he slipped from sight.

'Anyway, he's gone,' said Davies.

The Major scowled at him. 'I'll follow his example. You coming?'

Davies looked towards Dewi, crouched on the ground.

'Come on, Dewi,' he wheedled. 'Ride in the nice motor car.'

'He can ride in front with me,' said the Major, speaking to the mountains in general.

'Nice motor car,' said Davies unctuously. 'Poop-poop!'

Dewi shook his head. 'Then you can damn well walk!' shouted the Major, sick to death of the whole business, and started off downhill. Davies, after a pause, followed him. But at the car he said he thought he'd better go back. 'If you hadn't been such a fool as to give him the fox – ,' snarled the Major, though he'd been told a dozen times how Dewi stole it. 'I'm off!' He could have free-wheeled down, but revved the engine till you'd think she'd burst. 'Go, you – ,' muttered Davies, and climbed none so lightly back up the slope. On the next crest Dewi beat the turf with his hands and cried his heart out for llwynog bach. 'You – you,' said Davies, and sent a prayer down the valley. He sat down where he was, to wait.

The news, but not the details, went the rounds. Those with hens stolen or hens to steal said all was for the best, yet even they felt sorry for the silent Dewi who cleared the Llanvihangel rain-channels. The ingratiating smile, the foolish good temper were gone: the hecking walk and restless eyes remained. A small point – he had burned the Major's fishing hat. Some tried to stand him a drink or give him a hand-out of good food, but he never entered the Horse's Head, whatever the bait. He confided in no one, not even Myfanwy. They were all against him, he knew that now. Llwynog bach was his only friend, and he'd kicked llwynog bach and driven him away. Folk started to tap their foreheads and pull faces. Billy Stop-tap gave him three months.

– Then he began to perk up. And suddenly he was his old self, more or less. 'Damn fool,' they said, 'how could he remember anything from one week's end to another?' They reproached themselves for wasting sympathy on a crackpot.

But Davies had a theory he was keeping to himself. Not even his wife shared it – and there wasn't much in twenty-two years she hadn't screwed out of him. He did a bit of spying on Dewi, to begin with, and then a bit of thinking. The result was that in October, two days before full hunters' moon, he got the groom to run him up to Creigiau on his motor bike and then take himself home. It was on the cold side, and he had a longish wait before he saw what he was looking for. A shapeless, shambling man was coming up the road, and then climbing the bank. He passed Davies within twenty yards and went on to the second crest. There Davies heard him whistling the twisty little tune Morri Lloyd used to whistle before he bought it with the Welch at Givenchy. In a minute or two a fox appeared, a regular dandy he was, and came snakily forward. 'Llwynog bach!' he heard Dewi call. 'Oh my lovely little boy, mun!' The brute ran forward, right into Dewi's embrace. Then he brought a paper package from his pocket and held it out to the fox, who carried it some feet away and settled down to eat, Dewi meantime talking to him like a Dutch uncle. The meal ended, Dewi started to walk. The fox stayed for a last lick at the paper, but Dewi gave a sharp whistle, whereon he ran after him. Warily, Davies went to the second crest and peeped over. Tracks ran black through the dew, and some way off he could make out Dewi lying on his back, waving his arms all shapes, while llwynog bach circled deliriously or mock-worried his ragged sleeves. The keeper's face split on an oath and a grin, but he was concerned lest the fox get wind of him, so he slid back, stood up, and started on the long walk home.

It was about a week later the master of Lluest told him he'd heard all was well with the dafty down the road. 'So everything was for the best, as I thought all along.' He had shaken the black dog off his back by this time. 'Well, it's the old proverb come true, Davies: Where there's no sense, there's no feeling.'

'That's true enough,' said Davies. He couldn't very well say less.

And, since a job's a job these days, he couldn't very well say more.

The Green Island

~

THERE was a man lying on the headland over Ffald-y-Brenin.
His name was Merrill. He had been there for more than an
hour, sometimes smoking, sometimes shifting his weight from
elbow to shoulders, till the wild things had grown used to him. For
a time a tawny-yellow hare sat sideways on to him, his long dark
ears still as pitcher handles, his eye an unlidded jewel. High up
against the blue a hawk was watching. Black and distant though he
was, he looked filled with a compressed and savage energy. He had
seen the hare, but saw the man too, and was afraid to stoop. Once
only a lark began to rise, a short and struggling flight in the sun's
eye; then, as though touched by the hawk's shadow, he checked his
song, fluttered in a spiral, and fell like a stone to the ground. The
man sat up, twisting his head towards the lark's point of impact.
When he straightened, the hare had gone.

Winter had clung hard to the Welsh hills, spring was short and
bitter, but now in the last days of May sunshine fell like cloth-of-
gold over the western seaboard. Where he lay his heels sconched
the last short salt-bleached violets, there were cowslips half-
opened, and he saw the blue shield of the sea across a flame of
gorse. Near the cliff wall the bushes had been clamped to earth by
heavy winds from the south-west; their branches were tentacles of
grey and gold, the spikes gripping at the stub grass. Further back,
where Merrill was lying, the clumps were less compact, they grew
higher, with strong flowery arms curved upwards like the fronds of
ferns. When he sat up he could see to the north, between these
spiky arms, the far-off outlines of mountains, sharp jags and
rounded moels. Fronting him, out in the Bay, was Ynys Las, the
Green Island. It lay a couple of miles off-shore, its eastern cliffs
groined with shadows as the sun moved down sky. It had the look
of a fragment broken from the mainland, and the local story, he

knew, rested on this: how King Bleddri had flung a gobbet of his country after another king, Maredudd, who was sailing for Ireland with his, Bleddri's, wife. It had missed, of course. 'They always miss,' he said, getting to his feet. 'Always.' The thought pleased him and he repeated it as he brushed himself down. He shaded his eyes with his hand, staring westwards. 'Cunning,' he said. 'Or they think they are.'

He looked at his watch, then turned and walked slowly away from the headland. It was a country of low hills and wooded cwms, and from where he stood he could mark the writhing valleys of two rivers. In slow gradation the height of land changed from green to cyclamen and rose, and so faded into the purple masses of the water-shed. Here and there he could see a farm building, long, low, and white-washed. There was a drift of sheep across a near-by field, and from a farm away to the left, but hidden, he heard a dog barking excitedly.

At a step he was out of sight of the sea. A sheep-track wound down in front of him; he took this, in one place pushing breast-high through gorse and the soft white arms of bramble. At the bottom of the slope he trod a line of stones across a quag, turned right up a gulley hanging with crab-shaped honeysuckle buds, and so came to a ridge which gave him a view of the long southern arm of the Bay. He was looking into the sun, a million light-pricks shot from the water into his eyelids, he shook his head.

'Cunning,' he said again, and laughed less pleasantly. 'Or fools. Or we are.'

His train of thought lasted him over the ridgeway and down till he fell in with a cart-track leading to the sea. Soon he was among trees, oak with a feathering of ash, and infrequently the brilliance of young beech. All save those in the bottom were side-spilled by the wind, and where the tree-line ended in scrub and fern were less than twenty feet high. Their roots were enormous and exposed. It was as though they had cast out anchors, and these were dragging through a green surf.

He heard the brook before he saw it. It was on his left running strongly in a gulch, and as he came to the end of the trees it swung right in a curve, and he crossed it by a low stone bridge. In a minute or two he would be at Ffald-y-Brenin.

Unease made him stop here and light a cigarette. He drew on it without enjoyment, even without taste. 'What of it?' he said suddenly, and louder than he had intended. The narrow valley burst on to the Bay with blue violence; the Green Island lay basking like a seal. His arms reached out for it with a trembling passion. His jaw jutted, and he nodded fierce approval of the ideas farrowing in his mind. His mouth had dried so quickly that when he caught at his cigarette a sliver of rice-paper stuck to his lower lip. Then he dropped his arms. He had the feeling oil had run over all his limbs.

Flinging down his cigarette, he followed the brook to the house and workshop at Ffald-y-Brenin. These were under the one long roof, and fronted the Bay. The brook was imprisoned in a green-flagged channel for its last twenty yards, with a drop-gate to control its flow. Thence it ran to the black wheel which drove the saws and lathes, and after a tumble of ten or twelve feet went in wide transparent runnels through the shingle to the sea. He heard the soft roar of a saw as he came towards the workshop door, but after a moment's hesitation went on to the house. A board on the wall outside said: DAFYDD ABSALOM, TURNIWR, and underneath, obviously an afterthought, was written in chalk: *Wood Turner*. As he read, two dogs ran out of the house to welcome him, one with a huge ugly bucket-head, the other a cross-bred sheepdog in whelp. They pawed at him and barked till – '*Gad dy swn!*' shouted a voice from the workshop, when they dropped at once to four feet, their eyes rolled, and bucket-head went off round the corner of the house.

So he saw me come past, he thought, pushing at the house door. Well, he would.

Mrs Absalom was laying their tea. 'Oh,' she said, 'it's you, Mr Merrill?'

'Yes,' he said, 'it's me.'

'Well now – the men always come home for their eats, don't they?'

'They come home for everything they can't get elsewhere.' He spoke his sentence carefully, watching her the while.

She moved warily to the door. 'Dafydd!' she called. Merrill smiled ungraciously. But he didn't take his eyes from Mrs Absalom framed in the doorway, with the glitter behind her.

'Where's Mrs Merrill?' he asked.

'She's been resting. I knocked at the door a few minutes ago, and she'll soon be down. Ah, there's a busy man that Dafydd's been,' she went on. 'Finishing the spoons for the day after tomorrow – and there's the Wise Man's to go to tomorrow night.

No time, no time at all!' She looked over her shoulder. 'What are you staring at?' 'You,' he said bluntly. 'And you know it.'

Her lips moved soundlessly. 'Staring's rude, Mr Merrill.'

He looked slowly the length of her body. 'And thinking's ruder, Mrs Absalom.'

'We must control our thoughts. Everybody knows that. It's in the Bible. And why should you stare at me?'

'I'll tell you.' Her full lips parted, she patted her smooth black hair. He would have moved towards her, but – 'Here's Dafydd,' she said calmly. 'Beat off the mess,' she cried to her husband. 'Here's Mr Merrill back.'

He heard Absalom clouting the wood-dust from his clothes before coming indoors. Then Mrs Absalom brushed past him, smiling her sly smile, to wet the tea on the hob. 'Tea was always such a meal up at the Hall,' she said mincingly. 'All the things silver, and the lovely cups and saucers. Dear me now, weren't those the days!' Briskly she untied her check apron, smoothed her hips, patted her hair again. 'I wonder if Mrs Merrill . . .'

Her husband came quietly in. He nodded briefly when he saw Merrill, who was by the passage door. 'I'll just go up,' he was saying, when he heard the door open and close and his wife on the stairs. 'No, I needn't.' He stood waiting for her to enter, moved solicitously, and was annoyed by the swift downward flash of Mrs Absalom's eyes.

'Did you sleep?'

'No – but I rested.' She turned to the Absaloms. 'This is really the quietest place in the world.'

'It is not bad,' said Absalom, halting on each word.

'For sleeping in,' his wife added tartly.

Absalom seemed in one of his moods, the sulkiness of his face imposing silence on others as well as himself. His face was swarthy, with a coarse glow of health along the cheek-bones, the eyes black and slanting, the mouth red and hard. Some unresolved queerness of personality marked him as with a scar. When as today he came straight to table from the workshop, grey or ruddy sawdust fine as flour might be seen in the whorls of his ears, in the wrinkles under his eyes, and even threaded on his lashes. His hands were dusty as a miller's. A spot of oil had fallen against his index finger: he saw his wife's eyes on it and ostentatiously took out a red handkerchief and wiped it away.

'You are very busy, Mr Absalom?'

He nodded, hesitated, was driven to words. He had determined on resentment against his wife when Mrs Merrill's question came placidly in. 'Unless I've been wasting my time.' He was groping in his pocket. 'On this, say.' He laughed unexpectedly, showing an unpleasant scum of dust at the corners of his mouth. 'If you ever saw better than that up at the Hall,' he challenged Mrs Absalom, and sat back watching them all. He had placed on the table-cloth a small rimless bowl of a simple but beautiful shape, dull green and veined all over, with some of the pattern running to the greener shades of blue. 'Oh, may I touch? May I touch?' cried Mrs Merrill. Absalom's face ridged with a smile, yet as though against his will. 'Now, Mr Merrill,' he said rapidly, 'you are a college-trained man.' He pointed to the bowl between Mrs Merrill's long white fingers. 'What is it?'

Merrill took it from his wife. It was hard, heavy, cold as stone. He tapped it with the ball of his finger. It must be wood, yet this was like tapping a pebble.

'Would it be malachy?' asked Absalom, thrusting his head forward.

'Malachite?'

'Dafydd always gets mixed on those big words,' said Mrs Absalom.

'It's all the same thing. Is it?'

'I don't know.'

'Ah,' said Absalom, turning to his audience, 'then there's things after all even a college-trained man don't know.'

'A great many,' Merrill agreed, wondering what idea of a college Absalom carried in mind. 'It's wood, of course.'

'The colour?' cried Absalom excitedly.

He shook his head.

'The weight? The coldness? The grain – go on, look at the grain!'

To Merrill his triumph and mystery were overdone. He looked at the two women and realised with a shock that while Mrs Absalom regarded her husband's excitement with a cynical humour, his own wife was watching him, Merrill, with a withdrawn but real mockery. 'You tell us,' he said roughly.

'Whatever it is, Mr Absalom,' said his wife, 'it is very, very beautiful.'

Absalom's nod had to do for thanks. 'I thought a clever man like Mr Merrill would know it was oak,' he said, with what struck

Merrill as unpleasant deference. His gesture over-rode their surprise. 'Ffald-y-Brenin oak.' He took the bowl from Merrill, turned it gently in his hands, and went on to explain how three years ago, fearing it might have gone rotten, he had removed the block from under the mill wheel. 'My grand-dad's dad put it there, they tell me.' The block had proved hard and heavy as a rock, but the green of moss and slime and perhaps some mineral quality of the water had dyed it to the heart, and from this heart he had turned his bowl on the pole lathe. 'No doubt, I should have been making spoons for the Abermaid porridge-eaters,' he admitted belligerently.

'Is it for sale?' asked Merrill.

Absalom was staring down the table, and seemed to be thinking hard. 'Not for sale,' he replied shortly.

'That's foolish talk,' said Mrs Absalom. She pronounced the word 'fullish' always. 'What are things for if not to sell?'

But Mrs Merrill was shaking her head. 'I can understand that so well, Mr Absalom.'

He smiled at her, his eyes half-closed. 'Besides, I can show it at the Eisteddfod. This will make the Abercych men mad, I tell you. All over Wales I shall get a first with this.' He held the bowl to his ear as though it were a seashell full of music.

'But you can make another,' Merrill persisted.

'Can I?'

'From the rest of the block – of course you can.'

'If you think it so easy . . .'

'It wouldn't be, for me. It should be, for you.'

Absalom spoke pointedly to Mrs Merrill. 'It's because the wood is unnatural. It cracks on the lathe, or it cracks in the drying. This was the third for me to try.' He passed the green bowl back to her. 'This one may crack yet. Things are very different often from what they seem. And if it cracks who'd want it? No one would keep a flawed thing, would they?'

'It isn't flawed, is it?' Mrs Absalom asked sharply. 'So why a lot of old talk?'

'Why indeed?' Absalom had moved towards the door. The meal was over. Merrill took out his pipe, Mrs Absalom had reached for her apron. 'I'll help you clear,' said Mrs Merrill. Merrill saw how she stood tired and pallid in the shadow near the passage. We are made as we are made, he thought, watching her; and wondered whether he had been fatuous or profound. 'If you don't mind – ' said Mrs Absalom, bright and arch, with her Hall-parlour good

manners. She moved past him with the tray. 'Clean as you go –
that was always the rule, and such a good one, isn't it?'

He stood in the doorway, staring across the shingle and pebbles
and the water's dark edge. Ripples were rising a hundred yards
out, on a sandbank, but flattened as they reached deeper water.
Then once more they crumpled upwards, crawling in with hardly
any increase of height, till near the shore they curled into radiant
feathers, hesitated and fell over with quiet nudgings into the
hissing shingle. All was silent in the workshop, but the cross-bred
bitch sat against the wide door. Behind him he heard the women
talking as they washed up, and presently they came out to join
him, for a minute as they said, before Mrs Merrill went upstairs to
remake her bed.

'Would you like to go for a walk?' he asked his wife. 'Not too far,
just around the beach.'

She shook her head. 'Later I might. But I'm going to watch Mr
Absalom. He is going to make me a special spoon. But not a
sweetheart's spoon.' Beside her Mrs Absalom glowed with a svelte
good health; the sun which lost itself in the soft brown hair of the
one woman glittered on the twin raven wings of the other. 'What
lovely hair you have,' said Mrs Merrill at that moment. 'And how it
gleams in the sun!' Mrs Absalom turned, her red lips parting. 'And
how warm the sun is,' Mrs Merrill continued. She looked at her
husband. 'And how sad it should grow cool and dim and then dark.'

Merrill frowned, disregarding the commonplace, but not so Mrs
Absalom. 'Only for the night,' she replied cheerfully. 'And then it
comes again.' For a moment she rested her hands on her hips, the
very image of sly and jocund womanhood. 'That's the one thing
about the country,' she concluded, 'it makes you moody between
whiles.'

Absalom was coming out of the workshop. The bitch fell in at
his heel, grey-flanked and brindled down the spine and tail. She
was far gone, her bag heavy, the teats like huge red teeth under
her. Her tail swept slowly and unceasingly.

'Ask him again for the green bowl,' Mrs Absalom told Merrill.
'He will sell when he thinks it over.'

Absalom's teeth flashed. 'I am going to make your spoon,' he
called, all good humour. 'It will be something to watch, I can tell
you.'

'I'll leave the bed till later. I'm coming! And you,' Mrs Merrill
told her husband. 'We must all see.'

But Mrs Absalom was shaking her head. 'Not me. I had my spoon a long time ago.' Her glance passed through Merrill's as she turned back in and they went off to the workshop door.

Absalom was waiting for them there. It was a small square room he had to work in, without any windows, but with a door almost the width of the front wall. Inside there was room for two lathes, one the old-fashioned pole lathe, the other driven by the wheel. There was a pleasant mustiness in the air there. Just inside the door stood an untrimmed chopping-block, on which lay a short-hafted, heavy-headed axe. Merrill felt its edge as Absalom fetched three glowing rounds of cherry wood for them to sit on. He and his wife were opposite each other; Absalom had set himself to face the light.

'It is quite easy really,' said Absalom. At the same time he smiled rather cunningly. 'What you call a snip.'

'When you know how!'

'When you know how. Now watch me, Mrs Merrill, and afterwards' – he dropped his eyes – 'you shall make one for your husband.'

With a fast snaky motion he snatched on oblong of sycamore from the lathe-bed behind him. It went over to his left hand, slid and was gripped, and his right caught up the axe close to the head, his index finger lying along the blade. Without any pause he had begun to chop. *Chuck-chuck-chuck* went the axe: each stroke fell a half-inch above its predecessor till the block bristled like a cock's comb, and then a last and heavier blow prised the whole cut away. *Chuck-chuck-chuck* – against his will Merrill grew interested. He raised his eyebrows at his wife. A shape was already emerging, the handle and the block where the bowl end would be. So far Absalom had not appeared to give a thought to his work's end, but now for the first time he paused and let the whole thing lie on his palm. Then three savage strokes seemed to his watchers to ruin the whole block; the wood was rapidly reversed in his grip and a hasty feathering began anew along the handle and shoulders. He's showing off, thought Merrill; serves him right if he makes a mess of it – as he must. The spoon spun once more as in a conjuring trick, the axe hacked and gouged: as though in an instant the hollow of the bowl grew visible. Without a word Absalom set the axe down and reached for a thick-backed straight-bladed knife. Splints and shavings came whittling off the handle, again the shoulders were fiercely attacked, a dozen times Merrill could have cried: 'No, no, another cut will spoil it!' But a dozen times the cut was made till the shoulders carried a short spiky frill of splittings. *Crit, crit,* they were clear once more, clean and shapely. Absalom now caught from the lathe-bed a knife whose blade was first bent completely over parallel to the tang and then the bend contorted to a side-slipped S. With this he began to scoop at the bowl with that same apparent recklessness, the S-blade passing after each stroke within an inch of his naked wrist. 'Like to try?' he asked Merrill, grinning.

He picked up a spokeshave. 'A snip,' he said again. This was pure conceit and showmanship. His elbow and forearm hugged his side, the fulcrum for his flashing wrist; the spokeshave moved at a fantastic speed with a backhand motion; the sycamore peeled away in curls and tendrils. 'When you know how.'

Again he gouged at the bowl hollow till it seemed he would break through the thin wood. 'We must make this very special.'

The handle was now long and slender, with a spatulate tip; he had achieved an exquisitely simple angle at its junction with the bowl. By a lucky accident, maybe, the grain of the wood followed the shape of the bowl, wavy lines on white.

'Not bad,' said Absalom complacently. 'Now when we . . .' He went over to the lathe, followed by Mrs Merrill. 'It will be very plain,' he told her. 'I never decorate. I am like my dad – all for line.' He reached once more for his knife, pleased as a cat with Mrs Merrill's praise.

Merrill went outside. All for line! He thought of Mrs Absalom. Back at the house he found her folding linen on the kitchen table. 'I have seen the ninth wonder,' he said drily. 'It was a very pretty spoon.'

'If Dafydd put his mind to it then it was,' she agreed. 'I don't say he is better than the Henllan turner or those at Abercych, but he is as good.'

'Is he really?' He stood looking through the window. 'You are not going to Abermaid with Dafydd on Thursday?'

'I am not thinking to.'

'I'm going out to the Island.'

'You have quite a fancy for the Ynys, haven't you?'

'So you'll be able to come,' he went on calmly.

She shook her head, smiling. 'I'd be afraid, Mr Merrill, if I was on that island.' She spoke more slowly. 'I don't like being afraid.'

'Afraid of what?'

But she only smiled at him.

'Of me?'

'And why should I be afraid of you?'

'Of Dafydd then, if he knew you'd gone.' He persisted. 'Go on, say – would you?'

'I might be. Or again I mightn't. Anyway it's all a lot of fullishness we are talking. Why don't you go back to the workshop?'

'Because I'd rather stay with you.'

She had moved into the doorway as earlier in the day. 'I wonder why, Mr Merrill?'

'Oh no, you don't! I know you pretty well by this time,' he told her. He saw how she was watching him through narrow eyes. 'And you must know me too,' he added harshly. 'Or you think you do. And if you do, it saves me a lot of words.'

She took him up quickly on that. 'Then there's no more to say, is there, Mr Merrill?'

'Except that you'll come to the Island. I wouldn't eat you, you know.'

'I am not afraid of being eaten,' she replied, with a slow and tantalising smile. 'No, I am afraid of something quite different to that. Seasickness perhaps.'

'There are precautions,' he assured her.

'Are there now? I wouldn't know. But the best thing is not to cross the water, surely?'

He knew the pleasure this kind of talk gave her, these hints and veilings and indirections. For hers, he knew, was the twofold sensuality of mind and body that kept with her to the last minute of each day.

'And when will Mrs Merrill be coming back?' she asked him.

'Tuesday. And you know.'

'You will be quite the bachelor, I can see. And all fancy-free, I shouldn't wonder.' He thought wrily of his own hypocrisy in condemning her bad taste, momentarily saw himself mean and ugly. 'Quite a bachelor,' he repeated, 'and fancy-free. And so – the Island.'

'It's very pretty, I must say,' she said, shading her eyes. 'But dir annwyl, I shouldn't like anyone to throw the Green Island after me, Mr Merrill.'

'There's no danger. And they always miss.'

She laughed aloud and stepped out on to the doorstep. At once the bitch, greedy for affection, waddled over from the workshop door. Mrs Absalom began to sing 'Watching the Wheat,' her light and tender voice like a shaft of the yellowing sun. 'I'm going to the shop again,' he said at the end of her verse. She only nodded, her hand falling to the bitch's head. Behind him the song restarted, at once piercing and pathetic, the lyric melancholy of young love. Damn her! he thought. If it pleases her to play clever!

Inside the workshop door Absalom and Mrs Merrill were examining the pole lathe. The spoon, he judged, was finished. 'Look,' she cried, 'oh look! Isn't it wonderful?' 'I've seen it before,' he answered but covered his ungraciousness with a smile and by crossing to the lathe. He rubbed his fingers along the ash pole, testing its spring. 'The clever people in the Museum down at Cardiff they tell me,' said Absalom, 'this pole lathe would be thousands of years old – ones like it, I mean. Would that be right now, d'you think?' He didn't expect an answer. 'I sometimes think when I'm turning in here that I'll be the last man in Wales to use it in the way of trade. And that's a hard mouthful to chew on. I'm the only man of my age at it now.' He began to speak bitterly. 'It's all your shoddy stuff now. Well, I've never done it and I never will.' He rolled back some sacks in the corner, so that they could see spoons, bowls, egg-cups, butter-scoops and cream-skimmers, all simple and elegant. 'That's yew,' he was saying. 'There's a good wood for you.' He named sycamore, burr oak, yew again, and holly. 'And you'd never guess that – it's plum.' Objects turned with a peculiar swift stealthiness in his broad hairy hands. 'And here's a good one!' They all laughed. '*Llwy gam.*' This was a hobgoblin kind of spoon, with a huge bowl, thick round stem, and then a ridiculously disproportionate flattened end piece, all the parts fighting away from each other on a flowing double bend. 'Not quite your usual thing,' said Merrill, turning it over in his hands, and then: 'Yes, I see it!' – for centrally through all its grotesque curves there flowed the fine bold line he had come to look for as Absalom's sign manual. 'I like it. Can I have it? And don't be afraid to put the price up.'

'*Llwy gam* – the crooked spoon.' Absalom raised his head. 'All right, it's yours. But watch your chin when you eat your porridge.'

'But why should you be the last one to use the old lathe, Mr Absalom? Is it so very hard?' Mrs Merrill asked concernedly.

'It's all done in a hurry today. They can't be bothered.' His 'they' swung with his arm out from Ffald-y-Brenin, through Wales and the wide world.

'Then you must teach your son perhaps,' she said, 'to use it after you.'

His vivid tricky face lost all expression. 'Yes,' he said, and abruptly: 'Well, I must be getting on with my work.' It was blunt, direct dismissal.

'What you said about a son,' Merrill told his wife as they walked down the shingle. 'He didn't like it, did he?'

'He would like children, that's why. And he knows he will never have them.' She spoke with complete calm. 'Mrs Absalom will see to that.'

'Come, come – that's not for you to decide,' he bantered.

'No, for her. And she has decided. She will be as barren as myself.'

He stopped convulsively. 'Look,' he said, 'we settled . . .'

'I said that only by way of statement. If I can face it, you can.' He shrugged his shoulders. 'I've been wondering whether you'd be as pleased after all if I didn't come back on Tuesday. It's for so short a time. The journey is so long.'

'Why *pleased?* Is that the right word?'

'It was probably the wrong one.'

'It's for you to say. I'd want you to do what you wish – though that's not always so simple, I admit. Think it over, could we?' He hesitated. 'I'll come back with you on Thursday, if you like.' But he was thinking how stupid he was to say anything of the kind. As though anything could be solved by going back or unwinding the ribbon-pathways they had come. Not even pity – pity could solve nothing. He fell back on his earlier phrase: We are made as we are made – as though that explained or excused anything. 'Would you like me to?'

She shook her head. 'No, don't come. I'd rather not. Perhaps we'll both have time to think. For we'd better think.' But he looked stubbornly out to sea. 'Is it to stay as it has been?'

'It's what we said. It's no one's fault. It's happened, that's all. Anything I can do – anything I can give you . . .'

'I want nothing from you except what you seem unable to give.'

'Haven't we had this out before?' he asked angrily. 'It changed, it all changed. I didn't want it to.'

'And I didn't want it to. But it means I'll leave you.' He kept silence. 'We can't go on living a sham.'

'Why not? The whole world's a sham, God knows!'

'I am, I know,' she said quietly.

'I didn't mean that. You know I didn't mean that!'

'No?' she said. She shivered.

The breeze was freshening with the turn of the tide, and the waves were louder as, their height increased, they poised, revolved compactly, and then flushed out over the beach. And at the moment when the grey-green waters halted before their immemorial recession, the earth too stood hushed and all its creatures noiseless. Not a bird was singing.

Merrill made as though to speak, but checked himself, and it was in silence they walked back to the Absaloms' house.

II

They were walking up to Cornel Ofan where the Wise Man lived. 'Why Cornel Ofan?' Merrill asked. 'Why Terror Corner?'

Absalom halted and pointed. They had come up through the anchored oaks of Ffald-y-Brenin, the King's Fold, and were on the cart-track over Felindre land. High up and half-right and facing them was the Wise Man's house. 'You'll see the road at the back,' he explained. The hill was humped like a burial mound, rounded and soft with scrub and pigfern, but on its near side a buttress of rock crept its whole length, grey among greens. The house squatted seaward of the buttress, its windows flashing like spectacles in the sunlight. 'You'll see the view too, from the top,' Absalom went on to Mrs Merrill. He was wearing a navy-blue suit which vulgarised him. 'They say he lives high up where he covers all the roadways and paths, so that he can see everybody who comes. Then he slips indoors into a little place behind the ingle, and hides. But the caller comes indoors and tells Mrs Wise Man all about it, and there he is listening all the time. Then he comes swanking in and won't even let you start to talk.' Mrs Absalom began to imitate a deep male voice. ' "No, don't tell me, little one," he says; 'you don't have to tell the *dyn hysbys*. Your little cow has a bad tail – I know it; the Pembroke black. Take home this ointment in the brown box, and bite her tail to the bone in the middle of the bad. Then spread the ointment thick as home-made jam, and tie the tail up in a paper-bag from the Farmers' Co-op; and in four days if it isn't as clean as a leaf come to me for more ointment. Oh, and don't forget the two shillings, will you, little one? Even a Wise Man must live." '

They went on, half-jesting, to tell more of the Wise Man's remedies. To cure a burn, hold it in front of the fire – the heat would draw the burn out. To a bad cut apply a slice of home-cured fat bacon. He cured dogs of distemper by making a fold in the skin over the backbone, threading a cord through, and tying both ends in a fancy bow.

'So your Wise Man is a fake?' Merrill said.

The Absaloms shook their heads, shocked. No, he was very much the Wise Man. There were tricks to every trade. Apologetically, Absalom explained how he owed the Wise Man his life. He had had shingles when a boy, and the ends had almost met across his chest, and when the ends met (every fool knew this), you died. He grew excited and waved his arms as he described how the doctor from Dolau gave him up, and then the doctor from Pant, and at last the great Doctor Jones of Abermaid. And then his father had carried him in the dark, through a terrible storm, along this very track to the Wise Man, who plastered him from neck to navel, from nape to napkin-end, with hot mutton-fat and let it congeal into a life-jacket, and gave him to drink of the juice of the fleshy green herb which grows in wall-cracks at Cornel Ofan. He could take the evil eye off man or beast, but no one had openly accused him of putting one on; and he alone in the county could cure rotten bone by the old forgotten shepherd's maggot-cure. As the Absaloms grew more eager to defend and praise the Wise Man, Merrill wondered whether they were not a little afraid of him.

'We must certainly thank him, Mr Absalom,' he heard his wife say, 'that he saved your life, and you are now our delightful guide.'

This was a foolish Englishy sort of talk Absalom could never find an answer for. It puzzled Mrs Absalom too, despite tea at the Hall, as Merrill could see.

The shadows were stretching themselves when they reached Cornel Ofan. But first they went thirty yards past the house to the top of the hill, to admire how strategically the Wise Man had placed himself. And here the Merrills saw one reason for the name of the house, for the backside of the hill had been gashed by a stone quarry which ran right back to the mountain road: this approached it head on and then turned terrifyingly away without so much as a wire fence by way of protection. 'Wild Wales,' commented Merrill. 'Nice at night time.' Long elliptical banks, invisible from the valley, showed that the house stood within an ancient hill fort. The view ran out on three sides over the same country of wood and hill and cwm Merrill had admired from the headland over Ffald-y-Brenin, but the mountains of the north had swung into fresh focus. They were livid as a bruise and their outlines hard. Ynys Las looked flatter from here, and with the yellow ball of the sun behind it its nearer cliffs were the colour and texture of soot. Broad streams of light trembled in the water at its either side, their lemon brightness coarsening to steel-grey and the steel-grey to mackerel as they spread from the sun. 'What a throw!' said Merrill, thinking of King Bleddri. His thoughts shifted to Mrs Absalom standing by his side, and he smiled. She too was smiling, and he exulted to think she might smile for the same reason. What smooth black glossy hair she had, drawn back from her forehead and ears and rolled like a shell on the nape of her neck. Her throat was white and full. He thought of the flesh milky under the dark blue dress.

'Shall we go in?' asked Absalom.

Turning, they saw that the Wise Man had come out to welcome them. 'He's not going to hear us talk first then?' Merrill whispered to Mrs Absalom, but loud enough for them all to hear. 'Some things he knows without talking,' said Absalom.

The Wise Man looked half-prophet, half-charlatan. He was tall and heavy shouldered, with a massive head and thin white hair. His features were blunt and fleshy except for his nose which was bony and curved in the roman way and poked forward like a big beak. He gave Merrill the impression he did his listening with this aggressive nose, from the way he had of lifting his head in two or three short jerks when he was spoken to. This same trick gave him an air of extraordinary deliberation. He wore a well-kept suit of old-fashioned cut, with wide lapels and squarish trouser-legs, a soft linen collar and spotted tie over his flannel shirt, and his boots had lumpy polished toecaps crissed with little cuts. He was clearly on his dignity with guests he did not know, and after one Welsh sentence of greeting to the Absaloms stood waiting for the Merrills to be introduced to him.

'I have heard so much about you,' said Mrs Merrill, and this seemed to please him. 'They talk, they talk,' said the old man. 'You have not had those old shingles again?' he asked Absalom naïvely. In the Merrills' faces he read knowledge of the wondrous cure and nodded his satisfaction.

'*Fy nghartre bach i*,' he said, opening the gate, and then solemnly in translation: 'My little home, my dears.'

Merrill wasn't sure whether his manner held more of magnificence or absurdity, but found it worth watching.

They were shown into the small parlour. This like its owner was a showpiece. The walls were covered with a thick shiny yellow paper mellowed rather than sullied with age, but the ceiling was white-washed boards. On the floor was a bright red turkey carpet. There were half a dozen pictures, two of them enlarged and coloured portraits of an elderly couple whom he judged to be the Wise Man's father and mother. Hung where they could hardly be seen till the lamp was lit were likenesses of St John, with a huge quill pen, and a bearded St Matthew with a bull peering over his shoulder. There was a red mahogany table in the middle of the floor, and a harmonium with rosewood panels against the wall furthest from the fireplace.

Including the Wise Man there were already four people present. His wife was a shrunken woman of seventy, who wore an exquisite lace apron to honour her guests. Her fingers were worn with work, she had bright keen peasant eyes, but she was to surprise Merrill and charm his wife by a delicate formality in all she did and said. Next was a draper from Abermaid, twelve miles away; he had important business with the Wise Man, and had left his Austin Seven at the entrance to a field. He came naturally and volubly into the conversation with explanations why he hadn't brought her past the quarry. 'Over you go,' he told them dramatically; 'bump you go once, and still there you are. Bump you go twice, and still there you are – only not so much of you. Bump you go three times, and then – WHERE ARRU?' He roared with laughter. 'Collishon – therru are!' he cried. "'Sploshon – where arru?' 'Sploshon you have there – not a quarry at all. Oh dear dear annwyl!'

'Explosion?' This was the other guest, his life's story written in his face and hands. 'I could tell you about explosions too.'

'And you shall,' promised the Wise Man. 'Mr Thomas here,' he explained gravely, 'is a great one for reciting, and after supper he shall recite "The Explosion".' Mr Thomas nodded several times, his undamaged eye rested on Merrill as though to say: I will too – and what a treat! 'After supper,' continued the Wise Man, 'anyone who will may show his craft.'

Merrill saw Mrs Absalom smile. That's one craft I could show, he thought. And will yet. He turned his head, with the feeling someone was watching him.

'A difference between craft and crafty,' Absalom was saying.

'My English is not good,' said the draper. '*Yr hen iaith* I am at home in, the old tongue. Excuse me please, Mr and Mrs Merrill, our distinguished friends. But I say now they are damn scoundrels, those brothers. In fact, buggarrs.' The Wise Man held up his hand. But the draper was irrepressible, and perhaps the Wise Man didn't too strongly wish to repress him. 'Credit to all,' he cried, 'and first, credit to the Wise Man of Cornel Ofan!' He turned confidentially to the Merrills. 'If I wanted to, I could tell you – oh such things!'

'You could, Mr Meredith? Such as . . .'

'It is nothing,' said the Wise Man.

'Indeed it is not nothing. Those brothers – but you know Abermaid, Mr Merrill, do you not? You don't? Duw annwyl, Mr Merrill sir, and you a college-trained man, I'm sure. It is not such a small old world after all.' He seemed to lose his place but found it after a glance at the Wise Man. 'Those brothers I am talking about – I am a small shop, Mr Merrill and Mrs Merrill madam, in the drapery way of business, and I do very well until ten or twelve years ago, when those brothers who are also a small shop in the drapery way pay a *dyn hysbys*, a Wise Man as the English say, to put the evil on me. Consider now the change, Mr Merrill sir. Where I had a hundred customers I now had fifty, and soon where I had fifty I had ten. The Workhouse yawned before me like the mouth of hell when the fifth angel sounded in Revelations and there arose a smoke out of the pit – when I came to talk with the respected and reverent Mr Joseph Jones, the Wise Man of Cornel Ofan.'

The Wise Man made a gesture of tolerance and modesty.

'And what did the respected and reverend Wise Man do?' He screwed his chair closer to Mrs Merrill's. 'If only we knew the secrets of the ancient ages of the world, Mrs Merrill madam – but we don't. It is the Wise Man of Cornel Ofan alone who knows those. No, no, Mr Jones', – his voice dropped respectfully – 'the truth is always the truth. There was the Witch of Endor for one, and she knew her left hand from her right or the Good Book is putting it on a bit; and there was Myrddin whom the English call Merlin for two – he was no softy till he was taken in by a bit of a frittery wench; and there is Mr Jones here for a third – what a lovely man he is! He is better than the Witch of Endor as the male is superior to the female (with no offence to the ladies present, always excepted, as understood); he is wiser than Merlin, for no silly bit of a frittery wench ever put a pad of mist over *his* eyes; and in brief, he is exceeded in wisdom and fair dealing only by himself.'

The Wise Man rubbed his hand over the top of his head. 'Surely this is enough, Mr Meredith?'

'For Mr Jones,' continued the draper, 'came to Abermaid and took off the evil eye, and where I had ten customers I once more had fifty, and the fifty became a hundred, and the hundred waxed even unto two hundred, and so I have lived in peace and prosperity as a good Calvinist ever since. Till a month ago, in fact, when those two buggarrs put it on again.' He laid his finger alongside his nose. 'But I have brought my troubles to Mr Jones here. I could say a lot more . . .'

'You would be unwise to,' interrupted the Wise Man.

'But I shall say nothing instead. There is a time to talk and a time to be silent. I will now be silent. In brief, I will only say . . .'

'Say nothing!'

There was an astonishing change in the Wise Man's voice. Mr Meredith coughed and covered his mouth. 'Quite so,' he agreed. 'I am when I wish of a silence to make the grave sound noisy. I have a call of nature. Excuse me, please.' He rose, bending his back as though completing a sale, and went into the garden.

'He is a good man that Mr Meredith, but he talks too much,' said the Wise Man. 'And all because I was once able – but there, most of it is nonsense.'

The draper returned to find them all drawn up to table. There was cold ham and salad and a sage cheese which oozed yellow oil on to a paper doily. And over the meal presided the Wise Man's wife, in the hand-worked apron she had had these fifty years, and with a gentle, prim courtesy. Mrs Absalom was moved to a word of compliment. 'My dears,' said the old lady, to her and Mrs Merrill, 'if we have only a glass of water let us have it nice.' This was loudly approved by the draper, whose eyes were pricing all past his finger-ends and by Mrs Absalom; only the ex-collier looked baffled. Merrill felt the childishness in them all, couldn't help his sense of superiority. The Wise Man's love of flattery, the draper's eagerness to bestow it, Mrs Jones's pride in her apron and her silver teapot, Mrs Absalom – he checked on Mrs Absalom. They draw us, he thought, with single hairs, so deep she thinks herself and clever, but it's all in the flesh's red and white, our own incompleteness. Our own folly.

He caught the Wise Man's eyes, bland and unrevealing, and turned to look out of the window. 'You can't see the Island from here then?' He hardly listened to the Wise Man speaking of the round of the hill, for Mrs Absalom had turned too, to look over her shoulder. She looked amused.

'He is very fond of the Island, Mr Merrill is,' said Absalom, as though exhibiting a child's cleverness. 'He is very fond indeed.'

'You call it the Green Island but it looked black to me,' said Mr Thomas. 'This Bleddri must have had a collier's hand with you. I could tell of colliers too . . .'

'And you shall,' promised the Wise Man. 'The explosion and the colliers – tell them you shall.' Silently Thomas laid his hands on the tablecloth. They were twisted and sprinkled with blue scars, and on the left hand two fingers ended at the first joint. He peered at them with his one eye, and without a word spoken the atmosphere changed. 'Mr Thomas,' said the Wise Man gently, 'in his time has been in an explosion. He has composed a poem about it which he will recite to us later.'

And after supper he did. It was in all ways an astounding performance. The ex-collier began by taking off his coat. When he rolled up his sleeves they saw the hairy swelling right forearm and the blue fire-wasted strings of the left. His listeners had pressed back to the edges of the room, the reciter took his place confronting them. 'The Explosion,' he announced quietly, and in the fraction of time his face altered – terribly. 'The Explosion,' he said again. His words were Welsh with snatches of mongrel English, but his action and declamation so emphatic that the Merrills were never at a loss for their import. He began with a few humorous touches: Tal coming downstairs in the morning and drawing up the fire while the Missus got his breakfast and filled his tommy-box and jack. Then the walk to the pithead, greetings to friends, the cage, reaching the coalface. A word about the roof – No, no (this was the timberman, bass-voiced), the roof was all right. Tal looked at the flame of his lamp. Bit low, he didn't wonder. And now he was at work, balanced on his buttock, breaking out the coal. Once or twice he wiped sweat from his forehead and chest. He looked at his watch, told his butties the time, rested and reached for his food. Again the reciter's face altered: stupefaction, horror, despair masked him. He cowered down as the gallery rocked and roared in sheeted flame and blasted air, fell to his knees as the uprights snapped and the tough collars slewed and splintered, thrust up his broken hands against the world's shattered crust above him. O God, he panted, Arglwydd, Arglwydd, be with your children now! Merrill felt his heart bound and drop, his mouth was parched.

The uproar and destruction were past; and silence came crawling in, broken at first by the groan of timbers, the rattle of a stone from the quaking roof, little whispering rushes and compressions as the fall made solid the parting. Slowly men moved again, held up their lamps, blundered into speech, covered the faces of the dead. Time was there, and Silence, and the Dark. On his hunkers beside the fire he told how the lamps grew dim and died, and Blackness walled his eyes and stuffed his mouth, and his prayers grew dull and dead. In a sudden magic transition he spoke with sweetness of sky and sunshine in the living world, of birds singing free in air, of the women and old men at the pithead. A minister prayed, a crowd sang, and with them they sang in Cornel Ofan, a hymn that sucked the blood from Merrill's heart. The reciter held up his hand, silenced them on a falling note – he had heard something. Tap, tap, tap, the rescue party were at work, sending their question through the rock. Is anyone alive there? Answer, if you live. With the point of his pick he answered on the wall; the men spoke in low voices. And always tap, tap, tap, the blows of the crowbar ringing clearer till it rang into their heads. The tight crunching strokes of mandrils were heard in the fall, the hard slamming of a sledge. Men outside tore and battered, propped and lagged to make all safe; their nostrils dilated like stallions'. Then the shaft of yellow light, the breaking of the wall, men stumbling or carried out, the loud cry of grief and rejoicing.

The audience at Cornel Ofan sat forward, sighing. But the artist was not quite done. Tal's meeting with his wife again, his embarrassment at any show of feeling, some dry joke that gave them the chance to laugh. Then solemnly he raised his right hand for the ending. All the lovely butties, men of Lôn-Isa and Top Row, where were they now? The young men, the bloods, the football players and sweethearts; the strong colliers with wives and children; the whiteheads with bent backs and furrowed faces, where were they? He called softly through his hollowed hands, naming men: Twm and Dai and Eben and Llewelyn, where are you, lovely boys? But alas and alas! There they must lie in the sealed-off seam, and everlasting night enfold their flattened bodies. But their souls were with God, *yr Arglwydd Dduw*, on high.

The reciter reached hesitantly for his coat and put it on. He appeared dazed and asked for a glass of water. 'Our friend Mr Thomas has earned better than water,' said the Wise Man. 'I will fetch him beer. I am surprised,' he added in magnificent compliment, 'that the sun still shines in heaven.'

'It is a great talent,' said the draper sententiously. 'What a preacher you would have made, Mr Thomas man from South Wales!'

'I'm sure I thought I was there,' said Mrs Absalom. She looked innocently about her, smiling. 'Dear me, it is much nicer to be here.'

The draper was watching the Wise Man pour out a bottle of beer. 'Perhaps if I too could have a glass of water?' he suggested humbly. 'With Mrs Jones's permission kindly.'

'But if I said the sun was shining in heaven,' said the Wise Man, 'I was only just in time.' The corners of the room were brown and blurred, the far side of the valley softened from bright to gloomy green. 'A parting cup,' said the draper, setting down his foam-draped glass. 'I must be back before dark, for the way to Abermaid is as the hard and narrow way to the New Jerusalem.' He began to hum 'I'm Ready for the Other Side', while the Wise Man brought him his hat and a carton of brown eggs. The Wise Man was to see him as far as his car; everyone could understand that there were some last weighty words of counsel to be received, for even before he brought his tune to an end the draper was wagging his head and winking with the importance of a man set apart from his Abermaid fellows. 'God,' he said at his going, 'is with us all times, and now I have Mr Jones too. They shall need to grease their boots well, those brothers.'

All virtue seemed drained from Thomas still. He did no more than nod when the draper in farewell again assured him what a talent he had, and answered in a dull tired way when Absalom, suddenly all alive, began questioning him about his poultry run. The three women seemed naturally to fold together within the confine of their own affairs, and after a few minutes Merrill felt he could as well do without them all for a while as they apparently without him; with an excuse he went outside and took the road to the crest of the hill. He waited at the quarry edge and soon saw the Wise Man coming up towards him, his legs looking very short as he inclined his body to the slope. A brown bird hopped across the road and fell into space, startling Merrill.

'What was it?' he asked the old man. 'That bird – it was in the corner of my eye, moving.'

The Wise Man shook his head. 'How should I speak of what I did not see?' He jerked his arms in a vague but kindly gesture. 'You like Wales, Mr Merrill? You like Ffald-y-Brenin?'

'If it were not so lonely.' He felt the ungraciousness of this as he said it.

The Wise Man pondered. 'Yet two are always company. And three notoriously a crowd.'

'And at Ffald-y-Brenin we are four – a multitude, a stranded ark.'

'So long as the animals go in two by two it makes no difference.' He chuckled as Merrill turned to stare him down. His eyes were not to be held. 'Do you have Wise Men in England, Mr Merrill?'

'I have heard of Wise Women.'

'They are the deeper sex but not therefore the wisest. What do you think, Mr Merrill – are they?'

'There are as many fools among them as among men, I expect.'

'As many fools . . .' He chuckled again, bending to look into Merrill's face. 'Very good, Mr Merrill, I must say. And I expect a man like you thinks the number, the proportion as we say, pretty high too?'

'Pretty high.'

He nodded his satisfaction. 'As many as' – he began to count on his fingers – 'as many as three out of four, would you say?'

Merrill knew some childish strategem was being prepared against him. 'Or more,' he granted, humouring him.

The Wise Man looked shocked. 'No, no, Mr Merrill, we can't have more, can we?' His dignity was gone. With his antics and emphasis he was a white-headed buffoon. 'Not *four* out of four! Our company tonight, for example. Poor Mr Meredith who has such faith in the *dyn hysbys*. I am sure you thought him a fool, Mr Merrill, for I was watching you as he spoke.'

'I can't think . . .'

'An Englishman speaks!' cried the Wise Man with heavy humour. 'We may think folk fools but not say so behind their backs. I did not think you such a one for good form, Mr Merrill. And rest assured – our friend would much prefer we discuss him and call him a fool than that we ignore him.' He almost wheedled. 'Let us have him as our first fool – please!'

'So long as he won't feel lonely,' said Merrill as insultingly as he could.

'Never fear! Now there is our other friend, Mr Thomas of Pengaer, and one time of Senghenydd, Glam.' The Wise Man struck him off on a finger. 'He is a good one for the reciting, but what does that show? Only that he has a good memory.'

'So has a dog who sees the whip.'

The Wise Man threw up his hands. 'How true that is! He is our fool number two. Now let me think. You will understand, Mr Merrill, that we do not discuss our guests, you and Mrs Merrill who is so nice a lady though a little troubled tonight.' He had thrown the end of his sentence into the quarry before Merrill could turn on him. 'And would it not also be impolite to discuss the Wise Man and his wife? – though you have your ideas about me, I know it. Three out of four – and you thought a higher figure. But that leaves only the Absaloms! Now shall we start with Dafydd or his wife?'

'I think we'll change the subject and start for home!'

'There now.' The Wise Man walked along at his side. 'Mrs Absalom, well yes, but Dafydd – it would be a mistake to count on that.' Again he dropped his eyes as Merrill turned angrily towards him. 'I think I can hear the musical-box in the house there. It sounds very pretty in the night.'

Merrill heard it too, a tinkling as they drew near. Indoors they found all the party listening to 'Dolly Grey' and watching with attention the bright revolving cylinder.

'We have been talking of wisdom, Mr Merrill and I,' said the Wise Man when it ended. 'But I don't know that we are much the wiser.'

Merrill grimaced. 'I am sure we are not.' As he looked from his wife to Mrs Absalom he felt irritation and futility fill his breast like physical pain. 'Are you tired?' he asked, seeing the deeper lines of her face. And how had she shown she was unhappy? That old devil! With his talk of the Absaloms too. 'Wisdom,' the old man was saying playfully, 'is according to her name; she is not manifest unto many. That, Mrs Merrill, as I am sure you know, is from the Bible.' She laughed, disclaiming knowledge. 'It isn't such a bad old book after all,' he assured her, laughing.

'It isn't to be taken in vain,' said Mrs Jones reprovingly. She was changing the cylinder in the blue and gold enamelled box. 'Listen!' She held up finger, precise as a schoolmistress. Again the cylinder began to revolve, music as of a tiny spinet came enchantingly forth, and soon the melody had taken shape. 'Just a bird in a gilded cage.' Mrs Jones was obviously so proud of her treasure, and the Wise Man though he affected superiority so clearly gratified, that the sensation of their childishness came to Merrill anew. Thomas's one eye glittered at the revolving cylinder, a smile had lifted the grim corners of his mouth; the Absaloms sat engrossed; his own wife, he thought wryly, might be trusted to grace the occasion. The pretty box and its silvery runnels of sound diffused a charming sentimentality among them all, and he surrendered to it himself. All that had been ugly in his thoughts was tinged with romantic feeling; his thrusting sensuality slackened to tenderness; he contemplated his wife with pity and sadness and Mrs Absalom's bold profile without bitterness or desire.

The tune ended in a slurring of little bells. 'It's very,' said the ex-collier, and groped for the right word; 'it's very *artistic*, Mrs Jones.'

She shut the lid with a quiet, decisive click. The evening, it said, was over. Mrs Merrill smiled. The peasant woman had made a great lady's gesture.

And soon, their farewells made, they were on their way to Ffald-y-Brenin. The moon was lifting somewhere behind the hill, filling the valley with a soft and misty light, and breaking the pattern of distances. The trees still kept their green, a black and woolly green, and the beech trunks when they reached the bottom were grey and dull instead of shining vellum. Absalom carried a lantern which he had not troubled to light and was in front with his wife, while the Merrills came behind with an occasional stumble. They spoke hardly at all until they came to the oak wood, whose darkness encouraged them to walk closer together, and here Absalom on his wife's direction lit the lantern. It gave Merrill the feeling that at every stride he must set his foot into the glowing orange pool; he had to shake his head to defeat its hypnotic influence. 'I can't walk behind it,' his wife said suddenly. 'I feel, oh, I'm terribly sorry, Mr Absalom, I feel I'm going to fall forward into the light.' Absalom halted. 'There,' he said cheerfully, 'that's better, isn't it?' He swung the lantern to his other hand, clumsily took Mrs Merrill's arm. 'I'll lead, shall I?' Merrill had touched Mrs Absalom's hand as they walked together. Without design he lurched sideways from a dried mud-furrow and bumped softly against her. At once his arm had sought her waist, his hand pressed the sliding hip, for three or four paces her weight fell against him. Then she was away from him, he had fallen behind, again he stumbled. 'Wait for me,' he called to Absalom, as though he had been in the rear all the time. They halted. 'Almost there,' said Absalom, swinging the lantern. He could see the efflorescence of the water through the interstices of the remaining trees. 'Right. I've caught up. I was day dreaming.' He saw Mrs Absalom's face quite expressionless but avoided looking at her. 'Dangerous thing to do,' said Absalom. 'Better watch your step. Might come to harm. There!' he cried, and by pulling the lantern sharply up he douted it. They were clear of the wood.

Merrill took his wife's arm again as the brook splashed and bubbled alongside them. Ynys Las clung to the water like a cloud. The dogs had begun to bark their deep staccato volleys up the cwm; they heard a chain rattle. 'He's a good dog that Twm,' said Absalom with satisfaction. Then: '*Gad dy swn!* It's me!' he shouted. The dog fell quiet save for a couple of grunts as they passed the workshop, but the bitch went on whining her pleasure. 'Better have a look at her, I suppose,' said Absalom, taking the key from under a shell on the window-ledge. 'But she'll go a couple of days yet.'

They lit two lamps and the Merrills went on upstairs. But Merrill heard Absalom go outside and open the workshop door. He at once went back downstairs to find Mrs Absalom standing by the passage door. She seemed in no way surprised to see him, in no way surprised when he walked to her and set his hands to her waist. Yet she shook her head. He set his hands to her breasts, but again she shook her head. But his arms went around her and he forced her head back, forced her to kiss him. The blood was flooding at his temples, his throat was full, he had the feeling he was drowning, losing himself in her. Then she pushed him off violently. Someone was passing the window. He not only felt, he heard his heart gush and pound in that endless second before the door opened and Absalom entered.

'So I'm not last then?' To the listeners his voice was dry and steady, he closed the door and shot the bolt.

'Yes, you are,' said his wife coolly, and patted her hair. She yawned.

Merrill began to climb the stairs. But an impulse he couldn't control made him turn again to look at Absalom. He had been watching him go, he could tell, but a black bar of shadow was across his eyes and nose, and his mouth was tight and hard. Nothing to be read there. 'Good night,' he said again.

'Good night, Mr Merrill.'

This was Mrs Absalom, still yawning. Absalom's reply reached him later, when he was at the head of the stairs. 'Good night,' he said slowly.

III

Absalom and Mrs Merrill were away by eight o'clock in the morning. A thin mist was over the sea, and things of the night seemed neither real nor to be remembered. 'It will be a blazer later,' Absalom guessed. He swung the handle of his rusted Ford. 'She'll come. If she don't break my arm first. Try her on the starter, Mr Merrill.' The engine spat unevenly. 'Right. One more.' He made full contact, shattering the morning, then choked her down to an uneasy grumble.

Mrs Merrill's farewells were already made. She was taking the front seat alongside Absalom. 'You'll get a cup of tea at Abermaid,' her husband told her again, 'and lunch when you change at Maesheli. You'll be all right?'

'And Dafydd – ' this was Mrs Absalom. 'Look out for me by Felindre this evening. I might go up to Cornel Ofan. What time?'

Mrs Merrill wondered at the odd quality of Absalom's smile as he bent to the dashboard. 'Half-past eight do?' The clutch went in brutally, the car ground for a moment and then jolted forward. 'And don't forget the *Cambrian News!*' Mrs Absalom shouted, and ended almost on a scream. She turned to Merrill, beating her chest with her fist and choking. 'There never was a shout in me,' she gasped. They saw the car lurch over the bridge, and here the big mongrel Twm who had been scuffling along almost between the front wheels felt his duty done and came bounding back to where they stood by the mill wheel. The bitch, jealous lest he distract attention from herself, twitched her ears and showed the white points of her teeth, and knowing the signs and knowing her temper he slunk past, nervousness and conciliation all over his jowl. They laughed together, the man and woman. 'She's a one, that Shan is,' said Mrs Absalom admiringly.

That was three hours ago. Since then the sun had dug his fingers into the mist, combing it clear of the hillsides and the Ffald-y-Brenin oak forest. The shallow waves began to sparkle on the beach, the face of the sea came to glow with pink and rose and salmon, and high up against the blue sky a million globules of pearly light shimmered and danced before drying into pure translucent air. The high headland of Eryl Môr loomed baseless and unsubstantial, then hardened to the familiar brown cliff face protecting the cove from the north, and soon Ynys Las broke into view, a magic island in an old story, changing shape before one's incredulous eyes, from smudge to thin black reef, from reef to black bar, and from bar rearing and brightening till Merrill could see its upper limits burnt in a charcoal line against the intense air. The Island, the sapphire sea with its crystal pointing, these engrossed Merrill. He walked back to the house from the boat, his jacket on his arm, his neck bare. The strike of the sun, the wash of perfumed air from the sea exalted him; he flexed his fingers, marvelling at their suppleness and strength. Before him he saw two magpies beat from the near edge of the wood, the hen flying in a wide high curve towards Eryl Môr, the cockbird dipping and rising in gallant escort, the white horse-shoe on his back and wings a glory in the morning. The hen broke her flight, the bird following her, and they flew twisting and courting till they fell below the skyline. 'Ha!' he cried, a fountain of joy bubbling within him.

There was no one in the living-room, but he could hear Mrs Absalom moving about upstairs. 'Hello!', he shouted gaily.

It was like seeing her stop and listen. 'Hello,' he called again. 'Come down. What are you doing up there?'

'It's what they say.' She appeared on the stairs. 'A woman's work is never done.'

'But it's a holiday today!'

'I don't know that I want a holiday,' she said, with less assurance than usual. She was standing now on the bottom stair.

'You promised, remember?'

'Oh no, I didn't!' He held out his hand but she wouldn't take it. 'Besides, whatever would people think?'

'I didn't know Ynys Las was so crowded.'

'It wasn't the Ynys I was thinking of.'

'I tell you what,' he said, dropping his coat. 'I'll carry you to the boat, and then you can say I made you. Look!' – and thrusting under her arms which tried to repel him he lifted her struggling into the air. 'No,' she cried, 'no, no!' but he held her firm and started towards the door. 'Put me down, oh you must put me down!'

'When you promise!'

'All right then, I promise.' She was shaking with laughter when he set her down. 'Aren't we being awful, Mr Merrill?'

Reluctantly he let her go. 'We'll want food. And something to drink. You'll get it?'

From the boat he saw her tying the mongrel to the workshop door, where he had choice of shade or sun. She set down water, threw three or four square biscuits inside. The bitch, her wallow too distended for her to lie with comfort, was yawning prodigiously and sitting back against the door. Momentarily the Wise Man, his own wife, the evening at Cornel Ofan blurred and buzzed in his head like a swarm of blue-fly, so that he made slow brushing movements of his hands across his eyes to dispel them. No, he cried, No! This was a nut-shell world this morning, its limits the round green hills behind the cwm, the face of the headland, the sea-line broken by the Green Island. Outside these limits nothing should exist till evening. His head grew clear. All was moving to its consummation.

'I can't think,' said Mrs Absalom when she came down to the boat, 'why you don't go to the Island without me, Mr Merrill.'

'You can't?' But this time the dubious word-play jarred on Merrill. For we are not, he thought, like those marvellous magpies riding the sky because love and procreation whirl them to their natural joys; this was at once more sluggish and more febrile; and furtive. 'You'll find out,' he said briefly, and pushed out from the beach. Soon they had caught the breeze, but he was no expert and found himself fully busied with the patched red sail and tiller. The water was a hard, clean, greeny-blue, but behind them they left an unhealing weal which curved as he tried to keep course. Mrs Absalom was unusually silent. She must feel herself committed now, he thought – a trifle grimly for the occasion – but was surprised suddenly to see her smiling behind her hand. God, he told himself, what a fool I am to think she'd do anything except her pleasure. She trailed her fingers overside, so that inches under the surface there were frothy lime-green bubbles exploding upwards. 'It's cold,' she cried. 'You've no idea how it's cold! You won't tip us over, will you?'

'That isn't the idea,' he replied. 'I can't swim. And a death by drowning's too good for me.'

'If only the Seiat could see me now, Mr Merrill!'

'If only the Seiat could see you in an hour's time!'

158

She giggled. He expected her to counter with a question, but instead she began to hum a lively tune that soon struck down to the minor. 'No,' she said; 'it's sad on the water, because you always think how cruel it can be. Don't you think we should be kind one to the other, Mr Merrill?'

He could think of no reply fatuous enough for her. Instead he was watching the Island. 'We ought to make for the south side,' he declared. 'That's where the beach is. I wish I was a bit cleverer with the sail. Still . . .' The boat turned more into the wind. 'We'll make it all right.'

The rocky eastern face rose twenty to eighty feet above the sea. At the lower levels there were concave hollows of moss-blackened grass sinking rather suddenly from the skyline right to the cliff edge. But as they rounded the south-eastern spur they saw how a shelving beach of dark grey gravelly sand gave them their landing-place, while behind it a grassy cleft went upwards and inland. 'There!' he shouted, and in his excitement pulled the tiller the wrong way, almost spilling himself overboard. 'All right,' he cried, 'don't tell me! I know what I am.' And straightening course he ran the boat gently on to the sand. 'Nothing to tie her to, but the tide'll go out for hours yet. And I'll pull her up a bit too.'

He pointed up the cleft to where an outcrop of blackish rock was clamped to its own shadow. 'That's the place for lunch. Or look, there's a little cave that end of the beach. What a lovely Island this is!'

She watched him carry their things ashore. 'Why, what a boy you are, Mr Merrill, and I always thought you so – what shall I say?'

'Yes,' he admitted, 'I am a boy since I stepped ashore here. There's no age, no time, there's nothing except the Island and you and me. That's how I've thought of it; that's how I've wanted it; that's how it is.' He put the basket down where the grass met the beach, threw his jacket alongside it. 'It's like elastic,' he said, treading the tough spongy turf. They began to walk diagonally along the left bank of the cleft, climbing where the angle was easiest. There was a peppering of rabbit pellets and once only the open mouths of a burrow. The sun was very hot on their backs when at last they topped the rise. A furlong or so ahead was a swell of ground where rock broke the surface, and this except for some of the eastern cliffs seemed the highest point on the Island. When they stood there at last a great stretch of coast swam up at them east and north, but Ffald-y-Brenin was as yet hidden; westwards a second rift dropped to toothy rocks and a gravelspit. The sea out west was taut as a skin, with creeping greys and greens in the sapphire blue, and one huge patch of maroon where weed rose near the surface. Turning, they could see their own beach and their boat twenty feet from the water. There seemed to be no bushes or trees on the Island, but a pair of yellowhammers, of all birds, chased from one small rock to another in short quivering flights, never turning their mustardy heads towards the two humans, but observing them all the time.

'When we go down we'll bathe,' said Merrill. Catching Mrs Absalom's eye, he laughed.

'Oh,' she cried, 'so that's what you meant about the Seiat. Well indeed, Mr Merrill, if I'm not ashamed of you!'

'Go on,' he said. 'Think of all that nice water around you.'

'It would be very improper. Besides,' she added after a moment, 'it would be very cold.'

He grimaced at her, holding her hand as they left the mound. 'And you a Baptist!' But at the beach her scruples held firm, so instead of bathing they ate their meal and he smoked a pipe and threw crusts into the air for the screaming white-headed gulls, and they made guesses and bet halfpennies on where the cormorants would reappear which were diving for fish off the lengthening south-eastern spur. They could see the air trembling against the rocks, the gravel was like hot needles against his soles when he walked back from the boat. As he sat down again he had the sensation that Ynys Las was nodding like a gigantic tired head. The illusion strengthened with the heat, nodding, nodding, nodding, the grey cliff eyebrows sagging downwards, everything softened and loaded with sleep. But how could an Island . . .

He opened his eyes. It was Mrs Absalom, carrying her shoes and stockings. 'I wasn't asleep. I was thinking. Thinking what nice toes you have.' He rolled over against her as she sat down, his face pressed against her, his arms across her lap. The glossy grass-daggers fused and dimmed, through his lashes he saw one tiny orange flower on Mrs Absalom's frock bloat bigger than the headland, the weft of the material grow to furrows. Then he felt her fingers in his hair, heard her speak with all the tenderness of her singing; there were Welsh words he knew: *cysgu*, sleep, the gentle diminutives, *f'anwylyd*. For a moment only his blood stirred, his heart hammered, then he was falling towards unconsciousness, nodding into the dark as the Island itself nodded under him.

'Did I sleep?' he asked confusedly. 'What has happened?'

'Yes, you slept.' The short black shadows had wheeled. The cormorants dozed on the weedy rocks. 'Nothing's happened.'

He sat up, his shoulder against hers, and kissed her clumsily. 'No,' she said, 'not here. I couldn't here.' She looked guiltily out to sea as though they were open to the eyes of the world.

With no more spoken they began to climb the cleft as they had done at midday, carrying their shoes and she her stockings. As they hooked fingers at the steeper ascents he could feel the soft resilient pads under her fingers, the smooth callouses of the palm and inside the thumb. They were panting when they reached the top but went straight on to a smooth green hollow under the rock-scarred mound. 'Now,' he said, 'now.' She motioned him to undo the back of her dress, bending her head as he fumbled with fingers suddenly stiff and awkward. 'Hurry, hurry!' she whispered. Then he saw the pure white of her upper arms, soon her dress and slip and vest had fallen around her hips, and from this coloured calyx there flowered her fleshy sides, the full white breasts, the gleaming shoulders, the dizzy column of her throat where he saw the throbbing of a vein. She looked at him with dry, hard, smouldering eyes, her arms had dropped to her sides, their palms towards him in a gesture of desire and surrender both; he saw and kissed those little buds of flesh which grew between the crinkled inside knuckle-joints. And while he thought all his senses bound up in hers, everything in sky and earth and water was like a book opening before him, whose message was the urge to mating and fruition. They sank to the ground, and with a somnambulist's eye he saw behind her head waxy transparent stalks of stonecrop, the pale pink petals not an eighth of an inch long, and in the heart of each blossom a blood-drop. A pin-head spider clawed his way down an invisible line, then up, then down, unperturbed by these colossi who shut him from the sun, exhausting and renewing their loves in a rhythm nature now imposed on them and they not at all on nature. He went on with his spinning, and later Merrill was to see, when he looked from Mrs Absalom's bruised mouth and slumberous eyes, the long glistening outriders from blade to blade, the struts and cunning cross-pieces, then the sticky involutions of the web, and at its centre the spider, bunched and dry and brown. The spider, the stonecrop, themselves – he lay over on his back, wicketing his fingers across his eyes. It prevented self-importance, anyway.

When he sat up – 'Staring's rude, Mr Merrill,' said Mrs Absalom, pulling her clothes across her body.

'And thinking's ruder, Mrs Absalom.'

She put her hand to her breast. 'Ah, how my little heart beats, you'd never believe. And all your fault.' She drew his hand under hers, then smiled mischievously. 'You know what the poem says you hear there, Mr Merrill? It's best in Welsh, but it's in English too.' Her voice changed, grew charged with a stylised emotion, lyrical but restrained.

> Place your hand, if still you doubt me,
> Under my breast, but do not hurt me;
> And you'll hear, if you but listen,
> The sound of the little heart that's broken.

'I don't think it's broken,' he said sombrely. He was always embarrassed by the national trait of play-acting, and doubly embarrassed by this resort to poetry on what appeared to him no proper occasion for it.

'A cigarette?' he asked.

But she shook her head. 'It's not quite the thing, is it?'

He smoked silently, at her order looking away while she dressed. For that again was not quite the thing. And here, he thought, is where the difference begins. The stonecrop and the spider stay the same: no break, no end for them. But he would never return to the Island. He thought of his wife. The futile catchwords riddled his brain, preventing clear thought. It had happened – it was no one's fault – the failure, the humiliation – where there was too much pity desire died. And died, it seemed, for ever.

'I'm ready,' said Mrs Absalom.

He turned. Even her shoe-laces were tied, and she sat facing him with her back curved and her forearms wrapping her dress under her knees. She looked sleek as a cat.

'Not yet,' he pleaded. 'Don't let's go.'

'It'll be time.'

'No,' he said hoarsely. 'There's a lifetime ahead, but it won't ever be like this for us again. There's time, there's heaps of time.'

'It's all the same,' she said enigmatically. And when he reached for her she shook her head as she had done last night at Ffald-y-

Brenin. 'It's foolish,' she said, 'not to know when.' And when he persisted – 'You'll spoil everything!' she said angrily, and moved away from him.

He lay with his face on his arms then, filled as much with regret as revulsion. Yet, he felt sullenly, who was she to lecture him? Suddenly he felt jaded and drawn; his head was shaking with the blood-beat in his temples. He was in no mood for scolding. She'd better not say too much.

But that wasn't her intention. She was saying nothing.

He pretended to doze. Then he began to notice the ticking of his watch, time audible. He stretched his arm, so that the watch was farther from his ear, the dial upwards.

'It's getting late,' he heard Mrs Absalom say anxiously.

'There's plenty of time,' he muttered, glad to break the strained silence. He got up, reached out a hand to pull her to her feet. 'You don't dislike me, do you?'

The corners of her mouth drooped just enough to notice. Her lower lip was swollen, her eyes heavy but placid. 'I'm tired out,' she said.

'What about me?'

'Ah,' she said, 'that's your own fault.'

They were walking towards the top of the cleft. As they came out of the hollow where they had been lying they saw first the sky-line and then the dim mountains of Pembrokeshire enclosing the Bay to the south. There was a dimness on the sea too, its colours faded and streaked with white and grey. They looked down the steep green banks to the cove. The cormorants were gone, the south-eastern spur was shortened by the incoming tide which swilled waveless against the dark gravel beneath them. 'Oh, look!' he shouted, dragging at her arm. One frightened oath escaped him and then he was leaping madly down the slope. The boat was floating midway between the beach and the spur. Even as he ran he saw it spin gently in an invisible current. The next moment he stumbled and fell headlong. When he got to his hands and knees he was too dazed immediately to stand upright, he had bitten deeply into his tongue which was now a hard lump choking the right side of his mouth; a wet and fiery pain flooding his left ankle brought him near fainting. He shut his eyes, and when he opened them again masses of dark green swirled right, then left, before him. But at last he saw the sea and went haltingly forward. 'No,' he said, or tried to say, 'I can't. I can't do it.' He sat down and the puffs of air made his sweat cold as ice.

'The boat?' he asked thickly. Mrs Absalom shook her head frightenedly.

'It was foolish,' she said, 'I said it was foolish.'

'It was the fall. Anyone could have fallen.' He stood up, taking all his weight on one foot. The boat was thirty yards out, spinning very slowly towards the end of the spur. 'Oh well!' He sat down again, gasping: 'A bit awkward!' He began to untie his shoe.

'Awkward! A bit!' She had raised her voice unpleasantly. 'You know what this means?'

'It means we can't get off the Island.'

'You and your Island!'

He found himself thinking very slowly. 'What d'you want me to do? Wade after it? You know I can't swim. To say nothing of this ankle.'

Her mouth wrinkled like the bitch's that morning. 'What about me? What about Dafydd when he comes home tonight?'

'What about him? He'll have a bed to sleep in, which is more than we'll have. And look at this ankle!'

'If you thought more about me and less about yourself . . .' She tightened her fingers till her fists trembled. 'I'm afraid. Oh, I'm afraid, Mr Merrill.'

'There's a towel in the basket,' he said slowly, 'and here's a handkerchief. Go and wring them out in the water and bring them here at once.' He fought back his nausea as she did so. 'Now bind it tight. There's nothing to be afraid of. You changed your mind and came to the Island for a picnic. While we walked around it the boat drifted out. We'll wait till we see the headlights of the car, or we can see the house itself from the cliffs. Then we'll signal, make a bonfire, anything. They'll fetch us off in the morning, as soon as they get another boat, I'll say how sorry I am, and that'll be the end of it.'

'You think he'll believe that?'

'If he's wise,' he said, rather too cleverly.

'If he's a fool, you mean. No, he won't! Not after last night.'

'He saw nothing.' But the same thought was troubling Merrill. But I'll go, he thought meanly, I'll clear out – that will be best for everyone. Great God, he told himself, how we are tumbled out of our dignity and ease. An hour ago I rode the lightning of the flesh, and look at me now. And Mrs Absalom, frightened and ugly.

'She might come back in,' he said; 'the boat, on the tide.'

Mrs Absalom sat silent. She didn't even look at him. Yes, he thought, she's frightened all right. What a fool he'd been, what a gaping fool.

'I'm going for a walk,' she said suddenly, her voice trembling. 'No, I'm going on my own.' He felt guilty when he looked at her, she was at such a disadvantage, and as she climbed the long green bank again he noticed how the spring and tautness had gone from her step. 'We're a sad pair of sinners now,' he said aloud, jeering himself into confidence.

The sea was like wrinkled iron. A thick haze on the horizon was topped with cloud whose rims flashed silver. 'It's all very well her walking off,' he said. 'We've got to sleep somewhere. We've got to eat.' He counted their store and it was more than he had expected. 'Pity we fed those gulls.' With these words he knew how hungry he was.

He sat there for more than an hour till Mrs Absalom returned, resting his ankle, sometimes mumbling his tongue, thinking to no purpose. As she approached he stood up. 'Please don't be upset,' he begged. 'It'll be all right.' He knelt and spread the tarpaulin they had taken from the boat to sit on. 'Sit here, do! It's bound to be all right.'

'For you,' she said shakily.

'For you too.'

'You don't know Dafydd!' He tried some vague comforting sentence. 'No,' she cried, 'that's not right. He's – oh, he's deep. He could be – horrible.'

'You came for a picnic,' he repeated slowly. 'We weren't here more than a couple of hours – just as the tide was turning. I was a fool, I didn't pull the boat in. We'll signal as soon as he's back, and if he can't fetch us off tonight that's hardly your fault, or mine.' He went on talking, rounding out the story they must tell, till she just had to grow interested, add details, approve omissions, even invent dangerously. 'There you are,' he chided. 'Why, you're smiling again!'

'I'm not smiling inside,' she answered truthfully. 'Only anything's better than thinking.'

'Could you eat now?'

She shook her head. 'No – or yes, I could. The way I feel – yes, let's eat now, now.'

And afterwards, he went on, there must be a signal fire, they must decide where to spend the night if they were not brought off. They just had to be sensible. But not in the cave – she shuddered –

there'd be sea rats, huge ones, the sort you saw scamper towards the mill at Ffald-y-Brenin – what if they ran over your face? Laughing now, he patted her hand, her shoulder, welcoming the ascendancy again.

Then he hecked along with her, scrabbling in the sand and hollow rocks for bits of stick, dry grass, anything that would burn brightly. 'Merrill, his crutch!' he shouted across to her, waving a narrow strip of sea-smoothed boarding. He was glad of it: his ankle was more troublesome than he had shown. 'If you can carry these, I'll catch you up,' he told her. There was still the bank to be climbed.

It was a meagre bonfire they at last assembled on the cliff fronting Ffald-y-Brenin. Day was dead, except in the low west. 'I'm glad you've come. I was getting worried. Was there ever a place as quiet as this?'

'He should be at Felindre now. Perhaps he'll go on up to Cornel Ofan to meet you. If he does, then we'll see his lights.'

She stared forward. 'I wish Mrs Merrill was coming back with him.'

He had thought the same. 'Put my coat on,' he told her. 'Don't wait till you get cold first.'

'I wouldn't be surprised,' she said presently, 'if Shan has her pups tonight. That's another thing that comes of larking about.' This astounded him, but she seemed entirely serious and he wondered whether she had just been thinking aloud. 'And where can we sleep? Oh dear, dear!'

'There's a place . . .'

Her face was growing still and mask-like in the bad light. Against her pale and shining skin the eyes were soft black hollows under charcoal eyebrows; the mouth was swollen and sensual. A cold unimplicated observer within him condemned the swift riot of his memory, speculated on the change that darkness brought. Yet, he thought, yet . . . 'Quick!' she said. 'The headlights.'

A wide weak beam of light played against the sky, then dipped and was reduced to two yellow balls as Absalom came down the track to Ffald-y-Brenin. 'Oh quick, quick!' she cried. 'Light it now.' Thin orange fingers of flame crept then ran through the grass and reached the sticks. By the time the lights reached the bridge and pointed straight towards the Island yellow flames were all around the edges of the beacon-fire, while its heart was a hollowed-out redness of stalks and ash. If he stops now and dips his lights, thought Merrill – but no, the car stopped, the headlights turned away from them, he was putting her into the shed for the night.

'Has he seen us?'

'He must have. But what can he do till morning?'

Many things, they both knew, and were in their different ways disheartened. A light came on in the house and shone bleakly against them, to increase their isolation. No long time after a lantern was carried to the workshop. They watched in silence till it returned, the light in the house went out but reappeared briefly upstairs, then Ffald-y-Brenin was lost in the darkness. The rising moon kept it long in shadow, and at last Merrill rose to his feet.

'He's gone to bed,' said Mrs Absalom bitterly.

And left his wife with me, thought Merrill; but what he said aloud was: 'Yes. We'd better go down. There's a place by the rock.' He saw her shaking her head. 'What else can we do?'

'I would give a million pounds if only I was out of this.' She broke into passionate Welsh in which he caught 'Ynys, Ynys, Ynys!' Well, he thought, it's no news if she's cursing the Island.

'I thought here,' he said later, after a painful climb down. 'By the rock.'

When they lay down together she came into his arms for warmth and comforting. 'You don't want to be on your own?' he whispered. She turned half-heartedly and then consumingly to his will, but sometime, somehow, they fell asleep. He awoke cramped and aching. The moon, which had been clean as a cowslip, was now hidden by a spectrum of pink and green and sulphur yellow. She made no movement and her breathing was regular, but he knew she was awake.

'Thinking again?'

'I'm thinking how bad it will be when Dafydd comes to fetch us.'

He withdrew his shoulder, eased his foot and ankle. It seemed better. 'Try thinking how bad it will be if he doesn't.'

She made no answer and when he woke again, an hour or so later, the words were still in his brain. Now, however, he wondered whether they had been as clever as he thought.

IV

He wondered as much many times during the day. While the morning mists shredded and dispersed and the sea glowed like a hedge-rose, and the platinum sun deepened to the gold of midday; while the water crinkled in the afternoon breezes as though dapped with a million finger-tips, and then hardened and blackened for an hour before the western sky splashed it with orange, gold and furnace-red. While shards of hard cloud pierced the sun, jagging his shafts, darkening him down, and at last pressing him into the sea, so that the air browned with approaching night, the cliff-edge blurred, and where the waves capsized on shore was just a wavering suddy line. Every hour and all the changes of the day were for Merrill tainted with the vulgarities of doubt and alarm – and discomfort and the beginning of hunger. Yet he kept a good front, lying and sitting endlessly as he was, feeling his ankle strengthen.

'It takes time,' he said. Or: 'He can't do everything in a minute. He'll be fetching a boat from Abermaid.' Or, jocularly, 'You've got your story ready?'

But her answers were: 'You don't know him. I'm frightened. I'm hungry. Oh, I'm sick hungry!'

He grew tired of consolation, gave her her share of the food that was left, very, very little. She wasn't the only one hungry. He had plenty to worry about, without her whining. He'd be telling her as much.

But he always bit hard on the thought. It was rough on her, this. Rougher than on him. He could clear off – and would. She had Dafydd to live with.

He could read Absalom like a book. 'Like a book,' he repeated, for Mrs Absalom had gone up to look towards Ffald-y-Brenin. But it's no good to you, Absalom; you just can't do it! You can harass me, but you can't frighten me. You can frighten *her*, granted, and much good may it do you. All you can do to me is make me hungry.

Hungry. He flushed his pockets on to the grass. Not a crumb. Then his face filled with glee. He had found a chip of a boiled sweet, fluff-covered and tobaccoed. It was like a symbol of things going well for him, and somewhat furtively he slipped it into his mouth and crunched it, dirt and all. His tongue was sore on the side but back to its right size and he licked lovingly around his gums after the short sweet swallow. He would have a cigarette now. 'Eh,' he said, 'what's this?' For his lighter was sparking without taking flame. 'Dry,' he muttered, suddenly furious. 'Damn you, Absalom!'

He struck the lighter once more and hurriedly lit his cigarette as the flame dwindled.

He could read him like a book. He was going to leave them another night and morning. Great God, he thought, it's absurd: who'd think of a thing like that except some damn stupid peasant, some idiot of a foreigner? It was too childish. Left so much out of account – after all, his wife was on the Island too, and if jealousy came into it, or even property – he screwed up his eyes, thinking that Absalom might yet find it harder to see the thing through than he bargained.

A pity, he thought, Mrs Absalom hadn't more brains, and detachment of course. He would like to explain the subtleties to her.

'Isn't it time,' she asked when she came back to the cove, 'to light a fire again?'

He snapped his lighter, several times, till a yellow blob clung tiredly to the end of the wick.

'It's dry?'

'You can see.'

He hadn't meant to sound so irritable. 'I might have known,' she said hysterically. 'You think of nothing, nothing, nothing.'

'Perhaps I was thinking of you.'

'You'd never think of anything except yourself!'

'Crying won't help.'

'How could you be such a fool?' she cried, her voice breaking with tears. 'And what a fool I've been to listen to you!'

He turned his back on her, staring at the dusky rock-spur. 'You made your own choice. You may as well face up to it. We are here for the night again. It can be better or worse, as we make it.'

'Look at the place we're in. Oh, look at the place!'

'It's not a hotel,' he said. 'It's not solitary confinement either.'

'I wish to God it was!'

'You take me up on all I say. You can't see a joke.'

Her lip lifted. 'Joke!' He was reminded again of the bitch Shan. And if it came to that . . .

'Don't let's quarrel. That only makes it worse. I know it's my fault. I can't say fairer than that, can I?'

'You talk,' she said angrily. 'Like a gipsy tinker you talk the hind leg off a donkey, for what good it can do. And what about your wife?' She felt the contempt of his silence. 'I said: What about your wife?'

'I heard you.'

'Then why didn't you answer me! But she's used to this, she won't mind, her ladyship won't.' She watched his back, like a cat. 'Those washed-out ones never have any spirit.'

'Look here,' he said, 'you'll keep your mouth shut . . .'

'Or what?'

His hands slacked. This wouldn't do at all. He made excuses for her. But one thing was settled; he'd clear off without compunction the minute he was off the Island. Shabby it might be, mean as misery, but he'd go.

'You didn't like that, did you?' she asked unexpectedly. 'Then be more polite to me. I've got feelings too.'

'We are tired,' he said, 'and vexed. Oughtn't we to sleep? Or try to?'

'If I had a bed, and a roof over it. And food to eat.'

'You could smoke a cigarette – if we could get a light.'

'I'm worn out,' she admitted, 'and that's the truth. If I thought tomorrow would be all right I'd sleep like a little child. But when I start worrying . . .'

'Leave the worrying to me. I'm not unused to it.' And: No, he thought, I said the truth; I'm not.

He had cut a pillow of turf for their place behind the rock. 'If only we'd brought a rug,' he wished, picking up his waterproof, Mrs Absalom's thin coat, the clumsy square of tarpaulin. 'Like Robinson Crusoe – and it's Friday too.' But she showed no sign of understanding as they settled themselves and tried to sleep. Despite her silence and depression, still more despite the ugly side of her nature revealed so short a time ago, he could feel a renewal of tolerance, even friendship, between them; she must have felt it too, as though their need for comfort and companionship was too strong for hatred in a narrow place. Further into the night they might grow wide-eyed and restless, but now exhaustion and reaction, the strain and boredom of the day welcomed the dark and the warm and the promise of forgetting. And so, while one moment they said they would never sleep, and the next knew only their weariness, everything was falling away from them, and first Mrs Absalom was sighing and dozing, and then Merrill following her into long if broken slumber. When towards morning she awoke with a frightened cry he soothed her, muttering reassurances, thinking of her as his wife, not Mrs Absalom at all, reality having grown so unreal. 'It's too early,' he grumbled. 'Go back to sleep.'

170

Confusedly, yet with deliberation, he refused to know things for what they were. He remembered her saying she was cold and pressed closer to her back, a gesture fraught with domesticity as a cat on the hob. Happiness and well-being were in his mind as he fell asleep.

'Ah,' he cried, the light filling his eyes. 'What then?'

Mrs Absalom was coming back from where a slow drip of cold water had served her as washbowl and breakfast. She carried a wet handkerchief in her hand, her cheekbones gleamed, her eyes glittered after her chilly toilet. 'If only we had coffee!' he called ruefully, doubling the tarpaulin away from his legs.

'*Ach y fi*, the old coffee! Tea,' she said, 'with sugar, and fried bread and bacon.' She put her hands over her middle, groaned half in earnest. 'It's the sleep. It's done me that much good it has. Only it's silly to talk of food.' She hadn't looked so cheerful since the boat drifted out. Waiting with his hands cupped for water and then rubbing away at his face and neck he thought: She's tumbled to some trick for fooling Absalom. 'Cunning,' he grunted. 'Or they think they are. In his place . . .' But he couldn't be sure he was in Absalom's place, try as he would. The quality of mind was different, and flatteringly different at that.

'Got an idea for a smoke,' he told Mrs Absalom. He snapped his lighter in vain. 'Watch.' He unscrewed the base-plug and with a borrowed hairpin coaxed out the wadding, sniffed at it, smiled, and struck a spark into it. The sudden flare scorched his fingers before he could throw the wadding down, but he said nothing of this as he drew on his cigarette. 'From this,' he said solemnly, 'I can light my pipe, and from my pipe I can light another piece of paper, and so on till the boat comes.'

She had finished sleeking her hair and was making little pinches at her lips to redden them. 'I look so shabby. You think it will come?'

'You look very nice. Of course it'll come.'

'No, I'm a sight. You know I am!'

He began to chaff her, despite his hunger conscious of a cockerel gaiety. 'That's a trick,' he cried, 'pinching your lips, just look at you.'

She pouted at him. 'You are the one to talk. They'd be black and blue if you had your way. When Dafydd comes now . . .'

'Yes?'

'Oh, nothing. Will it be this morning, you think?'

'Or this afternoon.' He held out his hand. 'Come on, my ankle's fine; a last trip round the Island.'

'It sounds like a holiday at the seaside, doesn't it?'

'It is the seaside.'

She giggled. 'Only the holiday's over.'

They climbed the green bank, though it made him wince to do so. 'Only two days,' he said; 'it shows how relative things are.' The word went over her head but she nodded agreement and looked wise. And there, he said inside him, is the hollow and the crushed stonecrop, and if I had the nerve to go on my knees and look I'd find that same spider's web and perhaps a silly fly in it. He looked covertly at her as they went past the rocky central mound, but she was avoiding any glance at him or the hollow. For the holiday's over, he reminded himself. But: 'See,' he said, 'what's left of the bonfire. It looks terribly small, doesn't it? All odds, it was, and ends.'

He looked towards Ffald-y-Brenin, half-expecting to see a boat on the water between them. But there was no other boat at Ffald-y-Brenin, and Absalom would have to go up or down the coast to borrow one. Again he tried to enter Absalom's mind: He'd not ask for help, have others enjoying his tangle. What had to be done he would do himself.

The coast, he noticed with surprise, was both bold and indistinct. Its masses and outline were plain enough, but the details – the yellow stroke of low-water sand north of the estuary, the black mouths of caves under Eryl Môr, a shawl of charlock miles inland – these were rather remembered than seen. The soft pulpiness of heat had dried out of the air, which was now hard and deceptive as glass. Yet it's June, he thought with foreboding – June! as though the name were a key to unlock the sun out of heaven, gaol the winds, manacle the great rain. Temporarily he had the illusion that Ynys Las rode the water as the moon rides cloud, movement and no movement. He closed his eyes and when he opened them again avoided sight of the sea.

'There's so little to do on an Island,' Mrs Absalom was saying.

'When the holiday's over.'

'When the holiday's over,' she repeated brightly. 'Tell me about yourself, Mr Merrill.'

'There's nothing to tell.' Good God, he reflected, a man would feel a fool in broad daylight, in the morning above all, babbling.

'You mean you can't think up good lies in the light?' The words were perfunctory, not sharp. She was sitting with her back to the coast, shiny-eyed, stroking the wrinkles in her dress, beginning to hum the tune she had sung at Ffald-y-Brenin. When she sang the words it was in English, as though for his benefit.

> *A simple country swain am I,*
> *And love should be my pleasure;*
> *The whitening wheat I watch with care –*
> *Another reaps the treasure.*

It was a song of love without possession, the bride lost to another. 'She died for him,' said Mrs Absalom tenderly.

'Who did?'

'Ann Thomas did. The Maid of Cefn Ydfa. It's a beautiful book, Mr Merrill. It makes you cry all the time.' Her voice caressed her words, fluting the vowels like a blackbird's song. 'What a lovely man that Wil Hopcyn must have been. He loved her but they made her marry another. It's very sad, you'd hardly believe, Mr Merrill.'

She knows what she's doing, he told himself. She's listening to every lift and intonation of her voice, her eyes and mouth move as puppets dance. Why the devil can't they be honest: she, Absalom, that old fake at Cornel Ofan?

'Wouldn't the world be lovely if we were all friends?' she asked, out of her self-made sentimentality. He yawned, deliberately. He wasn't going to be drawn into that kind of fatuity either.

'If only the boat . . .'

She took off her mood as easily as a stocking. 'Yes, the boat. We mustn't forget the boat.' Standing up, they saw the sea move sluggishly into the land. 'You can feel the power,' he said; 'you can feel it in the Island, coming up into your body. I've never felt it before.'

'It's a meal we want, not power.'

'No, it's not hunger. It's the Island.'

She looked at him curiously. 'Why, Mr Merrill, you've always sounded a bit daft about the Ynys. But I thought you'd got over it, now.' The stress on the last word was faint as she could make it.

'The Island and you.'

'That's just making fun of me, Mr Merrill.'

'It isn't.' Taking her hand he stepped down from the skyline. The slow throb of the tide was in his veins. 'You,' he repeated clearly. 'They said it was a magic island.' Her eyes smouldered, he saw her face change as her lips parted, her hand melted in his, and he could see and feel her breasts burn towards him through the clothes she wore. It was but to blow on red ashes; they were consumed in a flame of their own making. Yet a little meanness came in: somewhere in his mind was room for the thought that he was revenging himself on Absalom, whom he had begun to hate.

'I don't know, I'm sure,' she said dreamily at last, 'why we did this.' She smiled slowly, her eyelids closing. 'When the holiday was over. Can you see the boat?'

As she fumbled behind her for a button-hole he saw her breasts swell against the stuff, the broad nipples. Over, he thought; that's over. If the boat would come now, this instant, make an end! Goodbye the Island, Eryl Môr, and Ffald-y-Brenin. And good-bye Mrs Absalom. Cynically he wondered: Is the word good-riddance?

But they must wait. He thought he had spoken aloud but she showed no sign of hearing. 'There was a spider's-web here,' he said boldly, as they went back past the hollow. 'Still is, I expect.' He drew his fingers over the grass. 'A little brown spider. They are lucky.'

'It's the red ones are lucky. They bring you money.'

'One the size of a boat would be lucky. With a pair of oars on it.'

'The waves are louder,' she replied, tangentially. But as though afraid of deduction, she added. 'Than yesterday, I mean.'

'We can only wait,' he said slowly. Every minute he felt change, the renewal of weariness and depression. As he stood on the top of the mound and saw the south-west horizon as though through smoked glass, doubt and fear smote him like axes. She must have been watching him closely. 'Oh,' she whimpered, 'Oh, Mr Merrill, what is it? What's the matter?'

He could hear the indrawn breath shudder through his nostrils. Christ! he thought, if only I were on my own. And anywhere but in this cursed place.

'Nothing's the matter,' he said roughly. 'What the hell should be the matter?' It was the first time for him to use an oath to her.

However, he wondered, did I find her all milk and roses so short a while back? An end of hair had fallen loose behind her ear. Like a rat's tail, he thought venomously. 'Your hair's down,' he said, his tone, gesture, expression, betraying him.

Her jaws hardened with anger, but her fingers caught instinctively at the loose strand. Vanity was too strong for her; almost humbly she tucked, patted, pinned.

'That's better,' he praised. 'It's pretty now.' He was ashamed of himself, would wish this to be his peace-offering, but she was walking away, silently down to the cove, leaving him there uncertain whether to follow her or not. At last he saw her standing by the water's edge and wearing her coat. From where he looked down he lost all idea of her identity as Mrs Absalom: for an enlightening moment he saw a lonely, frightened woman, a stranger to him, but her loneliness and fright a challenge to all he could give her of kindness and help. But the quixotries, the extravagances that crowded into his mind brought in their wake disillusion. 'There's nothing I can do,' he complained. 'Swim like a dolphin with her on my back – go down and kiss her shoe. Bah!'

He began to curse Absalom foully for doing him so much wrong. Words of the Wise Man's and words of his own wife's sounded on his ear: Dafydd was no fool, they'd said. Words of Absalom's too. Suddenly they seemed all round him, these childish treacherous ones he'd thought such clowns. 'But if he saw us,' he muttered, thinking of the night they returned from Cornel Ofan, 'would he have let us come?' Hunger and fear – how sick they made him! He sat down, holding his head tightly, for what he could see, clearer than the grass, the rocks, the sea, was Absalom sitting on his round of cherry tree inside the shed at Ffald-y-Brenin, his axe chucking at a porridge spoon, his glance now and again for the Island; and the Wise Man on the top of the hill peering out like some old druid, nodding benignly, and going back down to where the blue and gold enamelled musical-box threw into the murk tinkling handfuls of notes, notes of a ridiculous and maddening sweetness that told of birds in a gilded cage. And his wife – where was she? From what door or window, what corner of the garden was she staring west to Wales? They were all smiling at him, wagging a finger. 'I told you so; I told you so,' they were saying.

He opened his eyes and stood up. This was weakness. Strength was to see things as they were. Absalom wouldn't bring them off till his wife returned on Tuesday. Three more days. His stomach craved at the thought. And from the south-west across thousands of miles of black water, a storm was coming, the slashing gale of early summer.

But even this was not strength. Strength was to recognise that his wife might not return on Tuesday. He tried hard to recall her words but the exact edge of expression avoided him. 'But if you don't come back,' he said aloud, then – 'No, by God, Absalom wouldn't risk that!'

When he went down to the cove it was to find the cormorants gone from the spur and the gulls screaming and planing low. Mrs Absalom at once moved away from where she had been sitting. 'I'm sorry,' he said after her. 'I can't say more than that.' She had been crying, he could tell it from her reddened eyes, but when she still didn't answer and went to sit near the drip of fresh water he hardened to her at once. 'He won't come, you know,' he shouted, thinking with brutal satisfaction: Sulk that off, if you can!

Nor did Absalom come. For long and sullen hours he watched the sea change and move. By the end of the afternoon the waves in the cove were freighted and slow, the ground-swell rolling them up like metal tubes before they exploded into the gravel and seethed treacherously forward. To see them was to see the mid-ocean heaping up its waters under the mallet-blows of a cyclone and then shovelling them away to the western coasts of Europe. And every separate drop of this titanic flood had within it the violence and malice of its origin, though these polished, sucked-under waves on Ynys Las resembled the deep-troughed mid-Atlantic combers as a kitten's paw the talons of the tiger. But soon now some flick or offstrip of the storm would reach the Island, cut it from the mainland for an hour, a day, a week, the water piling high into the Bay, the wind funnelling through the cwms and broken valleys, tearing at the mountain heads, drenching all Wales with sea-spray and rain. High overhead cloud came driving in, the air grew colder, white water bounced and fell from the rocks. 'Now,' he muttered, 'it's coming now.'

One moment there was a breeze, the next the wind coughed and shouted in the cliff hollows, and then as Mrs Absalom ran to the shallow cave and he pressed against the rock where they had slept, the wind and the rain were one, grey, harsh, and slanting. The shower snapped like a whip, while the sea grew blacker and the sea smashed harder at the beach. In a dry minute he hurried over to where Mrs Absalom was sheltering. 'You can't stay here. It'll be filled at high water. But there's sand behind the rock. We could scoop a better place. Please come!' She seemed about to pull her arm away, but instead let him take it and lead her across. 'It could be worse,' he said eagerly. It was such relief to break silence. 'It's got the high ground behind it, and if we could only protect this corner . . .' He couldn't finish because she was choking with terror and grief. 'Oh God,' she wept, 'why, why did I ever come!' He drew her face to his shoulder but she twisted away from him. 'I'm hungry,' she sobbed, 'God help me, I'm hungry!' But what can I do? he kept asking himself, and along his blood beat the words, Three days, three days, three days.

'Sit down,' he said at last. He *must* do something besides think. With the big blade of his knife he began ripping out pieces of sand-hung turf, stacking them to flank their shelter. He carried sand and gravel in his waterproof, sheltering when the rain slashed in, talking to her. 'You see,' he urged, 'it's better than nothing. With the tarpaulin fixed . . .' He could never finish his sentences; he had looked seawards and the wind filled his throat. It made no difference. She was huddled now in silent misery. He felt a new grievance that she hadn't stirred to help him.

Crying doesn't improve a woman, he grumbled; real crying like hers. Features, complexion, the informing spirit, all smirched and smutted and bedraggled. Then he remembered what he had said about her hair and was ashamed.

His arm around her shoulders, pressed back against the rock, they waited for the end of day. 'I don't want to see it,' she muttered once, turning her face from the grey quaking walls of the cleft, shuddering at the wind which roared and ruffled and screeched overhead, the thud and hiss of the breakers. But was darkness any better? You could believe the elements alive, pitiless, gloating. Yet better, because you hoped to sleep, to awake from the dream, to find it ended. At the worst, there was forgetting for a while.

They were awake for hours before it grew light. After a time he began to tell her ramblingly about himself, his home, his wife, his job. There was peace between them again. He was aware of her sex only in so far as it made it easier for him to talk, almost to confess, about these simple and yet momentous matters. 'Oh,' she commented oddly, 'we'd never have done that, Dafydd and I.' He had spoken of his marriage in a registry office. 'I was married from the Hall, in a very old church. It seems more respectful somehow.' He thought she meant respectable. No, he said, there were no children. Yes, his wife had always wanted them – no, he didn't himself. But he'd been willing. It was the way things worked out.

Even as he spoke he knew he would bitterly regret his confidences later. 'Everything went wrong. I can't believe it. That it happened to us.' There had been a miscarriage, a long, long illness – 'Years,' he said. 'We were young. God in heaven, years!'

Then a second illness. 'My fault,' he said bitterly. 'Or no one's fault – what's the difference? Our life broke up on that.' How clearly he was remembering: he could have torn the world in two for her, destroyed it that she might be well and happy. 'She says she's better. The doctors say she's better. But it's too late. You live on pity long enough and everything else goes dead. I'm not making excuses. I've done some shabby things, and this is one of them.' He went on talking, telling her what he had never told anyone. 'She wants us to start again – or she'll leave me, she says.' How bald and unjust that sounded in words – he was overcome by longing to put his wife in the right, himself wholly in the wrong. And at the same time to win himself sympathy not blame.

But he'd been a fool to talk. There were no confidences in return. Abruptly he grew quiet, eaten by unease. The relief he had temporarily felt ebbed from him. For no one particular reason he grew convinced that Mrs Absalom was now stronger and surer of herself than he.

The same great wind was blowing sheets of rain over the Island, the sea still crashed and lathered the beach behind them. So far the tarpaulin had kept them dry and the narrow coffiny patch under them, but the wall of turfs was sodden and must some time collapse. With daylight he came to loathe lying still, yet to shrink from the notion of stirring. There was a knot of hunger in his stomach. He avoided looking at his watch as long as he could, for those early hours were the most unbudging. Yet the hands crawled round to eight and nine and ten and eleven o'clock. 'It's stopping,' he said. The sky had lightened a little, the spray-filled mist was thinner, and they stood up to rub their limbs, work their shoulders free of cramp, walk about again.

For a while he watched the waves flung huge and bristling against the black western edge of the cove, whence they bounded back to make a maelstrom of the centre. Then this whirl of waters yielded to the whale-back flow from the outer Bay, was borne high and tossing to the beach and flung in headlong till the ground trembled up into his legs. As it ground backwards, brown with gravel, the next wave would be bursting off the west face, hanging it with waterfalls, swilling to the centre where in its turn it felt the lift and drive of the tide and came hurtling inshore. It made him giddy to watch, increased his sense of helplessness, so he went despondently back to patch the turf wall and cut narrow drainage channels.

'What on earth have you done to your hat?' he asked, when Mrs Absalom walked back to join him.

She held up a round of wire unsmilingly.

'Well?'

'Rabbits,' she said, and her tongue came out to touch the middle of her lips. 'When we were children . . .' She began to twist the wire.

'But we haven't matches. We can't cook it.'

Her glance was cold humourless contempt, but she said nothing. Three or four hours later, during another break in the rain, she was searching for a stick at high-water-mark. All this was beyond his knowledge, she explained nothing of her purpose, though she borrowed and kept his knife, and he had the impression he was no more than a dog at her heels as she went up the grass bank, seeking a run that had been recently used. When she plugged the stick almost to its head in the ground his eyes widened, she was breathing hard through her nostrils as she tightened the noose and gave it its last touches. Some words in Welsh she spoke to herself, but when he stood staring she said sourly: 'We won't catch anything by standing here. Let's go down out of the way.' He followed her without argument. It was her affair, this.

The rain had stopped now. Twice during the evening they climbed to the snare to find it empty. A third time they had started up the bank when they heard a squeal. 'Quick,' she cried, 'run! Oh God, God!' His heart jumped at every stride, his ankle suddenly folded sickeningly. In the snare he saw a blue-grey scut, a struggling grey-brown body. The stick was coming up out of the ground, he thought, and he grabbed at the creature, pulling up the whole snare. 'I've got it!' he shouted, and groaning with pain turned to where Mrs Absalom clambered behind him. At that moment the rabbit was convulsed in his hand, he lost his grip, it fell to the ground and ran madly towards the top of the Island. 'I had it,' he said stupidly, gaping at the empty noose. 'It was in my hand. I had it.'

Mrs Absalom screamed with rage and disappointment. Then a torrent of filth burst from her lips and she struck him violently in the face. He felt her nails hot as fire from his eye to his chin. She was quite mad. It was all he could do to control her arms. When she stood glaring at him afterwards – 'You mad ugly bitch,' he snarled; 'I'll never forgive you for this.' With trembling fingers he reshaped the snare and thrust the peg into the earth; then after one look of disgust and defiance he hobbled in agony to the top of the Island. The wind threw him off his balance as he tried to see the mainland across a desolation of lunging water, and soon he was forced to the hollow, where he lay flat on the wet grass for shelter while the wind, like air turned fluid, went over him in a guttering roar. He retched with the pain of his ankle and must have fainted for the minutes which had been so slow had somehow rushed on to dusk when he decided he must go downhill. Much of the way he levered himself down with his hands and right leg, half sitting and forced to constant halts. When he came to the rock he could see that Mrs Absalom was lying there under the tarpaulin, so stubbornly he sat against the rock not far from her feet. He felt the wind cut like a knife to his sweaty chest. Like an animal, he went on repeating; like an animal. He touched the long hot scratches on his cheek. Like an animal.

He was awake and aching and chilled in heart and limb. Dazedly he went to the tarpaulin and crept under. He must have warmth. He lay close against her, shivering, put his arm around her. 'Leave me alone,' she said evilly. 'It's all you think of.'

'No,' he said, 'I'm cold. I think I'm ill.'

But she sat up violently, thrusting at him. She had been awake all the time. Everything that was cruel in her rushed to her tongue. 'If you've spoiled one woman, you can't spoil me. Get out,' she said shrilly. 'Don't you touch me!' He dragged himself round the corner of the rock; he had no will against hers.

Sunday night, he thought wretchedly. Christ, how I hate her, and how I hate the Island. The rain was beginning again, rattling against his clothes, splashing into this eyes. He licked his lips as an animal licks its hurts. Through the dark he could hear the boom and swashing of the sea and the wind scuffling off it. The ground began to heave and swing as he stretched himself out and huddled into the rock. 'I shall be lucky,' he said suddenly, 'if I come out of this alive.' He longed for sleep, but when at last it came he was to fall through the night into frightening dreams and panic awakenings. The Island, the snare, his wife, Mrs Absalom's words and lunatic face, his pain and hunger interwove, changed roles, clogged him awake and asleep with nightmares. When, he cried, oh when will the light come again?

V

Five days later a motor-boat approached the Island from the south. In it were two men and a lad of fourteen, who saw to the engine. The men were the ex-collier Thomas who had recited 'The Explosion', and the Wise Man of Cornel Ofan; the boy was Thomas's son. The morning was blue and white, the sea reflected the sky in greys and whites and creamy bluey-green; in front of them the Island was glazed and unreal, as though crumpled out of cloth. The boat rode the swell buoyant as a bird and threw white thrashes of spray high into the air. All three of them wore oilskins.

'We shall soon know now,' said the Wise Man.

His companion nodded. He was enjoying himself, he was greatly interested, but he had seen too much in the pits, in warfare, in slump, to get over-excited by what had happened to these love-me-quicks. When the Wise Man came for the boat he responded as he had responded in the old days to the call for a rescue party: you didn't ask Who, Where, Why – you caught up your cap and went. He touched the food packet with his mutilated left hand, felt for the hot flasks with his right. 'His missus,' he said, 'she seemed very nice, that one did.' He winked at his son, turned his wrist so that the coal-pocked thumb-ball rolled uppermost. 'The blueness of a wound cleanseth away evil,' he quoted – a family joke evidently, for the boy grinned before ducking his head to the engine.

The Wise Man nodded approval of them both. He liked an improving sentence even if it wasn't much to the occasion. 'A very nice lady,' he agreed. 'A man would like to do her a good turn. Now that other one . . .'

'But hunger is a good cure,' said the ex-collier, with the conviction of one who has tried it.

'It is sometimes a lesson,' said the Wise Man sceptically.

'The buckle-end of a belt is also a lesson,' said Thomas. He had dropped his voice confidentially. There were things children shouldn't hear. 'That Merrill now – a man wouldn't mind giving a clever buggarr like that a belting.'

'He is not so bad neither.' The Wise Man nodded into his oilskin collar. 'We shan't need to leather him off the Green Island, I venture.' He laughed, without Thomas quite knowing at what.

They were drawing close to the south-eastern spur. The tide had run down to low water and the cormorants were fishing from the rocks or slanting their long brown throats ecstatically skywards. A few minutes more and they were entering the cove, sliding in to the dark-grey gravelly beach. All they could see was the spur to their right running like a jaw-bone into the water, the harsh wall of rock to their left, and the dark grassy sides of the cleft running up to the top of the Island.

'Oi-oi-oi!' shouted the ex-collier. 'Who's about here?' The Wise Man followed him stiffly on to the sand. Almost at once Mrs Absalom came into sight, scrambling down the bank. She carried her crumpled hat in her hand, and ran to them sobbing and trying to talk all in a breath. 'Give her a drink,' ordered the Wise Man. The boy in the boat looked on marvelling as she gulped and sucked. She rubbed her chin where dribblings had run, then licked the fingers and back of her hand. 'Now give her food. Where is this Merril with you?' he asked. She pointed to the black outcrop. 'He's ill. He's very bad.' He saw how her eyes changed. 'We caught a rabbit. He couldn't eat it. He let one go. I ate it though. Take me off the Island! Oh, for Jesus' sake take me off the Island!' She screamed and beat with her fists at the Wise Man's chest, but he set her aside and went over to the rock.

Merrill was lying there under the tarpaulin. His face, when they drew the tarpaulin down, was greatly altered since the Wise Man last talked with him. But he was conscious and when they had poured hot tea into his mouth he opened his eyes on them.

'I knew you'd come,' he whispered. His eyes filled with tears of weakness and self-pity. 'She had food,' he whispered, 'chocolate and bread, but she wouldn't give me any. There was tea and milk, and she had meat and butter, but she wouldn't give me any.'

'Then we will,' promised the Wise Man. 'Only tell us later, not now. Now you must drink this.'

'It's lies!' cried Mrs Absalom. 'There was nothing, thanks to him. Only the rabbit. He couldn't even twist its neck, the soft fool he is.'

The Wise Man nodded. Of course it was lies. 'Eat more – a little more,' he told her. 'We must get to the boat.' There was neither pity nor condemnation in anything he said or did. Nor even surprise. Things, you could gather, had gone much as he expected.

Thomas's one eye peered at Mrs Absalom, swung up to the skyline, back to the rocks.. He made his deduction. 'It would get a man down on here, after a time or two.' He appeared to deal with what might be, rather than with what was.

'And where's the boat you had?' asked the Wise Man. He listened to angry explanations from Mrs Absalom. 'There now!' Watching him, Merrill saw only a humorous appreciation in his face. 'That was a poor trick for a college-trained man, Mr Merrill?' Thomas gave one brief hard bark of a laugh. Let them, thought Merrill, let them. Wasn't he eating their food? Cunning satisfaction took the place of a beginning rage.

But anger was to come. As the boy and Thomas took him to the boat they discovered how bloated his ankle was. 'And what's this on you now?' asked the Wise Man. Mrs Absalom told him, contemptuously this time. 'Well to be sure!' His words and gesture carried with them the tolerant but wondering comment: And what next shall we find this silly man has been up to? But it was a weak anger Merrill felt, tempting him to tears.

They brought off the tarpaulin and spread it for Merrill to lie on, put his coat over his shoulders and Thomas's oilskin over his legs and feet; the boy started up the engine. The smell of hot oil came to Merrill's nostrils as the loveliest smell he had ever known, the sourness of the boards was precious to him. 'And how many rabbits did you catch?' he heard the Wise Man asking. As though she'd tell, as though she'd ever confess to what she'd eaten on the sly, not sharing with him, throwing the pelts over the cliff. 'Very clever too,' said the Wise Man. 'A good thing that one wasn't in charge, I fancy.'

Thereafter they were talking in Welsh, and he noticed the change that was coming over all their voices. Contact was being re-established between them; Mrs Absalom's voice moved on levels of excitement, grief, despair; whatever her story, it lost nothing in the telling; the Wise Man's questions were free from that smug condescension he had shown on the Island; the comments of the ex-collier, which in English had been so indifferent, so unrelated to his own awareness of starvation and strain, grew eager, appreciative, astonished. Thomas's was the only face Merrill could see, the eye sunken and glittering, the mouth so impatient to speak that sometimes throughout a whole diapason of the Wise Man's his lips would be a-bubble. He too had been beleaguered in his time, let no one forget it. Several times they mentioned 'Mr Merrill' – he knew it, he was a million miles from them, right outside their Welsh world. There was something of Dafydd too. But whereas they spoke his own name often with a pause before it, as though they were jerking a hand or head at him, and always with some change of tone, Dafydd's flowed smoothly into the current of their talk. To them Dafydd was calculable. Even if he left two people on an island to starve, and whatever his plans for one of them now – they had the feel of him in their fingers. They were of a kind. But he, Merrill – only his resentment kept him from weeping. A man who might have died, *would* have died, wasn't he entitled to pity, a word of kindness, something better than jeers?

The firm outline of his thoughts wavered. Why trouble anyway? To be from the Island was enough.

He found himself thinking of his wife, confusedly and with distractions. For he thought also of food and comfort, and he felt safety, as an animal feels it which breaks from the trap and turns to its lair and scents the well-loved pungencies. And he was puzzled why he should be so weak and Mrs Absalom so strong. They don't know her cunning, he thought, they don't know how she starved me all the time. His mouth watered, and he was toiling towards food from one corner of the Island to another, hopeless as a dog on a treadmill.

He groaned and saw the Wise Man's face, huge and benevolent, hanging over him. Hating his weakness before these cunning strangers he tried to struggle up, but the old man's hand steadied his shoulder to the tarpaulin. 'You will feel better when you see your wife,' he soothed. He patted him as he would an animal he was tending, and Merrill felt suddenly eased as those animals did. Unexpectedly, he smiled. 'And what would be wisdom for me?' he whispered. But the Wise Man shook his head craftily, then bent to his ear: 'To preach from the text: And Adam was not deceived, but the woman being deceived was in the transgression.' His shoulders shook as at some famous joke.

He's a cruel old devil with it all, thought Merrill; and wondered what verse he had found for Mrs Absalom's case. It could hardly be complimentary to him, Merrill. What a humbug he was, with his scripture and quackery and posing!

The boy had cut the engine. The boat ground softly into the Ffald-y-Brenin shingle. They were taking him up, lifting him to land. Dafydd Absalom had come to look at him. 'Duw, duw, Mr Merrill,' he was saying blandly, 'and me thinking you were in London where the beds are soft.' The lift of his eyebrows was at once quizzical and cruel. He watched Merrill's face closely, nodding with satisfaction, once or twice stroking his chin. 'Fancy me being so foolish!' He turned to speak to the Wise Man at his side. 'I might have guessed, him being so fond of the Island out there. And there's nice to see the wife again.'

Merrill closed his eyes. He could hear Mrs Absalom's voice in low, passionate explanation, and a dog whistling and whining its pleasure. 'That's a bad bag she's got there,' came the full bass of the Wise Man. 'You let the milk come down, Dafydd. That was dull of you.' The bitch squealed but grew silent as the Wise Man examined her. 'See,' he said, 'see? I'll bring you some ointment for it, in a brown box – very good it is – you rub it in this way . . .' Mrs Absalom had stopped talking; he knew they would all be standing round the man and beast. For him, Merrill, they had no place, the foreigner, the outsider.

Before he opened his eyes again he knew his wife was with him. 'I knew you'd come,' he whispered. 'I know it's you.'

'Don't talk.' She fondled his hand, terrified by his thinness. 'We are going up to Cornel Ofan.' He shook his head. 'I've been there for days. I was frightened when I found only Dafydd here.' Again he shook his head. 'They have been good to me. He really is a Wise Man.'

'And I am a fool.'

She put her hand to his face and felt the hot tears there. At that moment she believed it possible to gather up the shards of their two lives and make them one. At worst, it could be tried.

'But why don't they move you?' she asked anxiously. When she looked round it was to find them all ignoring her.

'Mr Jones,' she called; 'Mr Jones.'

The Wise Man looked up. 'Yes, my dear?'

'We must move my husband – at once.'

He waved his hand in a casual, almost reproving way. 'In a minute,' he said, and went on with his explanations in Welsh.

'That's how they've all been treating me,' whispered Merrill. 'That's why I won't go to Cornel Ofan to be laughed at.'

'We'll see,' she told him. 'Mr Jones!'

'In a minute, a minute!' he answered testily. 'I am very busy, as you see.' She reddened at his rudeness; through Merrill's weakness there flared both indignation for his own sake and anger for hers. 'She is a nice bitch,' the Wise Man was adding, as though this were full explanation. 'She deserves care.'

'And doesn't my husband deserve care?' she retorted furiously.

'In God's good time.'

'Are you mad?' she asked. 'Are you mad, all of you?'

He stood up, shrugging his shoulders, inviting sympathy. The bitch lay at his feet, wagging her tail, the others formed a row behind him. The barrier, less of hostility than incomprehension, was complete between them. In the Wise Man's case she was lost. The ex-collier, battered and peering; the gaping boy; Mrs Absalom, white and ill-looking but smirking that her welcome had been no worse than it was; Absalom, his face never more branded than now with the inexplicable contradictions of his nature – from these she was prepared for indifference, even callousness, but the Wise Man! All her hopes had been on him; but now she felt her husband and her forced together, to answer a threat on their own.

Of them all, she appealed to Absalom. 'I'll give you' – she fumbled in her bag – 'I'll give you anything I have to drive us to Abermaid.'

He hesitated, his cheek-bones suddenly glowing. 'Go on, Dafydd,' counselled the old man; 'you couldn't do a better thing for yourself. And he could never walk it.'

He looked from one to anther of them and then amid their silence went to the shed and brought out the car; he backed her round to where Merrill was lying, the tyres scuffling in the sand. 'Take him to the old doctor's in Teilo Street,' said the Wise Man. 'He is not as good as the *dyn hysbys*, but he is no fool neither.' Seated beside her husband Mrs Merrill gave him a glance of bitter reproach, but he ignored it and held out his hand. 'No?' he said, as the Merrills stared at him without taking it.

'Hold the dog!' called Dafydd. 'One fool's enough at a time.' The gears ground, slipped, then caught. After a jerk or two the car moved slowly off, and Mrs Absalom walked into the house.

The Wise Man took off his oilskin and threw it into the boat. 'I am sorry Mrs Merrill has so bad a notion of me. It is for the best, but a poor thing to think of all the same.'

'You are a deep and depthy man,' said the ex-collier. 'He'll be all right?'

'Why not then?'

'If I was her,' said the ex-collier emphatically, 'he wouldn't be worth a po-tatto to me.'

The Wise Man chuckled. 'You are a great one for morals as well as the reciting, I can see.'

The boat backed out and turned in a swirl of green and white. The old man stood there for a while, watching it chug and spit its way south. There was a last wave of hands. Mrs Absalom was still indoors. As he passed the workshop door the bitch grovelled her pleasure, the mongrel Twm drummed his paws, thrusting up his ugly bucket-head. 'Did a little girl's bag hurt then?' the Wise Man crooned, and she followed him past the bridge to the beginning of the trees. When he turned he could see the long black roof covering the house and workshop, the black wheel, the untidy pebbly shingle and its broad glittering channels. From the beach the sea spread gay and apple-green, but out past the headland it was shaded to a dark foamy blue, and the sky was blue above it. Breaking the arc was the glossy seal-like bulk of the Green Island.

'What of it?' he asked suddenly, and louder than he had intended.

The bitch Shan, thinking she was spoken to, pressed against his leg, and he looked down. 'Home you go, little Shan,' he told her, and docilely she went. His lips pouted, made a wise little round red hole as he studied the awkwardness of her movements. For the Wise Man was a healer: he felt his power to cure her drip like fat from his fingers.

As he took the track between the Ffald-y-Brenin oak trees he was thinking equally of the Merrills and Absaloms and of Shan. He saw no reason why she should suffer for any of them. Then he sighed. His wife, he knew (that unsurprised, far-sighted lady with the formal manners and the work-worn hands) would want a full story, and he was the man to tell it. But first things must come first.

His brows sagged under their load of learning. Should he put a little more or a little less lard in the bitch's ointment?

When next he turned he neither saw nor wished to see the Island.

The Still Waters

~

'LET us now praise famous men, and our fathers that begat us.' It is a serious, almost a divine, call; but here in Llanvihangel we prefer a revised version: 'And the womenfolk that bare us.' We judge it more prudent, for one thing – we better know what we are about – and for another, here in Llanvihangel we are of the matriarchy. Our men are nothing, or at best but male spiders who exist to breed and be devoured. Nor shall we ever mend: in every generation the spear yields to the distaff. Today is as bad as yesterday, and tomorrow will be worse.

And first of today. Whoever approaches Llanvihangel from the Henllys side will have seen that hump of black barns under the shoulder of the Foel. A remarkable old woman lived there for close on seventy years, her name Lisa Owen. She had two husbands in her time, but the first gave her no children, and the second only a son. She frightened me terribly when a boy. I can see her now, a gaunt woman, with a green-and-black checked bodice, rough black shirt, and always a long black apron. Her hair was white and very thin, so that you could see the grey skin of her head through it, her nails were broken and her hands like hooks; she carried out of doors a tapering ash stick, and all my memory is of her cutting at the dog with it, or scattering the fowls, or whacking the rumps of the cows, or threatening her son Dafydd. Once only I felt it. I had been sent to Frongog with fourpence for eggs. I knocked at the door, but there was no answer, and I walked across the yard to the barn. Suddenly I could hear someone getting a hiding – not a good healthy hiding like the kind my mother gave me, with plenty of roaring and dodging, but a purposeful and unescapable hiding, with the slashes of a stick and sobbing and gasps. It went to my legs, the fright of it. I couldn't move. I saw a farm dog go half on his belly round the pigsty – he was well out of it, for the time being. Then Lisa Owen came out of the barn, with her stick in her hand. 'It's the devil's work,' she cried in English. 'O Cythraul Diawl!' Then she saw me. 'Well?' she asked.

I was dumb as a door-knob. 'Well?' she asked again, and her voice cracked like a branch. 'Well?' But my terror was a bait to her, and she struck sharply at my legs! 'Devil take the boy! Are they all bad?' A cruel stroke dulled my left thigh, and then without a sound I was running, running, running, from the gaunt woman and her black farm and the boy who'd been thrashed in the shed.

With such a mother, the boy Dafydd must grow up crooked or daft. And daft he was. The kindlier use of the term. 'A bit twp' was the Llanvihangel phrase. 'He's all right, Dafydd Owen – just a bit twp.' You could tell this by the people he touched his hat to: the minister at Beulah (holiness), the auctioneer (authority), and myself. He touched his hat as a cowed dog grovels, with a sly placatory roll of the eye. His *'Owbe's* were offered with a high-pitched nervous affability.

It was a good-bad day for him when the Angel at length prised Lisa Owen's hands off her holdings under the Foel. Good, because he was free of one tyrant; bad, because he was freed for another.

I saw his wife in Newport yesterday. With her children, of course. Three children – none of them Dafydd's. But by her former husband. Oh, *most* respectable. Those of us born between Rhymney and Wye will hardly need a description of Mari Owen; there are so many in her image. A woman within a year or two of forty, dark but not black, a slight wave to her hair, which is drawn back from her ears into a tight coil on the nape of her neck. Her eyes are dark brown, the lashes long, the glance slanting smoothly from your own. Her skin is white and healthy, the lower lip full and sensual, the upper a shade too thin for ease of mind. Not a tall woman, her body strong from work but with an agreeable roundness. How often have I studied such women in my native Gwent – the fool spider meditating his ruin! That smile which says 'Rush on disaster for disaster is sweet' – how well I know it. And how I feel its power. That voice which rides on words like a wave of the summer sea – it will call to my bones when we of today are with the bones of yesterday.

I ask: What chance had Dafydd Owen, a bit twp he was, when such a woman wove a web for him? A widow too. Three kids to call him dad. What chance for me, perhaps, without my schooling? Let us now praise famous men, and our daddas that sent us to college.

The names of Sarah and Maldwyn Price will fall flat on ears beyond Monmouthshire. Even there they fall flat on most. Let us, to the honour of Llanvihangel and the glory of its womenfolk, conjure them from the silence of two centuries. So limited a fame is Maldwyn's for hanging that he may well ask himself whether it was worth it. What Sarah his sister asks herself now it is hardly for me to inquire.

You will seek in vain for Maldwyn in *The Annals of Roguery* or *The Tyburn Chronicle*. He is not even to be found in so unfastidious a repository as *The Complete Newgate Calendar*. For he was a novice, obscure – and Welsh. But the Machen Collection preserves an abstract of his trial in an italic-sprinkled folio, between the sentence of transportation for shoplifting on Elen Jones and that of branding and transportation on Edmund Jackson, Esq. This seems to be the only time Maldwyn rubbed shoulders with a gentleman (or do I strain the significance of that *Esq.?*).

I could wish to quote. The day is the seventeenth of December, the year 1759, the place Monmouth town.

Mr Justice Fenton: The matter needs no dragging out. Put in the deposition of George Price.

This George Price, I interrupt to say, was Sarah Price's husband and brother-in-law of Maldwyn Price. The similarity of name was therefore, in a sense, fortuitous.

Clerk: If it pleases your lordship, the deposition was not properly witnessed.
Mr Justice Fenton: That point is not yet established. Put in the deposition.
Clerk: The deposition of George Price, farrier, of Llanvihangel in the County of Monmouthshire: Being now in prospect of death and desirous of a clear conscience, I throw myself on the justice of my Country and the mercy of Almighty God, etc., etc. Till fourteen months ago I was a farrier at Llanvihangel, but in the month of September I so burned my hand and arm that I have never since had their use and could not follow my trade. On that account my wife and three children have been subject to great poverty, and sometime to that extent we were the twenty-four hours with nothing to eat. My brother-in-law Maldwyn Price helped us as he could, but he is a simple-minded man and subject to fits, and so is but rarely in employment. It was in the month of June this year I opened to him a project that we might waylay a traveller on the South Wales road and so find food for my family. He was much upset by this, and talked

strongly against it, but my wife (his sister) urged it as strongly, and brought in the children that their want might plead with him, and at last he consented. He has always been a good uncle to my children. It was on Tuesday the fourteenth of August that we went towards dusk to a point on the South Wales road where three oak trees grow from one root. Here we waited, till a man on horseback came towards us, and him we robbed of three shillings and some pence. But I have said that my brother-in-law is simple-minded and subject to fits, and to our great misfortune he fell straightway on the road and did not recover himself for the best part of an hour. I was now frightened, fearing he would be searched out and known, and therefore, after we had delivered the money to my wife Sarah, I judged it best that we leave Llanvihangel for a while. We thereupon went north to the Beacons and had work of a kind on farms and gentlemen's houses. But one night, at Tre'rddol, we heard men at the door asking after us, and with that fled into the hills. There was a chase, and we were parted, and I have not seen my brother-in-law since. But I hear he is in custody, and now make this deposition that I did both originate and carry out this robbery with which he is jointly charged, and that he was at all times against it. He is a good man, but simple-minded.

Mr Justice Fenton: Pray conclude the deposition.

The Clerk now brought evidence that George Price had died of an injury to his back when he fell into a ravine during his flight. Mr Justice Fenton expressed himself pithily on a good riddance, and the case was taken further. It is all very matter-of-fact in that eighteenth century judicial English, and we must imagine for ourselves the plight of Maldwyn Price, alone, desperate, and hunted through the Beacons. Like other simple creatures he had the homing instinct. Where else should he turn save to his sister? Probably he went by mountain tracks along the bleak highlands towards Nant-y-Bwlch, turning in alarm from the coal workings below Tredegar, and so south and east to the known river and the gentler hills that look to the Channel. He was seen north of Llanvihangel, 'very wild and exhausted', by a tinker who, however, kept his mouth shut till his information was of no value. There was a reward of five pounds on his head by this time, but our tinker was maybe outside the law himself and unable to draw blood money. And now let Sarah Price take up the tale.

Sarah Price: It was after dusk of Tuesday, the seventeenth September. I was with my children in the house when someone knocked at the door. I called out: *Who is there?* and my brother answered. I was unwilling to let him in, but was afraid for my children and so gave him shelter.

Mr Justice Fenton: How long was he with you thereafter?

Sarah Price: For five days, until he was taken by the officers.

Mr Justice Fenton: You deny on oath that you were a party to this robbery?

Sarah Price: I do. My actions have proved it.

A brisk answer. To know what these actions were, let us turn to the evidence of Humphrey Jenkins, who made the arrest.

Humphrey Jenkins: Acting on information laid I went on the morning of Monday, the twenty-third September, to the house of George and Sarah Price. The door was opened by Sarah Price. We found Maldwyn Price between a piece of boarding and the water-butt. He cried a good deal when we led him off, and asked in God's name that he be permitted to speak with his sister and kiss her children, but this I had no power to allow. He was straightway committed to gaol, where he continued to cry after his sister for that day and the night that followed. Since hearing that his sister laid information against him, he has been very low.

How foolish of Maldwyn Price to be so very low. But there, we have heard he was simple-minded, a bit twp – like Dafydd Owen. And subject to fits. It was Mr Justice Fenton alone of surgeons who now took his cure in hand, a quick and bitter cure. If it was so bitter after all. For, to look on the bright side: this is no world for the simple-minded, and was there any other way he could have found five pounds towards the succour of his nephew and nieces? At three shillings and some pence a time it would have taken him thirty highway robberies to collect such a sum, and he simply hadn't the talent for it. Perhaps this weighed with Sarah his sister. Besides, we have a duty to the law.

But let us return to Mari Owen in Newport, with her children. Let us return to her with a sense of history. For how natural it is to think of Sarah and Mari together, of Maldwyn Price and Dafydd Owen. What chance, we have asked, for Dafydd when Mari came a-courting? He had been ruled so long he was glad to be ruled again – and this one was warm and kind, honey and milk were under her tongue, and her head upon her was like Carmel. They were married very quietly, as befitted a widow, and for a month the sun stood still in heaven. Then one bright morning, before the dust could dim Dafydd's wedding bowler, Mari marched her husband to the recruiting station at Newport Drill Hall. She did the talking, while Dafydd nodded and grinned and said 'All right too!' in his high-pitched affable way, and before they turned for home he was a '39 enlistment in the Welsh Rifles. We have a duty to our country, and Dafydd, though he hadn't fussed much before, was now in line to do his. He was killed in the covering action at Arras in '40 – no medals, no mentions, just another Daio gone to Catraeth with the dawn – and Frongog is now Mari's, and will be her children's in their turn. A good provider, this Mari Owen – like Sarah Price before her. Nor should we forget Dafydd's pension: Mari didn't – she was in Newport about that yesterday.

There are times, let me admit it, when I fear I am hard on these women of ours. Lisa Owen, for instance – it's a fine old proverb (it may even be scripture): Spare the rod and spoil the child. And Sarah Price – we can't hide that her brother *was* a highwayman. In old wives' wisdom: The quiet ones are always the worst. As for Mari – I have said that she made Dafydd happy for a month. We might perhaps count this as two, for to end as we began, with Ecclesiasticus: 'Blessed is the man that hath a virtuous wife, for the number of his days shall be double.'

Bad Blood

~

THE man walking in front stopped and pointed. He was about thirty, of middle height, with a hard clean-shaven face. He carried a shot-gun. Behind him was a farm boy in corduroys who picked up his feet and set them down even on grassland as though he was crossing deep furrows. They had walked the whole cliff pasture from Glan-y-Gors, looking for a sheep, along a mile of hillside spattered with fire-blackened gorse and winter bramble. Along the cliff edge the gorse grew thick and unscorched, wrapping itself round a rotten fence. He was pointing now at dirty white pulls of sheep's wool, strung along the spikes. There was a screaming of gulls below them.

He tapped his gun. 'I'll shoot her,' he said.

The boy nodded, cocking his ear seawards. 'Why not?' he asked eagerly.

The man from Glan-y-Gors set his gun against a post and began to press his way towards the cliff edge. The boy watched him silently. The gorse was rasping off his breeches, the older, drier fronds springing free with a hiss. Near the edge he went down on his hands and knees and eased himself forward between roots that smelt bitter and oily, while the dust of dead blooms pricked inside his nostrils and made him want to sneeze. Suddenly, his head was out in the hard grey air, hung over nothing, hardly belonging to his anchored body. The rock face, as he looked down, was black and crumbled, its base piled with debris left uncovered by the slack tide, and exactly below him was a tearing mass of gulls, its outer edges flurried as a snowstorm. He broke off a piece of shale-filled turf and flung it down, at the same time yelling with all his voice, and at once the mass burst apart, whirling up the rock like a smashed wave. He grunted, instinctively but needlessly protecting his face; then he wriggled back, got to his feet and dragged his legs through the gorse to the fence.

194

'It's her,' he said to the boy's eyebrows, 'what's left.' He bit gorse needles out of his hands, sucked at the blood spots, and then picked up his gun. 'That's it then.'

The boy's dull face was kindled with pleasure. 'You'll shoot her?' he asked excitedly.

'I told him,' said the man. 'Christ knows I told him, told till I'm sick. Told him twice, three times, must have.'

'Told him and told him,' agreed the boy. He raised an imaginary gun, levelled with his eye, pulled the trigger. 'Ba-bang!'

They began to walk straight up the pasture towards the top of the slope. There were a dozen ewes in lamb cropping among the bushes to their right, but to the man's eye, and the boy's, they looked uneasy, ready to run. They bore blue shoulder marks. 'It's the same thing,' said the man from Glan-y-Gors. 'She been running them too.' He licked the back of his hand, and then gently stroked the barrels of his gun. He looked to heel, then jerked his head. Except for Sunday chapel, it was the first time in years for him to be out without a dog.

From the top of the rise they could see the croft they were making for a quarter of a mile away, a black stone house, a tin-roofed barn, and a tarred pigsty. The man from Glan-y-Gors seemed to suck on alum as he watched the starveling buildings, the draggled hedgerows and the bracken-tainted ground. 'Farmer!' he said angrily. 'Preacher kicked out of his job more likely. Look at it. Christ's sake, just look at it!' His iron-shod heel thudded into a thistle root. They crossed another field and turned into the rough earth lane that led to the croft.

They were half-way along it when a black-and-white bitch ran through the open hedge twenty yards ahead of them. The men stopped, the bitch too; they looked at each other. Her dugs were down and swollen, her quarters hollow, the fur knotted and streaked with dirt. But the man from Glan-y-Gors had eyes only for her face. He walked nearer, opened the breech of his gun, felt for his cartridges, and the bitch stood still. Then she sat down, her haunches barely touching the ground. She began to shiver, her eyes turning inwards, and spittle showing around her mouth. She panted. She knew what she had done: she knew what would be done to her. Her expression was a frightful blend of guilt, despair, and resignation to human will. Then he fired. She jolted as if kicked with a boot, and as silence settled again her head sank slowly forward; then it dropped, and she fell over dead. The man from Glan-y-Gors felt hard as iron towards her, and yet a little sick with the memory of her face back of his eyes. The farm boy was grinning, and he went over to the bitch and pulled her head up.

The man from Glan-y-Gors snapped the breech open, blew wisps of smoke down the barrels. He cracked the breech to again, and walked on. As they reached the yard gate a fat man in black clothes was coming out to meet them, and they watched him with curiosity, as though they had never set eyes on him before. His face was soft and affable under oily flat hair, his shoulders sloped dejectedly, and his chest melted into a great swampy belly. His thighs were tight as bladders in his shiny trousers, and as he walked his buttocks shook and squirmed. 'I just shot your bitch,' said the man from Glan-y-Gors. 'I told you till I'm sick.' For a moment the fat man congealed in stillness, as though the air had solidified round all his limbs, then his mouth worked and he flapped his hands foolishly. 'She put one of my ewes over the cliff. With lamb too. I ought to put the police on to you.' He looked around him, and could see the thatch twitched and stinking over the house door, the blackened ends of straw hanging from the half-covered rick, the gate dragging on its hinge. A tidy man himself, nodding towards the thatch: 'You better – ' he began; then he bit short. 'What's the use! Where's her pups?' He followed the fat man's frightened eyes to the barn, and without asking leave walked over. 'Bad blood,' he said roughly, 'and the last of that damned killer from the Cross.' He caught up a bucket from outside the door and lifted the puppies into it. 'I'll do that,' said the boy, grinning. There were four of them, about a week old, crawling blindly, and their cries were like sword-points when they felt the water. 'Got a sack?'

But the fat man was crouching against the barn, his thumbs to his ears, his fingers over his eyes. The man from Glan-y-Gors opened his mouth, but shut it silently and shrugged his shoulders. He scraped his hands like a razor round his jaw-bone. He had taken out his watch and without a word spoken saw the second-hand tick its way through three slow minutes; then at last he swilled the bucket out on to the dung-hill, and the sleeked puppies settled softly into the filth with a perfect simulation of sleep. He put the bucket down with a clatter and scowled at the grinning boy.

The fat man had not moved. 'Look,' he told him, 'I'll give you a dog when mine whelps. A real sheep-dog, and sure to God! Only for Christ's sake, feed her. That other was a bad one. She oughtn't have bred.' He waited for an answer, a gesture, but got none. 'Look,' he said again, 'I'm telling you. I couldn't do anything else. No one's got a down on you. If only you'd show sense – if only you'd learn – ' But a loathing that was almost hatred welled up in him as he watched the smooth white sausage of a neck squeezed over the coat-collar, the fingers splayed over the podgy cheeks, the soft effeminate haunches loading the shiny black trousers. 'Oh to hell,' he shouted, 'have it your own way!'

He took up his gun and with a nod to the boy walked out of the farm-yard. In the lane they passed the bitch, and with his foot the man from Glan-y-Gors stirred her into the bottom of the hedge. 'He'll find her,' he said, 'if he wants to. I ought to have put the police on him. That's what I ought to have done.'

'You told him,' said the boy.

He watched angrily while the boy again levelled his imaginary gun. 'What the hell could I do?' he complained. 'She was bad right through. And a fellow with a father like him!' His voice was sour with irritation. 'What the hell could I do?'

'You told him,' said the boy. 'Christ knows you told him.' His face lit up with a loutish pleasure and he slowly crooked his finger. 'Ba-bang!'

Shining Morn

~

THE late morning sunshine fell hotly across the hillside. There was still rusty blossom on the gorse, but everywhere the seed-pods were cricking and cracking with their queer mildewed ripeness. A small boy was coming from the broken gate at the roadside, and a mongrel puppy, three-parts sheep-dog, was running earnestly ahead of him. Occasionally the boy shouted the puppy back to him: when it obeyed he put his arms about its neck, when it ran on he promised himself he would beat it within an inch of its life. The phrase pleased him, but he had no awareness of its meaning; he had heard it for the first time that morning. Occasionally, too, he kicked at thistle-heads and left them broken and oozing, or threw a stone, a twig, a piece of dried dung into the bushes. With all this he felt very important, for it was the first time for him to own a dog, and the first time he had been allowed to take it out on his own.

Suddenly the puppy ran furiously across an open patch of sheep-ground to a place where sloe bushes bent untidily over the exposed under-shale of the hillside. He saw it rush at the bushes as though in full chase; then it gave a shrill frightened squeak and came scuttling back into the open. Midway between him and the bushes it began to bark incessantly, its nose raised but all the time keeping the one direction. 'Quiet, Boza,' he called, then angrily: 'Quiet, quiet! I'll beat you.' The dog whirled in behind his heels as he approached the bushes.

He had a great fright. Something was there. Something alive. He saw its eye first – an eye round as a boot-button, quite unlidded. A snake, he thought; and his expelled breath left a heavy ache in his chest. He was not a country boy, but the son of the new schoolmaster. This was his first summer out of town. Then he saw fur, and knew that it was a rabbit. He wondered why it did not run away and slowly put out his hand towards it. He saw it convulsed at sight of his hand and noticed the extraordinary elongation of its back leg. Then he knew it was in a snare.

198

For a moment the rabbit's agony and terror became his. When the puppy darted in barking he shouted hysterically. The rabbit could go no further: it was at full stretch. 'Keep away,' he screamed, 'keep away!' And when the puppy still bounced near on stiff front legs he struck at it, missed, and then scrabbled for a stick with which to hit at it. All the time he could see the rabbit's eye rolled round at him.

His mouth had gone dry and he found himself trembling. He noticed a number of things at once: the notched peg driven into the ground, the thick brown cord leading from it to the dulled wires of the snare. There were three or four flies rising and settling along the rabbit's leg, and a dried raw place where the noose had sunk through the fur and ravelled it backwards for more than an inch. The rabbit had bellied a groove into the loose shale.

Watching the unwinking eye, the still ears laid flat, the close-tucked scut, the boy felt a great black cloud of guilt shut him from the sunshine. What he should do, he knew, was to break the rabbit's neck and put it out of its misery. This was another of the phrases he was fond of using; but until today this too had had no real meaning for him. Again he stretched out his hand, but the rabbit jerked so fiercely at the end of the wire that he recoiled, frightened, and fell backwards on to his behind. With this the puppy dashed in once more, the rabbit smell strong in its nostrils, but like the boy it was too inexperienced to seize and kill. And for another thing, it had for the first time felt fear of the boy, who screamed at it and caught it a furious blow across the jaws. It yelped and backed away, and stood shaking its head.

The boy's face was now a sickly white and he felt a great heat mounting from his stomach. I will free it, he thought, if it kills me. What he had to do was to ease the noose till the leg could be slipped through it. But to do this he must lift the rabbit nearer the peg, so that the wires would be slack and manageable. A new kind of fear grew in him: Would the rabbit bite? He looked at his hands, dismayed by their vulnerability. Dare he risk it? He studied anxiously the brown velvet softness of the rabbit's eye; it looked gentle enough, and he set his left hand firmly behind the rabbit's neck. It instantly slacked on the wire, leapt clumsily into the air, and fell panting away from him. At that moment he knew he could do nothing more, that he might not endure to touch that pulsing body again. But as he rose from his knees, he saw how the wires of the noose were now buried in the leg, and how the flies settled quickly where a black ooze of blood marked the deeper laceration.

He walked away, the puppy watching him nervously. 'Boza!' he called unnecessarily, and the puppy placated him with obedience. 'Come on, sir!'

The hot sun struck his face and shoulders. His sickness vanished. He began to think of himself as another boy, the kind of boy he read about in stories. This other boy would have done a number of things: he would have killed the rabbit to put it out of its misery; he would have freed the rabbit and watched it scamper happily off; or on the prairies he would have cooked the rabbit for his supper, on a smokeless fire for fear of redskins. He lived three lives before he reached the cliff pastures. The puppy too lost all fear and memory of fifteen minutes back, and ran and sniffed and surreptitiously devoured sheep droppings or little pellets. 'I'll beat you within an inch of your life,' the boy threatened him, but he wagged his tail and skipped blithely ahead. In the boy's fancy he grew up to be an iron-toothed ratter, a huge Newfoundland swimming dog who would save his life at sea, a lean and fearsome fighter who killed wolves. He gave him a variety of commands: Hold him, boy! Stick it, Boza, another hundred yards we are safe! Rip his gun-hand! 'Good dog,' he said aloud, 'good dog!'

His mind cleared. The sun streamed on to a sapphire ocean enclosing a golden island. The eyes of great cats glowed in the woods. Painted warriors paddled carved canoes. He withdrew to an impregnable fastness in a mountain of green basalt.

But as they turned at the end of the pastures, that bright world trembled and faded. He had to return past the rabbit. What should he do? Ought he to look again? Or ought he to walk straight by? Fresh from the slaughter of a thousand savages, he remembered with remorse the fly-pestered leg. Even if he freed the rabbit, it could never scamper happily off: the leg must now be dislocated at the hip-joint. Then why free it? he thought. It would only die miserably in a day or so. Would it not be more merciful to leave it in the snare for the farmer or poacher to pick it up that very evening? He nodded wisely, as another of his father's phrases beat to the forefront of his mind: We must be cruel to be kind. That was settled then. He would walk straight by.

With another breath he knew that he could not. The one thing he must not do was walk past and pretend that the rabbit wasn't there. He must kill it or free it. He thought in new fashion of the dryness of the raw leg; the rabbit must have been there a long time. How long? He began telling himself that to kill a rabbit would be rather a fine thing to do. He saw himself telling the story to all kinds of listeners, himself every kind of hero. Yes, he would kill it.

A pity, he thought, Boza didn't kill it. That would have saved an awful lot of bother. For how did one kill a rabbit? He shook his head, worried.

Where the shale fell away from under the sloe bushes he stood a long while hesitating. To keep in good face, he spoke sternly to the dog and saw that he came more or less to heel. But increasingly he came to feel a magnetic drag from the rabbit, and slowly he felt himself fill with a new and terrible excitement. Terrible and unholy. He must go down and look. What he would do was now of no consequence at all. But he *must* look.

He approached, quivering. He would put his hand on the rabbit's neck, and feel that dreadful throb of life throb through him too. His nerves were gnawing and grating, and craved the relief of some experience for which he had neither name nor image. He stooped over the rheumaticky branches, got down on his knees, peered forward.

There was no rabbit there! At once his heart filled with pure joy, with peace and exhilaration. It was free and happy! The morning was perfect and wonderful. 'Look, Boza, look,' he said over and over. 'He's gone, Boza; look, he's gone!'

When he looked closer he found the peg, the cord, and the snare, and in the snare the rabbit's leg bitten through at the first joint. His eyes widened and he looked stealthily round before pulling up the peg. This was a treasure past dreaming of. A snare with a rabbit's foot in it! He rolled the cord and wire carefully round the peg, and offered it, foot first, to the dog to sniff. But the puppy was madly excited by what he could smell on the ground, and the boy wondered whether a fox had been that way. For a moment or two he stayed on his knees, watching a striped fox as big as a tiger carry a three-legged rabbit through the thick tropical undergrowth. Then he ran madly down-hill, chanting at the top of his voice: 'Poor old Bun – ain't that fun! Poor old Bun – ain't that fun!'

The puppy started later but caught up with him by the gate. 'Back, sir!' he cried importantly, and was the first to enter the roadway. The broken gate thumped at its posts behind them, and at once the glow and stillness settled like enamel on the breast of the hill.

A White Birthday

~

WITH their next stride towards the cliff-edge they would lose sight of the hills behind. These, under snow, rose in long soft surges, blued with shadow, their loaded crests seeming at that last moment of balance when they must slide into the troughs of the valleys. Westward the sea was stiffened to a board, and lay brown and flat to the in-drawn horizon. Everywhere a leaden sky weighed upon land and water.

They were an oldish man and a young, squat under dark cloth caps, with sacks worn shawl-like over their shoulders, and other sacks roped about their legs. They carried long poles, and the neck of a medicine-bottle with a teat-end stood up from the younger man's pocket. Floundering down between humps and pillows of the buried gorse bushes, they were now in a wide bay of snow, with white headlands enclosing their vision to left and right. A gull went wailing over their heads, its black feet retracted under the shining tail feathers. A raven croaked from the cliff face.

'That'll be her,' said the younger man excitedly. 'If that raven – '

'Damn all sheep!' said the other morosely, thinking of the maddeningly stupid creatures they had dug out that day, thinking too of the cracking muscles of his thighs and calves, thinking not less of the folly of looking for lambs on the cliff-face.

'I got to,' said the younger, his jaw tensing. 'I got reasons.'

'To look after yourself,' grumbled the other. He had pushed his way to the front, probing cautiously with his pole, and grunting as much with satisfaction as annoyance as its end struck hard ground. The cliffs were beginning to come into view, and they were surprised, almost shocked, to find them black and brown as ever, with long sashes of snow along the ledges. They had not believed that anything save the sea could be other than white in so white a world. A path down the cliff was discernible by its deeper line of snow, but after a few yards it bent to the left, to where they felt sure the ewe was. The raven croaked again. 'She's in trouble,' said the younger man. 'P'raps she's cast or lambing.'

'P'raps she's dead and they are picking her,' said the older. His tone suggested that would be no bad solution of their problem. He pulled at the peak of his cap, bit up with blue and hollows scags of teeth into the straggle of his moustache. 'If I thought it was worth it, I'd go down myself.'

'You're too old, anyway.' A grimace robbed the words of their brutality. 'And it's my ewe.'

'And it's your kid's being born up at the house, p'raps this minute.'

'I'll bring it him back for a present. Give me the sack.'

The older man loosed a knot unwillingly. 'It's too much to risk.' He groped for words to express what was for him a thought unknown. 'I reckon we ought to leave her.'

Tying the sacks over his shoulders the other shook his head. 'You leave a lambing ewe? When was that? Besides, she's mine, isn't she?'

Thereafter they said nothing. The oldish man stayed on the cliff-top, his weight against his pole, and up to his boot-tops in snow. The younger went slowly down, prodding ahead at the path. It was not as though there were any choice for him. For one thing, it was his sheep, this was his first winter on his own holding, and it was no time to be losing lambs when you were starting a family. He had learned thrift the hard way. For another, his fathers had tended sheep for hundreds, perhaps thousands of years: the sheep was not only his, it was part of him. All day long he had been fighting the unmalignant but unslacking hostility of nature, and was in no mood to be beaten. And last, the lying-in of his wife with her first child was part of the compulsion that sent him down the cliff. The least part, as he recognised; he would be doing this in any case, as the old man above had always done it. He went very carefully, jabbing at the rock, testing each foothold before giving it his full weight. Only a fool, he told himself, had the right never to be afraid.

Where the path bent left the snow was little more than ankle-deep. It was there he heard the ewe bleat. He went slowly forward to the next narrow turn and found the snow wool-smooth and waist-high. 'I don't like it,' he whispered, and sat down and slit the one sack in two and tied the halves firmly over his boots. The ewe bleated again, suddenly frantic, and the raven croaked a little nearer him. 'Ga-art there!' he called, but quietly. He had the feeling he would be himself the one most frightened by an uproar on the cliff-face.

Slowly he drove and tested with the pole. When he had made each short stride he crunched down firmly to a balance before thrusting again. His left side was tight to the striated black rock, there was an overhang of soft snow just above his head, it seemed to him that his right shoulder was in line with the eighty-foot drop to the scum of foam at the water's edge. 'You dull daft fool,' he muttered forward at the platform where he would find the ewe. 'In the whole world you had to come here!' The words dismayed him with awareness of the space and silence around him. If I fall, he thought, if I fall now – . He shut his eyes, gripped at the rock.

Then he was on the platform. Thirty feet ahead the ewe was lying on her back in snow scarlet and yellow from blood and her waters. She jerked her head and was making frightened kicks with her four legs. A couple of yards away two ravens had torn out the eyes and paunch of her new-dropped lamb. They looked at the man with a horrid waggishness, dribbling their beaks through the purple guts. When the ewe grew too weak to shake her head they would start on her too, ripping at the eyes and mouth, the defenceless soft belly. 'You sods,' he snarled, 'you filthy sods!' fumbling on the ground for a missile, but before he could throw anything they flapped lazily and insolently away. He kicked what was left of the lamb from the platform and turned to the ewe, to feel her over. 'Just to make it easy!' he said angrily. There was a second lamb to be born.

'Get over,' he mumbled, 'damn you, get over!' and pulled her gently on to her side. She at once restarted labour, and he sat back out of her sight, hoping she would deliver quickly despite her fright and exhaustion. After a while she came to her feet, trembling, but seemed rather to fall down again than re-settle to work. Her eyes were set in a yellow glare, she cried out piteously, and he went back to feel along the belly, pressing for the lamb's head. 'I don't know,' he complained, 'I'm damned if I know where it is with you. Come on, you dull soft stupid sow of a thing – what are you keeping it for?' He could see the shudders begin in her throat and throb back the whole length of her, her agony flowed into his leg in ripples. All her muscles were tightening and then slipping loose, but the lamb refused to present. He saw half-a-dozen black-backed gulls swing down to the twin's corpse beneath him. 'Look,' he said to the ewe, 'd'you want them to get you too? Then for Christ's sake, get on with it!' At once her straining began anew; he saw the flex and buckle with pain; then she went slack, there was a dreadful sigh from her, her head rested, and for a moment he thought she had died.

He straightened his back, frowning, and felt snow-flakes on his face. He was certain the ewe had ceased to work and, unless he interfered, would die with the lamb inside her. Well, he would try for it. If only the old man were here – he would know what to do. If I kill her, he thought – and then: what odds? She'll die anyway. He rolled back his sleeves, felt for a small black bottle in his waistcoat pocket, and the air reeked as he rubbed lysol into his hand. But he was still dissatisfied, and after a guilty glance upwards reached for his vaseline tin and worked gouts of the grease between his fingers and backwards to his wrist. Then with his right knee hard to the crunching snow he groped gently but purposefully into her after the lamb. The primal heat and wet startled him after the cold of the air, he felt her walls expand and contract with tides of life and pain; for a moment his hand slithered helplessly, then his middle fingers were over the breech and his thumb seemed sucked in against the legs. Slowly he started to push the breech back and coax the hind legs down. He felt suddenly sick with worry whether he should not rather have tried to turn the lamb's head and front legs towards the passage. The ewe groaned and strained as she felt the movement inside her, power came back into her muscles, and she began to work with him. The hind legs began to present, and swiftly but cautiously he pulled against the ewe's heaving. Now, he thought, now! His hand moved in an arc, and the tiny body moved with it, so that the lamb's backbone was rolling underneath and the belly came uppermost. For a moment only he had need to fear it was pressing on its own life-cord, and then it was clear of the mother and lying, red and sticky on the snow. He picked it up, marvelling as never before at the beauty of the tight-rolled gummy curls of fine wool patterning its sides and back. It appeared not to be breathing, so he scooped the mucus out of its mouth and nostrils, rubbed it with a piece of sacking, smacked it sharply on the buttocks, blew into the throat to start respiration, and with that the nostrils fluttered and the lungs dilated. 'Go on,' he said triumphantly to the prostrate ewe, 'see to him yourself. I'm no damned nursemaid for you, am I?' He licked the cold flecks of snow from around his mouth as the ewe began to lick her lamb, cleaned his hand and wrist, spat and spat again to rid himself of the hot fœtal smell in nose and throat.

205

Bending down to tidy her up, he marvelled at the strength and resilience of the ewe. 'Good girl,' he said approvingly, 'good girl then.' He would have spent more time over her but for the thickening snow. Soon he took the lamb from her and wrapped it in the sack which had been over his shoulders. She bleated anxiously when he offered her the sack to smell and started off along the ledge. He could hear her scraping along behind him and had time at the first bad corner to wonder what would happen if she nosed him in the back of the knees. Then he was at the second corner and could see the old man resting on his pole above him. He had been joined by an unshaven young labourer in a khaki overcoat. This was his brother-in-law. 'I near killed the ewe,' he told them, apologetic under the old man's inquiring eye. 'You better have a look at her.'

'It's a son,' said the brother-in-law. 'Just as I come home from work. I hurried over. And Jinny's fine.'

'A son. And Jinny!' His face contorted, and he turned hurriedly away from them. 'Hell,' he groaned, re-living the birth of the lamb; 'hell, oh hell!' The other two, embarrassed, knelt over the sheep, the old man feeling and muttering. 'Give me the titty-bottle,' he grunted presently. 'We'll catch you up.' The husband handed it over without speaking, and began to scuffle up the slope. Near the skyline they saw him turn and wave shamefacedly.

'He was crying,' said the brother-in-law.

'Better cry when they are born than when they are hung,' said the old man grumpily. The faintest whiff of sugared whisky came from the medicine-bottle. 'Not if it was to wet your wicked lips in hell!' he snapped upwards. He knew sheep: there was little he would need telling about what had happened on the rock platform. 'This pair'll do fine. But you'll have to carry the ewe when we come to the drifts.' He scowled into the descending snow, and eased the lamb into the crook of his arm, sack and all. 'You here for the night?'

Their tracks were well marked by this time. The man in khaki went ahead, flattening them further. The old man followed, wiry and deft. Two out of three, he was thinking; it might have been worse. His lips moved good-humouredly as he heard the black-backed gulls launch outwards from the scavenged cliff with angry, greedy cries. Unexpectedly, he chuckled.

Behind him the ewe, sniffing and baa-ing, her nose pointed at the sack, climbed wearily but determinedly up to the crest.

Four in a Valley

~

THEY had been lying on the haystack for an hour outside time. He lay now, his face against her bare shoulder, as much asleep as awake, feeling the soft heat welling from the hay, from the girl's damp skin, from the yellow air that trembled so lightly round them. The haystack was in the eastern corner of the cleaned field, the hedges behind them of elm and hazel, and near their heads a golden sprawl of honeysuckle went through and over the contorted arms of a blackthorn. Its perfume saturated their nostrils like sweet wine. There were tall beeches breaking the hedge-line to the right, and lower down, where the field met the river, a pale-green copse with a blood-ring of foxgloves encircling it. Across the river the ground soon began to rise through steep fields, now emerald with after-growth, then through the dark fern belt, and so into upland grazing pocked with rock and tree-stumps. The sun glistened a narrow hand-breadth over the hill-top, and the first shadows stumbled black as water into the valley bottom.

The girl moved a little, caressing the man's hair. She could feel sweat between his face and her shoulder, the scratch and tingle of his day's beard. She looked down anxiously. He was a man in the middle twenties, thin-featured, with black wavy hair, his skin tanned and glowing. He was wearing shabby suède shoes, worn flannel trousers, and a khaki shirt. The shirt neck was open, and his jacket lay beside him. Across it had been thrown a green silk muffler covered with bright yellow greyhounds.

'Tom,' she said quietly, 'Tom?'

He heard her but made no answer. He breathed the half-sigh of a sleeper, moved his lips soundlessly, and pressed his cheek down to her breast. The girl too sighed.

He had been courting her for less than six months, and for a third of that time they had been lovers. She thought back confusedly, to days and evenings and the baffling hours of dark, troubled that it could be this way. She had been on her guard against him from the beginning: he had a bad name, and they said none of the Kemys lot were any good. There was his father, a fairday cockerel still; the quiet dim mother; the sister who cleared out of the county. She shook her head, her lips tightening. She would know one way or the other before she left him tonight.

He lay still, his face set. Behind the shut eyes he grew wide awake, thinking. He had felt her sigh, and knew what she was planning to ask him. He thought of himself with a disinterested clarity, as though his case were someone else's, thought of the girl at once sensuously and impersonally. Tonight, he guessed, would be the end.

He was extraordinarily aware of his surroundings. He could feel as well as hear a tight sustained creeping in the hay, as the dry shafts and beads of grass were rubbed together and compressed under their weight. In the red warmth of his eyelids he could see the tremble of elm leaves in the infrequent pulsation of air from across the valley. There were birds everywhere, the sharp *weep-wink* of chaffinches within a few yards of them, the chittering of hedge-sparrows, and far down the field the fluting of a blackbird, full, pure, and passionless. He could hear the scrape of her fingernails on his scalp, the intake of air into her lungs, its gentle expulsion. He smiled without his face showing it, smiled behind his eyes, deep in the brain.

The angle of heat on his face told him that the sun had dropped nearer the hill. Under his right cheek he felt the pucker and moistness of her skin, and the rounding like a pillow for his mouth and jaw.

The gold ring on the third finger of his right hand was locked painfully under the knuckle. Rings! His thoughts caught on that. They had their uses. He'd worn his the night the Lledrod boys rushed the Christmas dance; there was a split cheek-bone in Lledrod today for them to remember it by. That was the first night he saw her home. No arm round her waist, not even a kiss. Who would have dreamt –

He grew taut. The blackbird had stopped singing. And then, while his last note seemed to echo and throb in silence, all the other birds grew silent too. Into their silence he read their fear. He opened his eyes and sat up, screwing at his ring.

'Tom,' she said, and put her hand to the red patch made by his cheek.

He tilted his head, chopping with his hand for quiet. Hurriedly and as it were guiltily she thrust her arms into the sleeves of her dress. But he was gesturing away her fright. 'No,' he said, 'not that. Somewhere though – '

'What? Who?'

But he was kneeling now, tight-strung as a wire, his hand shielding his eyes. 'Listen,' he told her.

'Oh, why did you frighten me? I can't hear anything.'

'That's it,' he said. 'You can't. Nor me. Everything's gone still – and why? Ah!'

He had watched a black trail of jackdaws into the copse. Then, high above them, he saw a great brown bird glide across the valley, a winged spirit of lazy and disdainful power. 'That's him,' he said. 'No, her. I knew it. I heard the difference. They know what's good for them, those others. They shut up pretty quick.'

'Then you were awake,' she said reproachfully. 'And I wanted you to talk and answer.'

He laughed round into her face. 'Anybody'd want to stay put with you, Dil. What a girl!'

But she pulled his hand away from her neck. 'No, Tom, we've got to stop all this and talk. I've got to know, Tom.'

'Know what?' he asked. 'You know all you want to know. I've told you, haven't I?'

'You've told me what?' she asked, a little bitterly.

'Told you – well, how I feel about you. Told you you're the one for me. Told you how I reckon I fell for you, hard. You've got to be fair. I have now, haven't I?'

While he said all this, in short jerky sentences, he was following with shaded eyes the brown bird as it hung and glided and hung again over the opposite hill-side. The shallower level of his mind sufficed him for all he had to say; what was really present to thought and sensation was the buzzard in its arrogance and poise, and all the tiny creatures of earth now hiding from its eye. For not only were the hedgerows dumb and wary, but around the fields he knew how the rabbits had lolloped to their burrows and lay now with their eyes winking at the sunlit tunnel ends; the water-rats along the river's edge had plunged stealthily to their holes, and the long-tailed field-mice had withdrawn their quivering snouts under a branch, a leaf, or hidden them in the shadow of a grass tuft – each and every one of these certain that the fierce round eye was open for him alone. But his awareness of this pattern of frightened

life was untouched by sentiment or sympathy. That was the way of
it. That was how it was.

'That's something and nothing,' she retorted. 'I want you to
listen, Tom – now!'

'I am listening.' But he pointed upwards. 'You don't see this
every day, Dil.' A second buzzard was driving across the valley,
wheeling before the hill-side, and with a majestic wing-stroke
soaring across the sun. It was the male bird. Soon it joined its
mate, and the two superb creatures began to plane in vast arcs
over the valley's amphitheatre. The sun's ball was now exactly
balanced on the hill-top, and from time to time each bird would
disappear into the pale blaze and emerge jet-black and smaller, till
the eye recovered its discrimination of size and colour.

'If you won't listen – '

'I've said! I'm listening. I've got my ears open. I can't open
them any wider.'

The colour heightened in her cheeks.

'Well?' he asked.

She spoke nervously but with dignity. 'It's about when we are to
be married, Tom.'

'Married?' he repeated, almost absently. 'Well now, that's easier
asked than answered, Dil.' His eyes were bright and hard; she felt
them slip like lizards from her face. 'It's awkward,' he went on. 'It's
not as though I'm not as keen as you, Dil – you know how I feel –
I've been giving it a lot of thought, one way and another.'

She made as though to speak, but instead sat watching him. As
his head turned gently, now sideways, now forwards, she found
herself drawn to watch what he was watching. The she-bird was
swinging in huge irregular loops within the confines of the hills.
For a time the male would keep lazily with her, but now he began
to vary his courtship by taking in a higher, wider circumference,
from which he would ever and again glide smoothly to her rear. As
he re-mounted, he came to take an increasingly sharp angle of
flight, so that soon he was rising into the grey-blue vault of sky.
His glides grew correspondingly steeper, but still aimed into the
heart of the valley. Then she gasped and gripped her knees. The
buzzard had climbed higher than ever, for a moment he hung
motionless, his wings and tail stiff, and then he was falling like a
stone towards the point where his mate's nonchalant soaring
would bring them into collision. His speed increased; no longer a
falling stone, he was a spear hurtling from the blue. The female,

without a beat of her wings, sailed untroubledly towards annihilation, but in the last impossible fraction of time, when it seemed that the outstretched beak must already be piercing her, he drove sideways, like a plate turning, and passed swiftly under her. Again he mounted, though less high, and again dived his death-dive at her; again and again his wings spread flat and slashed the air beside and under her. Unflurried, she pursued her powerful, easy course. Their strength and certainty in that pure and translucent playground endowed them with a divine, unfeeling splendour.

'You said you'd been thinking a lot.'

He looked at her, smiling, ruthless, and clear-headed. 'That makes a man think,' he said, gesturing towards the sky. 'I'd like to be like that hawk, I would.'

'In a way, you are.'

This pleased him. He seemed all openness and affability, but she had seen his eyes narrow, the creasing of his forehead. 'Hawks,' he said slyly, 'they've never been before no parson. Look, Dil,' he continued, 'you know how things are with me. Why rush it? Isn't it fine as it is?'

'Fine.' Her tone was raised, between statement and question, but he was satisfied to take it for agreement. He stretched out beside her, put his hand on the round of her calf. 'Then why spoil it?' He began to stroke her, hoping to excite her, make her forget, or at least postpone, whatever she had in mind to say, but she sat still and unmoved. 'What catch am I?' he asked her. 'Haven't even a job to go to.'

'I have.'

'That's different, Dil. Things a chap can't do.' He grimaced. 'You know how it is.' He rolled over on to his back, his arms reaching up for her. 'Come on, Dil.'

'No,' she said, and could hear the primness in her voice. 'I've got to know. And I've got to know now.'

'God, Dil, what a funny girl you are. Haven't I told you?' He drove his shoulders deeper into the hay. 'Come on, Dil.'

She shifted away from his hands. 'Not again. Not until I know.'

With that he sat up coolly. 'All right, if that's the way you want it.' He watched the buzzards sinking into the valley. 'Only make up your mind. And don't blame me afterwards.' Try as he would, he couldn't spare more than half his attention for what he was saying; it was like the recitation of an old worn lesson. 'But I won't be fooled about with, Dil. There's as good as you tried that, and it didn't come off.'

She flinched. She would have spoken, but he cut away her words. 'We can pack it in when you like. There's nothing on my conscience, and nothing on your mind. I take my fun, but I know what I'm doing – always.'

'No,' she said then, 'there's nothing on my mind. And I think you do know what you are doing. I know now, too.'

He grinned, barefaced. 'Then we are back where we started. No hard feelings, Dil?'

She looked past him. The sun had sunk with a succession of little pauses behind the hill, the air was cooler, and everything shone clean and soft in the evening light. The buzzards had dropped almost to the valley bottom, their curving backs yellow-brown against the green hill-side. Twice the she-bird skimmed the front of a thicket of fir, the third time where was a short dull report, she appeared to be blown upwards in air, and then drifted like a rag to the ground. 'Oh,' she cried. 'Oh that anything so strong and beautiful should be broken and made ugly!' 'What is it? What happened?' The male bird beat upwards with frantic wing-strokes till he was clear of the hill-top. 'Dead as a stone,' she heard her companion mutter, his voice edged with jealousy. 'That'll be old Harris.' He pulled on his jacket, began to knot his muffler. 'I'm going down there. O.K. with you?' But he rose to his feet only to stand stockstill. 'Look,' he said. 'Watch this.' The buzzard had begun to descend into the valley. No, no she wanted to cry to him, fly away, oh, please, please fly away! For my sake, please! Several times he checked and swept uneasily sideways to recover height, but always he was drawn to the object of his terrible fidelity. His flight was losing its smoothness and power; he began to drop in short ragged stages towards the brown body below him. 'Don't,' she cried, 'please don't!' She saw the eye along the barrel, felt the tightening finger, heard the dull explosion. The buzzard made a rending effort to pull away, then an untidiness was blown through his wings, his strength left him, and he fell crumpling to earth.

'The damn fool! If he didn't ask for it.'

Her throat was too full for her to answer. He watched her, knowing nothing of the rage and pity within her. 'Well,' he said briskly, 'time to be off.'

'Don't let me keep you.'

He read only repartee into her words. He laughed aloud and slapped his leg. 'You're a one – and I mean it. I'll go, don't worry.' A tremendous and ingrained vanity made him add: 'Unless you'd like it to stay the way it is?' He lifted his eyebrows at her. 'No? Ah well, can't say I blame you.' Going down the ladder, his head and shoulders still visible, he gave her a brusque, humorous salute from over the right eye. 'I'll be seeing you.'

'You,' she said, 'a hawk!' She began to shake.

He had a skin thick beyond her piercing, and was not ill-content to be his own man again. She heard him whistling unconcernedly as he slipped through the hedge and made for the river shallows. What a fool I've been, she thought; oh, what a fool I've been.

She cried a little, and then some wry appreciation made her smile. She looked down. A rabbit had frisked to the dampening grass, she saw a branch move as a rat slipped through the hedge where the man had slipped before. Jackdaws began to scold and jabber from the copse, there were nervous twitterings filling out to song, and suddenly the blackbird threw a long cool note in front of her.

Their troubles, it seemed, were over. It was wisdom, surely, not to exaggerate her own. So thinking, she touched at her eyes and smoothed her dress, and after one rueful glance about her, set foot to the creaking rungs of the ladder. But, standing in the field – 'A hawk,' she whispered, 'a hawk!' She would have said more, as much to the world as to herself, but she saw the dew glossing her shoes and instead went hurrying homewards under the dusk-sanded sky – a sky she had never known so still, so rich, and yet so unbearably empty.

The Prisoners

~

I

THREE hundred yards of blue water was all that now separated the boat from the shore. The land here had run down from the maroon-sloped, flat-topped hills of the peninsula, and ended in a tangle of sand-dunes heavily cropped with the cutting triple-edged seagrass. There were five men in the boat, and a girl. Three of the men wore thick navy-blue jerseys and had their trousers stuffed into short seaboots with blocked rubber soles. Two wore caps and one was bareheaded. The fourth man wore light green trousers, patched with brown at the knees, a washed-out khaki shirt and jacket, and the forage cap of a German prisoner.

He was young, not more than twenty-two or three. His name was Kurt Lansing. He had seen this beach so close once before, when he and Klaeder were brought off to the Island almost a year earlier. Klaeder was the fifth man in the boat, but he had been wrapped in an old sail and lay in the stern, his head and shoulders, his buttocks and feet so many protuberances against the yellowing, salt-powdered canvas. Lansing's feet were braced against the cross-piece within a foot of him; once or twice he had toed him by accident. This had distressed him, but not on Klaeder's account, for Klaeder was dead. He had fallen from the rocks while gathering gulls' eggs, and had been killed as his breast met stone.

The boat was big, broad-bottomed and clumsy, smelling strongly of pitch and black paint. It had been heavy work pulling her across the water, even on a day as calm as this, but when they returned they would have the strong drag of the tide-race to help them most of the way. In the prow, away from the dead man, they carried three crates of lobsters, hung about with seaweed which had not yet had time to dry and curl. The lobsters were alive, crawling about each other, shuffling and creaking, and their broken

214

claws fumbling out through the salty apertures of the cages. Had Klaeder not been found before the tide could lift him off the reef, they or their kind would have eaten him to the leather of his boots; now they were to be eaten instead. The thought disturbed the man pulling in the bows, for as he slipped his oars a dozen yards out he swung silently but viciously with a short iron bar at a waving claw, so that it splintered and jerked in an ecstasy of pain. 'Why did you do it?' cried the girl; but the next moment they felt the squeeze of the sand, heard its gritty, sighing yield, and the men were clambering out and dragging the boat a yard or two in.

The girl had been at the tiller. She now screwed up her face as she contemplated the canvas-wrapped body, shifted her feet very carefully, and slid over the gunwale to the sand. She moved hurriedly away from the dead man, then stooped and brushed down her coarse dark skirt with such swift impetuous motions as might be removing visible and offensive dirt. A passionate and wounding spirit informed her gestures no less than it was evident in her fine-boned but haggard face, with the dark eye-sockets and the melodramatic mouth.

Lansing looked away from her to the lifelessness of Klaeder. Yesterday, he thought, only yesterday, and was surprised at his own indifference. Griffin of Pen-y-Garreg and his son Mel were tying the painter to a bleached post nearer the dunes; Powell (it was he who had used the iron bar) was rolling a cigarette from a flat red tin. Griffin and Mel were short and stolid, but Powell was the narrow-headed lean kind, a man in the early thirties. Lansing watched the flexing of his fleshless fingers, the black veins along the backs of his hands, the curling hair that almost hid the skin of his wrists. Then he noticed how Powell was watching him too, and flushed.

'Go on,' Powell told him, passing the tin (it had once held corn plasters) and the roll of papers, 'make one for yourself.' He shook off Lansing's thanks, and struck a match for them both. 'I'll have to phone them,' he said, half to himself. 'You'd better come along.'

'What about me?' asked the girl.

Lansing had begun to walk off, as unobtrusively as he could. 'Why, what about you, Gwen?' he heard Powell ask.

She was now out of Lansing's eye. 'You didn't bring me here to sit in the boat, I suppose?'

Powell made a baffled and half-angry sound. 'I didn't bring you here at all. I did my damnedest to stop you coming.' He paused.

'Can I help it if my damnedest wasn't enough? But come you, if you want to.'

They were interrupted by the Griffins returning. 'Ah well,' said the father solemnly, nodding his head at the shrouded figure of Klaeder: 'Pity, pity! All right, we'll wait, Johnny.'

His intention must have embraced the girl too, for in half a minute Powell had caught up with Lansing and was walking a pace or two ahead towards a gap between two large dunes. 'Pity all right,' he echoed Griffin's words. 'Wouldn't have been so long now.' He checked his step till the blond young German was alongside him. 'And the silly bastard had to fall over a cliff!'

'Is it as bad as they say?' the German asked quietly.

'What would I want to tell lies for? Lansing, it's true. Everything's in a mess.' His foot crunched on an empty crab-shell. 'And if you only know it, that's the news you've been waiting for a long time now.'

They had struck into a narrow but firm pathway into the dunes. The sand here was almost white, and so fine that it stirred and drifted under the lightest puff of air. And continually its pattern changed on the taller dunes as it slid soft as water to the lower levels. In one place the path had been carried across a dredged-up cleft on petrol-drums filled with concrete, and soon afterwards they turned left to the remains of some bathing-huts. Their doors were broken and hanging, their steps choked, their wheels buried; the sea air had peeled them of paint, and they were gently tilted from the perpendicular. 'Military secrets,' said Powell, and grimaced. 'It don't matter now, believe me.' He pushed at a door, it gritted open, and inside was a small olive-green telephone-box. This he unlocked and took out a field telephone. 'Wait outside, you'd better.'

Lansing strolled a dozen yards or more back towards the path, before sitting down on the warm sand. He began to stir it with his fingers, and then to lift it in fistfuls into the air and let it pour down on to his knuckles or his palm, so that the sun-irradiated stream glinted with greens and reds and peacock blue, all the colours of its parent sea-shells, till it spread and steadied and was confounded among the millions of grains from which it had been lifted. He remembered the path clearly, and even the bathing-huts. They had been brought this way, he and Klaeder, from the camp up on the peninsula, when they volunteered for farm work twelve months before. He smiled, for he was remembering how the truck had brought them to a side road, and how the side road gave out at a pink-washed, stone-walled farm far from the beach. There had been a sergeant and a private to see them on their way, and they had been offered donkeys by the farmer to take them through the dunes. He and Klaeder had plodded forward, light-hearted to be outside the camp wire; their guards followed less happily behind, the private too tall for his donkey and lifting his knees higher and higher as the sand grew softer. After half a mile they might have been in North Africa again.

Watching the sand grains creep and glitter on the golden skin of his forearm, he thought back to the Afrika Korps as to another existence on earth. Three years, he thought, three years. More than four years since he had seen his home, his father and mother, his sisters. Were they alive? Never a word, he thought, and then, 'Never a word!' he was whispering again and again. The strength of his longing brought him near panic; the grains which had crept, he saw them slip and fall as his arm trembled and his thumb locked the sharp finger-nails into his palms. He shuddered, and then his will was in control again; his fist slackened.

Powell had come from the hut. 'Best get back,' he said. He started off, ploughing with his feet till they were on the path again.

'They brought the path right down,' Lansing said, 'since we came before.' He got no reply and wondered whether Powell had heard him. Then the sky flashed brighter ahead, he saw the blue of the sea, and at once they were on the sea-and-air-washed beach.

'I asked them about the calves,' Powell began telling the Griffins, 'and they can take the lobsters up, and us too.' The father waved his pipe smoke away, wrinkling his placid eyes, while Mel nodded earnestly and thrust out his lips till he looked something of a calf himself. 'It's an ill wind,' he said complacently.

'What about *him*?' Griffin turned towards the stern of the boat.

'There'll have to be a statement. They'll send an officer down, or a sergeant or somebody. That's why there'll be a truck. We ought to get two hours in the village.' He looked at Gwen, who had taken off her shoes and stockings and was scraping her big toes deep into the damp sand at the water's edge. 'It'll be plenty.' But his tone made the words sound like, It will be too much.

With that she turned, hostilely. But all she said was addressed to Griffin. 'How long will it be? Before the truck gets here, I mean?' She patted her cheek, touched her hair nervously. 'Will it be long? It can't be long!'

Mel had cocked up his head and was making leisurely sweeps in the air, as though his arm were a pendulum to tell the time. 'Sure to be,' he began. 'Ah, couldn't be less than a half-hour.'

His father nodded as slowly as earnestly. 'Ah, possible,' he commented, with meaning enough for Mel but none at all for Lansing. How could these two be anything but father and son? he thought, watching them approve each other. The same heavy build, the same calm eyes, the same slow and self-satisfied manner, almost the one voice. Mel was now filling a pipe the same shape as his father's. In twenty-five years' time his ways would be no older. Twenty-five years ago his father had been no younger.

Their likeness, their amity, their matching of interests were so apparent, so palpable, that they acted as a touchstone for less harmonious natures. He began to walk quietly along the sea's edge, thinking of Powell and the girl. What lay between them seemed more significant than dislike, less strong than enmity. He flipped at the peak of his cap, feeling towards Powell friendliness and a dry hard interest, for the girl Gwen an intense and glowing curiosity. When for a moment he shut his eyes, it was to see the round knee-caps, the white legs, the toes curling into the sand, but with an effort that was little short of fury he drove his thoughts elsewhere, anywhere, back to the Griffins, to Powell, to the dead Klaeder. That was wisdom. And then he thought harshly: I am too young to have learned such wisdom with ease; I must respect it the more.

'Hi!' He heard the shout and turned to see Powell waving him back. Facing now west by north-west he could look out past the point of land, laid in pale yellows and greens upon the crystal-fretted water, to where sea and haze and sky created an indeterminate, uncharted world of their own. The Island lay peaceful and near on his left hand. He saw the men and the girl all watching him. The Griffins sat side by side on the edge of the boat; he saw soft ash-grey puffs of smoke float against their darkened faces. Powell was walking irresolutely up and down between the boat and the mooring-post; his legs were bare and his trousers rolled up above the knee; Lansing could see that the three crates of lobsters had been set down in the water where the transparent incoming waves swilled about their excited inhabitants. It was the Island practice to catch lobsters, crack the claws, and then tip the shellfish into these large woven hampers in tidal pools, till they were needed for eating or market. *Kriegsgefangenen-*

läger, Klaeder used to call these hampers, watching the mutilated creatures clamber and slide and wave their smashed talons through the apertures: Prisoner of War Cages. But this was a joke they judged it best to keep to themselves. 'Which one is me?' Klaeder would ask. 'And which one is you, Kurt?' He was no Apollo, that Klaeder, and he knew it. 'The ugly devil with the greedy jaws on him, that's me, Kurt. And look at this pretty little fellow here, that's you.'

And now Klaeder was dead, and he, Lansing, was smiling, if ruefully. Klaeder was wrapped in darkness, and he, Lansing, was walking in the sun. With luck and wisdom he would continue to smile, continue to walk.

The girl Gwen was half sitting, half lying on the sand away from the others. She had put her shoes and stockings on again, at which he was glad. Powell's walking took him within a few feet of her each time, but they had nothing to say one to the other.

'Thought we'd better have you near,' he told Lansing. He laughed, his contempt touched with something not unlike shame-facedness. 'Might think you were trying to escape – swim back to Germany.' Lansing could see how he strained to know whether Gwen was listening. 'You'll have to go back to camp with Griffin here, and make your statement. What happens after – I've told them we've got to make the tide right on four o'clock. They'll be bringing you back to us if you want to come, back into the village by half-three.' His tone was less sharp than his words. 'If you don't want to come back, you don't have to.'

'I shall come, if they let me.'

Powell shrugged his shoulders and turned away to Griffin. 'They'll have to bring you back, anyway. And that fixes the calves.' He was more like an actor than a man on a beach, thought Lansing, with his gestures, his brittle speech, his busyness. And for what audience? Certainly not for a German prisoner; as certainly not for the Griffins.

For the girl then.

Gwen Pellerin! With the safeguard of other men around him, he could think of her calmly, even look at her casually as his eyes moved from sea to sand-dunes, from Powell to the Griffins. Could think of her without emotion, or at least with emotion so banked down with other interests, with Klaeder's death, his own forthcoming visit to camp, the freedom of the moment, all the unusual and therefore precious experiences of the morning, that no trace of flame could break from under them. Gwen Pellerin then. He took no interest in her now that he would not have taken in any woman not utterly unattractive. Identity was but an accident to her physical presence. But surely, he thought, in her if in anyone might be seen the persisting blood of those dark and flashing winy men who three hundred and fifty years ago made their despairing way towards Spain down the stormy western coasts of Britain, their galleys cast away on every headland, their crews dragged from the sea only to feel the knife in their throats, except for the lucky few who found mercy and shelter and at last the favour of women, so that they grew into the native stock and added one more strain of darkness to the dark Iberians. Even the name, Pellerin – some other than Welsh pilgrim had left that to her, along with the glossy black hair, the violent uncertain eyes, the gaunt but luminous cheeks, the long but deeply-bosomed body.

And Powell? But the time was past for thinking of Powell, for at that moment a canvas-hooded army truck broke from between the dunes, and the blare of its horn sent the seagulls wheeling and wailing. It came bowling over the firmer sand of the beach, leaving behind it a sculptured tyre-track. Gwen stood up, Powell waved, the Griffins took out their pipes and looked anticipative. But Lansing stood impassive, just tugging his forage cap a shade lower on his forehead.

A lance-corporal was driving, a spruce and tough-looking little sergeant sat beside him. As the truck stopped dead on its brakes he jumped smartly out, and the door clicked to behind him with the exactly calculated force of his swing. The lance-corporal, an oafish youngster with a cow-lick falling from under his cap, got out more slowly, carrying a Sten-gun.

'What's it for?' Powell asked ironically. 'Us?'

The sergeant gave him a brief unfriendly stare, then turned to Griffin, his arms to his sides but his feet in the perfect at-ease position. His trousers had a cutting crease, his gaiters were speckless, his toe-caps were smooth as black china. There were two dull gold wound-stripes on his right forearm, but nothing to show his length of service save a black and green Palestine ribbon over the heart. 'You'll be' – they could almost see him throw aside the 'Mr' – 'you'll be the man, Griffin? Right! And this'll be Jerry Number One. Right!' His eyes had already travelled over the canvas-wrapped body in the stern of the boat. 'And that'll be Jerry

Number Two. Okay! Then gimme the Sten, and we'll want a hand to put him on board.' The corporal began to unload a stretcher from the back of the lorry. 'You,' said the sergeant to Lansing, and they could see him grope for a tense in vain, 'helfen,' and then with satisfaction, 'hinaufhelfen. And schnell's the word.'

'He speaks English,' said Powell. 'Almost as well as you speak, German.'

'Good,' said the sergeant, a glow of red along the cheek-bones. 'He'll be more useful than some others I see around here. All right, lift him out.'

It was now that he had his first full sight of Gwen's face, for she had come to stand alongside the Griffins, 'Ah,' he said brusquely but appreciatively. His splendid boots swivelled on the sand, he appeared to come up on to his toes as he saluted with equal respect and gallantry. 'Maybe you'd better look the other way, miss. Upsetting to a woman, death and all that.' He gave her a solicitous and confidential look, his very uniform seemed momentarily to relax, then his shoulders snapped back and he was executing his orders with a 'Lift, steady, hold it, I said hold it, didn't I, lower!' He was good for anything at squad level, a sound piece of gristle in the army's back-bone. 'Now *then!*' she heard him bark, and had to turn and look. The stretcher, bearing the nondescript burden of its dead, was being slid into the truck. Her eyes filled with tears, not for Klaeder but for herself and for the folk who would be weeping for him were they aware of his end, were they there to see his body so indifferently bestowed. He was married, she knew, and there were children. But above all she cried to think of herself and the sickness of Si Powell, the brother of the Powell then pushing Klaeder's body farther under the hood, Si whom she had come to the mainland to see, Si whom she loved. Self-pity and a half-imagined grief tightened and then closed her throat, and she heard herself sob. Awkwardly the men were turning to face her. Lansing too seemed of a sudden deeply affected, his face weary and pained, his eyes big and bright in the unavailing shadow of the forage cap. 'Pity,' said Griffin, 'ah, pity, pity!' and Mel's head wagged on his sturdy neck. The sergeant still had qualities unrevealed. 'Every soldier,' he said sententiously, 'has need of a good woman's tears.' The Griffins nodded warm approval, but Powell laughed jarringly. 'Where have I heard that one before – in camp concerts would it be, a dozen times or two?' The sergeant watched him, scowling. 'So you've been in? I wouldn't have guessed it.' Powell held his tongue, but Griffin answered for him. 'Johnny here came out two years ago – invalided out.' The sergeant, his face firm set but triumph gleaming through, caught only at what suited him. 'I know your kind. You couldn't take it. Thank God there's some real soldiers left.' He smiled grimly, his eyes flicking down to the wound-stripes. 'What's this I hear about lobsters?'

The dripping crates were brought up from the sea and set side by side in the truck, away from Klaeder's body. 'Wouldn't a-believed it,' said the incredulous driver. 'We should a-brought a fish-cart.' But the sergeant, with unmistakable malice, was making calculations. 'Can't overload the truck,' he announced unctuously. 'W.D.'s most particular about it.' He narrowed his eyes and lips at Powell. 'There's the man Griffin, I got to take him. There's the Jerry and the dead Jerry, got to take them. There's the lady – ' his mouth unbuttoned – 'I'll take her if I've got to walk myself.' He heard Griffin explain that Mel was his son and in charge of the lobsters. 'R-r-right, I'll take him too. *And* the lobsters. And that's a load. Sorry, chum,' he said off-handedly to Powell. 'More than my stripes are worth.'

His pointing finger made it clear he was waiting for everyone to get on board. But Griffin and Mel were protesting and explaining. They could have saved their breath, however, for all the attention the sergeant paid them: rectitude, malice and pleasure were equally apparent on his hard little face. But: 'He must come with us, Sergeant,' Gwen broke in. He shook his head, but: 'He must,' she repeated, 'he really must!' As her will met his, her eyes sparkled, her cheeks coloured, her voice betrayed an unconscious coquetry. The sergeant saw all this and misinterpreted it. He saw too, as did the others, that Powell was angered that it should be in Gwen's power to do this for him. 'Well,' he said deliberately, 'seeing that it's you. But for anyone else – ' He nodded Powell into the truck as though he were a recruit. 'You'll find it more comfortable in front,' he offered Gwen, a smirk starting at the edges of his mouth, but she hurriedly shook her head. She would travel with the others in the back of the truck.

'No accounting for taste,' said the sergeant.

He said it so meaningly and at the same time so offensively that Powell was provoked to do a stupid thing. 'Your mistake, Sergeant,' he called out. 'I am only this young lady's brother-in-law to be.' The vulgarity and folly of his words infuriated Gwen as much as it immediately distressed Powell himself. Why, he thought, why should I be such a fool? Such an unforgivable fool!

'I hope it wasn't twins,' the sergeant confided to his chuckling driver, in a loud stage mutter. 'Let her go!'

The engine rocked and roared, the truck shot forward in a tight half-circle and straightened out for the gap in the dunes. No one in the back had anything to say. The lobsters climbed over each other as furiously as futilely, and from the back of the truck a thin rope of water hung down to the sand. At first it lay between the tyre tracks like a wriggling black snake, then intermittently in splashes and flakes, and before Mel at last found tongue with some ponderous platitude it had ceased altogether. Then the dunes engulfed them.

II

The truck reached the village of Tresoch a little after one o'clock. It had been a glum, embarrassed journey for Powell and Gwen, Lansing sat sunk in gloomy thought, the Griffins alone broke the silence with anything more than perfunctory questions and strained uncordial answers. At Tresoch they braked to a halt opposite the blue-painted empty warehouses on the quay, and Powell helped Mel set the crates in the shadow of the stone wall there. The sergeant saluted Gwen in his own style of tough disillusion, his eye rested on Powell without favour, they saw him nod to the driver, and before his chin could lift again the broad scolloped tyres were bouncing on the cobbles. All three thought the same thing: This was no ceremonial ride of Klaeder to the quiet of his grave; but no one made comment as he went, or when they stood alone.

The quay was almost empty. Down below them a sailor was coiling a rope in an ever-widening spiral on the decked-in prow of a small grey launch, with a machine-gun mounted amidships. Farther out a couple of fishing-boats rested where mud met sand on the harbour bottom. The breeze was fresher here, and it brought a smell of brine and decay from the weed-covered rocks that buttressed the sea wall. Somewhere to their right a hammer and chisel beat music out of stone.

'We ought to eat,' said Powell. 'We've got till three-thirty.'

'I'm going to find Si,' said Gwen. 'He'll be on the wall.'

Mel fingered his lip. 'And I reckon I ought to get these to Josephy's first.' Powell knew him stubborn as stone over small things, for all his calm ways. He wondered too whether Mel would not be glad to be rid of them for a while. 'Ay,' he was continuing, 'I think I'll do that before grub.'

'I'll come with you,' Powell told Gwen. 'I won't stay though.'

Without replying she started off along the quay, and with a 'See you later' for Mel, Powell followed after her and caught her up.

But there was no Si on the sea wall. Half a dozen men had just broken for their midday meal, and were setting against sparkling blocks of grey granite their long red iron bars, their chisels and adzes, tapering hammers and vast shining sledges. A boy was hurrying from the nearest cottage with a bright green jack of tea, and at sight of him the gulls came screaming in from the fishing-boats. The sailor had straightened up from his rope and waved his hand as he saw them staring his way. A couple of the men knew Powell and gave him good day. Si? they asked. Someone pulled a face. He hadn't been along all the week. Not that it mattered. One of the younger men, pouring out thick brown tea for a mate, muttered words they were not intended to hear.

'Know where we'll find him?' Powell asked.

The men, biting into their bread and meat and dipping their faces into their mugs, looked at each other and shook their heads. They seemed troubled to have grasped that Gwen was no casual caller upon Si. Their spokesman was crumbling bread for a couple of feather-gaitered pigeons which had just arrived from the harbour end. 'It might be worth your while,' he began, in the bland and yet formidable fashion of a preacher about to set forth the heads of his sermon – 'Or there again – ' Then: 'Try the pubs,' he said bluntly, and began *prip-pripping* with his lips to the pigeons.

They hurried away from the sea wall, along a sandy alley into the village main street. Mel was waving his hand from outside Josephy's, and they saw the last crate of lobsters being taken inside on a hand-truck. 'We ought to eat,' Powell said again. 'We've got the afternoon for hunting in.'

'I don't want to all that bad,' Gwen replied. 'I want to find Si. You're his brother; you must know where he is.' Her voice grew sharper on her last words.

'You're his sweetheart. Why don't you?' He was speaking very slowly to her. 'You seem to think I'm hiding him from you. You heard what they said. Go on then, start in at this end of the town and keep going to the other. But if you are wise, you'll eat.' His voice grew edgy to match hers. 'Even a row is better on food.'

'There'll be no row,' she said fiercely, 'if you keep out of it. You've been against me all day. And I'll find him myself, thank you.'

'You think so?' He was prepared to say more, to invite her again to set about it, but she had turned and left him and was walking back down the alley to the waterside. For a time he stood looking after her, watching her shoulders, the set of her head; he wanted to follow and offer explanations, apologies, readiness to help, but he was still shifting his weight uncertainly from one foot to the other when she hurried round the corner and out of sight.

'Where's she gone?' asked Mel, sauntering up.

'How the hell should I know!'

Mel rubbed his left hand with his right. 'Those lobsters now,' he said. 'I never seen a finer lot of lobsters. They'll be swallowing spit in Brum over them. I reckon I'm ready to eat, Johnny. How about you?'

Powell drove out a great explosion of breath. 'I'm ready,' he said, and they turned into a half-cottage, half-café farther up the street. 'It's Si,' he began to explain when they were eating. 'It's my brother. He hasn't shown up for a week, and with him the way he is. She's worried about him.' He spoke bitterly. 'She needn't be.'

'I'm worried about my old man,' said Mel. 'He don't shine at the talking. I only hope what he says up there makes sense.'

'The German will talk. All the old man need do is keep nodding now and again.'

'You don't know my old man,' said Mel. 'He's a nice chap, that German. I've seen a damned sight worse at home, and that's putting it mild.' He paused and then said slyly: 'If only that sarge this morning. He was a boiling piece if ever I saw one.'

'I started it,' Powell admitted grudgingly. He began to count silver and coppers out on to the table. 'Pay the bill, Mel. I'm going to look for Si.'

Out in the street he stood in hesitation a moment before stepping into the bar of the 'Harbour Master'. There was no sign there of his brother, nor in the lounge. He went back into the bar and called for a beer. 'You wouldn't know my brother, Si Powell?' he asked the landlord, a fattish, round-headed man with incongruous weasly eyes. 'I would,' he replied briefly. Powell made his acknowledgement and drank. 'Any idea where I'd find him?' The landlord smiled shiftily, his eyes seemed of different colours, different expressions. 'I would,' he said again.

'Well, where?' Powell asked irritably. 'Or is it a secret?'

'No secret.' The landlord picked up his glass, gave it a pretended rinse under the counter, began to wipe it with a sopping cloth. 'Try the "Bell",' he said. As Powell reached the door without a word of thanks, he saw in a mirror advertising shag tobacco the landlord's weasly eyes following him with undisguised amusement.

At the 'Bell', pushing into the crowded bar, he had a surprise. A smooth-faced country girl with her sleeves rolled up was working two-handed on the pints and half-pints, and a woman with piled-up red hair was carrying a trayful of short drinks out to the parlour. He went quickly past the drinkers and through the passage door, where he stood waiting for her to return.

'Why, Johnny,' she cried, startled; 'it's you!'

'It's me,' he said. 'Where's Si?'

'He was here ten minutes ago. Isn't he in the bar?'

'You know damn well he isn't.'

She was a handsome woman of rather less than Powell's height, crested like a bird with her soft and glowing hair; her eyes, too, soft and warm, her skin clear as the underside of a sea-shell save where it was beginning to dry and coarsen over the cheek-bones and at the corners of the mouth. She wore a skirt of almost white stylish tweed, a blouse of dark green silk, and a gold trinket hung from a gold chain into the hollow of her breasts. There were small gold stud ear-rings shaped like flowers on the lobes of her ears.

'Why, Johnny,' she protested, with a false but attractive frankness, 'what do you mean? And aren't you glad to see me again?'

'Delighted,' he said. 'Where's Si?'

'Si, Si!' she mimicked, her pretty white teeth gleaming against her carefully made-up mouth. 'How should I know where he is?' Her eyes played at him, and she set the trayful of empty glasses to rest on a narrow oak side-board. 'Whoever would have expected to see you here!' She touched her hair. 'D'you find me changed at all, Johnny?'

'I'll tell you later.' There was an exhalation of perfume, warmth and softness from her bosom, as from a basket of ripe apples. It filled the short passage they stood in, his lungs were distended with it, it climbed through his nostrils into his brain. 'I haven't changed all that much, Johnny.'

'Nor I,' he said roughly. 'I still know trouble when I see it.' He put his hand to the door of the parlour. 'If Si's in there, I'm going in too.'

She put her hand on his. 'Is it urgent? D'you have to talk with him?' Her arm and shoulder pressed lightly into his side, but she could feel the powerful fingers begin to turn under her own. 'Then look – ' she pointed to another door. 'Go in there. I'll send him to you.'

He was in a small private parlour, most of the furniture old-fashioned but comfortable, though two flippant coloured glass figurines on the mantelpiece and a leather work-box mounted on shining steel tubes showed signs of a newer and alien taste. Si, he was thinking, my brother Si – with distaste, even anger, and yet with a gnawing affection. He felt his head clouded with perfume still, the back of his hand tingled from the soft and vibrant pressure set upon it. And her, he thought, meeting her! Si! He heard the door open behind him and turned.

It was his brother. 'Si,' he said, 'Si!' His vehemence surprised him. 'If it's not our Johnny! Hullo, Johnny.'

He came round to Powell's side of the table, his face loose with liquor, his eyes too big and bright. 'Say you are glad to see me, Johnny.'

'Si,' said his brother, 'for Christ's sake!'

Si waved his hand. There was no firmness in the gesture. He crossed to the deepest chair and sat back into it, sighing. 'Go on, Johnny, tell me.'

He was in the middle twenties, a thinner, more febrile version of his brother. Without effeminacy, he yet looked as though nature had cast him for woman rather than man, with his dark hair flowing back from a high pallid forehead, the clear brown eyes in their high-arched hollows, the long straight nose with its beautifully turned nostrils, the full clean lips. But his brother saw rather the soft girlish complexion and the way the shoulders had begun to slope forward, the rounding of the upper back as the chest caved in. And he saw with despair the signs of his drinking. Between anger and frustrated love he could find no words. But his face spoke for him.

'Forget it, Johnny, and give me a cigarette. But there, you roll them.' He took out a packet of his own and offered them, but Powell shook his head impatiently. 'Then give me a light instead.'

'Si, I came to find you because I want to talk to you. And I don't want either of us to lose his temper. Will you listen?'

227

'The listening I've done to you.' But he smiled good-naturedly. 'Go ahead, Johnny.'

Powell sat down facing him. 'I've been down the harbour. When were you there last?'

Si crossed one leg over the other, with a pretence at full ease. 'Don't say you've come from the Island to find that out, Johnny. Or even from the harbour. Did I do so much when I was there that anyone cares a damn? And can't an ex-private take a holiday at the Government's expense without his family badgering him?' He smiled again.

'If you'd stop play-acting – '

'Play-acting! And what are you doing?' The smile had gone, he beat his hand against the arm of his chair. 'Playing the elder brother. Playing the God-knows-what. What are you here for, anyway?'

Powell sighed. 'Gwen's here. She wants to see you.'

'And why the hell,' shouted Si, struggling out of his chair, 'should you bring her here? Haven't I trouble enough without you and her at me nine days out of ten?'

'I didn't bring her. I tried to stop her.'

'I wouldn't be surprised at that,' sneered Si.

'I don't know what you'd be surprised at,' Powell said, as calmly as he could. 'And I don't care. Have you forgotten you are engaged to her?'

'No. Nor have you,' he added cruelly, 'I hope.'

'Now listen, Si – I've already said I didn't come here to lose my temper. You have your say, and then I'll have mine. You are worse, is that it?'

'No,' shouted Si. 'Though you might like me to be.'

'Si, if there's anything I can do in this world to help put you right, you know I'll do it. But all this blasted foolery' – his voice began to tremble – 'boozing in the mornings, smoking your lungs away, messing about with women – Si, for Christ's sake why won't you show sense!'

Si had raised his fists above his head. Then, unexpectedly he clapped his hands to his ears and sat back into his chair, his eyes grown dull, sweat on his forehead. He swallowed two or three times. Then: 'Where's Gwen?' he asked shakily.

'She left us here in Tresoch, went down towards the harbour looking for you. We had words. But I'll easily find her.'

Si was wiping his forehead. 'Johnny,' he said, more steadily, 'I know what I am and I know what you think me. I even know what I'm doing. And I know that I'm worse. I don't want anybody to tell me that.' He sat silent for a full half-minute. 'But let's have it out for good. Johnny,' he said earnestly, leaning forward, 'what do you see ahead for your own life? Or never mind that – what do you see ahead for me?'

'More than you think, Si. Gwen's a fine girl, a very fine girl. I've known people worse than you, a hundred times worse, married, with kids, living full lives for twenty, thirty, forty years. It means taking care of yourself, that's all. And what's wrong with a chap taking care of himself?'

'That's fair enough, Johnny. And if you were God Almighty it might work out that way. But I'll tell you what I see. I haven't got twenty, thirty, forty months, Johnny. I know that. I know it *here*.' He struck himself lightly on the chest, and his face blenched with pain. 'I don't want kids. I don't want a woman being a martyr to me. I don't want any of the things you think I want.'

'But what do you want, Si? There must be something. Everyone wants something.'

'I've had either too much or too little, Johnny. I had the money spent on me, I had the education, I had the chances. And I had the family lungs, only more so. And they put me into the army, till I was spitting blood over half Italy, but someone on the other side forgot to shoot me, and now I'm out of hospital no bloody good to anybody, sneaking about a sea wall, and I've grown so weak that I can't even pretend any more.' His brother stirred anxiously as his voice became thin and high. 'So that's what the world has done for me, and now I want to do something for myself. I want six months, or a year if I can have it. And I want it my own way.'

'And Gwen?'

'She'll forget,' he said bitterly. 'The living always do.'

'That's fool's talk. You read it somewhere. And where does Mandy come into all this? How long has she been back here?'

'Six or seven weeks. It seems longer.'

'And her old man? Where's he?'

Si smiled unpleasantly. 'He's dead. She killed him, poor old sod.' He sat forward at his brother's contemptuous movement. 'I'm telling you, she killed him. You think I'm tight. All right, I am, I was tight, a bit. But go on, Johnny, ask me how she killed an old man like him. Or have you guessed? You know her as well as I do – better. Poor old devil, he lasted less than a year.' His voice dropped to a hoarse and brutal whisper. 'And now she's doing the same for me. Well, good luck to her, say I.'

Powell stood up, sick with rage. 'I'd like to – '

'Get wise to yourself, Johnny. You're still tied up with the ideas they sold us when we were kids. They may have been all right then. The world's altered, I've altered, why don't you alter too? Mandy's fine. She's all right, Johnny. With the booze and Mandy, it's grand how much you can forget.' He had begun to laugh, and went on chuckling and coughing through his next words. 'I owe her to you, Johnny. P'raps I'm a substitute; she talks about you enough, God knows. Well,' he concluded, with a sudden, naked viciousness, 'which of us is the fool, Johnny?'

'You're mad,' said Powell; 'you're mad! Try and get some sense, some hold on yourself. Or I'll go.'

'All right, go!' For Powell was moving towards the door. 'And don't come back. That's all I ask, don't come back, you or anybody.'

Without answer Powell left him sitting there in the arm-chair, handkerchief to mouth, crouched forward over his knees. The house was still and empty, save for a sound of glasses being put away in the public bar. He wished to get out unseen but had no choice but to pass through that way. It was the woman Mandy who was there, and she came quickly round from where she was tidying the shelves.

'How did you find him?' she asked, but her smile dried from her face at his look of disgust and hatred. 'Johnny,' she cried, 'why do you look at me like that? What have I done?'

'Open the door,' he said harshly. 'I want to get out.'

'Please, Johnny, don't go like this. It's not what you think. He can't work. He must have somewhere, and something.'

'Right,' he said. 'He's got it. Good luck to you.'

But she caught at his arm, and when he wrenched it away caught at it again. 'Please, please, Johnny,' she pleaded. 'I can't bear you to treat me the way you do. Don't go away hating me.' Her face began to work, her mouth to quiver, her eyes grew wet with tears. 'Can I never do anything right for you?'

He stood for a moment irresolute, watching the white bloodless fingers screwed into his sleeve, the nails reddened to a shade more violent than her hair, their pointed ends the colour of rich milk. The green silk stretched smooth and glossy over the forearm, swelled with the mould of the shoulder, and he saw the gold locket bump soundlessly against the shadowed rounds of her bosom. What message she read into his stillness, his silence, he could guess only too well, for suddenly he saw the fingers move on to his own, and when she turned up her face its grief was yielding to another expression at once shameful and pitiful. 'Johnny,' she whispered, 'please! Whatever I do, I do for you.' One great shudder ran through him from head to foot, then he had wrung his fingers free, pushed at her shoulder, so that she stepped back unsteadily, groping for the bar, and the next moment, with the image of her surprised and desperate face for company, he was out in the street. He had not walked twenty yards when he heard the chime of the harbour clock telling the half-hour after three.

III

The truck bringing Lansing to Tresoch was outside the blue-painted warehouse some five minutes late. It also brought Griffin, another German prisoner named Goerlicke, and on its way had picked up the two calves which were to be taken out to the Island. The same spruce compact sergeant sat in front alongside the same driver, and looked with the same cynical and knowing eye at Powell and Gwen where they stood waiting with Mel by the empty lobster-crates. But this time he didn't dismount, and gestured curtly to his passengers to get themselves and the crates on board. It was with difficulty that they all found themselves places, but at last, with Gwen wedged tightly between Griffin and Mel, and Powell and Goerlicke each nursing a black-and-white calf, they shouted 'Ready!' and the driver made his customary fierce start. Goerlicke was a youngster of an indeterminate dusty colouring, unlike the blond Lansing. Lansing was beginning to explain that he had enough English words to know what he might be told on a farm, but no ability to express himself. 'English,' said Goerlicke in confirmation, concentrating his effort on the quizzical Mel, 'no good, not so hot, eh?' Lansing raised his eyebrows and opened his hands at this equivocal start, but the speaker, content to get a conspiratorial nod from Mel, smiled cheerfully and stroked the bony back of his calf.

Griffin began to tell his son and anyone else who would listen how well he had managed at the camp. The commandant had been called away that morning, but he had been interviewed by a major, who insisted that he make a very good dinner. On the whole (he pronounced it 'hool') Griffin considered the major a very civil young fellow. And on the hool he thought the camp not too bad a place, though he wouldn't want to spend too much time there himself.

For Lansing's part it was with relief that he found himself back among the Island folk. Even a couple of hours at the camp had touched him with horror. Walking within the wire, it seemed to him the sun had stayed outside. A year on the Island had made the herded state of thousands of men brooding in a confined space as hateful as it was unnatural. The air was sour with their repression, the glaring tidiness that surrounded them as unwholesome as squalor. The blood thundered in his ears when the officer interrogating him had demurred at his return that day to the Island; the back of his skull ached with anxiety as the sergeant explained about the calves and the need for them all to catch the favouring tide at the end of the afternoon. Then the right paper had been found, mislaid by a clerk whose ears burned red at the major's bellow. Everything was straightway clear, Authority had expressed its will, and it was for majors and their like to expedite it. A senior German officer had been present throughout, documents were signed and sworn to, the German brusquely waved away the invitation to speak with Lansing in private and strode stiffly off without a glance at him. He was nothing at all, or if anything, then a nuisance. And the worst kind of nuisance, the kind that kept an officer from his luncheon. An officer of either side, it didn't matter which.

At a table in the kitchens, eating a half-cold meal, he found himself no more welcome to the cooks and their helpers. When finally he pushed his plate away and walked out of the babel of German, it was with an appreciation grown to longing for the quiet he and Klaeder had shared together, and the indifference grown to toleration and even to liking with which they had been treated by the Griffins, by Powell, by the other farming and fishing families, and by the Pellerins for whom he himself worked. He wondered who would accompany him back to the Island, and was relieved when he discovered it was to be Goerlicke. He was a Westphalian, and his parents were farmers in a substantial way.

The truck had now left the macadamed road and was running silently but evenly along the sanded track. Powell just had time to swing his calf's rump clear of his lap before it emitted a wet and greeny mulch. Lansing noted with approval that while Goerlicke half-opened his mouth, he closed it again without comment.

Gwen sat still as a stone the whole journey. Behind her tense mouth and straining eyes Lansing read great misery of spirit, and he had time and inclination to speculate why. It was past all question that Powell was in love with this girl, and here he was, Powell himself, for all his staccato jokes about the calf and his rough conversation with old Griffin, as unhappy as she. He was sorry about this, for he liked them both. Somewhere, he understood, there was a brother none too well. The corners of his mouth tightened with satisfaction: one learned wisdom, there were chains a-plenty without those one was tempted to forge for oneself. Then he sighed sentimentally, recovering his place after an unusually heavy lurch of the truck. In that close elbow-touching world of the Island one learned a great deal about one's neighbours, without even the pains of curiosity.

Within a minute there was a drumming under them as they shot much too fast over the bridged hollow. In as much time again they had broken through the line of the dunes on to the flat beach. 'Hold tight,' shouted the driver, braking the truck to a standstill, and the next moment he had thrust in his clutch and reversed in a swirl till the back of the truck stopped hardly six feet from the mooring-post. This time the sergeant jumped out and saw the truck emptied. He scowled at the mess made by the calf, wrinkling his nose like the townsman he was. He stood by impatiently while Griffin with an air of tremendous effort set his signature to a bill of delivery of the prisoner Goerlicke, then with a rapid *th-th-th* of his teeth and tongue he climbed back into his seat and the truck tore off.

The boat lay black and broad as a crab on the brown wet sand, with the water a hollow blue beyond her. The tide line with its fragments of weed, bits of whitened wood, and an occasional jellyfish the size of a hand, showed that she had lifted with the incoming flow and then settled contentedly at the full stretch of the rope. The scene was one of complete peace and beauty. The sun, fetching up from the south-west, shone with a golden glow out of a sky whose blue was beginning to fill with tall and snowy cloud-bluffs. Three or four herring gulls came drifting up from nearer the point of the peninsula to examine the newcomers, and one solitary yellow-billed bird went past them wailing and dangling its green legs across the sea's surface. They saw the pale sand above the water-line shimmer under a mirror of heated air. The crates were stowed, and a few purchases, and Griffin bound the calves' legs with broad loose swathes of canvas before placing them in the stern, where Klaeder's body had lain on their morning's journey. This done, he went complacently off into the dunes on business of his own. The German, Goerlicke, stood breathing in the sweet and briny air and stroking the polished handle of an oar. He looked out to the Island and could see plainly the bird-whitened cliffs to the south, the long inclined fields that fronted them, and near the sea-line a huddle of cottages and the square tower of a church. Then spontaneously and out of his happiness he began to sing, at first hardly above a whisper, then in a gentle and romantic tenor, a tender and wondering song of his own country. Mel, stowing some small packages under the empty crates, slowed his hand, nodded quiet time with his head. But Gwen, her eyes glistening, walked hurriedly away from the boat, till she was fifty yards down the beach. After his first hesitation Powell went after her.

'Gwen,' he said, 'don't be unhappy.' And when she made no answer, 'Gwen,' he said helplessly, 'Gwen!'

'Whatever you think,' he began again, 'be fair, Gwen. Didn't I tell you it might be better not to come? Why you should think I'd do anything to make you unhappy when all I want is your happiness – why should you think it, Gwen?' It was the nearest he had ever come to saying what he wanted to say to her. 'I saw Si, as I told you. He wouldn't see you. It was wrong of him, but he wouldn't. You must believe me, Gwen.'

'He was worse,' she sobbed. 'That's why he wouldn't see me. He doesn't want me to know.'

What can I say? he was thinking. What can I say, save the truth? And all the time the yearning of his own bowels towards her was something he could hardly master. And what, for that matter, was the truth? He grew confounded, as never before, by the conflicts and dubieties within the very heart of truth. 'What can I say?' he thought again, and was dismayed to hear his voice transform the thought into cold, hostile words.

'Nothing,' she said fiercely. 'Nothing at all! For God's sake, say nothing to me ever again till I leave the Island and all of you once and for all.'

He followed her back to the boat. Mel did not look up but busied himself unnecessarily with the crates. He wondered what Mel thought of it all: whether in Mel's eyes he was just a man after his brother's girl, without the guts to take Yes or No for his answer.

The elder Griffin, stolid as ever, had returned from the dunes and was untying the rope. Powell and the two Germans began to thrust the boat forward, the sand crumbling from the keel in tall outfolding ridges. Soon she reached water, Griffin climbed in, and with a shout and a heave the three men were clambering over the sides and reaching for the oars. At first they were poling from the bottom, but soon they had depth to row. Gwen sat in the stern again, her place at the tiller, her feet disposed about the prostrate calves. On the first bench were Lansing and Goerlicke, and on the second Mel and Powell. Old Griffin sat at ease in the bows. Later he would scull a starboard oar, to redress the drag of the tide-race as they neared the Island. The land began to recede, its contours defining themselves with precision above the rippling foreground. The colours richened, the water darkening to Prussian blue, the dunes white and glistening, the grasses cool belts of green.

For a time they pulled in silence, each man busy with his thoughts. Lansing, calmly happy, kept his eyes from Gwen; but Goerlicke, though with discretion, found it the crown of his afternoon to have a girl to look at. He was agreeably conscious of the colour of her hair and eyes, the deep bosom under the jersey, her long flat shin-bones. Or from her he would look with glee to the winking eye, large and liquid and inhumanly innocent, of the nearest calf. Mel and his father wore the same face of contemplative good-nature: what went on behind their foreheads, one judged, was neither strenuous nor vexing. But it was Powell's face which betrayed most to its beholder. Above all it betrayed that he was unhappy. Three people and all they had said pulled with each oar-stroke from arm to brain: Gwen, his brother, and the woman Mandy. 'Johnny,' he could hear her saying, 'I can't bear you to treat me the way you do. Can I never do anything right for you? Whatever I do, I do for you.' They slid in and out of his own words to Gwen. 'When all I want is your happiness.' And Si? Si's my brother, he thought. I can't do anything against Si. 'She killed him,' he heard Si say. 'And now she's doing the same for me. Well, good luck to her, say I.' And all the voices were frantic, sad, or bitter. How can it end? he thought. All of us wanting the thing we cannot get. And no one of us with anything worth having. The world full of our lies to others and ourselves.

Goerlicke had begun to croon to himself, taking breath between his strokes. Soon his voice strengthened and he was singing the same song he had sung on land. His voice was untrained but charming. Griffin had now taken the bow oar, and Gwen leaned heavily upon the tiller. They could feel the current press upon the boat like a hand. At first the singing pleased Powell, then it came to churn and distract and sharpen the grievous thoughts he suffered from. At last he could stand it no longer.

'For Christ's sake stop caterwauling!' he cried.

The two Germans looked round startled, their oar-blades raised clear of the sea. 'Keep going,' said old Griffin mildly. Lansing kicked Goerlicke's foot, and they recaught the rhythm of the boat. Gwen gave Powell one short glance that was nearer hatred than dislike, then looked away, and the boat made forward in silence. Already the current was easing its drag, in ten minutes' time Griffin nodded wisely and brought his oar inboard. He relit his pipe. When shortly afterwards Goerlicke stole a glance over his shoulder, a few hundred yards of blue water was all that separated them from the Island. His face, which had been downcast, lightened, he winked at the calf and drew in a great chestful of air as his oar dipped clean; and when he began to sing again it was so soundlessly that no one could hear him. Gwen alone, confronting him, saw and saw with envy the small and happy movements of his mouth.

Down in the Forest Something Stirred

~

A GREAT black double clap of thunder tore itself from the
heart of flame in the dead maw, the hell-gape, the tree-
toothed swallow of the oak-apple-starred, the moss-and-ivy
haired, the dead-bough-fingered woods of Supra Maelor. From its
fiery centre it spread and bellowed through the piny aisles, the
down-dropped bowing birches, the gnarled goblin thickets of the
oak. Its uprush shook down branches, made the leaves rain, and a
thousand birds rose into the dark with a whirring of wings and
with frighted and discordant voices. A double-barrel echo rapped
from the mountains and rolled under the sky. Then the noise
swooned away, the trees were shrouded in a midnight hush, and
soon the birds ceased from cheeping and chirking, and silence
settled upon the wood.

' – !' said a human voice.

John Lot Padog, the weasel-jawed, fish-eyed, horse-mouthed
poacher of Hedgerose Cottage, had tripped on a keeper's wire and
discharged both barrels of his shotgun.

Within the parish of Supra Maelor, two men that night watched for
a sign, listened for a wonder. The first of these was Manmoel Pliny-
Evans, who lived in the stable loft of the empty bleak mansion of
Capsant. He had lived there for ten years now, a saint subsided
from a varnished pew and the linoleum smells of holiness. A mild
and modest man enough, he could neither understand why he
alone of human kind might expect to inherit God's crystal houses,
nor why the Lord should have made his ungreased tongue the vial
of His truth. It grieved him to think of that universal error to which
his fellows subscribed, that the Garden of Eden was not visible in
their midst, and that the mischievous apple tree no longer bore
forbidden fruit amidst the lesser vegetables of Supra Maelor. For
had he not seen it there, and had he not seen the stoat lie down

with the rabbit alongside its bole? Oh blind generation of men, blindest since Pharaoh shut the lids of his heart against the showings of Moses! Oh dim and dusty vessels emptied of blessedness! And now mankind stood within eight nights of damnation, for by dividing all the letters in Genesis by the chapters of Deuteronomy, by adding Micah and subtracting Amos, he had found the exact day in this our year when the unbruised serpent would again tempt Eve to eat of the apple. And so far no man with faith and firearm had joined with him to shoot and slay. Always contempt and the eye-slidings of Sion. How long, Oh Lord, how long? He prayed for one disciple, one man of wrath, his red-palmed, knob-knuckle hands stretched out over the forest, his beatific basin of a face tilted on the long-strung neck. Send me the thunder and the lightning. Send me a sign!

High on the shoulder of the fronting hill Gellius Sant-Owen surveyed the velvet blackness of the low-breathing forest. His breadth from deltoid to deltoid was as his length from occiput to knee-ball. Nine jowls depended below his toadstool ears, his belly he bore as on a trolley before him. It was Sant-Owen's cross that he had never looked the ascetic he was, the smasher of fleshpots, the contemner of groaning trestles, the feeder on bread and chestnuts and wholesome pulse which trumpet their warnings against gluttony and surfeit. One luxury only did he permit himself, a sweet apple from the heart of the wood. For seven years now he had lived the life of a solitary in the battered sanctuary of Monkhole, high above the parish, and because the bats in his belfry wore the faces of wolves it was rare for any to seek him out. Yet there were times, and they had grown more frequent of late, when it seemed to him a sorry thing that all Supra Maelor should burn, and he with no butty in heaven. Not one from amongst so many? Not one just man in Sodom? He would not indeed ask that Sodom be spared, but oh for one sound apple in the barrel! Why not tonight? From his high hill, his broken doorway, and his full five feet of height he called on providence. Send me the earthquake, the voice in the whirlwind. Send me a sign!

The forest lit and split below them.

John Lot Padog had reached Hedgerose Cottage. Twice and thrice he scratched on his own back door till the gold-browed Becca, with whom he lived in tally, opened the window and looked down on him. She expected blasts, roars, and curses, when after some delay she let him in, but it was with soft-stepping feet and humble mien that he crossed the threshold and nuzzled in under the yellow light.

'What a strange look you wear,' she cried nervously. 'Did the keeper shoot you up? I heard a roaring in the forest.'

'Becca,' he said, blinking forward, 'I have seen the Glory of the Lord.'

Had he seen the Emperor of Africa's tigers she would not have been surprised. Yet when she sniffed it was only the well-known odours of dung and tobacco and gunpowder that seeped from off him, and nothing of strong drink.

'It was in the wood,' he continued, 'when I tripped over a wire put down by Jenkins – and for that may I soon see his throat cut from shoulder to shoulder. My gun went off, both barrels, and you will see from a dozen holes in my hat-brim and as many in my coat-sleeves that I was as near as ninepence to croaking myself. Becca,' he said earnestly, 'do up your nightshirt across your neck, for my thoughts are turned to religion. When the barrels went off and I was still falling, I seemed to be falling into hell. What wasn't red was black, and the brimstone was full of my nostrils. I knew at that moment what it is to fear the Pit, and as I dodged and crawled and side-stepped home, lest I meet with Jenkins and be led to club him, I determined that if the Lord spared me till morning I would go to talk either with Pliny-Evans, at Capsant, or the hermit Sant-Owen, up at Monkhole. I split no wishbones over it, Becca, I have been vouchsafed a vision, and I am not the man to shut my eyes to my own advantage.'

'Lot,' replied Becca, her voice deep and trembling as she thought of Jenkins then hiding in the big black coffer upstairs, 'what are our bodies compared with our souls? Why wait for the morning? The sooner, the safer. Why not visit one of the reverends tonight?'

'Alas, Becca, who am I to make my affairs a mote in the Lord's left eye? Besides, it is after one o'clock and I am disposed to slumber. But get you back to bed, my dove. I have a mind to sleep tonight like a little child, humbly, among the dogs.'

'I had myself expected an undisturbed night,' Becca admitted, 'and will keep you no longer. Ah, that Jenkins,' she scolded, 'it's little sleep he'll get this night if wishes of mine count for anything!'

Lot's boots fell thumping into the hearth. 'You are a good girl, Becca, though something of a slut, and nothing is too good for you. And that I may be revenged on Jenkins, may all your wishes come true.'

'Amen to that!' cried Becca, and her two white feet, like two white frogs, went pap-pap-pap up the ladder staircase.

It was with no surprise that Gellius Sant-Owen, trundling his tunbelly from the door of Monkhole, saw mounting towards him the rat-brow and rabbit-shoulders of John Lot Padog. He had been awaiting a disciple since cockcrow, and could hardly brush the bubbles from his mouth as his caller opened his case to him. 'And thou hast come, brother, to the one man in this soon-to-be-damned parish of Supra Maelor who can set thy face to the hills. Praise the Lord!'

'Praise the Lord,' said John Lot Padog.

'As to thy sins, forget them. Too long hast thou been dandled in the Fiend's bosom, and no present wickedness corrupts so much as memory. Do henceforth as I do, and all will be well.'

Surveying the bull's bulk of his preceptor, Lot thought indeed it might.

'When thou gettest home, first despatch from thy side that bundle of love, that load of delight, thy concubine. For the future thou shalt know nothing of woman. Thy night lines thou shalt set behind the fire, and thy rod thou must splinter over thy knee. The musket thou shalt smash against a stone, and thy great salmon gaff thou shalt break in three pieces with a hammer I will lend thee. Give over strong drink and live in innocence on turnips and water, and then,' said Sant-Owen, cleaving his huge chaps with a grin of benevolence, 'thou wilt have begun to taste on earth those joys which are laid up for thee throughout eternity.'

'But, Reverend,' said Lot, 'it is surely good scripture that the limb which is not used withereth away, and nothing could be more incommoding to man than your counsel – or less considerate of woman. Besides, is it for any one of us to hide his talent? Are there not rabbits that prey on the fields, and pheasants that guzzle the good corn?'

'Dost bandy scripture with me, brother?' asked Sant-Owen, baring his broad brown tusks. 'Wouldst teach thy grandmother to suck eggs?'

'Eggs or no eggs,' cried Lot, 'are there no salmon to gaff, no trout to tickle, in heaven?'

'Not in my heaven, brother. Thou art thinking, I can see, of the inferior and watery heaven of the Baptists. Brother,' he wheedled, in a voice like a waterfall, 'is it better to believe or burn? Tell me that.'

'A good question, Reverend, but I am not without theology myself, and I shall now go to Capsant to consult Pliny-Evans as to a less desperate salvation.'

'Pliny-Evans!' shouted Sant-Owen, his belly bouncing off his knees; 'that lugworm, that seagull's dung, that tail of a tadpole! Wouldst trust thy soul to him? Bibulous adulterer – ah, rightly art thou called Lot.'

'You have the wrong end of the stick, Reverend. For when I was born, a thirteenth child, and my father said: "Let him be John", my mother said: "Yes, and let him be the lot", and so I am John Lot Padog. But I will split no wishbones here, and offer you good-day.'

'Ay, go thou to Pliny-Evans, that goose's rump, and if in a week the devil have thee not by the heels, then 'tis I and not thou that am damned.'

'Amen to that!' cried John Lot Padog, and his heron-legs and web-feet bore him swiftly down the hill.

If Gellius Sant-Owen had awaited a disciple since cock-crow, Pliny-Evans had kept watch since the badger cried under the hill. It was with rapture that he beheld the flap and shuffle of John Lot Padog towards him, with exultation that he heard his duck-lips question of sin and salvation.

'My son,' he replied, placing his finger-tips together along the ledges of his nose to form a small arch of holiness for his words to bow through, 'the mercy of God is infinite. Now your sins are not infinite, in that they are but too well measured and known. Therefore I do not doubt that your case comes well within the compass of the Almighty. But it will be necessary for you to do penance, if only to show some seriousness in the affair.'

Lot nodded warily. 'I ask only that the penance shall be such as my weakness can bear.' And he spoke of Sant-Owen.

'It is not for me,' said Pliny-Evans charitably, 'to speak ill of Sant-Owen. The Lord made him, no doubt for some purpose as yet unapparent. That he is mad, oaf-headed, and a stuff-guts, and has unsound ideas about the Book of Genesis, may therefore be ultimately intended for good. Perhaps he was sent into the world as a warning. However! I understand, son Lot, that you would not choose to live in blameless chastity?'

'I am thinking of Becca, Reverend, and how any neglect of mine might imperil her virtue. For my own part – '

'The point is well made. Your night lines then?'

'Is it not good scripture, Reverend, that Satan finds work for idle hands to do? It is not for me to teach you your own business, Reverend, but Sant-Owen could do as well as that.'

'The point has substance,' Pliny-Evans admitted hurriedly. He thought a while. 'Could you give up strong drink?'

'What a hard man you are grown to me, Reverend! I had really best return and make my peace at Monkhole. If I must be made a pig of, then why not go the whole hog with Sant-Owen?'

'Stop, stop,' cried Pliny-Evans, catching at Lot's jacket. 'Your case grows clear to me. Do you, my son, ever make use of water?'

'Water?' asked Lot reproachfully, 'what is this with you now? No man has a cleaner record against water than I.'

Pliny-Evans rattled his teeth for joy. 'Then you are already by way of obtaining your robe in heaven. Your penance is never to drink water. Be strong, be resolute, have great faith, and all will be well.'

'Reverend,' said Lot with humility, 'what a thing is true religion!' But his eyelids drooped to behold the new nervousness of Pliny-Evans. 'True religion,' he repeated, 'without a catch in it.'

'Praise the Lord,' said Pliny-Evans absently. 'You have,' he remarked, 'a firearm or arquebus?'

'You mean a blunderbuss. No, but I have my shot-gun.' Lot slid his eyes round the steeps and declivities of his interlocutor's face. 'Why?'

'And you know an apple tree in the heart of the wood?'

'I did my courting there. But why?'

'Listen!' Hand to brow, Pliny-Evans scanned the yard, the hill, the forest, and the sky. 'I will tell you.'

He did, and the red fox-hair of Padog stood straight up on his head.

Exactly a week later a round black object descended the hill that stood to the east of Supra Maelor. It felt the strong pulls of wrath and gravity, and it proceeded by such headlong rushes and temporary arrests as mark the progress of a barrel down a stumpy bank. Now it rolled smoothly forward, now it fetched up against a tree or a turn in the path, then again it bounded onwards, momentarily a missile in space. A panting and a rumbling surrounded it at every stage. As it drew nearer to the waiting Becca, who had been gleaning eggs from the out-layers of the parish farms, it was revealed first as a fat rock falling, then as a solid balloon, and at last as the swagged jelly-body of Gellius Sant-Owen. The hermit of Monkhole was on his way to celebrate the damnation of John Lot Padog.

'Woman,' he demanded, confronting Becca like a vision of four Deadly Sins, 'what news of Padog the poacher? Has he been gathered to hell in a flame, or was he a lollipop betwixt the teeth of Beelzebub?'

'Reverend,' said Becca, 'I never knew him better in all his life. Religion has made a new man of him. All he does now is smoke and drink and clear his traps and wait on the Glory to be.'

Then am I damned? thought Sant-Owen. Did I speak a true word? And is that heat in my feet? 'Woman – Becca,' he began again, and knew with alarm that his eyes were staring at the pale skin which peeped through a rent in her skirt. Surely, he thought, I must be damned. My thoughts confirm me. And if damned, I must be wicked. And to be wicked is not to be good. How right the scholiasts were! Perhaps I have been good too long, and therefore wicked not long enough. Yes, he thought, looking on the comeliness of Becca, my heart inclines to sin. I long to taste a new kind of apple. But how does one proceed in these matters? Alas, my mis-spent seven years!

'This is a stealthy place, Becca,' he said, staring around him.

'But for my eggs,' she agreed, 'we are alone.'

'Eggs or no eggs, it is most stealthy. I fear for thee here alone. I fear for thy pearl without price.'

'If I understand you aright, Reverend, I have a pearl indeed, but,' and she rubbed her forefinger and thumb together, 'it is not without price.'

'Why, Becca,' said Sant-Owen, plucking his chins, 'as well ask a cow for fish-hooks as a holy man for money. But I am troubled nonetheless to think of thy loss should any in such a place as this think to take thy pearl with force.'

'I thank God, Reverend, that I was never so obdurate as to be taken with force. That would show great pride in a poor country girl like me. Come now,' said Becca, setting down her eggs, 'what must be, must; and the holier the man the holier the deed. I have always set virtue higher than profit, and I believe my present charity will be no small help to me when, all the world behind and done with, I rap my small white knuckles on St Peter's gate.'

'St Peter?' asked Sant-Owen. 'Dost tell me, Becca, that thou believest that papistical nonsense about Peter and his keys? Why,' he shouted, 'let me be damned, if such is my fate – and if the poacher Padog breathes still on earth, then damned I no doubt am – but let my damnation be an unheretical one. Oh Fool, Thief, Slut, Madwoman that thou art, thou hast dulled the edge of my resolution! Oh Curses! Devils! Brimstone!'

'Slut I am, and Fool I may be, but I am no madwoman. But should you change your mind,' called Becca, for Sant-Owen was now bundling himself back up the pathway to Monkhole, 'should you change your mind, I say, come to the big apple tree in the wood of Supra Maelor tonight, and maybe there we can swop our scruples. For even the best of men,' she concluded, gathering up her eggs, 'may see clearer by moonlight than in the gaudy eye of the sun.'

Five threads of sound tied the corners of Supra Maelor to the gaunt and clustered apple tree which marked the forest centre. From the north, with Assyrian assurance, came the gaitered legs and velveteen waistcoat of Jenkins the keeper. Under him the sward was almost silent: it knew its master; it sighed subvervience, more it dared not. From the west came the gangling shanks of Manmoel Pliny-Evans. He walked with great stealth, setting his foot at every stride on the small dry branches of the glades. 'Sh-sh-sh!' he would caution, as they snapped and crackled. From the east came Sant-Owen, bearing his belly before him and rolling like a castor-fitted octagon along the groaning pathways. All the way he was licking his lips and rubbing his hands, for he was minded to gather both an apple and a pearl. From the south came first the gleaming legs and luminous shoulders of Becca, her feet brisk as titmice among the moss and last year's pine cones; and far behind her the goose-necked shadow of John Lot Padog slid gun-laden along private trails.

The keeper and Becca stepped boldly out from the Venetian-blind shadows of the thickets into the white pool of moonlight that ringed the apple tree. 'Who's there?' said either. Said both: 'It's me.'

To Jenkins, a vain poetic sort of man, it was in no way surprising to find Becca in the wood. How better could she be employed than in looking for her Jenkins? To Becca the case was less simple. There was Sant-Owen for one, and John Lot for another, but 'Just wait till I place a few trip-wires to the south of us,' Jenkins was cooing, 'and then what joy, my little tomtit! Ah, Becca,' he continued fondly, 'what a treasure you are, and how cleverly you hoodwink the unspeakable Padog. Were I not already married, I should infallibly make you my wife. Remove that dress, dear Becca, which but hides your beauties from the moon, and be my Eve in this Garden of Eden. My chaffinch! My water-wagtail!'

'Chaffinch I may be, but wagtail I am not,' said Becca merrily. 'But when you talk poetry, how can a simple country girl resist you?'

Oh Death! breathed Sant-Owen, Oh Smell of Hell! Shall I see this and live? Trollop! Jezebel! Monster of Women! Was it for this thou broughtest me here? O impolite usage of my favourite tree! I feel the torments of the damned, my mouth is dry, my throat is parched. But if I cannot have a pearl, none shall deny me my apple. Surely while they are so busied – . He edged his way nearer.

From the other side Pliny-Evans saw Eve tasting of the Tree of Knowledge. He groaned like the groaning of great branches, for he knew the whole race of men condemned again to sin and pain and sorrow. John Lot, he muttered, John Lot, surely like your namesake's wife you have looked behind you this night and turned into a pillar of salt! Where are you, my marksman of fire? For here is your bull's-eye. He stepped towards the apple tree.

John Lot Padog, arrived by devious ways, saw a concourse of demons in the moonshine. I always knew that Jenkins was the devil, he thought gloatingly. I will now shoot him in five important places, cut his throat next, and hang his pelt up as a warning to all devil-kind. He saw the pale lubricious gleam of Mother Eve, and from either side stepped a spirit of evil, one short and round like Baal, the other tall and lean as Mephistopheles. It was no time for half-measures. He rushed forward for a nearer aim, tripped on the keeper's wire, and discharged both barrels of his shot-gun.

A great black double-clap of thunder tore itself from the heart of flame in the demon-haunted woods of Supra Maelor. From its fiery centre it spread and bellowed: its echo rapped from the mountains and rolled under the sky, and with it was mingled a wailing and lamentation. Then as the tumult swooned away, there might be heard the noises of flight from north, south, east, and west. To the north a man in gaiters ran cursing and hecking, his breeches filled with pellets; to the south a white wraith, dress in hand, flitted into the shades. Eastwards crashed a man whose breadth from deltoid to deltoid was as his length from occiput to knee-ball, and whose hand clutched a small green apple. Westwards hobbled a tall and gangling solitary whose face in the moonlight was as an upturned china basin.

' – !' said the man who remained.

Slowly he scraped earth from his eyes and blew grass from his nostrils. He gouged leaves from his ears and spat rotten wood from his mouth. He felt wet green moss under his fingers, and heard the bubble of a wood-fountain. For the first time in years he craved for water.

'Damnation be damned!' cried John Lot Padog.

He drank.

Guto Fewel

~

THREE men and a woman were sitting in the black-raftered kitchen of Pen-rhiw-gwynt, which in English is Top of the Windy Ridge. As they sat, they discussed in low voices the life and misdeeds of Guto Fewel, who lay dying in the next room. The woman, a hard-faced woman, was his sister; the fattish man nearest the fire was her husband, who farmed the wind-scraped acres of the Rhiw. Their name was Mardith. The second man wore a minister's collar and had kept his overcoat on indoors; the third, a wizened creature at once abashed and ingratiating, sat with his cap on his knee. The minister was in his late twenties; the others had little rent to draw from three-score and five.

'I just been in to him,' said the woman, her lips thin and blue. 'It's good of Miss Mabli to sit with him, I must say. Well, it can't be long now.'

The minister's throat and mouth moved with something between a cough and a benediction. 'It has been a great burden – a great burden.'

'None can say we haven't done our share,' said Mardith. He looked round the fire-masked faces for approval. 'I reckon we done our duty by him. There's some as wouldn't have.'

The wizened man with the cap squirmed on his chair. 'He got a good friend in you, Mr Mardith. I reckon you acted like a Christian all right.'

'There's many as wouldn't have,' said Mardith again. His heavy face soaked in their praises. 'I always been a God-fearing man, and be what he may, he's my wife's kin. I don't hold with him, I never did hold with him, but I know my duty as one Christian to another.'

'You have both been very kind,' said the minister. 'Is it – would it be three months now?'

'Come next Wednesday,' said the woman. 'We hadn't seen him to talk to for nigh on thirty years. You know how it was – ' Her husband gestured with his arm, and the firelight flung the shadow of it against the wall behind him. 'All them goings on! We every one of us finished with him. We had to, him being the kind he was. And then three months come next Wednesday, what was to happen? I went out after tea to the milking, and there he was, hanging on the door-frame. I never said a word. But I knew him for all he was altered.' She shook her lean head. 'His sins had come home to roost all right. I never seen a man so changed. And I'd heard too – I'd heard he was changed these years it would be – yet I never expected – '

'He got a friend in you all right, Mrs Mardith,' said the wizened man.

'She come back in,' said Mardith, 'as if she seen a ghost. "It's my brother," she said. "It's Guto." "Then he don't come over no threshold of mine," I told her. "Didn't I tell him, haven't I told him," I said, "that if ever I see him on my land again I'll set the dogs on him?" That was after that affair with the girl over in the Nant – you've heard of that, Mr Gideon? – she went in the river for him, right enough.'

'A dreadful affair, dreadful!' murmured the minister.

'Ah,' said the wizened man, 'he was always one after the women. Glands, I reckon. Even when he was a kid – '

'So that's what I told her,' said Mardith. ' "Don't bring no Guto of yours in here," those were my words. "I know," she said, "I know, but he's fallen on the floor outside. I'd hardly a-known him." "No more you'd expect to," I took her up. "A man that gives his life over to women and the drink. And I'll tell you another thing, my girl – it's a poor chance he stands to be known by One who is more important than you or me by long chalks." That's what I told her, Mr Gideon.'

'No doubt, he had his points,' said the wizened man. 'There's good in the worst of us, eh, Mr Gideon?'

'What happened then?' asked the minister. 'You brought him in?'

'I known life in my time, and I known death,' said Mardith. 'And I reckon I know my duty. But if ever I seen an old ram ready for the draft! "Well," I said, when I see him, "if I know my two-times-two, I know something here too. And I'll tell you what it is, my girl – he's as good as a goner. And the miracle to me is that he's lasted so long. So there is it," I told her, "and you may as well face it. It's up to you," I said. "He's your brother, and I'll do what you say. For I wouldn't like it to be said as any of our lot, not the worst of them, died in the poor-house, and if you want to, and on one condition only, he can have his time out here."'

'On one condition?' prompted the wizened man, though he had heard the story a dozen times already.

'I'm a farmer, Mr Gideon. No la-di-da about me, but I make it pay. I don't give stable room to greasy-heeled horses, and there's no place in pen of mine for a maggoty wether. "So long," I said – and you understand me, Mr Gideon – "so long as he *got nothing*, he can have my Christian duty."'

'Ah,' nodded the wizened man, 'gallivantin' and all that.'

'He's my brother,' said the woman, 'but the truth's the truth. We all finished with him. At least, Dad finished with him, leathered him out of the house twice before the last time; and my sister Meri she finished with him; and Mardith and me we finished with him too. And if Mam had been alive, she'd have had to finish. But she went on before it grew too bad, and she was spared that much, thank God.'

The young minister drew a hand down his troubled face. 'It's a sad story. It is difficult to judge. If it is our business to judge. We may well leave it to the Tribunal before which he must soon appear.'

'Funny though,' said the wizened man, 'I never knew him mean.'

'You didn't now?' asked Mardith, with ox-like irony. 'I wonder what you call mean? P'raps they done wrong to put him in gaol that time? And p'raps he wasn't mean to that poor girl over in the Nant?'

'I was only thinking – '

'Some,' said Mrs Mardith through her thin lips, 'ought to think twice before they say too much.'

The minister watched the fingers twist in the cap. 'I think perhaps – ' he interrupted. 'How old is your brother, Mrs Mardith?'

'He was the youngest of us. I was working it out the other day. There was me the oldest, then Llew who went to America, then Meri, and Guto came the last. It's a terrible thing to say of your own flesh and blood, but I often heard my poor Dad vowing it would be better if he'd never been born.' She began to ramble from the question. 'He come of a good home, and good stock even if I say it, but something got in him, I don't know what.'

'The Gadarene swine like,' said the wizened man. 'When they rushed down-hill there he was, waiting at the bottom.' He wriggled further into the firelight for the minister's approval.

The minister glanced anxiously towards the door into the passage and the next room. 'I don't think we ought – '

'Ah, it's all right, never you worry, Mr Gideon,' Mardith assured him. 'He can't hear, and if he did he wouldn't understand. He's just lying there, past everything. We don't have to bother. If there was any change, Miss Mabli would come out and tell us.'

'That's a good woman for you,' said the wizened man. 'That's a Christian if you like, minister.' He sat forward, squeezing his cap in exultation at the goodness of Miss Mabli, but as he encountered Mrs Mardith's eye sat back again.

'She knows her duty all right,' admitted Mardith. 'And that's the sort of people I appreciate, Mr Gideon. If we all done our duty always, the world would be a better place. That's what I told my wife that night. "If he's dying," I said, "it's different. We have a duty by him, be what he may. And on one condition – "'

'Yes, yes,' said the minister, and got to his feet. 'I am afraid, Mrs Mardith, I must be going now.' His swollen shadow billowed up the wall and on to the ceiling. 'There is nothing I can do for your brother save pray for him.' They all stood as he closed his eyes and muttered more to himself than to them. 'And I have other calls. If I can be of service later – '

'You shall have the burying of him, never fear,' said Mardith. The minister flushed, catching up his hat from the table. 'We'll see him into Christian ground all right. I don't begrudge him.'

'Though there's many would,' said the wizened man. 'There was good in him, no doubt, and bad. Only the tares strangled the wheat, that's about the size of it.'

'You talk too much,' said Mrs Mardith loudly. 'We haven't lost our memories, thank you.' The wizened man screwed himself downwards to his chair, nodding sheepish good-nights after the departing minister. As Mardith sank the latch home, his wife took a yellow-edged cloth from the dresser drawer and shook it out over the table. 'He's a good man,' she said, 'but I thought he'd never go. It hampers a woman, and me with him in there hanging on as helpless as a child. If he was married he'd have more sense.'

'He means well,' said Mardith. He tapped his forehead. 'We can't all have it up here. And he's got a lot to learn. I suppose,' he continued sideways, winking at his wife, 'you won't be leaving before you take a bit of supper?'

The wizened man grinned between brazenness and shame. 'If it wouldn't be too much trouble, Mrs Mardith – just a cup and a bite, p'raps.' He hastened to ingratiate himself. 'Now that Miss Mabli – any minister could learn a thing or two from her.' An indefinable but exciting edge came to his voice. 'You wouldn't think a woman like her would give the black of her nail to a feller like Guto. Her being so good, and him so bad.' He sighed. 'Not that any of us are perfect.'

The Mardiths looked one at the other. The wizened man was a famed repository of gossip: it was only right that he should earn his meal.

'No,' said Mardith, sitting to table, 'it wouldn't do for any of us mortals to claim to be perfect. There's an Eye that sees too much of us. Still,' he added invitingly, 'I reckon if there's ever been a middling perfect one around here, Miss Mabli might well be her. Eh?'

'I wouldn't want to hear nothing against her,' said Mrs Mardith thinly. 'Nothing as wasn't true, that is.'

'I'd be the last to try a thing like that,' said the wizened man. He speared a pickled onion. 'But it's funny!'

'What's funny?' asked Mardith. 'Come on now, don't talk in riddles or we'll be thinking you got something to say against Miss Mabli. Here, have some cheese.'

'Ah,' said the wizened man, 'it's nothing.' Mrs Mardith licked her lips, turning up the lamp. 'And it's so long ago. I don't know as I can rightly remember.'

'Not about Guto, is it?' asked Mrs Mardith. She quietly closed the passage door. 'We don't want everybody knowing our business. Not even Miss Mabli. It wouldn't be our Guto, would it – and her?'

'No, no, fair play now,' cried the wizened man. 'But that's the worst of a smelly name – it draws the flies right enough. But there was never nothing like that – you can take your oath in heaven on it. No, it was just something I happened to notice once' – he let them wait on his words – 'in Trisant.'

'Hm, down in the village?' Mardith pushed the butter-dish across the table. 'Go on, man, help yourself. We don't begrudge a man his vittles. In Trisant, eh?'

'But this'll surprise you,' said the wizened man. 'It was forty-six-seven years ago, I reckon, after fair-day. She's a fine woman to-day for her age. She's always been a fine woman – '

'If you like that style of woman,' said Mrs Mardith, her eye like acid on her husband's face.

'She's big, there's no denying it,' said Mardith slowly. 'Heavy like.' He laughed uneasily, pillowing out his hands. 'I never liked them Flanders mares myself.'

'That's enough of that!' snapped Mrs Mardith. 'That's no talk for a decent table.' But she was smiling as she turned to the wizened man. 'In Trisant, eh – after fair-day? I wouldn't want to hear no lies, remember.'

'If I tell a lie, Mrs Mardith, may this mouthful choke me.' He swallowed, grinning. 'Remember young Richard Lewis of Steddfa? The one that left for the big job in England? It was the day after that fair in Trisant he went. He was a handsome young feller, there's no denying, and she was a handsome piece, ah, my word she was! I never – no offence, Mrs Mardith – minded them big myself. It's different for Mr Mardith, I can see.' He sniggered. 'Well, to cut a long story short, it was about nine that evening I had a reason to go round the back of the "White Lion", and as a young lump of a feller will, if there's a light in a window and a crack in the curtain, he'll be sure to look in – and so I did. Now this is something I wouldn't tell to nobody else, and I know it'll go no further than this table.' The Mardiths nodded. 'Who d'you reckon was in that room? Yes, you got it, I can see: young Lewis and Jane Mabli. Whether it's right for me to say any more before Mrs Mardith here, that's a question.'

'I'm a married woman, ain't I?' said Mrs Mardith. 'I wasn't born yesterday. Don't you worry about me.' Her tea was growing cold, and she had forgotten to put milk in it. 'So long as it's the truth. Were they – eh?'

'Not exactly,' said the wizened man. 'But very near to it. Nearer than Christians ought to who haven't been before the parson, if you take me, Mrs Mardith.' He sucked in his lips, savouring their attention. 'I reckon that kind of thing's just putting yourself in the Devil's hand, and you can't wonder if the fingers close in on you. But I'll say this for her: she wasn't having any when he started to try his damnedest. She was as tall as him and strong as a horse. I never,' he said cunningly, 'seen a woman with such fine shoulders on her.' More cunningly still, he fell silent.

'What happened then?' asked Mardith. 'Wasn't he able to – '

'No,' said the wizened man regretfully, 'she was too strong for him, I reckon, and in a blazing temper at the end. The fur flew and away she went. But it was a fight all right, and if he'd looked like winning I don't rightly know what I ought to have done.'

'You got to keep out of things like that,' said Mardith. 'Otherwise you grow like Guto there. It's bad though, that sort of goings-on. I wish I'd been there!' But he felt the cut of his wife's glance. 'I mean, to give him the belting he wanted. Young swine!'

'It's never mostly the man's fault,' said Mrs Mardith angrily. 'She must have known what she was doing. I've often wondered about her, and all the place singing her praises. I want to sift this proper. Tell me,' she ordered, 'when you looked in – what did you mean about her shoulders?'

'A cupper tea's a lovely thing,' said the wizened man, reaching forward. 'Ah, thank you, thank you! I'll start at the beginning. As I was saying – '

In the downstairs back room of Pen-rhiw-gwynt, Guto Fewel was lying straight and silent down the middle of the third-best bed. He lay on his back, his uncut hair and pale-whiskered face against a high pillow. The sheet had been turned down under his chin, and the bedclothes went with hardly a wrinkle from there to the foot of the bed. His mouth hung a little open, and from time to time he made a gasping contraction of the throat. He was in the early fifties, but was dying of exhaustion and old age. The creased blue lids had fallen over his eyes, and he lacked strength to lift them again.

He knew that he was dying. He knew too that he had no wish to live. He knew this in periods of suffused recollection welling like moonlight through the surrounding dark. He judged he was nearer death because the nightmares had ended. Or were they memories? In either case, they were terrible.

It seemed to him that he was speaking aloud and audible to all creation. There was an audience, unseen, unknown, to whom he was for ever recounting the story of his life. But he could not get past his first sentences, for these were so important he must repeat them again and again so that never a hearer but would understand. 'I have never been a child,' the voice was saying. 'They thought me a child like the rest, but I was born an old man. Why didn't they hide things from me? I saw everything. God, oh God in heaven, I saw everything! "He's only a child," they would say. "He won't notice – he won't understand." But I have never been a child. They thought me a child like the rest, but I was born an old man!' Surely he was not speaking now: he must be crying, shouting, babbling along the rivers and the hill-sides, his voice a vast compelling instrument of sorrow sounding his woes throughout the earth and the firmament. 'I have never been a child. Why didn't they hide from me their horrors and their lusts? Great in heaven – for I was born an old man!'

The woman watching from her chair at the bed-end saw his mouth and heard him gasp and swallow. She was a tall and powerful woman crumbling in age, the hair gone thin and white, the shoulders grown round, the heavy bosom fallen. I wonder, she thought, I wonder! He is dying an old man, and he twelve years younger than me, and his name a by-word over the countryside. 'Listen,' she said suddenly, urgently. 'Do you hear me?' But he made no stir, the lids hung crinkled and worn over the unseeing eyes. She sat straight up on her chair, her thoughts moving through nearly fifty years to the fair-day in Trisant when she last saw Richard Lewis and first saw Guto Fewel. The firm-set puritan mouth set harder. What madness had possessed her? 'I was on the edge of the Pit,' she whispered, and the Pit for her was real and seen, like a crack in the mountain-side, from which her feet drew frightenedly back. By the mercy of God it lasted but an evening. No one knew, she had come to tell herself; no harm was done, she had come to hope. A lifetime of good works, with little of her own happiness: she could think back to it without complacency, and if her conscience still charged her with a great fault, she had made no small atonement. But her face grew sterner yet, and self-accusing, as she watched the movements of Guto's throat. If only she might know!

Guto could hear his voice booming between earth and heaven. Each sentence he uttered filled centuries of time. The unseen listeners waited on new words to come. But the words would not come; always the revolution of his thoughts flung him back on those same tremendous sentences. An unendurable anxiety pierced him, to think that they might not hear the thing he had to say. Miss Mabli saw sweat wet his forehead, the eyelids twitched, there was a tremor in the bedclothes from his arms. She moved round the bed to wipe his face, and at that moment he opened his eyes.

How clear and sweet the evening was! He was almost light-headed as they went to fetch the pony and trap from the stable behind Trisant Cross. Oh so happy, he thought, so happy; closing his eyes as he hung on his mother's arm. The painted stallions galloped out of blackness into the yellow light, rose and sank on thick golden rods, their nostrils blew out blood and steam, and oily manes swung on their swelling necks. Flowers of tawny flame roared and trembled from the flare boxes, saturating the night with sweet and greasy perfumes; the air was a blare of red-and-white music. And there had been black-eyed, black-haired girls with long silver ear-rings coaxing wary young labourers to the rifle-range and cockshies; the swing-boats were rushing skywards with their screaming crews; on the edge of darkness a lion grumbled in his deep African throat. And when at last they left the smell and the glare of it, there was the magic street along which they walked past kings and princes and the executioners of the East. 'Happy?' he heard his mother ask, and rubbed his face along her camphored sleeve. Coming into the lamplit stable he stumbled and yawned and the smell of clean horses and polished leather washed his nose and mouth. Importantly he held on to a shaft while his father backed the pony in; he tightened a strap or two but his father went over these after him. They were ready to start when Miss Mabli came round from the Cross and asked whether they could take her home their way. He couldn't take his eyes from her face. He had never known a woman could be so tall and noble and worshipful. Her parents, she said, would grow anxious if she were not home soon, and after some politeness it was agreed that she and Guto should share the back of the loaded trap, and the others be in front. There was only the one seat and Guto must sit on the floor-boards. As she settled herself near him, her shirts brushed his face, warm, sweet-scented, and soft as doom.

Most of their way lay down the vally, and the pony settled briskly to his load. It had grown dark, there were stars but the moon was down; their lamps threw a weak brown light ahead of them. On the close-metalled winding road the pony's hoofs tapped out a gentle clop-clip, clip-clop. The hedgerows were a moving blur, but the tops of the tree-less hills showed hard against the faintly-twinkling sky. The night hazed, grew dreamlike, his head nodded with the trap, soon he was leaning heavily against Miss Mabli, with his right arm thrown across her lap. It was then it started. He began to shiver with an excitement he dreaded but could not control, a shivering as much of his frightened soul as his body. He felt Miss Mabli stiffen and hold her breath unnaturally long. 'Push me away,' he wanted to pray, 'oh, push me away!' But: 'Are you cold?' she whispered and put her hand to his head and pressed it hard to her thigh. And then he felt the same soft shiverings in her. 'He's only a child,' the great voice intoned; 'he won't know – he won't understand.' But how terribly he knew the use to which he was being put, the fury of the appetite he must now satisfy. Why didn't they hide such things from me? The horrors and the lusts they made me see! Why could I not be a child like the rest?

He heard himself groan with ecstasy and grief. It was safe now to groan. But then, that night, all that happened happened in the unnatural silence of guilt, reaching up from the trap-floor to the stars. He was drowning in the memory of it, the warm musky smell of the night and the lavender of her petticoats, the feel of the soft flannel and the softer flesh. And through the silence that guarded them from his parents he heard still the crunch of the wheels on a gravelly corner, the hoof-clops of the horse, the pantings of her breath.

'Listen,' said Miss Mabli. 'Can you hear me?'

All my life, he was crying aloud, all my life it was so. What could I do? I had seen, I knew too much. And at that age, at that moment, I lay as in the embraces of Eve. God, he shouted, oh God, have pity on me! I have never been a child. They thought me a child, but I was born an old man.

He was back in the trap. The woman, watching, saw the pillow darkening with sweat, the death-rattle had begun in his throat. I should call the others, she thought; but she did not move. His eyes opened again, but she could read nothing into them. 'Can you hear me?' she asked again, in a whisper.

The wheels were whining over the hard roadway, the hedgerows fled into the dark. Below them the earth, above them the heavens, streamed backwards to the void. He felt himself and Miss Mabli caught up in the rhythm that rolled the planets and swung the tides. This is death, he thought, and longed for it. Her limbs opened for him, he was floundering in seas of bliss and pain. I was born an old man, he mumbled, and I die as a child. Oh God, have pity! Give me rest and the dark.

And then he was falling into untellable depths, and the dark was all about him.

Miss Mabli came out into the kitchen. Their shadowed faces turned up at her, curious, furtive, hostile. 'He is dead,' she said harshly. 'I shall never forgive myself.'

'Don't you worry,' said Mardith, but his wife's face was snaky with pleasure and malice. 'We all make mistakes at times,' she said. 'All of us, Miss Mabli.'

'I was sitting there,' said Miss Mabli, 'and then it had happened. I should have been more careful.' She's grown an older woman, thought the wizened man. 'I am much to blame.'

'Times when we all ought to be more careful,' said Mrs Mardith. 'Even the so-called best of us.'

'They say Death pays for all,' said the wizened man, mocking all three of them.

'Only some,' pursued Mrs Mardith, 'gets away with it better than others.'

'No one can say we didn't do our duty by him,' said Mardith. 'But it's out of our hands now.' His glances slimed her. 'Life,' he speculated, 'is a very funny thing.'

Miss Mabli moved heavily to the door. Her face was working. 'I shall never forgive myself,' she said again, brokenly. And with that she was gone from among them.

The men nodding, the woman smiling, the three who remained went into the back room, and Mardith took a clean white scarf from where it lay against the big Bible. 'The Lord's been kind,' he told them, tying up the dead man's jaws. 'It's a good riddance, I reckon. I seen many an old tup look just like him.' For once he over-rode his wife. 'He's a goner, ain't he? He can't hear, and if he did,' he added, knotting the scarf, 'he couldn't answer back.'

'Now what makes some good?' asked the wizened man, smarming the Mardiths. He looked at Guto Fewel. 'And what makes some bad?'

'He was bad from the start,' said Mrs Mardith. 'He never was a child like you and me. And he's died an old, old man.'

'Old he might be, and wicked he was,' said her husband. He took up the night-light, motioning them out before him. 'But he can't be needing this any more.' And nipping the still flame, and leaving Guto Fewel in silence and the dark, they returned with relish to their talk in the firelit, shadow-filled kitchen.

Goronwy's House of Gold

~

One hot morning in May Goronwy Morgan was lying in a field between the sea and the Cardigan Road. As he lay, he counted his blessings and found them but few. For forty years he had pursued wisdom in the two-roomed school which serves the black farmsteads and pink cottages about Rhydfelyn; he had escaped that penury which grinds down loving-kindness; had cheated no man and wronged no woman. But with it all he was unhappy. In all the days of his life he had washed his own head, and the pillow showed ever one dent of a morning. And now even the inks and the chalk and the slippery black-board were behind him. The life that is lonely is assuredly empty; the life that is empty is not worth the living. So thinking, he took his nose out of the grass, knelt up and looked about him. To the north lay Dyfi, and Cader floating like a whale, and the long finger of Lleyn hooking at the tide; eastward were the soft rosy lumps of Plynlymon; he looked south to golden hill-slopes and barren creamy beaches; he looked west and saw his own shape drowning in the sea.

'And some there be,' he heard the preacher drone, 'which have no memorial; who are perished as though they have never been; and are become as though they had never been born.' For all the glow and swoon of the morning, he shivered and found his forehead dry. With a sigh which was half-way to a groan, he rose hurriedly to his feet, outstared the winking diamonds of the in-shore water, and turned his face sadly towards his home on the fronting hill of Goleufryn.

From grassy base to rock summit the hill was braceletted with walls of dark-green stone on which the yellow lichen grew. These walls were cunningly set about triangular patches of grazing land, but these had long since been given over to rabbits and crows, or to such sheep and goats as wandered there from unhasped gates or mildewed fences and were collected towards nightfall by whooping lads from the Rhydfelyn farms. Year after year the gorse had rooted lower, hawthorn and nettle and fat offshoots of bramble thrust to meet it. It seemed to Goronwy that his house would soon be but a stone in the wilderness. Time was when it shone like a ball of gold. It needs life, he thought, which I am too old and too dull to give it. At that moment he saw a stoat cross his path, a half-grown rabbit hanging from its jaws. The weight of its prey and the dangling legs forced it to hold its head high, so that it moved with great insolence and pride. 'Aye,' said Goronwy sombrely, 'such is the world,' and he looked neither right nor left till he passed through the gap in the wall which brought him level with his house.

It was built of such stone as braceletted the hill, but the bulging walls had been washed with ochre, and the black slate slabs of the window-sills carried boxes of drooping valerian and mignonette. The lintels had been cemented and then stuck about with silvery cockle-shells. A thin brown steam of mountain water slid away to the right, and to the left in the rear a cow-byre and hayloft stood unused but clean. Once I judged it snug and joyful, thought Goronwy, but now it is void and vast. What am I to do? Oh, what am I to do?

It is my loneliness, he thought indoors, which is so unnatural. How wise was he who said, The solitary man must be god or devil! That I am no god, how well I know, nor shall I ever become one. That I am no devil, I hope; but I have no guarantee for the future. Why, I have not even a cat. And he told himself afresh the story of that holy man of old who knew no companions but a cock and a housefly. The cock would wake him at the first light of dawn, and when he read in the Bible the fly would move like a directing finger from word to word of it, so that he never lost his place.

It should not be hard, thought Goronwy wistfully, to get oneself a housefly.

At least, he thought, snatching at hope, this is a vast orange of a world, with no small variety of creatures crawling on its rind. Maybe if I look abroad, I shall find one desirous of my company. I shall not look too high – a human is as much above my port as an archangel would be – and I want nothing to do with stoats and all such masters of barratry. 'But,' said he, thinking aloud, 'I shall now collect such food as is in the house, pocket the thirty-one pounds and sixpence which is hidden under the hearthstone, and set out on my quest. Nor shall I return until I find some humble creature to share my teacher's pension with me.'

As he made this resolution, misery and heartburning left him, and before the sun clanged noon he was tramping south on the Cardigan Road. It was perhaps an hour later that he saw three boys squatting round a stick fire where the plank bridge crosses the Rhigos stream. He was curious to know why they should endure both heat and stifling, and stepped aside to talk to them. One held a captive thrush in his hands, and the other two were heating needles in the fire.

'Boys,' said Goronwy, 'what are you doing with the little thrush?'

'It has been silent since we caught it,' they complained, 'and we are going to prick its eyes with red-hot needles, to make it sing.'

'Do no such thing,' he cried. 'Set the thrush free!'

'We will set it free if it doesn't sing when we have blinded it,' they promised.

'Free it at once, or I will make you!'

'Not you,' they answered. 'For it is ours, and we may do with it as we please. Besides,' added the oldest among them 'we know you. You are the old schoolmaster of Rhydfelen, and all the world calls you nuts.'

'Nuts? What have nuts to do with it? Free the bird!'

But the boys ran a short way from him and brought the needles near the eyes of the thrush. How he strained and he struggled, and opened wide his beak. 'Stop, stop,' shouted Goronwy, 'and I will buy the bird from you.' For he knew that those most deaf to mercy have no flaps on their ears when there is talk of profit.

'Money has a loud voice,' said the boys. 'We ask threepence – '

'Agreed, agreed!'

' – An eye.'

'Agreed, agreed! Here is the money, and give me the bird.'

The boys laughed. 'From all we hear, the world's been giving you that this many a year. Besides,' whispered the oldest, 'when we get the money we will run away and blind the thrush just the same. Give me,' said each of the three, 'the money.'

'Me,' snapped the oldest, 'because I hold the thrush.'

'Me,' leered the middle one, 'because I stole the needles to prick out its eyes.'

'Me,' screamed the youngest. 'It was I stole the matches to light the fire.'

But Goronwy spun the sixpence to fall midway between them, and the thrush flew to the open from the grasping hand. He heard the three heads crash together, saw the fists thrash and flail, heard the squealing and squalling, and thought it a pity the thrush had not stayed to hear it too. For a moment he had wondered whether the thrush was the one to share his house with him, but he reproved himself for the selfish thought. He drank of the Rhigos stream, broke bread from the loaf in his pocket, and went back to the high road. Behind him the noise of greed and fury died with the distance.

'But nuts?' asked Goronwy. 'Surely a very foolish as well as a very wicked boy, that.'

It was late into the afternoon when he came to the wooded lands of Argoed, where a thousand laburnums spread their leaves under the sun and dripped liquid light from the yellow chandeliers of their blossoms. He turned from the road into cwms and clearings where a breeze moved the bluebells like the waters of an inland sea, and was sitting at last to rest against a broad smooth bole, when he saw a man come into the glade ahead of him, followed by a thin-faced brindled bitch. The man carried a rope, and Goronwy observed with interest and then with horror what he proceeded to do with it. For he selected a strong bough standing out square from the tree at a height of six feet from the ground, and threw the rope over it. Then he made a running noose at its one end. This done, he called to the bitch, which advanced unwillingly and with ingratiating quivers of her tail, and set the noose about her neck. He was about to pull her up over the bough when Goronwy shouted and ran forward.

He had the uncordial face of a herring-gull, and wore a dark-green celluloid patch over his left eye. 'And who are you?' he asked slacking the rope.

'I am no one and nothing,' panted Goronwy. 'But why, oh why, should you hang this little dog?'

'Because she is mine, and because I choose to, and because rightly is she called bitch.'

'But has she done wrong?' asked Goronwy, and patted the sad head.

'No,' swore Greenpatch, and kicked her in the ribs, 'she lacks spirit for that. I am sick of the miserable looks of her. God knows I have beaten her enough in the attempt to make her spry. But my patience is now ended, and I'll waste no more of my time and strength on her than it takes to swing her up on this branch.' And he slid the rope through his hands.

But Goronwy caught at the slack of it. 'I can see how you have beaten her – her poor sides, her hanging head, the scar under her eye. Ah, little bitch,' he said, 'and would a creature like you choose to live, if life might be? Or shall I do wrong to spare you for more pain and grief?' The bitch looked up, her clotted eyes dilating with hope. 'Then live you shall, and henceforth have no fear.'

'You are either mad,' said Greenpatch, 'or nuts. But take your hand off the rope, for I will certainly hang her.'

'You are a ruffian!' shouted Goronwy.

'I am a property owner,' replied Greenpatch. 'The two things are quite distinct. Let go the rope.'

'Not I.' The bitch licked his hand and cowered. 'But I am a law-abiding man, more's the pity, and I will buy this dog from you rather than see her come to hurt.'

'Money,' said Greenpatch, 'chimes like a bell.' He nodded his head slowly, made a purse of his lips. 'What is your offer?'

The bitch crawled to Goronwy's boots. 'I will give you half a crown.'

'For so intelligent a bitch as this?' He twitched on the rope.

'I will give you five shillings.'

'A bitch so well-trained, so obedient, so clean about the house?' The rope slid upwards.

The bitch raised her eyes to Goronwy's. 'Then ten shillings – but that is my last bid.' A sudden jerk drew the bitch up on to her back legs. 'I have the law with me,' said Greenpatch, 'I know my rights. A dog of which I am so fond as this one – I'd rather leave her for the crows than be robbed.'

The bitch whined and scraped at Goronwy's thighs. Quick, said the whine, oh quick, I'm choking! 'Then a pound,' said Goronwy. 'And as God is my judge, if you pull further on the rope I will fell you to earth with my good stick – if I had one.'

'I am a man for honest dealing,' said Greenpatch. 'A pound it is, and when I see the colour of your money you may take the rope from round her neck.' Goronwy fumbled in his pocket and slid the outside note from his bundle, and as he handed it over the brindled bitch sighed and trembled against his legs. 'But you are a fool,' Greenpatch said, laughing. 'She will come sneaking home by evening, and I shall hang her then, as a stray.'

'If you again lay finger on my little bitch,' said Goronwy, fondling the head, 'I will hang you in turn, from the tallest tree in the forest. You are a stoat and a pimp and a barrator, and Argoed would be well rid of you. And with that, little bitch, we will wish him good day.'

'Good day, is it? Aye, good day to you and good riddance to her!' And Greenpatch kicked at the bitch so that she ran yelping into the forest. 'So much for the pair of you!'

Rage and pity filled Goronwy's head and heart, but the bitch's vanishing squeal banished all save pity, and he went running clumsily through the trees in hope to overtake her. Soon the sound of her grief was lost among the green curtains, his heart beat heavily from exertion and pain, and he sat wearily on an ivy-wrapped stump. 'I shall never see my little bitch again,' he lamented. 'For a second time I have parted with my money to no purpose – to no purpose of my own, I mean. How nice she would have been about my house! But like the thrush she has left me.' He sighed. 'I am clearly a fool – I may even be nuts. The sun now shines from over the sea, and it will be best for me to eat my words of this morning and go emptily home.'

It was so he went back to the road and plodded northwards. But in an hour's time he saw ahead of him a man with no forehead sorely beating the rump of a fawn-and-white cow. As he drew near he could see the udder taut and dripping, so that the beast might hardly move her back legs.

'Why beat the cow, friend?' he asked urgently. 'You are a man not unused to beasts – indeed, you look much of a beast yourself. Surely she needs milking more than beating?'

Had the cowman a forehead, one would have said that he scowled. As it was, his eyes disappeared under his hair. 'I will beat her, and no one shall stop me. If her bag bursts, then burst it may. For I hate and loathe her.'

'How so, friend?'

'Because all the morning I drove her to market, and all the evening I have driven her home.' The cow lowed. 'Answer me back would you?' And he whacked her anew on the rump.

'Friend,' said Goronwy, 'you would not punish the cow for your failure to sell her. Stop now and milk her.'

'I begrudge her the labour.'

'Then allow me to milk her for you. I cannot endure to see her in pain and hear her moaning.'

'Milk her? On to the ground? And pour good money in the dust? Do you think I am made of gold?'

'Not for one moment,' said Goronwy. 'But I hope you are not made of stone neither.'

The cowman cursed. 'She lost me thirty good pounds at market today, and all because she was grieving after her calf. Ah, that I had my thirty pounds,' he wailed, hammering the beast in front of him, 'and were rid of this curdle-milk, this she-devil with horns, this moaner and groaner.'

'Friend,' said Goronwy then, though he could hardly believe his own voice, 'I will give you thirty pounds for your cow, but first let me milk her.'

'Money,' said the cowman, 'is a trumpet. But thirty pounds for a cow like this? The best milker in Cardigan, the gentlest feeder, a comely beast. And what a mother! Look at that bag. Feel those teats – no, hands off!' For Goronwy already had his shoulder into her flank, ready to ease her. 'Thirty pounds! Why I wouldn't sell my wife for less than thirty-one pounds ten.'

'Thirty,' said Goronwy, 'is all I have.'

'I know you now,' said the cowman, scratching his thatch; 'the schoolmaster from Rhydfelyn who is nuts. A man like you wouldn't stick for thirty shillings. Don't be mean to a hard-working man. I love that cow. I'd weep bitter tears for her even at thirty-one ten. At a penny less I'd break my heart.'

'Thirty,' said Goronwy 'is all I have.'

'Look at those hocks,' said the cowman, 'feel those flanks – no, hands off! What a build – small enough for the mountain, big enough for the flat.' The cow looked round and bellowed her pain. 'What lungs!' cried the cowman. 'I'd give the skin off my thumb for lungs half as good.' He saw Goronwy about to open his mouth on the old formula. 'Thirty-one,' he said, 'and I'm robbing my children.'

'Thirty,' said Goronwy, 'and this lump of beeswax.'

'Thirty-fifteen, and a lump of beeswax, and I'm taking the clothes off my bed.'

'Thirty and a lump of beeswax and my hat.'

'All that and five shillings to spit on for luck.'

The cow moaned.

'All that and my last piece of bread,' said Goronwy.

'And your waistcoat,' said the cowman.

'And my waistcoat,' agreed Goronwy from his dream. 'Here is the money, and here is the beeswax. Here is my hat, and here the waistcoat. And here is the bread. And now let me milk my cow.'

'I know when I'm bested,' said the cowman, 'and since I have no forehead to wear your hat on you may have it back instead of luck money.' And as Goronwy bent over and eased the glistening bag, the cowman went ape-like on his way.

'I think, cow,' said Goronwy, as the milk spurted into the dust of the road, 'that I have done a very stupid thing. You, I am sure, think it is wise one.' She grunted content. 'Soon you shall eat a little grass and drink a little water, and then we must make for home. The ways of Providence are beyond me. The thrush I could bear to lose, for who would keep a wild thing from its haunt? The little bitch I should love to have kept, but if you don't think it uncivil of me, I am much puzzled what to do with a cow.' The cow lowed and turned her head towards him. 'Well, we shall come to an understanding, no doubt. Now, if you are ready, shall we proceed?

'You know, cow,' said Goronwy later, 'I feel the day is by no means over for me.' The cow lowed. 'You are a most sensible cow, I must say. Yes, when I recall the events of the day, how I started off with thirty-one pounds and sixpence, and ransomed the thrush for sixpence, and the bitch for a pound, and you for the other thirty (and the beeswax and my waistcoat, though it is warm enough for me not to miss it, and don't for a minute think I begrudge it you), I feel there is a meaning yet to be made clear. Already here I am, talking as I have not talked for years, and only this morning I was the glummest man alive. What do you make of it, cow?' The cow lowed. 'I am of your mind. We must wait and see. Perhaps we shall not wait long, for surely,' said Goronwy, as they were approaching Rhydfelyn, 'that is someone crying ahead, and someone else bullying. I have no longer a farthing in my pocket, but I think we should go ahead and look.' The cow lowed. 'You think I should pick up this ash-plant? Maybe you are right.'

And right she was, for when Goronwy turned the bend it was to find a man driving a frightened girl before him down the road. The man was big and strong, with black hair slicked down in front, and his paunch like a pear in his navy-blue trousers, but the girls was small and tender, as though cut by nature for his chopping-block, and her face under its terror was meek.

'Bitch!' shouted the man. 'Cow that you are, to the poorhouse with you, or follow the gipsies! Sing like a thrush for your living, for I have done with you.'

'Friend,' said Goronwy, 'what goes on here? Are you not treating this girl worse than she can bear?'

'Bear's the word,' he jeered. 'Let her bear her brat in the ditch, but first she'll bear the weight of my hand.' And he hit her a great blow into the hedgerow. He would have hit her again, but the cow had walked in between.

Goronwy felt his right hand and arm a-tremble. 'I know this child,' he said softly, 'and I know you. She is the orphan Mair, from Llanfair, and all she knows of arithmetic she owes to me. Why do you beat her?'

'Because she has brought shame on me who gave her a home and asked nothing but work in return. Because she is to bear a sailor's brat without a ring to her finger. If she can bear anything when I have finished with her!'

'Friend,' said Goronwy, 'you have finished with her now. What I am not sure of is whether I have finished with you.' He looked over the cow's back at the girl. 'Who is the baby's dadda, little one? And who has done you wrong?'

'No wrong,' she sobbed. 'It was Lewsin Tirnant, but he went to the wars and was killed. There was no wrong. I loved him and he loved me.'

'He was another of the lonely ones,' said Goronwy. 'Like you he had no dad and mam. I have seen and heard too much today of the world's stoats and barrators. Cow, keep watch on the child, for I have work to do.'

The next moment he was sprawling in the dust. 'He'll kill you,' screamed the girl, as Blackhair drew back his heavy boot. But on that stroke of time, as Blackhair's boot swung in the balances of assault, a thin-faced brindled bitch jumped through the hedge and bit him in the calf. He turned bawling, but the bitch slashed his other calf. And now Goronwy was on his feet again, swinging his great cudgel. 'One,' he said, 'for this girl you have so cruelly dealt with!' – and he landed a bone-cracker on his right shoulder. 'And one,' he chanted, 'for Lewsin Tirnant, who was a good but lonely boy!' – and he bowed him groundwards with a gut-melter on the left. 'And finally,' he sang aloud, 'one for the babe unborn' – and he gave him so gruesome a whack on his skull that the echo of it crackled round the hills like thunder and Blackhair rolled three times over to end on his back in the road. And straightway Goronwy sat on Blackhair's belly as on a throne and embraced the little bitch, while the cow came over and ate of his adversary's hair.

'But it is time for home,' cried Goronwy, 'for all of us save this heap of vomit here. You, cow, whom henceforward I shall call

Megan, will lead the way, and you, little bitch, who shall from this day forth be called Betsi, shall follow behind her. And last will come Mair, leaning on my arm where the way is steep. Are you crying still? There is nothing to fear. Look on me, child, an old man they call nuts, and see whether I am not much more in need of you all than you of me.' He felt his load of loneliness fall from him as trust and happiness grew in her face. 'And when the child is born, if he is a boy we shall call him Lewsin, and if a girl Lewsina – my own invention!' They began to walk. 'I thank the Lord that I am better treated than Elijah. For he had but ravens to feed him, and I have a cow and dog. If I had my thrush, my cup would be running over.'

'Your thrush?' she asked.

'It is nothing,' he said regretfully. 'Ah me!'

The quiet blue of the evening was all about them as they passed through the black farmsteads and pink cottages of Rhydfelyn. The cow mooed with contralto satisfaction, the little bitch talked in her throat. Soon they had entered upon the path to the lower slopes of Goleufryn. 'The house,' he cried, pointing. 'Oh, how friendly it looks to-night!' The bitch barked joyously, and a stream of golden melody poured down the hill-side to meet them. 'It's Dicky Thrush,' he gasped. 'Look – he's perching on Megan's back!'

Megan lowing, Betsi barking, Dicky Thrush singing, they bent their knees to the incline. One last gleam of sunlight broke from over the darkening sea, and as they threaded the lichen-draped green walls, and Mair leaned on Goronwy's aching, proud arm, it was a little house of gold which laughed its welcome from the hill.

Shepherd's Hey

~

I

IT WAS soon after dawn that the first flurries of snow blew out of the north, where the mountains had shown white for almost a week. Nothing was visible up there now: the north had disappeared, earth, sky and water, under the blue-grey snow pall. Not that the man standing in the doorway of Penhill had eyes for the north, anyway. He was watching a ewe in the field before him, a black-faced ewe with yellow in her fleece, whose time was upon her. She had just risen from her side and was moving uncertainly forward before beginning to crop at the stiff grass. Again she lay down on her side, and again she arose, heavy, panting, and unsure of herself. This would be her first lamb.

Craddock felt the dog rub lightly against his leg, and with a dropped forefinger warned him to stillness. On a thought he turned his head to peer into the cottage behind him; saw his black kettle squatting on the fire. When he looked out again, the lamb was born.

He had come like a little red diver, curled and sticky, into the March morning. The ewe was struggling to her feet; she stared at this undreamt-of visitant with surprise and alarm, and when his tail made its first feeble flip she scuffled backwards as though from danger. But soon she came forward again, the drag of all the world's time upon her, sniffed cautiously, and nervously licked at him. Her eyes began to roll, puzzled but possessive; she licked a second time, and from that moment he was completely if incredibly her own.

'Good girl,' said the man in the doorway and stepped back inside, stretching his arms and yawning. He was still heavy after his four hours of rest, and in want of his breakfast. The dog watched him round-eyed as he lifted the kettle to the hob and slid the frying-pan over the glowing peat, stepping back deferentially as the eggs and bacon spluttered in the fat. In turn the man watched the dog as he filled his own mug and then poured tea and milk into a thick brown basin. Slowly, as befitted a ritual, he blew into the basin and tested the heat with his finger before setting it down. When he began his own breakfast, it was to the tune of the dog's tongue slapping at the luke-warm tea.

'I don't know,' he said suddenly. He looked at the dog, dropped him a hunk of bread soaked in bacon fat. 'If I did, then I'd tell you.'

He was thinking of two things; the lambing flock and the pall in the north.

He was a tall man, this Craddock, heavy-shouldered, round-headed, with a smoulder of red in his coarse thick hair, and his moustache bushed along the upper lip. His eyes were a pale, hard green, and there was a three-day growth of beard over his face. He was wearing an old battle-dress as he cleared away the breakfast, using the last water from the kettle to wash his mug and plate, and before he went outside he thrust himself into a drooping army greatcoat and a cloth cap. The refilled kettle he set on the hob, and over his shoulder he drew a respirator case stuffed with medicines and bits of greasy cloth.

'Now then,' he said, and the dog slid silently ahead of him through the cottage door.

He had already milked his two black cows and turned them out of the shed, but he saw that they had not left the shelter of the wall. 'Don't like it, eh?' he asked, and the dreamy heads and great moon-eyes turned towards him questioningly. 'Don't worry,' he said. 'You've got me.'

He walked over to where the ewe was cleaning and sheltering her lamb. As the dog drew near she squared round at him, stamping her feet, her head jerking. The lamb's upper side was white and crinkled, and his two ears twitched like butterfly wings. 'You'll do,' he said. 'Fine little ram.' He talked this way to all his animals, because he felt god and father among them, and because he had no one else to talk to.

There were sheep all over his fields, half of them his own, half of them yearlings from a farm in the uplands. Perhaps a hundred and fifty altogether. The yearlings, hardy and nimble, were dotted over the furthest fields, some grazing as high as the bracken, and others near the gorse-rimmed cliff edge. They should have gone away a week ago, but someone had broken a leg at their home farm, and they were not fetched.

The home field ran between low stone walls from either side of the house as far as the cliff, three hundred yards away. He remembered it when he came there, the walls falling, the land sour with gorse and tall thistles. And the ragwort in late summer! Now a firm green sward swept the whole distance – his back, his arms, had done that. Season by season, year after year, he had exulted in the work, regretting the lack of money only for the time it might have saved. My place, he thought now. My creatures. And as the snow began to whirl out of the north against his face and breast, he confronted the wind and the cold and the white smother as though they were listening enemies. 'Nothing of mine,' he challenged them; 'you'll get nothing of mine!'

In another moment he could not see his cottage. It was as though all Penhill was at the bottom of an immense chute, and down this chute snow rolled and twirled and fluted. It hung like wool from his eyebrows and moustache, plastered his greatcoat, and when he opened his mouth he felt flakes melting against his tongue and gums. He began to plod forward, making for the stone wall, as though to satisfy himself that there was still something black and solid in this streaming whiteness, and as he bent his back almost in line with the ground he could see the dog advancing determinedly with him, his ears flattened but his tail a-flare.

Along the wall he found most of his sheep. He must move them to shelter, gently. Among them were the first lambs, frail as knitting and seemingly unboned, and ewes which could hardly go another hour or two. Patiently he made his way cliffwards till he reached the last of them, then drove them up before him, the dog collecting stragglers and nuzzling them to the wall. With a loud baa-ing they turned in behind the cottage to the hurdles under the hillside and the sheltered barn. 'They'll do,' he said at last. Adding worriedly: 'Why not?'

With the dog he began sorting and counting the sheep. There were five ewes missing, and these he would bring in presently. Meantime he had plenty to go on with. A barren ewe was claiming a lamb from another with twins, and her he had the dog drive headlong into the weather. A couple of the weaklings he carried into the cottage, to bed them on an old overcoat near the fire. It was as he was about this that he remembered the ewe which had given birth to the young ram earlier that morning. She was nowhere near the barn, he remembered her too well to have made a mistake over her, so he went hurrying out to where he had seen her before the wind grew fierce. She was still there, stoical and half drifted over with snow. He felt the lamb and it was cold as a stone and dead – and no reason for it. For the first time that day he swore, knowing that deep in his heart he had believed the young ram the flower of his flock, even associating it in some unspoken way with himself. He stood upright in the blinding wind, wiped snow from his forehead and eyes. He should have carried the lamb to shelter at once, he told himself – and then, Nonsense, he said: he had only the one pair of hands. He left the lamb and ewe lying together and walked straight down the field with the dog. Near the cliff he found one of the missing ewes, just delivered. She was dying in the stained snow, but the lamb looked well enough. It was another ram, and through its trembling helplessness he saw or thought he saw the promise of mighty bone and heavy fleece, of increase and strength. 'Right,' he said joyously, defiantly, to the wind and sky. 'Right!' He was getting to his feet when the dog half-purred, half-growled, and stood pointing. He turned his head and saw a woman with a small bundle over her shoulder walking down the field towards him.

A woman unmistakably, for all the whirled shapelessness of her, the bowed head, the bunched shoulders, the wind-whipped, snow-fluffed body. But no one he knew. Besides, he was too busy wrapping the lamb in a piece of cloth from the respirator case and tucking it under the breast of his greatcoat to do more than glance at her as she came up to him. He had an impression of dark eyes, that was all, and dark hair under a hat tied down with a scarf. 'Go back to the house and wait,' he told her, staring at the ewe on the ground, kneeling again to lift her head. No, there was nothing he could do for her. But he would come back and try, all the same, once the lamb was in safety. As for him, the ramling, he wouldn't make the same mistake, if mistake it was, twice.

'Back to the house!' he ordered more loudly, and went hurrying on ahead to where he had left the other ewe and her dead lamb. 'Here,' he told her, opening his coat, 'carry this one' – handing her the live lamb, anxiously watching her hide it under her coat. Against the protesting stamp of the ewe he picked up the dead lamb and stuffed it into his pocket, the head and forefeet dangling outside. Next, with a quick grab he laid hold of the mother and swung her up on his back. The dog had already rounded up the other missing sheep and on a handwave and whistle headed them towards the barn. He was back in time to fold the ewe in a tiny pen by the cowshed, where the two blacks were moaning with satisfaction at having been allowed to re-enter their warm, dark shelter with its knee-deep bracken.

Craddock had lifted the latch, motioning the woman inside. 'The lamb,' he said, 'quick!'

Softly he set him down near the fire, letting the heat play inside his wrapper. The other two lambs lifted their heads, and one even sat up and bleated. 'In good time,' said Craddock, 'all in good time.'

'Hey!' protested the woman, for Craddock had pulled out his knife, slit the dead lamb, and was now peeling the skin from him as from an orange. 'What are you doing to him, mister?'

'Giving his butty an overcoat,' replied Craddock, too intent on his work to look up at her. 'Look!'

He had picked up the other lamb from near the fire and was fastening the skin loosely over him. 'Now,' he muttered, 'we'll see.' He went round to where the dog guarded the single pen, leaned in and put the coated lamb near the ewe. The woman had followed after him, shaking the snow from her head and coat. 'She'll never be such a fool,' she said.

For the second time that day the ewe pondered the unfamiliar scrap before her. She was sure this was not her lamb, and yet there was her own smell all over it. She sniffed disbelievingly and turned her head away, but was drawn despite herself to sniff and scent again. Her irresolution was at once comic and pathetic, for above all she desired to deceive herself that what she had lost, and knew she had lost, was miraculously restored to her. And so, the deepest needs of her nature conspiring against her judgement and her senses, she nosed him all over till he staggered in under her woollen valance.

'She's giving,' said Craddock joyfully. 'She's taken him.'

'Trust a woman', said the watcher at his side, 'to take the second best.'

And now he looked at her, the dark-eyed, leaned-faced stranger. 'Who are you? How did you get here?' He watched the snow burying his field. 'In this.'

'I lost my way.' She could tell that he did not believe her. 'Anyway, I'm frozen. And am I blooming well hungry!'

For answer he nodded, leading the way to the cottage door, kicking clots of snow from his boots, and beating his cap free of

272

white before he entered in front of her. 'My,' she said, 'ain't you tall!' Smiling warily, edging towards the fire.

'I could do with a cup myself,' he said. And again: 'Who are you?'

'Me? Oh, I'm Mrs Trent.' She took off the scarf and then her hat, looked round and pointed to the towel behind the door. When he nodded, she began briskly to rub up the tails of her hair. 'Got a mirror, mister?'

'Trent?' On his own he would have eaten bread and margarine, but now he was sliding the frying-pan once more over the peat.

'All right, you don't know no Trent. Well, I'm not from round here.' She hesitated. 'I was going north.' She watched the dog back out of range as the fat spluttered. 'He knows what's what, that dog of yours. What's his name?' And without waiting for an answer: 'I'm fond of dogs, I am. Though I know some as aren't. Well,' she asked, 'how do I look now?'

He turned, astonished. Of all the questions! But she seemed concerned to know his answer, her eyebrows lifted, her lips pouted a little, the backs of her hands on her lean hips. Woman, he wondered, or girl? 'Wrong question,' she said, 'eh? You can't face it at twelve in the morning.'

'I've got to feed these,' he answered, not knowing which way to take her. 'Cut me off a round, will you, while you're at it?'

'God strike!' she exclaimed, watching him with the lambs. 'From a titty-bottle, what next? You're a proper nursemaid, you are. And don't you ever take a rest?'

He was getting into his greatcoat again, drinking his tea standing. 'It's my busy time. And now there's this storm. I'll be back later and take you down to Lerry – that's where you came from, wasn't it?' He didn't wait for an answer. Where else could she have come from? 'If I'm not back', he went on, 'in an hour or more, you could give these lambs the bottle, the way you saw me do it. Could you?'

'You're the boss,' she told him, with false brightness. 'Leave it to me.'

The wind tore at his cap, his eyes, his mouth, as he went outside. The dog was already wallowing in the drifts, yet parts of the field were hardly more than speckled. Lerry? He pondered this, fighting his way down to the dying ewe near the cliff. His duty was more to her than to this woman, more to every creature about his farm than to a tricky stranger. For she was a queer one: he

273

knew that as surely as he knew the temper of any other animal. And if he did set off with her and reach Lerry, how could he get back? The lambing at its height, the yearlings in the furthermost fields, cows to feed and milk: no, she'd have to go herself.

And what was she? Some soldier's wife padding north to the big camp? He must ask her. Oh, very odd.

The ewe was dead when he reached her. He felt troubled, even guilty, though there was nothing he could have done for her. Time wasted, jawing with that woman. He shook his fist into the whether, a gesture not of rage, but defiance. Anyway, he had the lamb.

Still, he thought, someone to talk to, a voice to hear. And when next he went inside the cottage he said nothing of Lerry.

'What's it like up north?' she asked.

'You can forget the north,' he answered. It was dark indoors, but too early yet to light the lamp. A swift-sinking halo of crimson sparks shot over the fire as he dropped on another piece of turf. 'I've never seen it thicker.'

He was gone again, for a last look round his ewes before trying to collect the yearlings and bring them nearer home. He was thinking back to a March snow-storm of his boyhood, in another part of the country, when for almost a week his father stayed home from the pit, no trains ran, and the deepest drifts lay more than a month. What if this were as bad? He couldn't risk it.

It was a long task fetching the yearlings into the home field. The dog was beginning to drag his legs, and at times was helpless in deep snow. He himself came to feel that if once he stopped working he would be too tired to restart, and there were many things waiting for him at home, yet to be done. The lambing ewes, the cows, the weaklings indoors and in the hurdles – and beyond these he faced the irritation and fatigue of preparing food and keeping the cottage clean. Small things loomed large and worried him; but the true worry was the woman from Lerry. What could he do with her? What would he wish to do?

He had put off returning home as long as he could. What would she be doing when he came in? Had she, he wondered, gone away? But that was impossible: it was still snowing, the shape of wall and field and cottage unbelievably changed, the path buried, grass buried, only the gorse bushes still struggling for air through the piled whiteness.

He saw an orange gleam from the cottage window. He grew nervous, approaching his own door, as though he were the intruder there. The wind had slackened and he moved slow and upright, a snow-caked monolith through the dusk. As he drew nearer he saw her limned against the window, as though she were looking out for him, and at once there was the door opening.

'Is that you?'

'Me,' he assured her.

'I was getting frightened on my own. God,' she said, 'don't you ever knock off?'

'Soon I'll be done.'

But he picked up two buckets from inside the door and went off to attend to the cows. 'Twenty minutes,' he called back to her. 'I'm hungry, too.'

He had forgotten the lantern. Not a thing he often did. As he fetched it, there was a loud impatient mooing from the shed, and despite his tiredness he smiled to hear it. The air was soft and sweet and warm inside, the bracken crackled under his feet. 'All right,' he said soothingly, 'the old man's here.'

Having finished there, he walked once more among the hurdles with his lantern jerking at his belt. One or two things to do, but nothing as pressing as his own needs. He would come back after supper and tidy up for the night. He noticed that the dog was no longer with him. Well, he'd earned his keep today.

Darkness had fallen black and heavy. No moon or star limbecked the snow to silver, the very flakes looked black as they flitted into the lantern. There was much less wind, but he shook his head gloomily, feeling as an animal feels the unseen burden of the skies, the loaded air. It came into his mind that he had not heard a bird-cry since morning.

'You said twenty minutes,' she reminded him as he came into the cottage. Her nervousness shrilled in her voice.

'There was a lot to do,' he said mildly. He opened his blunt fingers, looked downwards. 'And only one pair of hands.'

'I've got your supper,' she contradicted him sharply. The dog was eyeing him apologetically from where he lay between the succoured lambs and the fire. Then his eyes changed, grew brighter, his tongue flashed round his muzzle as she lifted the lid of the pot and the smell of potato soup came steaming out. 'I cut all the bacon rind into it,' she told him, and held up a protesting hand. 'All right, Mr Busy, I can spoon it out!'

He grinned, shoving his hair off his forehead, his green eyes peering at the lambs. Then: 'Lord,' he sighed and filled the dog's bowl, blowing on it furiously, testing it with his finger, while the dog tried to press its behind through the floor. 'All ready, are we? Let's eat.'

'You've finished for today?' she asked, when he was plugging his pipe and rubbing his stockinged feet before the fire.

He looked at the clock. 'Always something to do. Take these lambs back, for a start.'

It was her turn to sigh. 'God strike, I thought my job was hours enough.'

'Your job? Aren't you married?'

'Sort of,' she said perkily. 'Of course I'm married.' She held out a ringed left hand. 'The gold one,' she said. 'Not the diamond and sapphire. That was my engagement ring. As if you'd know the difference!'

'As if,' he agreed gravely, looking back to the fire.

He smoked in silence, the prey of his unchanging habit. It was too much for her and she began to fidget. 'Is it always like this here?'

He was surprised. 'Why not?'

'God strike!' she said eloquently. But she had sharp eyes and sharper wits. 'You don't like a woman to swear, do you? I can tell that.' She mused. 'One of the old-fashioned ones, are you? I thought they were all dead and buried long ago.'

He was knocking out his pipe, pulling on his boots. He signalled the dog back to rest.

'Off again?'

'I'll leave you the dog,' he promised, lighting the lantern.

'The dog!'

The words touched him on a nerve. Contempt? Provocation? Amusement? What was in those words? 'You can sleep in there,' he said steadily, pointing to the small off-room facing the fireplace. 'There's a curtain you can pull across.'

'But that's your bed!'

'You needn't worry.'

'Me? Worry?' She gave a silly little laugh.

But that was not what he had meant. 'I'll manage all right. Let the dog out for a minute last thing, and put a piece of turf on the fire – and don't stir it.' He was into his greatcoat, picking up the lambs. 'I'll say good night.'

He had gone. He stood for a moment outside the door, and then went round to the hurdles and the barn. In half an hour he was satisfied that all was well, and made for the cowshed. In the empty stall there was straw piled a yard high and he had his greatcoat, soggy though it was. And it would be warm here all night. He saw the cottage door open and the dog slip outside. He stood unmoving till some minutes later the orange light fell outwards again, and he could see the dog give himself a brisk shake and nip back in.

The cows paid no attention to him as he thrust in past them with the lantern. The shed was warm as the cottage itself. With the lantern safe on its hook, he climbed up on to the straw, heard it hiss up round him, bunched it for a pillow. For a moment he wondered about the woman making ready for bed, about the young ram that died in the morning, about the million morrows awaiting the tired world, but everything was merging and sinking down, the woman, the animals, the snow from above, time and place, all one and the same, and all of them a soft enfolding dark.

II

The woman in the cottage slept late and woke frightened. The window, the light, the brightness of fire – where, where was she?

She was remembering, seated upright in bed, her shoulders shinning in the half-dark, her hair unkempt and wiry. There was the fire, new-peated, a hot glow at the heart of it; a grey light seemed frozen throughout the outer room. She thought: Do I have to get up? What a life!

She pushed back the bedclothes and swung her legs out of bed. The bed was not a big one but it filled three-quarters of her room from end to end. It had a built-in look, with space underneath for a sack of potatoes, nailed boots, ten or a dozen rusty mole-traps. She was still only half awake, yawning and sighing, and beginning to wish she had a cigarette to face the day with. That had been a mistake if you like, but who would have thought of it? If she'd got near the camp up north she'd have been – 'Stuffed,' she muttered, 'I'd have been stuffed out with fags by now.' But she was in one sense of the word a philosopher and prone to turn swiftly from the ideal to a contemplation of reality.

The kettle was blowing up its lid on the hob. 'Oh, good,' she exclaimed, 'that's good!'

She began to pull her clothes on, careless of anything that would not show, twisting a quick knot in a garter, perturbed by what the snow had done to her shoddy shoes. The toecaps looked quite mildewed, and she feared lest they were ruined. But tea was the thing now, and toast, if only she could make it.

God strike, she thought, eating and drinking and warming her flat shins, if Harry could see her now! Stinking toad, she called him. Crocodile! She wasn't sure what a crocodile was, save that it was slimy and yet hard, and very unpleasant. That was Harry all right, Harry to a crossed 't'.

This other chap here, this farmer – she didn't know his name. Didn't seem a bad sort, and he'd certainly done the handsome by her last night. According to his lights. Would he be good for a touch, she wondered? Something worth while? But they said these country chaps were closer than coffin lids with their money. The ones that stayed at home, that was. For she'd seen many a strawboy throwing out his shillings on a show-ground in her time.

Where was he now? And what was the time? She couldn't believe it. She put the kettle on again and went to the window to look on the world. But where it was not thick with snow the glass shone with a ferny glaze which prevented her from seeing anything at all. So it was from the doorway, soon after, that she watched Craddock with a towering bundle of hay on his back plodding down the near side of the northern wall. She closed the door quickly, before he might notice her, and prepared to wash her face and comb the tangles out of her hair. Looking into the mirror, she found her face, for all its out-of-bed staleness, fascinating. 'I can see what they see in me,' she told herself, tilting her chin, arching her brows, squinting sideways in hope to see her profile. She was vain, hardened, romantic, and incurably good-tempered and optimistic, a tricky barque in breeze or shallow water.

It was two hours later when he marked his return by clawing the snow from the window. His red fingers and blunted nails made the noise of an iron scraper, alarming her, so that she twisted her head round to find him looking in at her. The doorway was low for so big a man, and as he entered, capped and greatcoated, he seemed bowed and yet filling it.

'Strike,' she said, 'I bet you got muscles! What's it like this morning?'

'Haven't you looked?' he asked, puzzled, amused, distrustful.

'At a lot of blimming snow?' She grimaced. 'What for?'

'It's stopped,' he said. 'That's one thing. Stopped soon after five.'

She was silent as he for a time. When he did speak, between mouthfuls, it was in answer to her thoughts. 'No,' he said, 'you won't be moving on today.'

'What d'you mean, moving on?' she answered sharply. 'I'm not a tramp, mister. Moving on, I like that!'

'No one said you were,' he said calmly. 'But what are you?'

'What do I have to be? I'm a married woman, aren't I?' She looked complacently at her rings, turned her wrist to make the stones sparkle.

He looked at them, too, looked from her long strong fingers to the bone of her wrist, following the line of her arm to the shoulder, the throat, the marked jaw and hollowed cheek, the dark-brown eyes and puckered forehead, the hair dark as a roasted chestnut.

'And what's your name?' she challenged. 'Funny you never told me.'

He laughed. 'Craddock. And now I'll be moving.'

'And what do I do?'

He stared at her.

'I don't see a wireless. Haven't you got any mags or comics or something? Can't you read or something?'

'There's a Bible,' he told her. 'Somewhere.'

She bit back her words, for it was bad luck to speak ill of the Bible, and he saw slyness overtake the impatience on her face. 'Ah, yes,' she retorted, 'I'm well up in the Bible. I'm *in* the Bible, I am – least, my name's there.' She waited for him to show interest or disbelief, but he merely hung like an oak trunk in the doorway. 'You'd never guess in a fortnight. Salome Trent!'

He went out on her dramatic disclosure, but as he cornered the house she was tapping on the cleaned window, and he saw her mouth open wide on the three syllables, 'Sa-Lo-Me', her finger jabbing at herself for a further identification. He swept his hand downwards, half farewell, half derogation, but he was grinning as he went on to the barn. She was a tricky one all right!

She found the Bible at last, in a drawer of the brown dresser. It was with no less dismay than surprise that she discovered every shelf and drawer lay open to her search. Surely there could be nothing worth the taking where there were no locks! She uncorked his small shelf-full of bottles, wrinkling her nose at the sheep nostrums, and rushing to the wild conclusion that he was a secret drinker when in the two endmost she found gin and whisky. 'For his barmy sheep more likely,' was her dejected correction. She replaced everything and sat by the fire with the Bible, starting in at Genesis to find Salome. But increasingly she found her mind on the spirits, and at last, after a quick look outside and through the window, she poured herself two fingers of gin and topped up the bottle with water. The Bible proved surprisingly full of interest as she skimmed through the leaves. Beautiful are thy – how come, she wondered, that they let you put stuff like that in print. And so wondering, she helped herself to the tiniest of whiskies.

But the day was long till evening, and she had too much sense to drink more. 'Stay in', she said, 'and talk to me. You're only keeping out because I'm here.'

His expression changed just enough for her to know that she had spoken truth. The thought at once exasperated her and gave her confidence. If he avoided her, then he was aware of her, and in however small degree, and from whatever motive or shade of a motive, afraid of her. 'I'm the cheerful sort,' she chided; 'I like a talk, and I like listening, too. You don't have to keep on the go, night, noon, and morning. Tell me,' she asked, 'that lamb we took to his new ma, how's he doing?'

The two young rams! It was a lucky question. She drew him on to talk of his stock, his farm, himself. No, he hadn't always lived here. He was born down south, among the pits. He showed her blue pocks on the back of his left hand, then rolled up his sleeve over a forearm glinting with red hair, on up to the biceps where an anchor and scroll told their tale of years at sea. 'Coal,' he said, tapping the back of his hand, 'that's what it is. It's a thought that I'll carry coal into my coffin with me.' But his mother had died; he saw his father killed by dust on the lungs, and straightway he left the long black valley between the brown mountains and made for the ports and a new life. He was strong ('Strike,' she said, 'you *are* strong' – her fingers moving towards his forearm but quickly withdrawn), and he was never out of a job. 'Where you get to?' she asked. Where not, in five years? South America chiefly, sunny ports and oily rivers, white birds screaming and fish that flew out of the sea. 'No good to me,' he said abruptly, staring at his visions in the fire. 'A furrow in water can't last. Nothing of your own in the whole wide waste of it. And we all want something of our own.'

He talked slowly and clumsily, but once he was started, inexhaustibly. His life moved before him, disordered, gapped, and yet coherent, and what he saw of it he described with bold, uncunning words. Animals now – sheep he had, and cows, and one day he'd have a pony. All of them living things, and the land was alive, too, the grass on it alive and growing; even the weeds, gorse, even ragwort, it was a kind of killing when you tore it up, you heard the roots groan. And the soil itself, the brown feel of it over your hands, every grain of it alive and life-giving. The very stones – nothing you'd call deader than stone – he smiled at the fire, smiled at her; you had only to live with it, and see how it lived with you. Build it into a house, stack it in walls, watch the mosses putting out their little noses, not out of earth, but out of stone itself. 'Oh, yes,' he told her confidentially, 'there's nature in stone.'

She heard it tolerantly, for she liked the feeling of company his words gave her, and the novelty of his ideas flattered her with a sense of her understanding.

'So you came back to this?' she asked.

'That's right.' He looked around him, and the farm instantly asserted its mastery. 'There's a ewe,' he began, And hung his head at her gesture of disillusion. 'Shan't be long, honest.' A change had taken place in him, so that he was anxious to come back, if not to talk then at least to sit and think, with her for company. 'It's only', he explained, 'that with sheep you can't be too sure.'

When he had gone out, in his great boots and hulking coat, she sat on by the fire. After a while she reached for the poker but put it down again unused. That was a thing you had to learn about peat. 'But stone,' she asked, 'alive? Sounds daft to me.' She laughed. Not many she knew would have taken in as much as she had.

'That's right, Crad,' she greeted him when he returned. 'This is better than in with the cows, isn't it? Go on, Crad, it's not a crime to laugh.'

'I don't understand you', he said, 'and that's a fact.'

'Nothing to understand where it's glass right through. Got a clean towel? I think I'll wash my hair. And for suffering's sake, man, you don't have to run out again!'

He fetched her a red towel. 'Wash it in here?'

She was pouring water into the only bowl. 'Hot it up again,' she ordered. 'I'll want it swilled.'

Her fingers were at the buttons of her bodice, her shoulders and then her arms came honey-yellow out of the black dress, which she drew down outside her slip to her waist. She set the bowl on a chair and knelt in front of it. 'Don't look so frightened,' she said sideways out of her mouth.

The clock ticked more loudly, the whispering of the fire grew harsh as a flock of starlings. Blood was prickling in his face, his hands lay iron-heavy on his knees. 'I used to see my mother wash her hair,' he said in a slow, slumbering voice, 'and I've never seen anyone do it in all the years since. I used to swill her hair.'

'Then swill mine, too.'

From a black enamel jug he did so, pouring the water through her tensile fingers into the lathered hair. The flesh of her shoulders was richly mellow in the lamplight, the bones of her spine were shadowed and round; the graining of her skin finer than sea sand. Soon snowy suds were running through her hands into the bowl or dripping to the stone floor, and as they cleared away she squeezed the wet hair and pressed it up from the nape of her neck. 'Don't run away.' She pivoted on her knees to before his chair, thrusting the towel into his hands. 'Dry me, Crad!' She held on to his knees as he towelled her hair into wiry springs and coils. As she bent before him, he could see the golden globes of her breasts swinging in the white cage of her vest, their purpled shadows swelling or narrowing with each rock of her body. Harder he rubbed, harder and harder, till the hair crisped and crinkled with life. 'You'll kill me,' she protested, her scalp afire. 'You'll have my head off!'

She struggled to her feet, her face flushed by the fire, and straightened the straps over her shoulders. 'You've made me a gollywog,' she cried, tilting the mirror to get the best light. He heard her curls crackle as she tugged at them with the comb. 'I wouldn't trust you with this job,' she grumbled. 'Strike, you'd pull my head off, you would!'

He had thrust back the kettle and was dropping a turf on the fire when he heard her say: 'Look at me in my ear-rings, Crad. Real diamonds!'

He dared not turn and face her. 'I've got to go. I've been here too long.'

She was pulling at his shoulder. 'What's the matter? Don't you like me, Crad?'

'Like!' he said roughly. 'What's like got to do with it? I can't let my animals go hungry just because – '

'All right, Crad, you go. You see to them, and then you come back.' She spoke quietly, gently, surely. 'Don't be too long, that's all, for I'll be waiting.'

She helped him into his coat, while the dog scrabbled up and ran to the door. 'I'll leave him in the shed,' said Craddock, not looking at her. 'Hand me the bag there.' The brilliants flashed in her ears as she obeyed him.

When he came back the cottage was in darkness, save for a strong glow from the heart of the fire. She was not in the room with him, and he washed his hands in the water where she had washed her hair, dried them on the same dank red towel. He had fumbled his boots off his feet and his eyes had grown used to the dimness when the curtain of the bedroom was violently pulled back. The firelight glowed upon her in crimson and shadow, blazoning the long lean legs, the snake-supple torso and shoulders. Red fire struck from the pendants in her ears, and on her uplifted right arm glowed a broad copper-hued bangle. Her hair was a dark crown.

He stood silent and unmoving (daughter of Baal or maiden of Ashtaroth?), but: 'D'you like me?' asked this vision of barbaric splendour, in the accents of a fair-ground. 'Salome. I'm in the Bible, I told you, remember?'

III

She had been at Penhill a week and a day. At first snow and more snow, then a tightening frost, and now for two days and nights long soft showers of rain. Yesterday he went down to Lerry, taking three hours each way, but bringing back a week's supplies. The drifts, he reported, were still prodigious to the north. What they received as rain was yet more snow on the high ground. But he was jubilant enough, turning his sheep down the open middle of the field, driving the yearlings into the long green lanes the far side of the wall, slapping the cows' rumps as they left the dark of the shed for the beckoning daylight. And now, on the Thursday, there were hours of sunshine. He stood with her in the doorway at the afternoon's end, pointing out the mountains, naming them, not a little irked that she would not even pretend to be interested.

'It's all snow to me,' she checked him. 'And who wants a lot of snow?'

'But look,' he urged her, 'look.'

In front of them runnels and ponds of green grass gleamed amidst the snow, and over these moved the anxious ewes, cropping and baa-ing deeply, while the white lambs skipped and ran and on every mound played king-of-the-castle. A pungent, blended smell of spring exhaled from the earth, and high above them the gulls planed and lamented. The sea was a pale cold blue, stretching to a smoky horizon, and north and north-west in the distance the mountains lay low and serene under their gold-infused mantles of unblemished snow.

'All right,' she said glumly, 'it's pretty, so what?'

He was too genial in his hour of ease to resent her tone. A ten times rehearsed arithmetic of losses and blessings filled his head as he watched his lambs and the ewes that were still heavy. It was thus Abraham felt, and Isaac, and Israel's seed in Gerar and Hebron and the plain of Mamre. He saw the young ram jostling his playmates, butting his woolly skull at a contender who gave way before him. The flower of the flock! The one he had waited for. The one he needed.

'Fine little flamer, isn't he?' He had turned but she was no longer beside him. Far to the left, rounding a drift in his own track of yesterday, he saw a man approaching. 'We've got company,' he called into the cottage, but there was no reply from her. He could not know that she was sitting on the bed's edge, her face alert but uncertain, wondering what she would do. 'I'll keep him out though,' he called. But she set her finger-tips to the point of her chin. 'That's what you can't do with Harry,' she whispered.

She had spied their visitor well before Craddock did. 'Here's a fine packet of peas,' she told herself. And with relish she thought: I hope the walk's done him good. I hope it's blistered him up fine and proper.

Craddock was watching the new-comer find the gate to the home field. Who could he be? Some government twister if only the weather was better – but you wouldn't find them out just yet, he reflected wryly, with the contempt of those who live on the land for those that live on *them*. And there'd be a car to keep the muck off his boots!

He had a wizened middle-forties look about him, a grey soft hat, waisted blue overcoat, sopping boots. Perky, too. A weasel, thought Craddock, and stood monumental and unwelcoming as he stepped along to the cottage door.

'Hullo, guv,' he said cheerfully, and his vowels were weasels too. 'The dog now – is he O.K.?' Craddock nodded silently. 'Not that I'm against dogs, but I was bit when a kid. Bit by a horse once, too.' He appeared to offer this with confidence, as a claim on a country-man's regard, but when Craddock showed no interest he nodded and held up a soaked trouser-leg. 'Wet, ain't it?'

The woman inside was listening hard and grinning. 'Nice little place you got here.' She knew he would say that, and she knew what he would go on with. 'Nothing like the country; I've always said it.' For he always had, when he wasn't saying: 'Nothing like the 'Igh Street, nothing like the Old Smoke, nothing like the north or south', or wherever else he happened to be. The soft approach, he called it, milk for the cat.

'What do you want?' Against the new-comer's chesty tenor Craddock was full bass.

'I'm in your hands, as I see it, guv'nor. I mean to say, here we are, a million miles from nowhere. Definitely, it's up to you.'

God save the seagulls! she was thinking. He'd jaw the ears off a donkey, that Harry.

'I don't take tramps,' said Craddock's bass. She could tell how he was bulking himself out till his shoulders filled the doorway.

'Who's a tramp? I'll show you something, straight I will. Here's my wallet, look at it from there, guv. Is there money in it, or is there not? Do I look like a tramp?' She heard his ingratiating snigger. 'Don't tell me I smell like one.'

'What are you here for?' asked Craddock, massively unyielding.

He's in for a surprise, thought the woman, and it won't be long now!

'In a manner of speaking,' said the new-comer, 'I'd say I was here on business.'

'I've got no business with your sort.'

'I always say one never knows, guv. Now I haven't a card to do the thing right, but my name's Harry Trent.' There was a short pause. 'I said Harry Trent, guv.'

'What of it?'

'It's what the lawyers call a case of locum tenens, guv – that's Latin. Phoo,' he said, 'and could I do with a sit down and a cupper!'

'You'll get one in Lerry. If you start now.'

'I wouldn't do that, guv, not if I was you.' She knew just what kind of a grin would be spreading over his face. What she was not prepared for was his squeal of terror. 'Keep that dog off me! Keep him off!'

'The dog won't hurt you if you go.'

Strike, she thought; old Crad is talking to him like he wants. But it won't pay dividends with Harry. He'll be back.

Craddock must have stood there watching him out of sight, for it was all of five minutes before he came in and closed the door. It was as though each was waiting for the other to speak first.

'Anyhow,' he said, 'he's gone.'

'He'll be back.'

He frowned. 'He'll go quicker next time.'

'And what'll that solve?'

Her words seemed to him to hold more of rebuke than question, and he put them from him unanswered. They were part of that drag-net of problems through which soon he must break or thread a way. Soon he was outside again, to clean the shed and milk the cows, to cast his benedictory appraisal over every item of the day's work and night's rest, but the woman stayed by the fire, coaxing brilliance from the glass jewels of her ring, whipping her bangle round her wrist, and pondering on Harry, that stinking toad and crocodile.

Crad could tread him under, or pull him apart like a cracked peg, but where did that get you?

'This Harry Trent,' he began, when next he saw her. For he had failed to drive him from his mind. 'He looks old enough – '

'To be my father, I know. Ask no silly questions, mister, and you'll be told no lies.'

'I won't?' More because of the 'mister' than the sharpness of her tone, he fell into an uncordial silence. The lamp was lit and the evening heavy on their shoulders when the dog growled and stood up, the hair lifting along his spine till she felt her own back crawl and chill in sympathy.

'It's Harry all right!'

Craddock rose with great deliberation. He always stooped a little indoors, and now his shadow loomed like an ape's across the wall and curtain, the head round and featureless, the shoulders humped and monstrous, the arms protruding and hooked.

'Let him in,' she said.

He stopped, turned round to her, his weight bearing down oppressively in the small room.

'Let him in,' she said again. 'He's a rat, Crad.'

He nodded his understanding of why he should keep a rat in sight rather than outside in the dark. And he nodded, too, at some remoter speculation of his own.

Harry's hand on the door was like the scratching of a thin claw. 'Keep that dog back! I couldn't make it, guv, and that's the truth.' He used hardly a sentence that was not infested with gabble. 'Look at my poor perishing feet. Look at my legs! I'll get my death from this, sure as eggs. Look at my – Gaw, look at my Sally!'

Craddock's huge hand shovelled him forward till he stood shivering in front of the fire. The dog stalked fastidiously to the furthest corner, and from there watched the new-comer with a lifting lip.

'It's what you're used to,' said Harry. 'I'm a delicate-bred man myself. But cosy once you're in,' he commended, rubbing his hands together, his trousers beginning to steam. 'I've always said it, there's something about the country – haven't I, Sally?'

'Have you? Then give me a fag.'

'What do you want?' This was Craddock.

'What do I want? I'm not kidding, mister, so don't think that I am. I want food bad, and, help me, I want a cupper.' He winked at the woman. 'And then I want to talk – business, let's call it – man to man.'

His mouth dipped snout-like into his mug as he drank by the fire, his close-set tiny white teeth nibbled their way through round after round of bread and jam. Then, his food destroyed, he began at once to talk, with a boundless faith in his gift of the gab and a deathless confidence in the power of repetition. 'It's a matter of principle,' he said from time to time, or 'Talk it over reasonable, that's my motto.' And the words which passed queerly from this out-of-hole rodent to the big work-stained farmer: 'We're men of the world, you and me, that's what I say, are we or aren't we?'

To all this jabber Craddock said nothing. It was a trait of his which the woman had taken days to get used to: that when he had nothing to say, he stayed calmly silent. So what answer there was came from her, briefly and crudely. 'You give me the croup,' she announced, and crossing to the off-room drew the curtain and vanished behind it. A moment later her face reappeared. 'Good *night*.' For the time being she was out of it.

For Harry it was as though she had vanished not merely from his sight but out of the house. 'What a thing to say to your husband, eh? But she's a one, Mr Cred, as I'm sure you've found out. Like all women, supple as a snake.' He smacked his pale lips over the phrase. 'And if the supplety of the snake deceived Eve – bless her shirt! – then what about us poor old Adams, answer me that, Mr Cred!' He laughed as though he were blowing through a keyhole, *thoo-thoo-thoo*. 'But it's a curious go, come to think of it. Here's me, her husband. Here's you, a *locum tenens*, as the lawyers call it. And here's her, the *corpus delicti* – Latin again.' I could squash him like a cockroach, Craddock was thinking, burst him like a flea, a sheep-tick: to what end? And what was this? 'You'd better listen, mister!' Harry was getting angry, his rat-eyes showed malice. At his change of tone the dog, which had curled up nose-in-tail, sat suddenly upright. 'It's as I was saying,' continued Harry, moderating, but his eye sparing one fearful flicker of hatred for the dog; 'if we can't take the human line, where are we?' And her, thought Craddock, that one in there, where does she come into this? 'Lawyer,' said Harry again, bullying; 'reasonable', whining; 'men of the world', imploring; 'clod-hoppers who don't listen', spitting venom. 'Not so innocent, so don't you pretend,' said Harry. 'Have your fun, that's only human, but what I say is, play the man and pay for it. Haven't I got my feelings, like any other husband?' He pursued his monologue, mean, hateful, bitter, utterly unable to gauge the withdrawal of the man in front of him, his tree-like remoteness from the words showered over him. His indifference, which at first served as a challenge to Harry's oratory, ended by rousing him to fury. Who was this stupid ox to resist his cajolery, ignore his subtleties, rebuff his sweet reason? If I had him tied, thought Harry, wouldn't I warm him! His glance fell on the poker: he saw it red-hot, and he was pressing it to Craddock's feet. That great trap thing on the wall – to crush his fingers one by one. Razor-blade him! He'd do it, too. Not for nothing had Craddock seen him first as weasel: cunning, malignant, and cruel as hell. He came to hate this great dumb animal before him; but for his craven fear he would have struck him in the face, knuckled his eyes, dragged at his ears, that he might see, hear, and obey the superior intelligence of which he so maddeningly sat in ignorance. Threats, wheedling, insinuation and sweet reason: the whole barrage of intimidation fell harmlessly about him, cold, stone, brute that he was.

From within the curtain the woman heard the familiar whirr and whine of his chesty voice. She lay there thinking, not sure of the part she should play, sure only of Crad's stubbornness and bull's strength and the rat-like persistent evil in Harry. It was always easiest in the end to buy him off. Meantime she savoured the hour of his exasperation, his loss of the first round, his panicky greed, till in the end even she, who knew him so well, sickened at his performance.

'God strike,' she cried at last, tearing back the curtain, glaring out at him, 'don't I get any sleep to-night? Finish it in the cow-house!'

They stared across at her pale face and tangled hair. 'If she's not a picture!' cried Harry. 'I wouldn't change her for a duchess and her crown. But bed it is, guv, and no mistake. Ah,' he added, as the dog ran to the door, 'nice old Toby!' He struck a pose of curdled innocence and goodwill. 'I'm reasonable,' he announced. 'Admit I'm reasonable.'

Craddock had done his thinking while Harry gabbled. 'I'll see to a place,' he told her, and went out after the dog.

Harry was alongside her with a quick skipping step. 'What's in it?' he rattled. 'What's the touch?'

'There's no touch.'

'There's always a touch,' he answered threateningly. His trembling little white-knuckled fist was near her face. 'Every time you run, there's a touch.'

'The dog's back,' she reminded him, yawning.

He glowered at the door, where she had heard the paw-stroke. 'I'll dout your bleeding lamps, my beauty,' he whispered, 'see if I don't! Ah,' he went on to the opening door, 'nice old Toby. What's his name, guv?'

'Bring your coat,' said Craddock coldly.

Harry looked back at her before he went outside, his face tightened with rage but his voice oiled. 'Sweet dreams, handsome!'

'Watch he don't milk you in the morning with others,' she jeered.

He would have liked to drive a knife into Craddock's back as the farmer walked before him to the cowshed. 'What are they? Bulls or something? Are they chained up?' But he climbed on to the straw jauntily enough. 'It's what I've always said, the morning's the time for business. There's nothing a little talk can't put right, Mr Cred.'

Craddock dropped the bar into place outside the door. He was deeply troubled, standing there in the dark, for he could smell evil as the barn-yard smells the approaching fox. Fox, he thought, aye, and weasel and rat. Queer creatures to have on a farm. He walked past the front of the cottage and stared out before him till he could discern the pale hummocks that were sheep, hear their stirrings and breathings, and far beyond them hear the murmuring of the invisible sea. Slow-footed and sure he started on his rounds, moving like a huge worried parent among his own, his green eyes true as a cat's. Every creature, every stick and stone, was as it should be; nothing appeared to share his unease. When he returned to the cottage the lamp was burning but the woman was asleep within the curtain. Taking great care to be silent, he hung up his coat and cap, dropped a fresh turf on the fire, so that a crimson rain of sparks rushed downwards to the hearth, and when the lamp was out sat patiently back in his arm-chair. His rest tonight would be light as a dog's. He would keep good watch. He was the farm's stay, and must see to his own.

IV

'Where is he?'

It was Harry, sliding his white and waxy nose round the door-edge, his livid eye winking.

'Where d'you think he is?'

'I've been working it out,' he told her, 'in that cow-house last night and all the perishing morning. There must be a touch somewhere.' This was the first article of Harry's religion: that there was always a touch. 'If not, by Gaw, I'll pay him out, I will!' That was the second. Without this twofold faith in profit and revenge Harry's life would have been duller than a hen's; for to be on the make was his soul's peace, and should he be what he called simpled, twiced, done down, cheated, he always paid them out. That was why many had found it best to buy him off; as though by tossing a crust into a rat-hole you held mischief at bay. 'And you,' he menaced, 'running off again. If I wasn't so fond of you, I'd learn you, too.' He began to pluck open the drawers and cupboards, sifting them with a claw-like hand, while she watched him calmly. 'I might have known you'd be through this lot first. Where's he keep it, Sal? Be a good girl now and tell me.' Evidently he expected no answer, for he continued poisonously: 'I've come to hate the whole lugging hulk of him, that I have. I hate him because he's big and stupid and won't listen to reason. But if he does me down, I'll leave my mark on him!'

'How could a lump like him do you down?'

He ignored her words whether as question or irony, but went on fingering behind the clock, drumming on the ceiling boards, frantic for a cache. 'What's that?' he asked, turning his head.

'Gunfire. From the camp up north.'

'Camp up north!' he said. 'Don't think I'm not wise to you, because I'm acting reasonable.'

'Ah, you still give me the – '

'Go on,' he invited, 'say it – and I'll belt your face.' He began to rummage the medicine shelf. 'Poison, half of it, I bet – too risky. What's this? Stars and cripes, it's gin!' He took a cautious sip, then a second. 'Watered down, but it's the right old stuff. And what's this? Whisky? Too good for the likes of him, I'll say it. Well, it's something saved from the wreckage, eh, Sally?'

'He's coming back,' she said from the window.

'He's coming back!' he mimicked. 'Him and his flaming dog together. Broken glass I'll take to 'em if they won't talk reasonable. Why, hullo, Mr Cred? Top of the morning to you, Mr Cred.' Hadn't he always known it? He ought to be on the stage. With his talents he'd have had them splitting. His vanity thus placated, he set himself out to be insolently affable – 'winning them over' was his own description of it.

'If there's one thing I've learned in my job, Mr Cred – '

It was after dinner and Craddock had filled his pipe. 'What is your job?' It was his first word to either of them.

'Sometimes it's a bit of this, and sometimes it's a bit of that. I'm what I suppose you'd call a kind of an impresario, eh, Sally?'

'Salome and her seven veils,' agreed the woman, in her raised fair-ground voice. 'And for every bob a veil drops off. Step right up, you lucky gents, and smack your shillings down!'

'Best partner I ever had,' said Harry with studied rapture. 'What a talent! She's artistic. We're both artistic, that's the truth of it. Got the temperament, too – hence the 'ump and run-away act every now and again. And that's the whole point, guv, that's what I'm trying to tell you, it's a matter of business as I said, in a way it's my living. If I was only a husband, or if I was only a showman, Mr Cred – but I'm both, I'm cut both ways, and without some little plaster of damages I'll be bleeding to death.' He was into his litany, explaining, expostulating, nagging, but in the middle of it Craddock knocked out his pipe and made for the door. 'Before I show the other side of me,' Harry half whined, half threatened. 'In the interest of every creeping one of us, that's why I'm asking.'

'Crad,' she called. But she had to follow him outside, he wouldn't stop for her either. 'Give him something, Crad. It's easiest, I tell you.'

'Give him this, shall I?' He balled his fist.

'Honest, Crad, that would only make it worse. He's loopy in a way, he's got to feel he's clever and smart. It's his vanity, or call it pride, or just plain lopsidedness. Even a couple of pounds and he'll go.'

'He'll go without.'

'But he'll come back. Tonight, tomorrow, in a year's time, I don't know when, to do something that'll show him he's still top of the act.'

'And you,' he asked hostilely, 'what do you want? Are a couple of pounds enough for you?'

'Not if I can get more,' she said tartly. 'And you wouldn't be robbed, at that.' She watched his bull's back as he walked away from her. 'Don't say I haven't warned you.'

'Been making the touch?' asked Harry as she came back indoors. 'I can see you had no luck though.' She smelled gin on his breath, and reaching for the bottle took a small drink herself. 'Not a wireless, not a daily, not a comic in the place! What's he do when he's not working, I wonder.'

'There's a Bible,' she said. 'Here.' And remembering her search for Salome, she added: 'It don't seem a full one, though.'

'I've read the Bible,' he boasted. 'I was brought up on it. Gentle Jesus meek and mild, Pity me a little child. Yards of it I've got in my head, Sal. Gimme the gin.' He poured the weakened mixture down his throat, coughed hoarsely, and put the whisky bottle into his overcoat pocket. 'I'm going out to have a last word with his lordship. I'll give him one more chance to be dazzled by intellect, and if he don't I'll fix him proper. And it's only my good nature, my girl, that I don't fix you proper, too.'

'Mind the dog,' she shouted derisively.

His nose slid back in through the door. 'He can mind me instead. I wouldn't have his insides tomorrow for a fiver.'

One thing came of knowing Harry. She hooked the dog's bowl out from under the table. It was full of scraps, put there by Harry, and in every piece of bread and meat had been embedded glass splinters, thin as thistle stings. Levering the fire forward, she scraped the whole mess of it to the back of the grate, shredded turf across it, and then wiped out the bowl before refilling it. She drained and refilled the water-bowl, too, and then went to look on the two men in the further field.

'A kind of property tax I'd call it, guv,' said Harry. Craddock's stride, deliberately lengthened, forced him now and then into a skipping pace to keep up. 'A kind of pay-as-you-go. There's plenty of husbands would take another line, the courts, damages, correspondence and the like, but I'm human myself, and I'm reasonable if I'm anything.' Craddock ploughed on through a drift near the fern-line, and without a glance for Harry went ahead through the snow-laden bracken, aiming for half a dozen sheep in a green clearing higher up. The dog, working things out his own way, made a wide and complicated detour which would keep him out of deep snow and yet bring him on duty by the time Craddock had need of him. From below, Harry in his thin shoes, grey hat and waisted overcoat sent wails, oaths, protestations and pleas reeling up the hill behind them. The nearby sheep bolted in alarm, and when Craddock looked down from the clearing in the fern, he stood alone and shunned, a flat insect rather than a man, mouthing his imbecile trivialities in a vast arena of snow and grass, thirty miles of sea radiant behind him, and further still the mountains, sublime, inviolate, serene in the light of the sun.

'You scab,' he called quietly downhill, and his voice did not reach the babbling Harry; 'you maggot, you sheep-fluke.' With that he had said his shepherd's say, not as abuse but as statement. 'And now I'll put you off my land.'

The snow, wet and cloggy, shot off his thighs as he burst downwards through gorse and dead fern. The dog went bounding over his former tracks, his red tongue flaming from his black muzzle, till Harry sickened lest Craddock should not be the first to reach him. He scrabbled in the snow for a stick, a stone, some weapon, but there was no need for one: the dog ignored him utterly. So did Craddock as he made briskly for the gate in the wall and the cottage.

'Where are we going?' gasped Harry. 'What's the hurry, Mr Cred?'

'I'm going to the cottage. You are going to Lerry.'

Harry's hatred burned like bile in his throat. His head grew fumy with the bitterness of his hopes, the fury of his plans. To be beat by a clod-hopper – him, a man like him, Harry. By a great, stupid, hulking lump of an animal. It affronted nature to admit it. And yet the touch was out, he knew it. Zealously he turned to the second article of his creed.

'You've settled it?' she asked, at the cottage.

'Give him food,' said Craddock. 'He's going. Are you?'

'You're a fool,' she said, marking the whiteness of Harry's face, the blink of his eyes. 'But I'm damned if I'm going with him. Unless you throw me out.'

For a moment she thought he would, but: 'Food's civilized,' said Harry unexpectedly. He had control of his throat muscles and spoke quite cheekily. 'So let's all have an eat, I say; you, me, her, and the dog.'

'I'll eat when you've gone,' said Craddock, but the dog had scented his day's bonus and was choking on the lumps of meat and bread.

'Now that does my heart good,' said Harry, winking rapidly. 'I can enjoy my cupper now, I can.'

Within a quarter of an hour he was on his way, and she could have written out in advance his parting platitudes. 'Well, guv, even the best of friends must part. No hard feelings, eh? If you can't win, what I say is, you can always be a good loser. And I'm nothing if I'm not a reasonable man, Mr Cred.' He had turned in the doorway, and she expected this too. 'Good-bye then, Sally. And don't never forget: I'll be seeing you.'

He was half-way across the field. 'Give him something, Crad. It might still be in time.'

'Who are you for?' He was as hostile as he was suspicious.

'Have it your own way,' she said resignedly.

Before he moved out of sight Harry turned, as she knew he would, and waved. Half-heartedly she waved back. 'No harm in waving, is there?' she demanded of Craddock's scowl.

He breathed the cooling air with something like a snort. 'Well, he's gone.'

'He'll be back.'

'Back!' For had he not seen this miserable Harry from a hill top, against a background of all nature, a maggot, a worm, a sheep-fluke? 'Not he. But there's another thing – I've been wondering a lot how he found you here.'

It was less than a question, and she gave it less than an answer. 'He always has. He always will, I fancy.'

'What do you reckon to do?' he asked. 'Even if you wanted to stay – '

'Where? Here?' Her arm made a sweep at the emptiness, the sea, the horns of the bay. 'Not me. I'll be moving on tomorrow.' She was still the optimist, with a better time round the corner. Guns boomed in the north, and when they looked far out over the sea there were black smoke-balls bursting round the yellow air-hung target flares. 'Strike,' she said, suddenly brisk and cheerful, 'what are we fighting for, Crad, you and me? We only live once, don't we?' She watched his face slacken and smile. 'Tell you what we'll do; after supper I'll put in my ear-rings, like we did before, remember? And you,' she cried to the watching dog, 'aren't you the lucky boy?' She sent him scuttling with a snowball, and her high spirits lasted throughout the evening.

He groaned with the dog's first bark. A great brown horse had reared at him, a horse that filled the sky. The polished hooves pounded his chest, its swollen head with the yellow teeth and reddening eyeballs grinned as it sank to destroy him. 'No,' he groaned, 'no!' His fist drove at its breastbone, sank through unstayed. 'No. Oh, no!'

It was a woman, trying to suck out his heart, lean-limbed, snake-smooth and writhing. If once her lips reached him – horrible, a-drip, the image of lust and death. 'No!' he groaned again. His fists struck, sank into nothing, and he could not pull them back. 'Crad!' There was a yelling. 'Crad, Crad, Crad!'

He was awake, wet and shuddering. The shouting woman beat harder at his shoulders, and the dog's barking, shrill with fright, volleyed between ceiling and walls. There was a soft red flicker throughout the room, and her bosom seemed loaded with roses.

He was out of bed, huddling on his clothes, snatching for his boots. 'Turn the cows out,' he shouted, and ran through the door.

It was the barn and hay-loft, burning with a bright incongruous gaiety. Flame was sweeping from the loose and scattered hay up to the main mass, from which fell lovely crimson rivulets and gouts and splashes of red. In the nearby pens four ewes dashed madly against the rattling hurdles, which shook and stood firm, throwing them in heaps to the ground, whence they arose and made their furious springs again; and with them there skipped and fell their desperate weak-legged lambs. It was to them he ran first, tearing open their prisons, bellowing the sheep forward so that they bounded wildly past the cottage to the home field. And now a drape of merry flame masked the hay-pile, hung like a cyclopean brocade crackling and roaring from roof to floor. The timbers of the barn had started to snap and flower. He ran round to the back of the barn, began to tear out armfuls of hay, raced stumblingly and half-seeing, flung them on to the grimy snow; but already the first arms of fire were thrusting through the roof, driving their openings wider, scooping at the steaming boards, dragging them down to destruction, while lumps of snow fell hissing into the blaze below. He hurried back to between the barn and the cottage, and saw the woman standing as though on watch out past the cowshed. He shook his fist at her, at the fire, at the world, but she showed no fear as she walked over to him. 'It's Harry,' she said. 'I'm afraid for the house.'

The dog skulked behind her. 'Get him!' he raved. 'Bring him in, can't you?' But he only cowered till Craddock signalled him in a language he understood, when he straightened and with his tail tucked in slipped furtively away.

Again Craddock ran to the back of the barn, but by this time that, too, was ablaze. The flame here was redder and mingled with black, the dislodged hay flaring outwards to ruin. Smuts rained all about him, and from the heart of the fire fountains of sparks were lofted by the quick-falling timbers of the barn. He confronted this destruction with the brute puzzlement and black hatred of a bull. Why should he alone suffer this, his barn, and his beasts? On whom, on what, should it be avenged? His hands were opening and shutting; what next they closed on that was alien and hostile they would crush and destroy. Seeking a victim, he glared from the fire to the cottage, from the cottage to the sky, from the sky to the hill slope and snow banks. And it was then that, pale, floating, and instantly withdrawn into the dark, he saw the face.

For a while he made no movement. Another redness than the fire's burned behind his eyes, the red rage of the bull. His sensations ceased to be human; his moving hands were the bull's feet pawing before the charge. He began to groan, his chest rose and fell, spittle gushed from his mouth, fouling his chin. And all the time some red and furious residue of the brain told him of terrain and slope, ruse and surprise, the moment when he would roar and make his charge.

Across the smoke and sparks Harry saw him too late, rose in terror and fell again, and as the great hands seized him squealed like a rat that feels the stick on his back. From Craddock, as he lifted him, swung him, dashed him to earth, came a wild and broken roaring. The rat and the bull had their true voices now. Alongside the cottage the woman heard their bestial notes of terror and triumph, and ran to meet them. Craddock had Harry like a sheep across his shoulders as he lurched back down the slope, making towards the fire. 'Don't,' she begged; 'Don't do it, Crad!' Did he hear? Did he see. Did he know? 'Crad, oh, Crad!' She struck at his chest, beat upwards at his face, clawed at his waist, but he came on. 'Crad, don't, oh Crad!'

'Burn,' he groaned at her then. The one word. 'Burn.'

Sparks showered over them, and she smelled her singeing hair. Tiny puffs of smoke rose out of his clothing, and she saw a thread of hay burn from red to black on his right hand. She fell on her knees, gripping his thighs, so that he dragged her forward, sobbing. 'Crad, oh Crad! Don't do it.'

She felt his muscles tense for the heave. The man on his shoulders felt it too, and gave again his high inhuman squeal. 'Crad,' she cried, 'Crad, look at the sheep!'

He stood still, held by the strongest word in his life. He stared past the sinking fire. Thirty or forty ewes with their lambs were being driven nearer the blaze by the half-maddened dog, growling, worrying, snapping behind them. He had worked to Craddock's gathering signal, mistaking its object, and crazed with fright himself. A great hullabaloo of frantic sheep, caught between dog and fire, dinned into their ears; their distress pierced his very brain. She felt his thighs slacken, saw his jaws close; his knees bent and the man on his back fell off him to the ground. 'I'll see to Harry,' she said. 'I'll take him away. Go to the sheep, Crad.'

He was rubbing his face as he went blundering round the fire. She heard his voice, cracked but masterful, bringing the dog to heel, ordering everything anew; the bawling of the sheep receded, they were being driven gently into the home field. She pulled at Harry, dragged him on his knees out of the drifting sparks. 'Wait here,' she told him. 'I'll be back.' He looked round him, still on his knees and dazed. 'My hat,' he said piteously; 'can't go without me titfer.' And fainted again.

As she collected her belongings from the cottage she saw the dim shapes of Craddock and the flock moving towards the gateway that led to the outer fields. 'God strike!' she said devoutly. When he came back he found the place empty. He was carrying a dead lamb in his left hand. The dog, ashamed, slunk at a distance behind him. Only a few tongues of flame were left now, but the great heap of ash glowed and quivered with every brush of air. From its blackening rim a sour and horrid smell had begun to poison the dawn, and he turned from it, sickened. An intolerable dejection weighed him down; he knew himself befouled with evil, Harry's and his own. His legs hung heavy as he went into the cottage, lit the lamp and put the kettle on the fire. He took up the lamb from where he had placed it by one of the table legs: it was the young ram, and it had been kicked to death by one of the cows in their frightened gallop down the field. With its body across his knees he sat by the fire and began to cry, for the lamb, for himself, for all the events of the night. But he stopped this with an immense effort of will, stumbled across to the bed and lay down. Half an hour later the rattling kettle-lid roused him, and he saw through the window that it was pale day. A small, sharp object had scratched his neck as he moved. It was a 'real diamond' ear-ring. Unvindictively, unregretfully, he dropped it into the fire and made himself tea. He saw how the dog looked anxiously at him, and slowly he blew into his basin and tried the milky tea for heat with his finger. The dog wagged his tail, knowing that they were friends again.

His breakfast done, he stripped to the waist and washed. Then he went into the doorway and was vexed to find the home field full of sheep, his own ewes and the yearlings. Bad, he thought, that he was too careless to secure the gate last night. And it was more than time to fetch the cows in and start the day's round.

Suddenly he flipped his fingers for the dog and walked excitedly among the sheep. Overnight his last ewe had lambed, and he had the dog distract her while he picked up her trembling youngster. It was not the ram he hoped for, but what matter? It was alive and young and clean and whole. Calling to the dog, he set the lamb on the grass again and laughed to see it rush for its mother's milk-bag. The sun was clearing the hills behind him, it already sparkled on the water a mile out from land, and beyond the water the mountains were benedictory and white. The two black cows were lowing to be milked, and by the time that was finished the sun would be on the flock and the night, by them, forgotten.

Best, he thought, forgotten by him, too. He would rebuild the barn, half of stone this time, and do it with his own hands and the friendly aid of neighbours. No man had better neighbours in need than he.

But this was no time for dreaming. Followed by the dog he set briskly off, with one backward glance at the flickering tail of the lamb. He was the farm's stay, he had only one pair of hands, and there was blessedly much to do before mid-morning.

The Brute Creation

~

THIS was the field. The white tents, the four hundred yards of
grass, the hurdles and the pens flashed at his eyes, the flags and
the bright dresses of the women. The first dogs had already gone
out. He was suddenly sober, a shepherd with a job to do. He knew
that most of his fellow competitors disliked him, and that some of
them feared him, but to be feared was honey on his tongue. He
knew, too, how they hoped to see everything go wrong for him this
afternoon: he wouldn't trust those scabs down the field not to
loose a tough one when his turn came. They said it was the run of
the game, the sheep a man had to work; he growled to think how
often he got bad ones. Some of these farmers, squat, basin-bellied,
fat-legged, he'd like to see them on the mountain. That's where
you showed whether you could handle sheep, not on a green
handkerchief like this.

He was a red-headed one from the farmstead up under the
Black Rocks. A scurfy, thin-soiled place with the whole mountain
for a sheep-run. Sometimes he had a woman up there, but never
for long: they could stand neither the place nor its tenant. The tall,
black rocks rose up behind the cottage like a claw; the mountain
sprawled away thereafter in bog and stream and the rush-ridden
grass of the grazing grounds. Lonely – too lonely for everyone save
him – too lonely sometimes even for him. That was when he would
come down to the town and haggle with some sly or trampled
creature to come up for a week, a fortnight – no one had ever
stayed longer than that. And they all left him the same way: they
waited till he was far out on the mountain after sheep and then
fled downwards, from home field to path, from path to mountain
road, and so to where the lower farms spotted the slopes round
Isa'ndre. Fled, they would say, as if the devil were behind them, a
devil with big hands and red hair.

He lumbered his way to the stewards' table. There were thirty or
forty dogs entered for the different classes, the air quivered with

299

their excitement. Their merits and failings were as well known here as those of their masters, and even more discussed. He saw men eyeing his black-and-white bitch as she moved close behind him. 'Novice?' asked one of the Isa'ndre shepherds, jerking his thumb. 'Novice!' he sneered, and then, savagely: 'Open! The Cup!'

The Cup! That tall white silver thing on his shelf for a year, his name on it for ever. A wide smile covered his face and he looked down at the bitch. 'You better,' he said. 'You better, see!' Her tail went tighter over her haunches, her eyes seemed to lose focus.

They were ticking his name off at the stewards' table. They were looking down at the bitch, a fine-drawn, thin-faced youngster. 'You ought to have entered her for the Novice. It's not fair to a young 'un.' 'She's going to win,' he told them, grinning. 'She better!'

He was walking away, swinging his stick. Behind him they shook their heads, shrugged, went on with their business. He grew restive and arrogant among men who seemed always to be moving away from him. Crike, he'd show them.

And then he was out at the shepherd's post, and far down the field they were loosing the three sheep which he and his bitch must move by long invisible strings, so that his will was her wish, her wish their law. A movement of his fingers sent her out to the right on a loping run which brought her well behind the three sheep. She sank instantly, but rose at his whistle and came forward flying her tail and worked them swiftly through the first hurdle. No one of them attempted to break as she ran them down towards the shepherd, turned them neatly round to his right, and then at a wave of his stick fetched them down past his left hand and so away to the second hurdle. They were now running too fast, and he whistled her to a stalking pace while the hurdle was still seventy yards away. The sheep halted, their heads up, and at the whistle the bitch proceeded with short flanking runs which headed them into the gap.

The shepherd was now five separate beings, and yet those five integrated so that they were one. He was the shepherd, he was the bitch, he was the three sheep together and severally: he could hardly distinguish between them as aspects of himself. The sheep had been turned across the field towards the hurdle in front of the spectators' benches at a moment when a string of children ran madly towards a stall selling drinks and ice-cream. As they faced the benches, the shepherd could feel alarm and irresolution grow in the sheep. The bitch felt it, too, and showed by a short, furious spurt that she was worried. Her worry moved simultaneously within the shepherd's mind.

The bitch steadied on his whistle, crouched, rose again, and raced out to fetch a straggler back. At once a second sheep broke away on the other side. By the time she had them once more in a group her anxiety was apparent to every shepherd on the field. They broke again and it looked as though they would pass round the hurdle, but a fierce whistle helped her cut them off. The pattern renewed itself: yet again the sheep faced the hurdle and the fluttering benches behind, yet again the bitch sank in their rear. The time was going by, she had lost the benefit of her quick work at the beginning and the shepherd brought her once more to her feet. She raced to their right, but grew confused on his signals and sank at the wrong time, letting a sheep escape. The crowd began to laugh, for she seemed little better than a fool to them now. She collected the sheep for the last time, but they at once strung out across the face of the hurdle, and at the shepherd's furious whistle she openly cringed and began to creep away from the sheep. Hoots of laughter and miaowings pursued her across the field; only the shepherds were silent.

The red-headed man turned from the post, his face like murder. The time-keeper's whistle had blown to clear the field, and at his own whistle the bitch came slowly to within thirty yards of him. Nearer she would not approach. 'That bitch,' said the steward who had spoken to him before, 'you want to go quiet with her. She'll make or break after this.' The red-headed man hardly looked at him, but gripped his stick and made for the gate.

First he went to eat food and then began a round of the back streets, the spit-and-sawdust bars where the legginged touts and copers drank, and where the policemen walked in twos. When he entered a pub he moved ponderously, swinging his weight from side to side like a Friesian bull, and he had a bull's eyes, gleaming, reddish, ill-tempered. At the *Hart* he pushed across the counter a corked medicine bottle. 'Fill this! All whisky. No water.' He slid his ten shilling note into a spill of beer, grinning into the landlord's cloudy face.

Behind him, wherever he walked, slunk the bitch. She was hungry and thirsty, but too terrified even to lap water. From time to time he stopped and looked at her; he had no need to threaten; her bones had softened inside her. He could wait for the reckoning; delay would add to the pleasure. And the more he drank the blacker-hearted he grew. She'd make him look a fool before them all – all right, they'd see.

Later in the evening he went down to the woollen mills where before now he had found someone hardened or needy enough to accompany him back to the Rocks. He avoided the women who knew him, and struck into a bargain with someone he had not seen there before, a woman in the early thirties with an old, used face, dressed in country black. 'Come back to my place,' she wheedled. 'We can talk there. P'raps I will, p'raps I won't. We can settle it after.' They were both smiling, his face cunning, brutal, hers set in a mirthless coquetry. 'All right,' he said thickly, his hands opening and shutting. 'Where?'

They were walking down a dingy, low-fronted street. 'There's a dog following us,' she said.

He began to curse the bitch, his luck, everything that had happened that day. 'Eh,' she said, 'you don't want to take it that bad. She looks frightened.' She patted her knee, clicked her tongue to call the bitch to her, but the creature stayed at the same distance, sitting and shivering.

'Leave her,' he growled. 'She'll follow. She better!'

The bitch turned away at his tone, but when they went on to the woman's room she trailed them behind, like a lost soul. Hours later when the woman slid from the bed and went to the window overlooking the street the bitch was still there, outside the house, lying uneasily at the edge of the shadow. Behind her the red-headed man stretched and groaned in his sleep and she looked round at him, his huge lardlike shoulders, the thick neck and hairy hands. 'Swine,' she whispered, 'filthy swine!' Moonlight fell through the window with a pale green radiance, so that she could stare down the swollen whiteness of her body to her spread feet and the greasy fringe of the mat on the floor. 'Great God,' she whispered, 'Great God in heaven above!' She went quietly to the cupboard in the corner and hunted through her food-shelf till she found a piece of meat and a cake crust. She was back at the window with these when he sat up and asked what she was doing.

'The dog's outside,' she said, afraid of him. 'I was giving it food.'

'She don't eat tonight,' he told her. 'Nor p'raps tomorrow.' He leaned back against the bed-head, savouring her fear of him. 'I'm a bad 'un to cross. She got to learn it.'

'P'raps I got to learn it too, up at your place.' She reached for her raincoat and pulled it over her. The action, the covering her nakedness, gave her resolution. 'You can get dressed and clear out, and the sooner the better.'

He shook his head. 'I don't take orders. Not from muck like you, I don't.'

'I'm muck,' she said bitterly. 'Christ knows, but I'm too good for you at that. I'm wise to you, anyway, and I'm not coming.'

He closed his fist. 'I got a mind – ' he began, but she had opened the door and stood half on the landing, staring in at him. 'Don't try anything,' she said. 'If I call, I got friends.'

'You!' he jeered. 'Friends!' But he got slowly out of bed and dragged on his clothes, swaying with exhaustion and drink. 'Muck like you,' he said, tying his laces. 'Friends!' He coughed and hawked with his heavy laughter.

Warily she watched him out of the room, backing away from the head of the stairs. He began to clump his way down, his boots hammering the boards, making all the row he could in that listening house. Then he was through the door with a shattering slam. She went back to the moon-filled window and looked into the street. For a half-minute she saw him leaning against the wall below her, then he began to walk away. The bitch emerged from shadow and, disregarding her low whistle, slunk after him.

The night air, cool and clean, drew him briskly forward. His head felt loose and large, but his legs moved steadily, his weight back on his heels, so that his progress rang and echoed between the houses. He felt he could walk a hundred miles. A brief good-humour filled him. Hadn't he been too clever for everyone? That landlord! He rumbled with beer and satisfaction. The woman he'd had – he swallowed appreciatively. If only he'd had a fair deal in the Field!

His good humour was gone. He looked round for the bitch. That woman. The judges. That blasted landlord scowling at him. Crike, he'd take it out of someone before he was through.

The houses had changed to hedges. There was no pavement, nor now a strake of dusty grass to walk on. The ring died out of the road; his boots were beginning to drag. He struck angrily at an ash branch which had missed the hedger's bill. If only it were that woman, the judges, the landlord – he thrashed it till the branch hung torn and a faint bitter odour of greenery tinged the air. He turned and called to the bitch but she kept her distance, her haunches tight, her head hanging forward.

It was then he heard the clopping of a horse, the scrape of wheel rims, and saw away behind the bitch the yellow blob of a headlamp. He went into the middle of the road, stood waiting with his stick raised.

'You, is it?' said the man in the trap. The words were uncordial, the voice unfriendly. 'All right, get in. I'll take you to the usual place. That your bitch behind there?'

He was a compact, dried-out man nearing sixty, spry with gaiters, side-whiskers, and a hard hat, a big farmer from higher up the valley. He was a great one with the chapel and the local bench, and the red-headed man at once despised him and stood in awe of him, for he was the kind who could put the police on to you. The kind who would, too, if you touched his pride or pocket.

'She won't come,' he said sullenly.

'Not the first time today she made a fool of you,' said the farmer coolly. 'All right, if she won't ride I reckon she can run.'

He drove the mare smartly, as though she were before judges in a ring. The hedgerows were dipping past them, the mare's hooves tapped sleep into the red-headed man's brain. First his head rolled sideways and then he was canted on to the floor, groaning with discomfort, the sourness of drink rising into his mouth and nose. He was thinking, or dreaming, of the woman in her room when the shaking of the trap became so intolerable that he must open his eyes and struggle up. But the trap was stationary, and it was the farmer kicking hard at his feet to wake him. 'We are there. I was just going to tip you off.' He snaked the whiplash out sideways, gathered it neatly back to the handle. 'This bitch of yours now – '

'Where is she?'

He pointed with the whip to where she lay gasping thirty yards down the road. 'I'll take her off your hands as a favour.'

For a moment the other couldn't take this in; he stood staring at his hands as though they should contain something. Then, 'Not for sale,' he said abruptly.

'I'm not talking about a sale.' His hard little eyes stared into the red-headed man while he reached for a wallet with a wide rubber band round it, opened it and drew out a note. 'Still, I'll make it legal.'

'Legal, hell,' said the red-headed man. He leaned so heavily on the back of the trap that the mare pawed uneasily. 'She's worth five, ten pounds. What's this? A scabby ten bob!'

'Take it,' said the farmer. 'I'm doing you a favour.'

'Favour, hell. I'll see you stuffed first!' He leaned forward into the trap, closed his fist. 'I got a mind – '

The man in the trap had made his decision. Instantly his whip cracked and the mare bounded forward so sharply that the red-headed man fell floundering on to the road. He came on to all fours, cursing and threatening, but the trap was disappearing round the next bend before his hand could close on a stone. 'Chapel bastard!' he swore, and turned to the bitch. This was her fault. Everything that had happened today was her fault. He'd see that she paid. 'Come here, damn you!' he called.

Suddenly he thought of the whisky in his pocket. The medicine bottle was undamaged and he took a long, noisy suck at it. Whisky was a whip, he told himself, and began to lurch up the mountain road.

But tired! After three hundred yards on the steep road he felt that till tonight he had not known what tiredness was. His legs were moving against rather than with his will. Only the pattern of resentment shaping in his mind drove him on. All the faces of the day, he saw them staring at him, landlords, stewards, judges, the woman who'd thrown him out – he ought to have smashed his fist into their grinning mugs. He'd been too soft, he'd let them outsmart him. Tomorrow he'd go back and find them, his fist like this, see, smash them all. Smash, smash, smash!

His head swayed with thought. The bitch was the cause of it. Well, that was something he could take care of tonight. When he came to the path, to the peat stream, there'd be a pool big enough. He turned to look at her. 'Come here then, little 'un,' he said, wheedling and hoarse. 'Come to the old man.' Exulting in his stratagem, he began to coax her forward with soft words and endearments. Once she moved so much as a foot she was lost; she was powerless against the god she recognized in him, helpless against her craving for kindness after so horrible a day. 'Well then,' he said at last, stroking her head and slipping the leash on to her collar, shoving her frantic tongue from his face. 'We shan't be long now.'

Crike, but he was tired. 'I'm drunk,' he said aloud, and she wagged her tail with joy. 'Owl drunk. Where's the whisky? Crike, but I'm drunk!'

This was it! He must find a stone, a big stone. There it was, shining in the water, black with a glitter on it, just under the surface. Careful, he said, careful now. He heard a curious slapping sound and was puzzled what it could be. It was the bitch drinking. 'That's right,' he grinned. 'Plenty of water.'

He slipped the leash because it wasn't long enough for him to hold the bitch and reach the stone. But she wouldn't run away. She was ingratiating herself with him, frisking her tail, fawning and slobbering.

'Crike!' he said vexedly. There was a bright ringing weight in his head from where he had been stooping. And dimly he was aware that this was no real pool, just a couple of inches of water over pebbles, and they moving treacherously under his feet.

He shouldn't have stooped. He reeled as he straightened up, and saw a blinding moon flash from the heavens. His heels shot from under him, and he fell face down into the water. Still the great moon flashed and pealed, only it was all about his head now. He must get his head up out of the moon. It blinded and deafened him. He heaved with his back, thrust with his great hand, for a moment his mouth gasped air.

From the bank the bitch watched his play with increasing excitement and delight. She was barely a year old. She dabbled the water with her forefeet, whined and then yapped her pleasure. She wanted to join in the game. Emboldened now and dizzy with joy that the black of the day was behind her, she leapt for his arching back, and stood proudly with her two paws on his shoulders. She could feel him moving in muscle and lung, and she tried ecstatically to lick his face. But always her muzzle was repelled by the water; so she retreated to the bank and sat for a while wagging her tail in expectation that he would play with her again.

The shadows had shifted a broad handbreadth when she paddled out to him a second time and sniffed at the back of his head. Soon her paws were once more on his shoulders, for long seconds she sniffed and whimpered. Then the hair rose along her backbone, the muzzle pointed, and briefly she moaned in her throat before her long and lonely howl went tingling to the moon.

Old Age

~

O N WHAT morning, in what golden summer, had he come to
the big house first? And why, why, should he have come to it
now? Thinking of it, he sighed, and saw his breath steam thin and
white in the wintry air. The gravel drive was speckled with rime,
and there were ferns of frost over the front windows. He moved his
feet feebly but resentfully on the iron scraper. It would be cold in
there, and he was not such a youngster now.

He stood all hunched as the bell called tremulously into the
hall. Everything looked smaller, but he was used to that. And
everything looked shabby and more worn – and he was used to
that too. He had a habit these last years of forcing his tongue
rapidly against his upper gums, which gave him, as now, a
champing monkey-like look. *Chup-chup-chup* was the sound he
made, as he stood there waiting. *Chup*, oh *chup-chup-chup*.

The door had opened, a middle-aged woman (he thought she
looked like one of the Lloyds from down by the sea) was offering
to take his hat and coat and stick. The hat he gave up with
misgiving, but he kept his coat close-buttoned, and the rubber-
shod stick squeaked its owner's protest through the chilly hall and
up the yellowing staircase. He gave the balustrade a hostile rap:
houses like this were nothing to him now, for he had come a long
way from the mountain. He felt inside his coat for his watch-
chain, chupping with satisfaction as he found it safe. Nothing like
gold, he told himself. And nature's other gold, the sunshine – he
shivered – that too was good for old fellows like him.

And then from the head of the stairs he saw the door, white-
painted still, with its gold-edged panels and the same white china
knob. 'She wouldn't hear you,' said the woman, polite and
indifferent. 'Would you please to go inside?'

But he knocked, as he had knocked before, and his fingers grew
cold on the door knob before he turned it and the door opened.

He had come down from the mountain, all that life-time ago, looking for a pony. A scrawny pony rising twelve hands, with a bushed yellow mane, which had thrown him the day before and galloped down the mountain road. He remembered still the sickness of heart with which he reached home after hours of walking. His father said little that night, but in the morning, before the sun rose over the hill, he had climbed to the loft and shaken him by the shoulder. 'Get up,' he said roughly, 'and find the pony.' There was barely light enough to see the gaunt face bent over him, but he knew him by the leather and peat and sheep-ointment of which he always smelled. 'And don't come back without him!'

The words frightened him, as well they might, for his father was a hard man since his mother died. He rose without a word, reaching for his clothes in the summer dark, huddling himself into them. As his stockinged feet touched the ladder that led downstairs, he heard the outer door close behind his father. He ate cold potatoes and bread, drank buttermilk, and then went out on to the hillside. The plain lay dark and slumbrous far below, and away beyond it was the gloomed and lifeless sea. He knew no time by the clock, but the first daylight was now fingering its way over the crags behind him. Somewhere up there, their feet delicate among moss and heather, moved his father and their dog Fan, for it had been a bad year for sheep, and sheep were their life. Stooping, he rubbed his hands on dewy grass, and at that moment felt the earth heave and wake, and straightway a light hard as flint glittered past the rocks and into the sky.

He began to walk, following the brook to the mountain road. A sheared ewe with a lamb bigger than herself glared at him from yellow eyeballs, then bleated and ran off, her black feet scuffing outwards on the lumpy turf; the first birds were twittering in the birch bushes. By the time he reached the top farm folk were astir; dogs walked out at him, yawning and then frisking a welcome. But as he walked downhill, neither at farm nor at house was there news of the pony. Most of the head-shakers clearly thought him a fool to have lost it. His spirits, which had brightened with the July morning, were clouding again. The sky was an early-day blue, but milk-hazed at the verges, and the sea sparkling out to the horizon. Coming near the plain, he wondered which way he should go. He felt himself a foreigner here, as though people would laugh at his hill clothes and not understand his speech. So he was careful to call only at the cottages of those who looked poor as himself, or to speak on the road with labourers or those who carried burdens. Some were curt with him, some over-friendly, but none could tell him of his pony.

The morning was wearing on, he had walked a long way and come to feel hungry. By a stony bank he stopped to gather whinberries, and soon his lips were purpled with their juice. But this made him yet hungrier, and he had not a halfpenny in his pocket. His one treasure, a hare's foot, hung from his neck down on to his chest, and he was continually making sure it was next his skin and safely out of sight. For the gods of the humble serve best when close and hidden.

It had grown hot. Even the haze was now burnt from the horizon. The roadside grass was soiled with dust, the ash leaves hung sapless. Down on his hands and knees, he drank deeply from a brook, splashed water over hair and neck, grimaced when he saw the sleek drowned body of a rat a few yards further down.

And then he saw the horses. Or did he dream them into life? In a white-railed meadow, on a flashing sward, how proudly they cropped the emerald grass or arched their lovely necks. Creatures of fire and air they seemed, all golden in the golden light, and young as the day's dawn. He stood a long time counting them, seven mares and their stallion, strong and slim as a sunbeam. He called to them, and they looked towards him with their huge soft eyes, and the stallion shrilled and whistled his way among the mares, their master and their slave. But the boy went on calling gently, and holding out his hand, and first one and then two and then three of the mares came shyly over to him. He stood with his thighs and chest pressed to the rails, rubbing their heads, combing and stroking their manes. Never had he seen heads so slender, felt hair so flowing and fine. From a distance the stallion watched him keenly, ever and again throwing up his head and snorting through his sunny nostrils. His mane tossed in the air like aureate rain. He was curious, a little piqued; he would await this new human if he entered the meadow, but was too proud to seek him out at the rail.

This the boy knew, watching his sparkling eye and restless head. And he sighed for joy as the stallion swept against his favourite mare and made little love-bites along her haughty yet submissive shoulder.

He had forgotten his tiredness and hunger. He lived in the animals before him. The sunshine which glossed their backs glowed on him too, the same grass grew about their feet, their nostrils stretched to the same scents of summer. In his neck, his back, his legs, he felt the muscles of the stallion. And as the stallion bared his creamy teeth to nuzzle the mare's shoulder, his own teeth showed between his purple lips and snapped laughing at the air.

'You laugh, animal, do you?'

The voice, like a wet black strap, slashed the sunshine from his back. He turned, frightened, and saw a man with his stick raised as though to strike him. 'Please,' he cried, 'please!' The stick clattered on the rail and the mares went kicking over the turf. It was a red, sodden, moustachioed face which stared into his. 'What are you, animal?' And before he could speak: 'Pan,' said the slapping wet voice, 'it's Pan!'

'Please,' he said again, finding no sense in the words, and his eye sideways on the stick. One of the mares came cantering back to them, and he felt her nose push at the small of his back. 'It was the horses when I saw them. For I have lost my horse.'

'For he has lost his horse!' mimicked the voice. He pulled an ogre's face, so that the eyebrows sprouted and spread and the long horns of his moustache looked threatening as a bull's. 'I say you are a horse thief, God damn you!'

'No, please,' he said anxiously. 'I was looking for my horse, that is all.'

The eyes in the red face were small and blurred and cunning, the breath that seeped from the sodden mouth was hot and sweet. 'Thieves everywhere,' he said. 'Can't trust your best friend.' The boy was growing harassed by his stare till he noticed that the eyes had changed focus. 'Look,' he said suddenly, 'look!' He made juicy clucking sounds against the roof of his mouth, and the stallion whinnied. Then he came up to the rails with a swirl of mane and tail, seeking the sugar the man took from his pocket. 'Give him this.' The stallion looked at the boy suspiciously, then soft as moss his lips fumbled over the palm, found and closed, and they heard the teeth crushing ecstatically. The boy licked the sweet, damp place the horse had left.

'An animal from where?' the man was asking. 'But that's ten miles away!' He pulled his ogre's face, nodded rapidly. 'Come to the house, animal.'

And so for the first time he saw the big house behind the green meadow. He saw it in silence, clutching his hare's foot, frightened still of his guide, who shouted through the hall, 'Anna, Anna!' and when an aproned woman appeared, said roughly, 'Bring this boy food and, yes, by God, milk. In here.'

Books, hundreds of books, a world of books to one who had seen only his father's bible, were on the walls. Pictures – would he ever forget them? – one of a beautiful woman with bare shoulders from which he must be always forcing his eyes – and flowers in vases, and soft carpets, and carafes of yellow liquor – things he had never seen and did not know existed. The small blurred eyes watched him eat as they would watch a dog; and as with a dog which has been given all that is good for him, there was no offer of more.

'So the animal is afraid to go home?' He poured whisky and drank. 'Then I'll give you a horse, God rot me!' Fright and rapture tore at the boy, and a vision of the stallion free on the mountain. 'No, by Jesus,' swore the red-faced man, 'but one with four legs all the same!' Whisky splashed on the table top. 'Did you ever hear of Black Cherry? As though you would! The Consort Stakes, which year was it? I rode that horse, I brought him home like thunder when no other jockey finished the course. Christ, if I wasn't a fat sack of misery and guts, I'd do it again with the stallion!' He groaned, toasting the bare shoulders in the portrait, and the boy thought him like his own lost pony come to a bad place in the bog, the whisky his rope-end. 'What will you do for a horse, eh?'

'Anything. Anything I would do, please.'

'Then God damn me, so you shall! Go upstairs' – the voice grew sludgy – 'into the room I shall show you. Take off your clothes there and get into bed with the mistress' – he swore oaths which made the boy wince – 'and then I'll give you your horse.'

His words had no meaning for the boy. And before he could find one, the hot strong breath was on his face, his arm was caught in a thick red hand, and he was being forced out and upwards along the silent stairs. 'There, ahead of you,' said the man, pointing. 'Knock and go in, or you get no horse.' And as the boy stood puzzled and alarmed, 'Go,' he said savagely, 'now it's gone so far, or by God I'll break your neck!'

And because the boy thought he meant it, and because he was used to obey, he walked slowly to the white-painted door with the gold-edged panels, and knocked, and knocked again, and with a bent head stood waiting.

She heard the knock. So quiet, so timid, hardly more than a scraped finger-nail it sounded.

It was not *his* knock then. Neither the furious fist blows by day, nor the furtive drumming in the dark. She sat upright in bed, staring at the door, wondering what to do. Mistress of the big house, but no mistress of herself. Marry him she would never, with his red face and gross hands, his voice and monstrous oaths. Half schoolboy lout, half swine in the garden of his own hopes.

Again a gentle knocking. 'Who is it?' she called.

There was no answer, and still she stared at the door. Earlier in the morning she had risen and dressed to go downstairs, but suddenly felt unable to face him. Her day clothes lay about the room where she had taken them off again, the yellow dress on its hanger outside the wardrobe, just where the sunlight fell, the long white stockings with her shape still in them over the foot-rail of the bed. 'Is it you, Anna?'

'Please,' said a voice she did not know, 'it's me, a boy.'

Did he say a boy? 'A minute. A minute then.' She slipped from bed, stood with her hand near the bolt. 'Did you say a boy? Who are you?'

'It's me,' the voice said forlornly. 'I've lost my horse.'

After silence he heard surprised laughter, and felt his face go hot. He had never heard laughter so clear, so sunny, as that. 'Come in then,' she called, from where she was back in bed. 'If you think your horse is here!'

The door opened slowly, and she saw a boy in outlandish clothes, his hair the colour of wheat straw, his eyes brown, his lips pouting and empurpled. And oh, but he was frightened of her – of her, who had herself been frightened of so many. She thought he could not bring himself to look at her.

And yet he saw her and her clothes and the sunny room more clearly than he had seen anything in his life before, save the horses that morning. And when he saw the pouring gold of her hair and the whiteness of her shoulders, it was the horses he thought of, and the caressing teeth of the stallion.

'A boy after all,' she said. 'Well, what is it, boy?'

He looked towards her, and did not see the tautness behind her smile. 'The man said – ' But he could not go on, for what had been meaningless downstairs was now a sacrilege so terrible that he could not speak of it.

'He said?'

'No,' he cried. 'I am ashamed!'

'Tell me,' she said sharply. 'And tell me at once.'

Her tone was so imperious that he fell into his habit of obedience. 'He said that if I came into this room and undressed and got into bed with the mistress, he – he would give me a horse.' Seeing her face whiten, he hung his head, hiding his eyes. 'It was bad of me, but I was afraid.'

'It was not bad of you,' she answered, 'and we are all afraid sometimes.' She was silent for a long time, wondering at the brutish and pathetic oaf downstairs, wondering too at her own folly and weakness. And all this time tears burned the boy's eyes, that he should insult this white and wondrous lady – and that he should be so far from a man as to cry at all. 'Well,' she said firmly, but her breast a-flutter, 'you shall have your horse.' When the boy looked up at her, he saw her cheeks reddened but her eyes bright and blue as harebells. 'You must undress and lie here on the edge of the bed.' She set her lips primly. 'On the edge, you understand? You must not touch me. And then we shall send for him and see his face.' He noticed the queer lightness of her voice. 'Shall we, boy?'

Though she could not see him, she knew he had not moved. 'Oh, hurry up,' she called impatiently. 'We cannot take all day!' There was a loud and troubled sighing as he obeyed her, and her heart bumped violently as his boots fell to the floor. In a panic she moved to the far side of the bed, spoke angrily to hide her fear. 'Will you never be ready!' He got into bed as softly as a cat, lay rigid on its edge, a deep channel between them. 'At last then!' He did not look at her when she moved, but he heard the distant silvery tumbling of a bell.

It was the red-faced man who came to the room. 'So you've done it!' he said, rage and wonder choking his voice. 'I ought to kill you both.'

Her hand caught at the boy's as she felt him flinch.

'It's too late for threats,' she said. 'You've lost. So give the boy his horse.'

He struck the bed-rail with his fist, that mad dazed gambler. 'I haven't welshed yet,' he said furiously. He looked at the boy's peeled whiteness. 'So it's Pan first and the rest of the field nowhere.' In the mirror he saw his own bloated face and body. 'God blast me, I was never a starter!' He began to laugh, the folds under his wet eyes, the fat under his chin trembling.

'Get out!' she cried, more furious than he.

He stopped laughing, looked at the blood which oozed from his hand. 'Are you sure you know the odds, mistress?'

'Get out!'

The door slammed behind him. 'We've won,' she whispered. 'Boy, we've beaten him!'

She sank back on to her pillow, still clutching his hand. 'He was afraid of me!' She in her turn began to tremble and laugh, and the boy saw the inside of her mouth pink as a hedgerose, the tiny glistening pebbles of the teeth, and the foxglove bell of her tongue. White and soft her nightgown as the lining of a bean-pod, and her neckband finer than bog-cotton. 'You laugh,' he said, 'but it is the same, I know, as crying.' His fingers tingled as they touched the golden hair; her cheek, her chin, her throat were softer than the dove's breast-feathers. 'Do not cry,' he begged. 'Please, you must never cry!'

Did her arms enfold him? Or had he sought, so clumsily at first, to calm her shaking body? He did not know, nor by what miracle his lips were in the hollow of her throat, his forehead under the hair's waterfall. Nor could he tell, till his hands sought and found it, what heart it was that throbbed and leapt between them. They lay in a whorled and shelly chrysalis of light, time fallen from them with their garments. O bright young stallion trampling his lilied plain, his teeth on the mare's white shoulder! Pasture fair he found her, long fields of flesh and rounded flower-topped hills, the smooth white ridges and warm luminous slopes, and golden mossy caverns out of the sun's sight. All these she yielded up to him, and these he ranged in rapture and pride, till at his strength's end faltering and falling he entered the tenebrous valleys of sleep.

How long thereafter till like a white rod he sat upright beside her? Her eyes were closed, her lips were fallen apart; sweat-drops lay like pearls within her bosom. A strake of yellow sunshine reached out to her feet, and he knelt down to clasp and kiss them. Words, he prayed, if only there were words in this wide golden heaven which was yesterday only the world!

There had been words enough. Dully he heard them again, their hot and broken torrent thin now and brittle, tinkling like brook-ice. Words, but for whom?

The old woman was drawn up high against her pillows, a white shawl gathered with a silver brooch beneath her chin. The hand lying outside the bedclothes was mittened, the fingers blue-skinned, transparent. Had the bed stood just there? The yellow dress hung here? The shaped white stockings? He did not turn his head, but sat with his hands grey as parrot-claws over the crosspiece of his stick. Did it matter?

Indeed, anything there could be between him and this white and wintry woman in the bed, had it ever mattered? Surely it was a dream! Only the horses were real.

Sighing, he closed his eyes. He was a creature, that stallion, all of gold and fire. Something you could never forget. What height had he been now? His mane and tail, what length?

He found he did not know. It was only at night he knew these things again. And he had learned to wait.

How withered she is, he thought. He was not half so dried and ugly as she. And never would be. Besides, he told himself meanly, he had his eyes, he could see, and he could hear. He measured his blessings against her, as though she were his enemy.

'If I could see you,' she said gently, 'how changed your face would be. If I could hear you, how changed your voice.' Her face moved, she was smiling. 'Yet you were younger far than I.'

The bones were aching in his feet. He was growing anxious for himself, here in this cold room, and he could not look at her without distaste. He rose stiffly, carrying his stick lest it squeak on the floor. Her eyes were closed, her blued lips fallen apart, and he looked wryly away. She is asleep, he lied. And stiffly he went out through the white door with its gold-edged panels, and downstairs to the waiting car. Flakes of snow had begun to fall, they stroked at his cold cheeks, marred his glossy toecaps. He must take care of himself, great care. 'For indeed, I am not so young as I was,' he mumbled.

Upstairs, for a moment it seemed to the old woman that her room was filled with sunlight. 'You will not get a horse this time,' she jested, but the bed-clothes made no stir at her laughter. And then all was cold again. 'You are not gone?' she asked. 'Say you are not gone!'

Tears burned her sightless eyes, ran down the furrows of her cheeks, touched her mouth and chin, and fell against the woollen shawl. They fell soundlessly as the snow outside, the quiet tears of age. And in her age she wept with a new sorrow, not that she was old and blind and lapped in hideous silence, but knowing that her golden hour had died from willing memory. Better to die, she whimpered, oh, better to be dead!

But time which had been so cruel to her was now growing kind, and her tears did not last long. Soon she was dozing, and soon she would sleep, and after sleep this new, small death at the heart would be less than the pain of waking again, to one so old, so tired, and herself so soon forgetful.

Copy

~

Miss Silvia Ede to Mr Geoffrey Keames

The Elms,
Brunton Friary,
Flintshire.
April 1st, 195–

Geoffrey Keames, Esq.,
c/o Messrs Wiggins and Blow Ltd,
Sweetpea Street,
Covent Garden, WC2.

Dear Sir,

I am writing to tell you what great pleasure I derived from your novel, *The Rainbow Montage*, which I have only just finished reading. I don't think I have ever enjoyed a book more, and I am still quite unable to say whether I think most of the extraordinarily clever plot, the brilliant characterization, or the rare quality of the style. As one who dabbles herself, I really feel I am qualified to greet your great achievement, and to recognize the work of one who should yet place himself among the ranks of the greatest masters of our literature. You must have letters from a great number of admirers, but never from one who more sincerely wishes you well.

Once again, with many thanks and with sincerest wishes for your future,

Yours very truly,
SILVIA EDE.

II

Mr Geoffrey Keames to Miss Silvia Ede

April 7th, 195–

Dear Miss Ede,

I was very pleased to get your letter, and to know that you thought so highly of my novel, *The Rainbow Montage.* There is no greater satisfaction for an author than to know that his work is bringing pleasure to those who really care for literature. I thank you for your good wishes, and trust you will allow me to offer you mine, just as sincerely.

Yours very truly,
GEOFFREY KEAMES.

III

Conclusion of a letter from Mr Geoffrey Keames to Mr Nigel Whiteruff

April 7th, 195–

. . . have just been replying to my fan mail. To be precise, a letter from some woman in the worst kind of provincial hole. How do people survive in these places, Nigel, when even in Swiss Cottage one feels at times so far away from the hub of things? But this is fame – I'll be finding admirers in Walham Green next!

See you soon,
GEOFF.

IV

Miss Silvia Ede to Mr Geoffrey Keames

April 10th, 195–

Dear Mr Keames,

I was very pleased to receive your charming letter yesterday. You see, after I had written to you I felt quite ashamed I had done so, and if I could have called the letter back through the post, then I'm sure you would never have received it! I thought an author like yourself would be too busy to bother with it, though I'm certain if

318

I received any letters after the one or two things I have had published, I should be quite wild with delight. Certainly I never expected to be lucky enough to receive a letter in your own handwriting. Most authors, I'm sure, would have sent just a typewritten couple of lines. It makes me wonder whether you use a typewriter, or whether, like me, you find it easier to compose with the pen. But now, perhaps, I am just being curious, and I must stop.

With sincere thanks for your good wishes. I hope you didn't mind my letter.

Yours very truly,
SILVIA EDE.

P.S. – I have been reading your book again. I can't think how you thought out so clever a plot, so clear and yet not a bit ordinary, and so completely unvulgarized!

V

Mr Geoffrey Keames to Miss Silvia Ede

April 12th, 195–

Dear Miss Ede,

Of course I did not mind your letter. I was very happy indeed to receive it. Every one likes to have his work praised – the author who doesn't can't be human. As for the typewriter – I must confess it isn't often I answer even so pleasant a letter as yours by any other means, though, after what you say, I'm glad I broke the rule in this case! I should advise you, though, not to read my novel any more. There are only a few books – all masterpieces – that grow better and better with re-reading, as I expect you've found. I am interested in what you say about finding it easier to compose with the pen. It shows how different authors are, doesn't it?

With best wishes for your writing,

Sincerely yours,
GEOFFREY KEAMES.

VI

Miss Silvia Ede to Mr Geoffrey Keames

April 15th, 195–

Dear Mr Keames,

It was very kind of you to wish me well as a writer, though I don't know, I'm sure, whether I shall ever do anything worth while. Sometimes I have hopes, when I think I've made what most people would call a good start, but more often I'm a little downcast to find that I cannot see my way clear to produce a distinctive, cleverly-contrived piece of work like yours, for example. At least, I don't mean to say I could ever write anything so powerful or, in places, so bitter as *The Rainbow Montage* (it is far above anything I have in mind), but I mean something on a smaller scale, only with a fine subject. Sometimes overnight I seem to think out the loveliest plots, only in the morning they don't quite work out. Still, I feel sure I have it in me to do something out of the rut. I'm sure I envy you your gift of working out a strong story so beautifully. My own work so far has been so much slighter – so much less immense, if you understand me – and though it has been praised highly by some very good judges, I cannot really feel satisfied with it. I expect you are one of those lucky people who never feel like that. You know the value of your work, and that is everything. As I say, I envy you – though not in a mean spirit, naturally.

But I am talking far too much about myself. It could hardly be expected that the author of *The Rainbow Montage* should be very interested in the work of one who probably presumes when she styles herself a fellow writer. It is like the story of the Lion and the Mouse, with me as the mouse – and a very daring one at that!

I have not yet thanked you for your second letter. It was so very kind of you to write it. You need not fear I shall think less of *The Rainbow Montage*, though I read it again and again. I have settled now what I admire most in the book – it is the character of Edith Bellen. I believe that in her you have created one of the great heroines of fiction. She is the Juliet of the novel, and I'm sure I was never more affected by a real death than by hers. Her relationship to Evan too, though perhaps illicit, is not only wonderfully portrayed, but is absolutely true to life – a rare thing! I feel inside me – and in these matters a woman can trust her judgment – that it is exactly how a woman would act in those circumstances. A true woman, that is, and one not afraid to live!

But I am writing far too much. As it is, I expect you will be bored with this.

Yours very sincerely,
SILVIA EDE.

VII

Mr Geoffrey Keames to Miss Silvia Ede

April 20th, 195–

Dear Miss Ede,

I wonder why you should think me bored with your letter? I found it most interesting. What you have to say about your literary labours has quite caught my fancy. I wish you would tell me more about them, or better still, let me know where I can get hold of them. You see, I've been at work on *The Rainbow Montage* so long and so intensely that I'm rather out of touch with contemporary writing. I'm sure I have a great treat in store. Be comforted – you are not the only one to know that sense of dissatisfaction and inability to get at the best inside one. I know how I felt while writing *The Rainbow Montage* – as though I could never get down on to paper the brilliant ideas that were always occurring to me – as though they must be dulled in the expression.

I think you are right about Edith Bellen. She is the best thing in the book, though, myself, I can't help a sneaking regard for Louisa in Chapter IV, that rather outspoken bit where she gives herself to Evan's father. There's the symbolical passage towards the end too. Perhaps that cost me most to write. The emotional strain was almost unbearable. I could hardly sleep for it, I remember – my brain white-hot. But you are right about Edith. Your judgment is sound there – which makes me think your own work far better than you would lead me to believe. Do let me know more about it.

With sincerest good wishes,
GEOFFREY KEAMES.

VIII

Miss Silvia Ede to Mr Geoffrey Keames

April 21st, 195–

Dear Mr Keames,

Your letter was really too kind. I feel awfully nervous at the idea of you reading my work. Somehow one doesn't care when it appears before the world of strangers, but after your letters I can no longer think of you as such, and that is why I feel as I do. I hope you get the parcel safely. I have registered it, of course. I have included two unpublished pieces too, though I really oughtn't to take advantage of you like this and impose on your good nature. I confess I'm too excited to write any more, and must now be as patient as I can while awaiting your reply.

Yours gratefully,
SILVIA EDE.

IX

Part of a letter from Mr Geoffrey Keames to Miss Silvia Ede

April 30th, 195–

Dear Miss Ede,

More than a week has gone by since I sent you a bare acknowledgment of the safe arrival of your publications and manuscripts, and here I am at last, writing to tell you how much I enjoyed reading them. It would be unkind of me to delay that statement to some later passage of my letter, for I know you must feel as I did when first I exposed *The Rainbow Montage* to the criticism of a friend. I could hardly wait for his considered reply. Twenty times a day I felt like running across London to see him and hear from his own lips the inevitable praise or blame. Perhaps, too, it would have been better had I done so, for I remember he sent me an ill-judged and envious letter which put an end to a very dear friendship. But you need have no fears of that sort, for I hasten to state my pleasure at having this opportunity of reading and then passing judgment on your literary productions. To take them in order – I think with you that the story in the *Flintshire*

Evening Gazette is the best. It has that charm of perception and delicacy of craftsmanship which are the most valuable feminine traits in literature, and the delightful, unstrained humour of the characters is above all praise. I am not surprised that the *Flintshire Evening Gazette* asked you for a companion story. They say sequels are never so good as the original conception, but yours, like Daudet's immortal Tartarin volumes, is an exception to the rule. Then the story in the *Countryman's Round* – just the thing to convince me of the work you will yet produce. I thought the character of Effie in some respects like that of Edith Bellen – perhaps in the way she stakes all on her chance of love and happiness. The passage about the healing influences of the countryside was both tenderly conceived and warmly expressed. I don't quite know what to say about the poetry. It has the authentic note, the true *vis vivida*, but might I say, in the friendliest spirit imaginable, that few are capable of the highest flights in both prose and verse – or so it seems to me. 'That with no middle flight intends to soar etc.' You remember the passage? To which do you feel yourself most drawn: 'The poet's eye in a fine frenzy rolling', or 'The other harmony of prose', as the great poet so finely calls it? In either, I think you have a future, but ought you to expend your strength between two such exacting masters? . . . If any sentiment here expressed seems to you a little severe, please remember that if I were saying it and not setting it down in cold black and white, it would have no such connotation.

I am returning your manuscripts by this same post. Thank you so much for letting me keep the published work. I have been greatly privileged to read it.

Yours, indeed,
GEOFFREY KEAMES.

X

Part of a letter from Miss Silvia Ede to Mr Geoffrey Keames

May 1st, 195–

Dear Mr Keames,

I opened your letter with fear and trembling, desirous and yet afraid to see what it contained. And now – however can I thank you enough? All the kind things you say – I know I don't deserve them, and yet I am woman enough to be delighted and thrilled! Is this silly of me? Or can you understand it? – As though the creator of Edith Bellen could not. . . . Indeed, what you say about the desirability of personal, verbal criticism is absolutely true. Every inflection of the voice means something, does it not? When I feel how well you understand my work and me, I do wish that I might be fortunate enough to one day meet the author of *The Rainbow Montage* in the flesh. Am I too bold? Not in these days of a more sensible relationship between the sexes, surely!

Perhaps I ought not to send this letter. But I will, even though you think it terrible of me! Again with thanks and best wishes,

Your sincere friend and well-wisher,
SILVIA EDE.

P.S. – I have split a very bad infinitive, I see.

XI

Mr Geoffrey Keames to Miss Silvia Ede

May 2nd, 195–

Dear Miss Ede,

I write on impulse, with your letter before me. If, as I think, there is in Silvia Ede much of my own Edith Bellen, I ask you to meet me at Liverpool next Saturday evening, May the fifth. What happens thereafter is on the lap of the gods.

Yours,
GEOFFREY KEAMES.

XII

Miss Silvia Ede to Mr Geoffrey Keames

May 3rd, 195–

Dear Geoffrey,

You see! That is my answer! I shall be at Liverpool to meet you. I have told my people that I shall be away over the week-end. It is weird to think that when first I read your wonderful novel I thought of myself as Edith Bellen, and dreamed that you might be Evan. I felt, indeed, that if ever I could share love's sweet mystery with anyone it would be with the author of that wonderful book. But do not be alarmed by that word 'love'. We are modern people. We can meet and, if fate so wills it, we can part at once for ever. Which will be the case? That is what we shall soon know.

Not adieu, but au revoir!

I am (Edith, I would say),
SILVIA.

P.S. – I suggest we meet on the landing stage, where the Egremont ferry comes in. At six o'clock? You will know me by my fur coat of grey squirrel, with a red flower, small red hat, and small hand case.

XIII

Mr Geoffrey Keames to Miss Silvia Ede

May 4th, 195–

Dear Silvia,

I have your letter before me as I write. We will meet as you say. You will recognize me easily. I shall be wearing a brown overcoat and hat, and I too shall wear a red flower. Strange to think I am to meet one who might have been the original of my Edith Bellen. I will write no more now. Does it seem quite real to you? But that it will *prove* a precious reality, I am confident.

GEOFFREY KEAMES.

XIV

*Conclusion of a letter from Mr Geoffrey Keames to
Mr Nigel Whiteruff*

May 28th, 195–

. . . Too long already, I know, but I must tell you about a rather queer business I've taken part in these last six or seven weeks.

Remember I told you I'd received my one and only fan letter from some crack-brained female in North Wales? Well, that's the beginning of the story. I wrote back the usual thing (or what in my ignorance of the fan world I thought such), but that didn't satisfy her ladyship, who wrote to me again. I just can't bear to be cruel, as you know, Nigel – I replied a bit more fully, and that led to more letters on either side, until within three weeks she was sending me drivel of her own to read, and I was necessarily giving it my blessing. I judged her a product of spinsterhood, the parsonage plus Freud, poor thing – felt sorry for her, and all that. Anyhow, this went on till at last she suggested I should meet her in Liverpool, on the landing stage by the romantic river, and (I quote from her), 'What happens thereafter is on the lap of the gods'. As I say, I felt sorry for her, so I agreed. Not quite my *métier* you will say, Nigel – and how I agree with you – but a man must try everything once! And now imagine me in Liverpool, waiting at the trysting place fifteen minutes before the hour. You know how it is, one gets a little troubled, thinks better of it, that sort of thing? Well, I stepped aside and determined to see without being seen, and heaven be praised that I did! She was there to the second, looking older than I'd expected, but dressed exactly as she had said, in a cheap-looking fur coat, with a red hat and one of those horrid little fibre cases. Fibre, Nigel! When I'm so sensitive to every kind of imitation and sham! I don't want to say anything caddish – you know me better than that – but honestly now, what would you have done? So did I. After all, can I help this damned fastidiousness of mine? Came back that night, quids down on the deal. Since when I've heard nothing.

But at least I can salvage the quids. After all, it's a story. I kept copies of my letters, and with the least doctoring they'll do. Life is all grist to us writers. *The Rainbow Montage*, you ask? It's a mystery to me it didn't do better, considering the boost you and the others gave me. It was too high-brow for the motley, I suppose, and too subtle. I think I'll stick to laying down the law for others yet awhile. It's not as though I'm too old, or too proud, to learn.

See you next Wednesday at the usual?

GEOFF.

XV

*The Literary Editor of 'The Best of the Month' to
Mr Geoffrey Keames.*

June 21st, 195–

Dear Sir,

I return herewith your story *Copy*. The circumstances of its rejection are, I think, such as to merit more than the customary rejection slip. I think I should inform you that our July number, which will appear in three days' time, will contain a story precisely similar to yours, save for the circumstance that at the end it is the lady who waits near the meeting place and goes away when she finds that her idolized author is – I quote her words – 'a complacent, petty figure, with a face too weak to be wicked, too vacuous to be menacing, too effeminate to interest a true woman'. Naturally, we communicated with the writer, Miss Silvia Ede, who assures us that her copy is in every way original, and that she will undertake full responsibility for any difficulty that may arise from its publication.

Yours faithfully,
JOHN FRIENDSHIP,
Fiction Editor.

All on a Summer's Day

~

A WOMAN stood outside the black-hasped door of the farm
Greenmeadows, listening into the north. She stood very still,
her neck rigid, her chin a little lifted and aligned on her right
shoulder. She had set down a bucket of swill before her; some
liquid and boiled potato peel had splashed over her boots, but
within the bucket the swill had lurched to rest under its mesh of
odorous scum.

It was the declining hour of afternoon, with a first paleness
infusing the high blue sky, and brown shadow standing against the
back wall of the house. To her left, on the south side of the valley,
the ground billowed up in soft timbered rises, with fields of grass
and green oats stitched in amongst them. Northwards was a flat
and luscious river bottom extending almost a mile to hills that were
taller but no less cushioned with oak and ash and rowan. The river
flowed sluggish and unseen in its sunken channel, bridged only at
the lower Fonlas meadow. Fonlas itself, the great stone house, lay
back against a crescent of elms, whence its masters had surveyed
and controlled the valley for five generations. Her brother Job was
up there now, for some of the elms had perished in the bole and
were to be felled, and with him was her grandson, the five-year-old
Wyndham. The boy's mother must be at this moment coming
home by way of the bridge. In the long field further down the river
the red-and-white Fonlas herd would be starring the rich grass; she
knew exactly where they were, though she could not see them from
Greenmeadows. Fonlas Pride, the huge swinging Fonlas bull, had
for days been bellowing grossly from his fenced and wired padlock,
but now he was down in the lower meadow. The listening woman
was the only person in the valley to know this. She knew it because
a short time earlier she had untwisted the wire and pulled the bolt
and dragged back the gate which gave him his freedom.

She was listening hard. This moment, her blood told her, it
must be. Now, oh now!

A thrush's song dripped from the nearest hawthorn. Her foot rasped on the dry earth. She put her hand to her mouth. Let it be now, God, she prayed. Let it be now!

Then she heard it, a screaming from the meadow. Scream upon scream, so baffled by the summer air that it might have been laughter or the crying of birds. And it seemed to her that she heard the roaring of the Fonlas bull.

Time snapped. Now she heard only the thrush in the hawthorn, the jet and tumble of his notes, and her own heart sucking in her breast. Picking up the swill-bucket she carried it over to the sty and emptied it into the trough. Her hands were unsteady, and small dribs of swill spattered the yard behind her. She avoided setting foot on them as she went back to the house, set the bucket down carefully alongside the water butt, and stood for a moment listening in the direction of Fonlas. Was that the shouting of men? The corners of her mouth moved downwards, she caught her hands together; then she hurried into the house and closed the door behind her.

I'm married, Mam, he had written, married to a girl in England. And from that first moment she knew her world in peril; knew it with a threefold jealousy and suspicion – as mother, her heart answering every impulse and sensation of his being; as peasant, frantic for the possession and transmission of her fields; as a remote and lonely woman, frightened of the stranger. She had long forgotten how to write more than her name, and it was her brother Job from the cottage past Fonlas who painfully set down her few sentences of inquiry and anxious caution. 'Not very *war-r-rm*, is it, Esther?' he had asked, rolling the adjective across the roof of his mouth. 'Not quite the thing, p'raps. Shall I read it out now?' She listened, coldly. 'It will do. And I can put my own name, thank you.'

He need never have been in the English Army at all. But he had gone off one afternoon, three months before the war started, and joined up with two other young labourers, friends of his. He came home, half-sheepish, half-defiant, smelling of beer, and felt the rough edge of her tongue even before he told his news. 'What's here for me?' he retorted. 'Not a damned thing from one year's end to the other, except a cow calving and a kids' treat at Whitsun.' 'Your home is here, isn't it? I'm here, aren't I?' 'Aye,' he agreed sullenly, 'aye.' And then, stupefyingly, 'I'm clearing out, Mam. I've joined the Army.'

How distant, how hostile, seemed England to her who had rarely ventured to the next county. And war, when it came, how frightening and unfair – her own son taken, the sons of her neighbours hard-rooted in their soil. London she's from, he wrote; a Cockney girl. Her stomach sickened to hear it read. 'You'll like her, Mam. She don't talk the way we do.' 'Wait and see,' her brother advised her, worriedly. He saw the world, over at Fonlas. 'I knew an Englishman once, a man I met where-would-it-be; he was all right, he was – as good as us any day. Don't be hasty-thoughted, Esther.' 'And they called him Job!' she said sharply, and frowned at his inoffensive grin.

But when Luke came to Greenmeadows he came without his wife. Her suspicion leapt again. 'But you didn't ask her, Mam,' he explained. 'And the journey – her the way she is. There'll be a baby, Mam, soon.' 'It can't be that soon,' she said, excited and angry. 'You've only been married since autumn.' He rubbed his hands in patience over his knees. 'Look, Mam, the world's changed. There's this war on, and I'll be going overseas any time now. Does it matter?' 'It always matters to be decent,' she told him stubbornly. 'But I'm not blaming *you*, Luke.' It was what she had thought all along. 'No, no, it's not your fault.' He stood up brusquely in the dark kitchen. 'Don't say it, Mam – whatever it is. She's all right, is Addie. If there's any blame, I'll take it, see? I love her, Mam. It's my kid she's having and I'm happy about it. That's all that matters.' Then he smiled. 'Don't you want a grandson, Mam?' 'Yes,' she said fiercely, 'always I've wanted you to marry and have children – but here!'

Uncle Job was ready with the Fonlas trap early the next morning, to take him five miles to the railway station. A silver web of dew clung to the grass, the valley was smudged and hazed and so deadened that the coral-combed cock led his hens in silence across the yard. 'It's good here,' he said fondly before exile, 'and when the war's over I'll come back for you, Mam.' His haversack was already bulging with food but she pressed a further package of her round cakes into his hand. 'If she'll let you. She'd never come to a place like this, Luke.' 'But she will, I tell you! And there's one thing: if they start bombing London, she's got to come here with the baby. I've told her, for the kid's sake. Mam,' he pleaded, 'if she comes, her and the kid, will you be kind?' She nodded, staring at the fidgeting Job. 'That's the one big thing you can do for me, Mam, because I'm going a long way off, for a long, long time.'

At this going there were tears of blood in her breast but her eyes were dry. It was only when the trap had disappeared that she cried quietly before turning to the day's work, desolation a clawing thing inside her. Soon she heard of the birth of her first grandson, and then of Luke in Asia. 'Be good to Addie,' he wrote, 'and our Wyndham. I've told them to come.'

Wyndham! He won her deep and selfish devotion from the moment she saw him. She had not loved even Luke more. 'Yes,' she said, seeing the green eyes, the soft clusters of brown hair, the long cheekbones, 'he's Luke's boy all right.' Her daughter-in-law stared, and went on staring at the iron-grey hair over the low forehead, the guarded eyes and severe mouth. She had not put on her best to meet them: let them take her as they found her, let them find her as she was, in her thready black blouse and rubbed black skirt, the stained black apron and the scratched black boots. 'We are rough down here,' she said, almost tauntingly; 'this isn't London, is it?' She saw Addie glance away to the woodlands enclosing the valley, with mingled admiration and misgiving in her pretty, silly face – Addie in her blue costume with the short skirt, the yellow scarf tied over her bleached and shiny hair, the shoes of imitation lizard skin, the thin stockings now bagging at the knees and ankles. Her skin was sweaty under the powder and her made-up eyelashes were stiffened as with alarm. 'He'll be safe here,' said Esther, taking the child from her. 'He'll be well looked after now.' 'It's the bombs,' said Addie, in mild protest. 'He's always had the best of everything.' The child laughed merrily, gripping his grandmother's forefinger, and with it her heart.

She was a cheap and shiftless thing, that Addie, as she had guessed from the beginning. How Luke had come to marry her – but there, that was only too clear. Useless about the farm, frightened if a goose hissed, each heifer was a bull to Addie. And soft – even the dog had his meal put out each day and straw set for him to lie on in the shed. And her clothes – 'That blouse,' said Esther brutally one day, 'the way it shows – with men about it's not decent.' 'Men?' asked Addie, flushing. 'Are there men about here?' 'There are eyes,' said Esther, 'and tongues.' 'Then that's all,' Addie cried. 'What a crib! Not a pictures, not a wireless, we don't even get a newspaper till it's too late. I'm sick of it I am, sitting about knitting socks and mittens!' 'Only lazy people get bored.

And why shouldn't you knit socks and mittens for Luke?' 'He's in Asia, Asia, Asia – if you've ever heard of it. They don't wear mittens in the jungle,' said Addie scornfully. 'And leave my clothes alone. They were good enough for Luke. My God,' she burst out, 'what wouldn't I give for an evening in a pub and a talk and a glass of beer!' 'There's only one sort of woman goes into a public,' sneered Esther; 'I'm learning fast.' 'There's lots you could learn,' said Addie heatedly, 'and do yourself no harm. Isn't a girl ever to have a bit of fun down here?' Her words carried only one meaning for Esther; it was as she had all along thought, Addie talked like a streetwalker because she was one. Soon she could not remember when she had not *known* that Addie was bad.

The cleavage that resulted in her mind was both deep and ugly. For the child all was love and worship; she doted on him; his whim was her law. And the little tyrant knew and enjoyed his power to the full. *Mamgu* he was calling her now, the soft Welsh for grandmother, and she was winning him to the language. When he hung at her skirts about the farm and she talked of tools and places and animals, it was the Welsh words she used. For the only time in her life she would leave the work to look after itself while she talked and taught till he thought more in Welsh than in English. 'When your Dad comes home,' she told him, 'you'll be a proper little Cymro for him.' All that was English, alien, tainted in him must be exorcized. And so Addie must sit many a trying hour without understanding his prattle, and wonder from what secrets and confidences that slippery maddening tongue shut her out. 'Talk in English, can't you?' she cried, and when in mischief he refused she slapped him. He turned weeping to his *Mamgu*, and in her weak and foolish way Addie was frightened by what she saw in Esther's face. And the grandmother was crooning in the unknown tongue: 'When she beats him, when she frightens him, the dove, the darling, the mannikin, he will always come to his *Mamgu* who is good and kind and will protect him.'

At what point, and for what last reason, will hatred grow from dislike? Esther could not have said. 'Why don't you go back to London for a change?' she asked one day during the second great bombing. 'You are always grumbling about it here.' 'You think it safe?' asked Addie. 'Oh,' said Esther, 'if you are afraid!' 'Safe enough for Wyndham?' Esther stiffened. 'Oh no! Wyndham must stay here, for his Dad's sake.' 'Then so must I,' said Addie spiritedly. 'He doesn't think less of me than the boy.' But for days she was silent and moody. London! A bit of pleasure, even if there was danger, might be better than this dreary life among fields and cows and nothingness. The streets, the people, the pictures – she shut her eyes to see them. Christ, she groaned, I'm bored. You'd think they'd have a pictures or something in a wet place like this! And the old woman hating the sight and smell of her. But it's life, she concluded perkily, and can't go on for ever; better eat grass than have a headstone of jasper. She would stick it for Wyndham's sake, and Luke's, and to spite that old bitch his mother – but oh, it would have been nice! And so thought Esther, setting the dream behind her, it would have been nice just she and Wyndham at Greenmeadows. For Wyndham belonged. He was bone of their bone now. The farm was freehold: when she went, Luke; when Luke went, Wyndham. But Addie? She hated her about the place, that slut who had trapped her Luke. The more cruel her unspoken words, the sweeter their taste on her tongue.

The women spoke less and less together, which weighed the heavier on Addie, for Esther had always been a woman given to silences and brooding. In one thing only were they in league together: they let Luke guess at nothing of their true feelings for each other. 'I'm glad, Mam,' he wrote back, 'that you and Addie are getting on fine. And our Wyndham can talk Welsh then! They call me Taffy in this mob. We've got you-know-who just about taped by now, and believe me, dear Mam and Addie, I'll be home sooner than you think.'

Luke home! She looked suspiciously at Addie who had read the letter to her. 'Is that all it says? Doesn't it say when?' Addie shook her head. 'Give me the letter!' But Job read it out exactly the same. 'When he comes home', said Esther, 'all the place will be different.' She drew her fingers along the stone wall. 'A farm needs a man. He never ought to be in the Army. There'll be a lot for him to do.'

'He won't be doing it,' said Addie.

Esther's fingers were suddenly still.

'He won't be doing it, I said. He won't be staying here. We'll go back to London, the three of us. Greenmeadows! Who'd stay in a dead end like this unless they had to? Not me for one!' She grew shrill with triumph and contempt. 'You've got to be born to it to stick it. And even then Luke ran away.'

'He didn't run away! You little carrion!'

'Go on,' shrilled Addie, 'call me names! Of course he ran away. And he will again. I'll make him, and Wyndham and me, we'll go with him. I'll dance all that day,' she cried. 'Oh, life will be lovely then!'

Life, said Esther into her pillow that night, would be no better than death then. She rose silently and went to the other bedroom where Addie and the boy lay asleep. There was moonlight but the window was small, and she could no more than distinguish their shapes in the big bed and the little. She stood there till her feet were cold as stones, the long white folds of her nightgown stiff and still, and when she went back to her own room it was to pray at her bedside to God that Addie should never take Luke's boy away from her. Even if it meant – but there was no need to put one's thoughts in words to God. He knew, and would do what was right.

It was in the summer following, almost four years since they had come to Greenmeadows, that vanity, good nature, and boredom dug a pit for Addie's feet. She had been into the market town with Wyndham, and as she faced the weary walk home from the station was passed by a car whose driver stopped and offered her a lift. He was a soldier with a scarred forehead, on leave from Normandy. He was recovering from his wound. His home was at Maeshelig, ten miles away. He got all the petrol he wanted from the local farmers. 'If you would like a drive round one afternoon,' he said, and nodded at the drowsy boy, 'bring him too. It will do him good.' He was full of chaff and slang and laughter, and her spirits freshened to hear him. 'Stop here,' she told him, a quarter of a mile from Greenmeadows. 'You'll come?' he begged; 'I've got another ten days.' There could be no harm in it, and swiftly she nodded. 'Here,' she said, 'at three. Just for an hour's drive. But if I don't turn up, please don't call for me. Will you promise?' His answering nod established a conspiracy between them.

And now her life which had been so drab and tired tingled with excitement. On the third afternoon of their companionship this became a guilty ecstasy when he lay with her under the trees. She was lost at the first touch of his hands; her starved body craved the act of love, she flowered and glowed with that delicious relief. And later, walking home by way of the Fonlas bridge, 'I have done no harm,' she told herself. 'We are young and lonely, and I love Luke just the same.' She met him each afternoon thereafter, for the week that was left to him, and always by half-past five she was crossing the Fonlas bridge. 'Soon he may be killed,' she said, 'and I have given him what I could.' And more frankly: 'I was desperate to be loved. I was frozen inside me. Four years it's been – and who can ever know?' She felt sleek as a cat, and cunning as one. Esther had not once asked where she went of an afternoon; only too glad to be rid of her, she thought. And now that it was all over, and tomorrow he would be gone, she felt neither sorrow nor guilt nor regret. 'It's done me good,' she said, patting her hair. 'I can stick the old bitch now till Luke comes home.' How warm the sun was still, how brown and slow the water! The Fonlas bull was bellowing as usual, except that he sounded louder and nearer. 'Poor old fellow,' said Addie. 'It's not much fun being tied up, don't I know it!' Some shameless recollection of the afternoon made her smile, stepping on to the bridge.

I did not let her see that I knew anything, said the woman waiting inside the house. She thought she was deep, but I was deeper. The child talked to me, her own child, and so I knew. Washing and ironing she was, bleach on her hair again, and her eyebrows skinny as a fowl's – and the different look on her all the time. Sleek she was, contented as a cat. The house stank of her wickedness; it rose about her like a cloud of flies. But Esther could be as free of anger now as she was of pity. Soon they would be knocking at the door, and she would go out to them. It was wise to send little Wyndham up to his Uncle Job – she would always keep from him what was hard and ugly. Nothing would be too good for her grandson. And all that lovely future for Luke, for Wyndham, and for her.

Now! She heard the rolling of trap wheels from the home field into the yard. Suddenly she was suffocating, there was no strength in her legs, and her bowels were dissolving within her. She was looking into the red-rimmed eyes and scarlet nostrils of the bull; his up-curved horns and pounding knees were into her; his breath was sweet and rotten as death. 'Oh, no,' she whimpered. 'Frighten her I meant. No more, before God!' The door lurched open and her brother was there, looking in at her. 'Esther,' he said, his voice broken as his face, 'Esther!'

She stood up and went outside the door. It lay there in the back of the trap where last she saw Luke, unexpectedly small under the white sheet. 'He went down to meet his Mam at the bridge,' Job was sobbing. 'And I let him. Oh, why did I let him!'

'The bull was free,' said the man who led the pony. He held out his arms. 'You mustn't look. We heard his Mam screaming.'

Then Addie screamed again, tearing at the sheet which covered her son. 'For Christ's sake,' said the man with the pony; 'For Christ's sake!' He looked to them for help, and Job ran forward and caught at Addie's shoulders. 'Esther,' he pleaded; 'please help!' But the older woman, her face grey as ashes, tottered into the house, and in the first ring of silence they heard the weaker scream of the thrusting bolt which shut her cowering from them.

Two Women

~

THE black labrador which had been lying against Costin's legs suddenly stood up, whistling and trembling, and started to tear with hard nails at the floorboards. 'Cut it out!' called the man at the wheel. He looked in the early thirties but was already fat and balding, with the red skin a-gleam over his face and much of his head. He turned grinning to Costin. 'Always does that hereabouts, the old fool!'

'I wouldn't mind whistling myself,' said Costin, and blew soft doleful notes between his teeth.

They were spluttering their way into the small dead harbour, between a cracked breakwater and a scoured yellow jetty. The paleness of a late September morning rested everywhere, and a smell of weed and decay crept upwards to their nostrils.

'Don't whistle too loud', advised the man at the wheel, 'or the breakwater'll fall down. And when the breakwater falls down, we all fall down.' He jerked with his chin, affection and contempt in his voice. 'Well, there's St Clair for you. Pretty, would you say?'

This still village! He looked away from the weed-slimed blocks of granite under the cracked wall and saw first the genteel once-much-more-elegant frame round the harbour, long stone sheds and three-storied offices with Georgian windows, faded little houses with their blue flower-boxes, the neat withdrawn inns, and the slate-covered spire of a church. And behind was a rocky hill with farms squatting on its lower edges, and higher still, on the sky-line, a folly in shape of a ruined castle, with the sky staring out of its windows.

Costin sat frowning, a hard young man with a naval beard, brown-haired, brown-eyed, brown-handed. He ought to know this place, recognize each corner of it. Wyn had talked of it so much, there were the drawings, the snapshots. But no, he was remote from it, quite alien. No pulse beat from it back to him. Why had he come?

'It's quiet,' he said, patting the black dog.

'You bet your thumb it's quiet!' replied Harris, with what sounded like relish.

No need to ask why he had come. He owed it to the two women at Manordy, and he owed it to himself. He hadn't expected it to be pleasant, but at least it could be brief.

'Battleships,' said the man at the wheel. 'Ruddy great things I always thought them!' Delicately he nosed across the shallow green water and felt for the dried steps under the harbour-master's office, which was now also an ironmonger's. 'You couldn't love a battler now, could you? Like loving a girl nine feet high it would be.' He speculated. 'Though that might be something. Just once.'

'Just once it was,' said Costin. 'And once too often.'

But he didn't want to talk about it to Harris. You cheapened things with talk, and you kept them rawly alive too. He fingered the stone wall as though it should be steel plate, watched the black labrador scuffle up the steps ahead of him and lift his leg against the iron post. 'Be with you in five minutes,' said Harris. 'Are you taking your bag?' The dog ran back down the steps to join his master in the boat.

The harbour side was cobbled for ten feet or so, with heads of groundsel and dandelion contending for the joins; then there was a wide roadway and a yellow-gravelled promenade in front of the houses. A housewife looked out from behind one of the blue flower-boxes, eyed his beard and hold-all tolerantly and decided to say good morning; men in jerseys or navy-blue jackets were gossiping near the jetty; there were children playing in front of the church. He walked slowly up and down past his holdall, screwing his heels on the dandelions, on a whim sparing the groundsel. The land was as silent as the sea.

Yet to Wyn it had all been alive, pantingly, passionately alive. He tried to see it with his friend's eyes but could not. Gulls mewed overhead, and he saw them planing disconsolately to the north.

Harris had rolled up over the side, followed by his dog. He went down to swap greetings with the gossiping men and had soon begun waving his arms jovially; they were chaffing him by the look of it, and he saw one of them catch at Harris's sleeve and detain him. 'Stay then!' said Costin sourly. He caught up his hold-all and began walking to the inns beyond the church. 'Hiya!' he heard Harris shout from behind him, and when he turned there he was, swinging forward like a new-coopered cider barrel. 'Try *The Dolphin*,' said Harris. 'Nice landlady, nice grub, nice view of the harbour.' 'You sound as though you own it,' said Costin brusquely. Harris rubbed the red blades of his hands together, 'Boy, wouldn't I like to?'

The Dolphin had a handsome fresh-painted sign. Amid bright blue billows a jolly red fish carried Arion towards the inn door. Arion's face had been painted with love and detail. 'I'd know him if I met him again,' commented Costin, and Harris opened his mouth and shut it again without speaking.

A good-looking sulky girl with black hair and a made-up mouth was sharpening a pencil behind the desk.

'Hullo, Sue,' said Harris.

'Hullo,' she answered indifferently; 'It's you, is it?'

'Prince Charming himself,' said Harris, licking at a patch of tar on the back of his left hand and grinning all the time. 'And how's the Sleeping Beauty?' She gave him the lift of her shoulder by way of answer and turned to Costin, but 'The Admiral wants to leave his bag after we've eaten,' continued Harris. 'Anybody in?'

'Mr Wolfe is in the bar.' She patted with red-nailed fingers at a bored yawn. 'I think.'

'Then what are we waiting for?' asked Harris, pushing on to the frosted glass door ahead. 'After all that salt water too! Now, meet my friend Mr Wolfe.' He appeared to anticipate a pleasure.

It was Arion on a red-leather settee instead of a dolphin. A swollen belly of a man in a black suit and white linen, with an artist's bow holding up his chins, and the petals of a silk handkerchief falling out of his breast pocket. His face was smooth as though the skin were stuffed with lard, and white, and the nose blobby. With it all there went an air of sweaty distinction and noble acquaintance – Costin rather missed the astrakhan collar, but no doubt he had one upstairs in camphor. And the voice when it came, he was ready for it, a whisky-washed bass-baritone.

'My friend, Admiral Costin,' said Harris impudently.

'A friend of my friend Harris,' intoned Arion-Wolfe, extending his short fat arm, 'should be a friend indeed.' His delivery gave his words the effect of false epigram.

'You mean, a friend in need,' countered Harris. He had already taken the head off his pint and was dipping his finger into the beer and offering it to the labrador to lick. 'Wolfe paints. You'd be surprised – real pictures.'

'As Harris thinks,' Wolfe retorted comfortably. 'Real thoughts, at intervals.' He was lifting his glass to Costin. 'Your good health, Mr Costin. Or as the natives say, *Iechyd da!*'

'So you are not a native?'

'The Welsh', said Wolfe, 'have many good qualities. To them I am a mad Englishman.' He began to smoothe and fondle his belly's overhang as though he had eaten and were digesting his joke, not speaking it. 'To the English, on the other hand, I am a wild Welshman. But in sober truth,' and Harris groaned at the announced fatuity, 'I am a citizen of the world.'

'But you paint?'

'I paint,' admitted Wolfe, with an air of manly frankness. 'As to how I paint – '

'For the lord's sake', interrupted Harris, 'let's eat. All right, the whole boiling of us, if we must!' He was away and into the dining room and slapping on the table top before Wolfe had wheezed himself upright. 'You there, Admiral,' he directed, 'and the poor cabin-boy here. Two chairs for Wolfe, and Billy Boy under the table.'

'We were talking of painters. Maitland,' Costin asked, 'did you know Maitland? Here, in St Clair?'

'Wyn Maitland?' Wolfe shook his head. 'Not exactly know him. No one did know him, really, before it happened. I know his work, of course. And that so many others know it too has been very largely my doing, Mr Costin.' He took up an imaginary brush, dabbed languidly at the air in front of him. 'The boy had a knack, let's admit it – and a sense of colour too. I don't suppose you saw my thing in *Paint Today*, Mr Costin?'

'But you didn't know Maitland yourself?'

'I didn't come to St Clair till 1940, as it happened.' There was no need of an explanation but he felt himself challenged to offer one. 'A lot of people were advised to get out of London at that time. Most painters would have gone to Cornwall.' He blew on his soup. 'I have always liked to be a little different, Captain.'

'Damned brave of you,' said Harris.

'There were other wars,' Wolfe reminded him. *Wa-ahs*, he pronounced it, *Wa-ahs*, with plumed lancers galloping through each syllable. He caught Costin's look of disbelief. 'I too have done the State some service, sir.' His pudgy hand reached for his left breast, as though to assure himself that his decorations were still hanging. 'Sad, unhappy far-off things, and battles long ago.'

The thick lips, the swelling chins, the bobbing adam's apple went on moving, making sounds, but Costin was not listening. Battles long ago! The roar that beat one's head in, and the fountain of fire out of the sea, the black washes of pain. Where was the ship? Where were the men?

His knife clattered as he set it down. He heard his chair scrape and fall behind him, saw their eyes staring, the men's puzzled and alarmed, the dog's interested and friendly, saw too how Wolfe checked Harris's move to rise and follow him as he walked stiffly out of the room and along the passage to the air and light and bright pale water of the harbour.

And then he saw his own hands, brown and tight-knuckled, gripping a faded iron rail near down-running worn stone steps. And again the questions moved cold and wormy in his heart: Why was he here? Why had he come?

Yesterday morning he had left the north of Scotland on his last service leave. A long train journey to the Midlands, a wretched night's lodge on a waiting-room bench; then the stopping train across Wales to Abermaid and a lucky meeting in a pub with Harris had brought him to St Clair. And now the sooner done with the better. For what, after all, could one say? The whole world knew the story as well as he. The great ship, struck in the magazine, detonating into the northern sky: no tales of heroism or failure, no premonitions even. Not even a tale of action; the bracketing rounds from the enemy, and then destruction. Five survivors from that vast company of men, his own back flailed and ribboned, his left arm peeled and broken, his ear trimmed to a grotesque wing. And somewhere in that moment, by blast or fire or drowning, with fourteen hundred others, Wyn Maitland met his end. He, Costin, a freak to be alive, like a two-headed calf or a one-legged hen, only his was a spiritual deformity – he had robbed death, and with death his comrades.

('You have no right to be alive, you know,' said many a well-meaning fool.

'Shall I kill myself to please you?' he had snarled.)

He sighed. It had not gone yet, that guilt of survival. And terror could return. He had fought it the hard way, with service on many seas, his eyes open on disaster and other men's deaths. And he had fought it by himself, with his back often on the ropes but letting no one throw in his towel. And he had fought it in silence.

Heroics! He smiled wryly. He was like Wolfe feeling for his medals. And yet, 'Talk about it,' the doctors had told him. 'Write it all down.' Cry, they said, if you must. Take off the rein. As if a man could!

His fingers lost their rigidity, rubbed softly along the worn rail. Mrs Maitland – that was Wyn's mother – a fine woman she must be. And Bronwen his wife: if he had nothing to tell them, why was he here? Bronwen! A pretty name he thought it in sound and meaning. The White-bosomed. Once more it brought a tang of sensuality to his thinking of her, a hint of pleasure and quest to his long journey. 'If this were a world to paint beauty in,' he heard Wyn say angrily, 'I'd paint my wife and nothing else.' But you'd expect a husband, and a young husband, to say no less. Bronwen! He felt as though he was falling forward into the embrace of water, his forehead laved in milky whiteness, his eyes enfolded. That would be rest indeed, a good journey's end.

Illusion! He dropped his arms, suddenly tired and harassed to think of the hours ahead. Oh, let the long day end!

A dog's nose was in his hollowed hand, a tail swished the backs of his knees. 'When do we go, Admiral?' It was Harris taking up station behind him, the smell of beer on his breath. When he turned, it was to find him grinning as if nothing had happened, a circumference of good fellowship to a core of tough self-interest. 'I said I'd take you, remember?'

The black labrador bundled himself ahead of them as they walked from the harbour side, his nose of wet sealskin snuffling an inch above the cobbles. For a space they walked in silence, then: 'It was the *St Michael*, wasn't it?' asked Harris. 'I had an idea it was that all along. I heard about her when we were down in the Sea of Siam, and knew we'd none of us see Wyn Maitland again. It must have been the biggest news for St Clair since the breakwater cracked open five years before the war.' They had reached a small grassy knoll and he pointed towards the sea, which was pallid as milk, with all the warmth and glow of summer creamed from its surface. 'Anyhow, you are sure of one thing, Costin: you'll never die by drowning.' White feathers of foam frothed through the pebbles. 'No, by God, not if they tied brass lanterns on your feet. Though by the present look of your physiognomy, Costin, I'd guess you were destined to hang.'

'For you?' asked Costin. 'I think not. It isn't in the St Clair pattern.'

'Most things are,' Harris assured him, 'if only you live here and find out.' He turned away from the blues and yellows of the village, rounding the knoll by a narrow gorse-edged path. 'Look at the St Clair folly now: the world's wisdom in stone. My grandfather put it there, and don't let anyone tell you he was off his nut, Costin, for he wasn't. D'you know what he did? All right, I'll tell you. He took a boat out of St Clair when he was a twelve-year-old boy and saw the world the hard way another twelve before striking it rich. He and two others, they found gold in America up north, millions of it, in the river, in the tree roots – you couldn't walk a horse through that valley, according to the old man, unless he came out with gold hooves. That was the time, not later, when he was off his nut, and the other two with him. They sang, they holla'd, they threw gold dust in each other's hair, they went raving mad as they planned to squeeze the future like a juicy orange, drip, drip, drip. Only they had to get back to a town somewhere for tools and food and more horses, and would you believe it? the fools got drunk and talked, and when they were let out of prison six weeks later every claim had been staked and all the gold they got could be carried off under your eyelid. He made his money in steel ten years later and managed to lose most of that before he crawled back home. Women, children, all over the place – and he ditched the living lot of them. And what did he do once he was back? Build a hospital, a school, litter the place with more empty chapels? Not old man Harris! No, sir, he built a folly, one-wall thick, and he built it overlooking this pale little village to show his opinion of St Clair, the world, and everybody in it, including himself. Any comments, Admiral?'

'Only that if you aren't talking for the sake of talking, then he was dead right about himself. You have nice relations, Harris.'

'Everyone has nice relations. You and me, and Wyn Maitland too.' He expected a question but it did not come. 'And soon you'll be meeting them.' He snapped his fingers at the labrador. 'That's how we humans ought to be, free, like dogs, and to hell with the rest of the litter. No fathers, no mothers – especially no mothers! – no brothers and sisters in better shape than yourself because they get most of the milk. Everyone's life his own. You'll see!'

'All right,' said Costin, 'I'll see.'

He heard again Wyn's sharp angry tenor. 'No one could have a better mother,' he was confiding across a coffee-slopped table. 'When I think of all she did for me – that small poor farm – it's frightening what we owe to other people, what we'll never be able or willing to repay.'

'You said that twice,' said Harris, 'so perhaps you'll see double.' They were approaching a patched gate, a gapped hedge. 'We are on their land from now on.'

Two bony fields away he saw the dark stone walls and slated roof of the farm Manordy. Hardly more than a cottage it looked, the barns low and haulm-like, rimmed by a dozen stunted trees, their heads combed north-east by winds off the sea. 'In a place like that,' said Wyn, 'you must surrender or be selfish. So I was selfish, and she made the choice right for me. The story's in our hands, hers and mine. One day you'll come there and see them, like fern roots, black and cracked. And these white silken things are mine!'

And these, thought Costin, these hard brown hands are mine. Here on their gate at last. I had to come. I was close enough to him for that, it was her due, the mother's. And yet, what could a man say?

'The grand old sacrificial mother,' said Harris into his thoughts. He was untying the wire that held the gate to the mouldering post. The dog had already climbed through the hedge and was waiting for them on the other side. ' "O ye men, how can it be but women should be strong, seeing they do thus!" The best text in the Bible,' he jeered, 'and the one they never preach from.'

Thumping the gate against its creaking post, they crossed the hard dry fields. As they came near to the farm four or five black-and-white cows bumped their way from the sheds towards them, and they heard a man's voice shouting out of sight behind the farm. 'Nothing there a gate couldn't mend,' said Harris scornfully. At that moment the dog dashed in behind the cows and began to chivvy them, even jumping up joyously to bite the hindmost's tail. 'Cut it out!' shouted Harris. 'Damn your eyes, come here!'

A man, a youngish man still, ran round the building towards them. He had a pitchfork in his hand. 'I'll break your back for you!' he yelled. As the dog whipped away towards Harris he flung the pitchfork at him off his shoulder, missed badly, and stood facing them, his tongue a-stutter with rage. 'I've told you about this, Harris. You and your filthy mongrel! I'll put a prong through you both if you come here interfering, so help me!'

Harris stabbed with his foot at the still quivering fork. 'Not you, Fred. Not today anyway. I've brought you a visitor, Wyn's friend Costin off the *St Michael* – if you ever heard of her. Is the old lady in?'

'Get off my land,' ordered Fred, 'and that dog of yours with you, before I fetch a gun to him.'

'Not to him, Fred. Not to my boozing chum Billy.' The dog sat wagging his tail at this mention of his name, and Harris, taking his foot off the pitchfork, kicked it contemptuously aside. 'I can't think why we quarrel, Fred, with all the things we've got in common.'

Fred's eyes moved to the pitchfork and then to Harris's turned back. Man and dog were sauntering away towards the gate. 'You'll try me once too often!' he shouted after them, and the threat had more of weakness in it than if he had sat down and cried. 'See you later, Admiral,' called Harris, and walked indifferently on.

'I shouldn't lose my temper,' said Fred Maitland, 'I know. But the cows get all excited with a dog.' The voice that had sounded like Wyn's weakened on the ridiculous excuse. He held out his hand on what was obviously an afterthought. 'I'm Fred, by the way, Wyn's brother. I don't suppose he ever spoke of me?'

'Often,' said Costin, answering the wish in his voice. 'He spoke of you all.'

'I'm surprised he mentioned me,' said Fred doubtfully. 'I'm like the fire, I always say: no one notices me till I've gone out.' A new thought came to trouble him. 'I think you'll have to go over to the house yourself. I just don't know how it is, the way everything's left to me. Would you mind?'

He stood there ladling his long hair back under his cap, his mind bemused with Costin, Harris, the straggling cows and heaven knows what else besides. 'Why should I mind?' 'Oh well,' replied Fred, 'that's all right then, isn't it?' And shouldering the pitchfork he went off with an air of urgency.

To the grey eyes watching him from behind the front curtains Costin looked hard and purposeful as a gun barrel, but his feelings as he watched Fred strut away were much more those of anticlimax and grievance. To have come all the way from Scotland for this! If only he'd known! He left the childish phrases as incomplete as they were futile. He had a good mind – but he left that incomplete too, easing the stiff white collar from his throat, gauging the set of his black tie. At least it would soon be over.

The grey eyes watched him walk briskly the grass-stained pebbly path towards the house. Mrs Maitland felt her face flush and then chill: this was he who was with Wyn when he died, in that grey iron coffin which carried him struggling to the sea's bottom. But this one had escaped. Five had escaped. O Justice and Mercy of God, five! And not one of them her Wyn. The blood again heating her face left her heart cold and dry, and something close to hatred arose in her for this alert spared person stepping so assuredly towards her. She had no wish to hear him speak. What could he tell her of Wyn that she did not know, what of his end that could be other than dreadful to her? And deepest and most disturbing, his coming was out of the pattern she had woven so unceasingly about Manordy, about Wyn and Fred and Bronwen, during the lean and empty years of their loss.

But she was at the door before he could knock. He saw her stand there three stone steps above him, gaunt and dark as a tree-top rook, and utterly unwelcoming. He saw the blood move into her cheeks and was disquieted by the emotion revealed and as suddenly frozen there. The shock of her dislike stilled his rehearsed greeting, and again the thought turned like a worm in his brain: What can I do? What can I say?

She had spoken his name, with a word of grudging explanation. 'We had your letter, Mr Costin.' The door squeaked on the linoleum and she was motioning him into a narrow passage papered a soapy yellow and smelling of milk in the churn, opening thereafter a parlour whose windows leaned from the eye of the sun and whose corners were plushed with brown shadow. WE SAT DOWN, YEA, WE WEPT, said an embroidered text, WHEN WE REMEMBERED ZION; and a horse and foal in coloured wools were framed on the longest wall. To his right as he entered, above a round-legged mahogany table, hung a bright and violent painting of St Clair, its hill and sea and houses drenched in sunshine.

'Wyn's,' he exclaimed, startled by its brilliance and the incongruity of the setting.

She nodded, gratified against her will by such spontaneous recognition. 'Please sit down,' she invited, 'for I know you have come a long way. Though lots of people come to Manordy', she went on, 'to see his paintings they come and the place where he lived, or to talk to me and Fred and his wife Bronwen. And a lot have come trying to buy his paintings.' Her mouth relaxed. 'But you have come just as a friend.'

Her words and tone assigned him to a low rank among visitors, but he nodded and half smiled. 'There were things I thought you and Bronwen might want to hear, Mrs Maitland; you and Wyn's wife.'

As she sat down, with two neat strokes she folded her apron on to her lap. 'I was in service once,' she said, and he could tell from this how closely she was watching him. 'In those days we learned to be tidy. My hands were whiter then.' Before he could control it his glance had fallen, but her hands were hidden beneath the apron. 'You spoke of Wyn's wife?' she asked coldly.

'His widow,' he corrected stubbornly and rudely. 'Is she here?'

She frowned away the distinction, and his question along with it. 'Up there, when it happened, were you hurt too, Mr Costin?'

She must have known! 'A little. I was lucky.' But he could not leave it at that. 'I don't claim that I deserved to be.'

'No one begrudges you your luck Mr Costin,' she said grimly. 'Me least of all.'

He kept back the quick-starting cynical thanks. She'd drown him in an egg-cup, he knew, to save Wyn's little finger. And could he say he blamed her?

'Up there,' said Mrs Maitland again. 'Was it dark?' The question made him grope after words for the things he knew too well, the endless arctic night, the fog, the wallowing black water. The snow that died on its seething surface, the ice-sheeted steel – how describe them? But there was no need after all. 'Wyn loved the sun,' she said suddenly, interrupting him as though his words were a thrown switch to her own more engrossing thoughts. 'That text behind you', she said, pointing, 'was Wyn's work too. He did it when he was a boy in the school, and I kept it like everything else he ever made or painted. He didn't like this room, I don't know why, but the text has been here always.' He saw her adjust her eyes as though she were reading from a big printed bill. 'He spent two years in France, did you know? It was necessary for him to study there, they said so at the college, all of them. So I sent him. It's all in his pictures, that's another thing they say, the sun and glow and colour of Provence – those are the very words the critic said, Mr Costin. I have them on a paper written out for me by someone who was there when he said them at the exhibition in London, in a very big gallery they used for him. I have lots of papers, newspapers most of them are, and they all say the same thing, that France was good for him, and that it was right for him to be sent there.' The work-twisted claws of her hands came open and upturned from beneath the apron. 'So it was right all the time for me to send him.'

'He spoke of it,' Costin told her, 'he spoke many times of all you did for him.' The wired gate, the rotting post, the dry lime-hungry fields: even a war had not put heart and blood into this stripped Manordy. He thought of the jeering Harris, that sucked-out petulant Fred. 'He knew all the sacrifices that were made for him.'

But again she was not listening. 'To think of Wyn month after month in the dark. He couldn't have been happy all that time out of the sun. They must have known that before they sent him,' she complained.

He was saved from answering by the entry of Fred. 'I've wiped my boots,' he told his mother. 'Jack Harris was here again, did he tell you?'

'He brought me over from St Clair,' explained Costin. 'And from Abermaid in that boat of his yesterday.' With no need in the world so far as he could tell, he found himself drawn into an excuse. 'He was in the Navy too, wasn't he?'

'There's very little Jack Harris hasn't been in in his time,' said Mrs Maitland.

'Except an honest job,' added Fred righteously. He pointed to the sunny picture. 'Nice of St Clair, isn't it? See the folly, Mr Costin – exactly the way it looks from down by the beach. Harris's grandfather was the beauty who built that.'

'It has been made to look very attractive!'

'As folly often does.' Mrs Maitland was smoothing down her apron, rising with a swift straight-backed movement, brushing down her heavy black skirt. She was less tall than he had thought her on the steps, and less old, and strong as a wintry sea. 'Would you like to see Wyn's paintings now that you are here?' Her words set a limit to his visit and of this he was glad as he nodded and followed her from the room.

But where was Wyn's wife? That would be better than this ingrown woman and the ungrown man, her son. She was the one he must talk to, and not leave Manordy with everything unsaid. He wondered at a girl's life in this starveling place. Could she be happy, a white gull among daws? Happier than Fred? Than Mrs Maitland? He grimaced. Or than he, Costin?

It was odd, he thought, how they walked in single file round the dark farm with its clumps of blue daisies fighting the drabness of the walls, past the dunghill and an empty pigsty to a fresh white barn still acrid with whitewash. Ahead of him Mrs Maitland moved in silence save when she shooed some white chickens from under their feet; and behind him Fred had the pretended nonchalance of a new hand penning a bull he has been told is harmless so long as you handle him right. The barn's black door with its three iron cross-pieces was locked, but Mrs Maitland took a key from her skirt pocket and opened it for him to enter.

A clear unchanging light filled the barn from its inserted north-eastern windows, a light pure, cold and sterilized. The air itself was light, and light lay without glitter or smile along the smooth white walls. And on those walls hung fifty or three score drawings and paintings, embalmed in this flawless light as in transparent ethereal liquid, landscapes that flashed blues and yellows and green of the fresh leaf, vistas of sun-washed seas tumbling on a coast of gold, still-lifes of flowers and fruits in deep-rimmed antique bowls, portraits of old men and girls, and a great naked negress sprawled on a silvery couch. He cried out with surprise to see his friend's life spilled before him thus prodigally, and as he cried the door closed behind them on the bloom of September sunshine with a soft immolatory thud. Immediately he felt as he had felt that morning when he saw the still gentility of St Clair. There was the same remoteness about these canvases of flesh and flower and splintering water. Where was the life, the pulse that had beaten from St Clair to Wyn and from Wyn to the world? As he shook his head, puzzled, he saw Mrs Maitland's face stiffen in disapproval, so he began to walk from painting to painting, finding words of praise and sometimes of recognition, admiring aloud the shadowless light and gleam-free walls, the simplicity of the hanging, yet troubled anew by the flatness he could hear in his voice. 'It was Mr Wolfe saw to it all,' said Mrs Maitland, and 'We paid him plenty for it too,' put in Fred, with his customary filling-in of his mother's thoughts. 'It was a man down from London though who suggested the white walls.' 'A man who came to buy,' said Mrs Maitland. 'Not that we sold,' added Fred, notes of doubt and regret clouding his clear tenor.

'Nothing is for sale,' said Mrs Maitland, thin-lipped. 'And nothing ever will be.'

He knew that she was waiting for him to go, that for a reason unknown he was no fit visitor to the shrine she had built to her son. Of course! that was it. Why the pictures were filmed, the barn dead, the very light without gleam or tincture: the whole place was a shrine, an empty tomb, and these patches of colour on the walls the stiff waxen offerings of an old-fashioned Palm Sunday.

'You have made a shrine, Mrs Maitland,' he said drily.

'A shrine,' she echoed, and for the first time he saw her eyes fervent and clear. She looked almost pleased with him, he thought.

He was turning to the door when he heard her again. 'There is a book to sign, if you will.' He picked it up from the table, and his nostrils twitched to the damp creamy smell of its leather as he furraged the opening leaves. There were names there he recognized, but far more he did not: fine imposing signatures most of them. Wolfe's name flopped like a broken blackberry branch across the foot of page one. *Frank Costin*, he wrote, the letters angled because he was standing, and after a pause he filled in the date. *A survivor of H.M.S. St Michael*: he could already see the words added in a stiff grey feminine hand the minute he left St Clair. And that, he thought, will be all the good my coming will have done her.

'When are you leaving, Mr Costin?'

His pen was moving again as he answered. H.M.S. *St Michael*, he wrote this time, within brackets under his signature, and as he did so he recovered his good temper. It was like winning a petty victory, and he planned to win another with his next curt words. 'As soon as I can, Mrs Maitland.'

She was unperturbed. 'Then I suppose we shan't be seeing you again.'

There was no question in her voice and he did not argue his dismissal. 'You were very kind to come so far,' she assured him, at the same time making a neat dusting movement over the visitors' book with the corner of her apron. Her expectancy that he would go, and go quickly, was in itself enough to propel a man from the room. 'If I could say good-bye to Wyn's wife,' he protested, and at once thought: What's the use? If he spoke more his voice would show how foolish he had been made to feel, and he wouldn't gratify her so far. 'Good-bye,' he said instead. 'Don't trouble to see me off.'

'It's no trouble,' put in Fred, as so often on his mother's behalf.

His hand was reaching for the iron latch, in seconds now he would be gone, when there were quick footsteps outside, the door opened and a girl came hurrying in. He saw the face of Wyn's drawings and snapshots, the eyes, the corners of the mouth, and the dark framing hair.

'I know you,' he said. 'You are Mrs Maitland. You are Wyn's wife Bronwen.'

He saw her breast rise smooth as doves against the white silken blouse, her hair trembled with her breathing. 'I was afraid I wouldn't be in time, and I ran some of the way back.' She had a smile so gay and friendly that you must smile with her. 'Look how I'm panting, everybody! I'm so glad I found you here, Mr Costin.'

'Mr Costin was just going, Bronwen.'

This was one, he knew, who did not want him out and away. 'After I ran? After you came all this way?' she asked anxiously. 'You can't mean you are going now, this minute? I wanted to talk and listen – there are things I want to know, and only you can tell me. Please, Mr Costin!'

'But Bronwen – ' He had to close his opening mouth or talk Mrs Maitland down. 'Is that fair to Mr Costin?'

'Fair?' She looked surprised – and then she surprised Costin in his turn. 'And that reminds me. Fred, why didn't you tell me it was Autumn Fair at St Clair tonight? I met Tom Evans and he reckons you are going together. It wouldn't have been much of you to tell me too, would it?'

'I suppose', said Fred, with an uneasy eye on his mother, 'I just forgot. Anyhow, I've got to have a bit of time off sometime, haven't I?' He started for the door, kicking his feet defiantly over the floorboards. 'Why should I be like an old horse about the place, with nothing but work, morning, noon and night? Can anyone tell me one good reason?' But before anyone could, he had gone.

'Hadn't he told you either?' Bronwen asked Mrs Maitland. 'He's a funny one, is Fred.' Her soft, charming smile played over her face. 'Or are we all funny ones down here, Mr Costin?'

He put the question by with a quick shake of his head. A spirit of mischief was working in him, so that he had come to feel light-hearted, pleased, a little predatory. 'About the fair,' he said, his voice once more full and resonant, 'if you are going tonight, couldn't I come with you?' His lifted eyebrows offered a challenge more than a plea. We are young, his face sang, and the world is old: let us have happiness while we can, the sun and glow and colour that are our right and that none should take from us, Bronwen. Did she nod back in answer? All at once they were laughing together, the two young people, under the grey eye of the mother. 'It's a very little fair,' she warned him. 'It's a very little world,' he answered. Again their laughter came with their voices, hollow-sounding in the hollow barn, but charging its ghostly air with something of joy and youth, so that the paintings glowed brighter from the walls, moved nearer to the laughers, shared in their pleasure.

'Oh dear!' Bronwen was turning to Mrs Maitland. 'It seems such ages ago when Wyn and I used to go to the September fair.'

Mrs Maitland flinched from the words and a silence fell upon them all. 'If you want to go, Bronwen, and if you think it right, then of course you should go.' Her delicate and exact emphasis made even Costin feel stupidly in the wrong. The girl's hand was laid imploringly on her sleeve and she began caressing it with her sacrificial claw. 'Well, there it is. Mr Costin has already said that he must go back at once – as soon as he possibly could, those were his own words – but the decision I can see, Bronwen, is yours more than his.'

'I see,' said Bronwen, and as she hesitated it seemed to Costin that once more there was a fading and cooling all round them. 'Well, I wouldn't want to be a nuisance to Mr Costin.' She looked quickly towards him but he refused, or spared, her any denial. There was another silence before she began again with an air of false decision as betraying as Fred's first outburst. 'In any case, Mr Costin can't possibly go yet. He must stay to tea, and there's time to talk first. Let's go for a walk before tea, Mr Costin, shall we?'

She was young, she was pretty, she was Wyn's wife asking him, so he nodded, yes, he would like to. 'You'll be back to tea,' Mrs Maitland thought proper to remind them, 'in fifteen minutes, you think?' 'In half an hour,' replied Bronwen, with the Manordy gesture of self-assertion in surrender. 'In half an hour then, Mr Costin,' Mrs Maitland told him, 'I shall be expecting you.' It had the sound of an ultimatum.

They walked together through the farm yard, through a field where the half-dozen Manordy cattle were grazing unharassed among a flock of rooks. The birds rose resentfully at their approach, made short grunting flights, then settled again behind them and restarted pecking for grubs.

'Let's be friends, Mr Costin, not strangers.' He saw her quick glance sideways at his face. 'Even if I haven't made the best start.'

'Friends,' he agreed, holding out his hand on the impulse; and hers was strong and cool and more friendly still than his.

'I'm sorry about the fair, I am really. But I know you will understand?'

The faint questioning seemed to invite reassurance, but 'Understand?' he repeated unhelpfully. 'What is there to understand?'

'Oh, everything! Mrs Maitland, me, all kinds of people.'

'I understand her, yes. She's a type you meet.'

'She's a person too, Mr Costin, and a very wonderful person. I want', she said earnestly, 'never to forget all she did for Wyn, and I hope she never finds me ungrateful.'

The sincerity and affection in her words held him from his answer and he was content to nod. They had come to where the sea meadow ended in white pebbles, St Clair lay behind them, and facing them to the south a green-capped ledge of tall rock offered them a walking mark. 'I've come a long way to Manordy,' he told her, 'and all the time I've been asking myself why. Yes, I know I was Wyn's friend, but even that was by accident and wouldn't have lasted once the war was over – oh no, it wouldn't! – and as for what happened to the *St Michael*, I'm like everybody else, I read about it later. So why did I come? What can I tell you?'

'One thing I've longed to know,' she answered, 'and I can only know it from someone who was there. You were hurt, Mr Costin, when it happened, I know that.' Her eyes, he could see, were brown rather than black, her hair brown too where the light quivered in it. 'All five of you were hurt terribly. I've had to keep telling myself night and day that Wyn died before he felt pain.' He looked away as she controlled her mouth. 'It's no good pretending. He was frightened of pain, Mr Costin, and he was frightened of fire.'

'There was no pain,' he said. That had come later. To the living.

'If only I could be certain of it! You must tell me, please tell me, what happened.' Her eyes changed, gave him the warmth of her sympathy. 'If you can, only if you can.'

He stood shaking his head, troubled and caught up in her emotion. 'There was fog', he said, 'and a big swell on. We'd been in the hunt for days on end and never a sight of anything.' He frowned at the unreal pale sea, the pale blue sky. 'Then we saw them, a battleship and two others, biggish ones. They didn't want to fight us – that's the irony of it! – they wanted to run south into the convoys, get away from us without any fuss. I was up in Control, supposed to be spotting, not that I ever saw anything more than fog and patches of water. Wyn must have been forward somewhere with the ack-ack, but you know all that. If he wasn't checking the ammunition for the tenth time then he must have been just staring at the fog, or chatting perhaps, or how do I know what? There was a petty officer standing alongside me, a queer fellow I'd always thought him, as though he'd come a long way down in the world and was trying to come back up by joining for hostilities. Everybody looked so calm, I must have done so myself, but I was all excited inside, tight and compressed, waiting for the start. That's how Wyn must have looked too, and felt. I tell you he must!' he insisted to her doubtful eyes. 'Then all of a sudden there was a roar, a swish, overhead – how can I describe it? – as though the air had been ruffled like a gigantic venetian blind. It was his first broadside and had come pretty fast. "Well, well," said the gunnery officer quietly, almost as if to himself, "and what do you think of that?" And this queer chap Moran, the petty officer I mentioned, he took it on himself to answer. "Naughty old fox," he said, "he wants to bite back." And I remember thinking that he sounded quite fond of foxes. And that was the last thing I did remember, for it was then he hit us in the magazine. No one could have felt pain, for we disintegrated. Turrets, guns, flesh and armour-plate and water, you couldn't tell them apart. Remember what our other ships saw – there's never been anything like it before. Wyn couldn't have felt or known more than I did – which was nothing. I tell myself there was a great noise I heard, as though the explosion was here, here, here, inside my skull, and that the noise was all red, and that I was touching nothing with any part of me, inside the red noise and in space at the same time, and yet the noise was inside me too.' He had been beating at his forehead, *here, here, here.* 'But in fact I know nothing. Whatever I think I know I imagined later, because there was an explosion with noise and fire, and because I must have been flung headlong out of the middle of it. But at the time it was annihilation. Life ended the same way for us all. Only five of us, the lucky ones,' he added bitterly, 'had to come back to a new beginning.'

('He's lucky to be alive and sane,' whispered many a well-meaning fool.

'Shall I go mad to please you?' he had snarled.)

'I've never called you lucky, not even in my mind, Mr Costin. I could think clearly enough for that. I know that two of you were blinded, and that for a long time you must all have found life much worse than dying.' She was remembering Wyn painting in the shabby old barn, and because of the light reflected from its walls, because they were together, and because they knew nothing of the future, it seemed to her now that in those days the sun was always shining, the days a long dream of happiness. How could life change like this? Without any fault of your own how could it grow so black and horrible? 'If he had been one of you five, blind or with his hands destroyed, that would have been far worse than death. But that's something I've never dared say to Mrs Maitland. She would have wanted him back blind, mute, a cripple. Oh,' she cried, 'why should the world treat us so cruelly, when we did nothing, nothing at all! So when I prayed at night for him – I still don't know whether there's a God to pray to, but I prayed – it was always that he should come back safe and well, never that he should just come back. For with me he had never pretended – you can't pretend when you are like us. He was afraid twice over when the war started: that his work could be over almost before he had begun, and that he might have to suffer great pain. That is why I wouldn't pray for him to come back on any terms except his own.'

'And now the war's over,' he asked her, 'what happens now?'

She recovered from her emotion as resolutely as he from his. 'There's plenty to do on a farm,' she replied evasively.

'For you?' he pressed her. 'Here at Manordy?'

'And there's a lot to be done for Wyn. And', she added warmly, 'for his mother too.'

'And when that's done?'

She showed surprise. 'Isn't it a little early to be thinking about it?' They had reached the green-capped rock and she rubbed her hand against it affectionately before they turned to walk back. How many times, he wondered, had she walked this way with Wyn, and with how many memories the rock was stored. The fields here, the hills and the beach – he had begun to ponder sentimentally when she broke into his mood with a sentence so prosaic that he jerked his head in mock disgust.

'We'll be late for tea, I'm afraid, Mr Costin.'

'Why be afraid? But there, I've remembered: we mustn't offend Mrs Maitland.'

'Is there any reason why we should?' Her counter was so quick and so reasonable that he had no answer for it. 'I don't think you like Mrs Maitland, do you?'

'Should I? And do you?'

'Like?' she said after a pause. 'What kind of word is like? No,' she said, her face suddenly enriched, 'I love her, Mr Costin, as Wyn loved her, and for the same reasons. I told you before she's a wonderful person, though you don't seem to think so. Yet, Mr Costin, you've seen the farm and the land here and that might have given you some idea. But what you don't know is how she lost her husband, Wyn's father, in the first years of her marriage, when the boys were so young she had to work the farm herself as well as bring the two of them up to be something. Think of her sending Wyn to grammar school and then to the college of art, and afterwards she even sent him to France for two years, and wrung every penny of it out of Manordy and herself. Do you think that was nothing? Or that it was easy?'

'I think it was hard. Too hard,' he said, 'and too much.'

'That was for her to decide,' she reproved him, 'not you or me. Why, ever since I've known Mrs Maitland she's not had a selfish thought. Always thinking of Wyn – and it's been the same even now she's lost him. The barn was her idea, because it's where he used to paint, and it cost a lot of money to put it in order and decorate it and frame all the paintings and get them properly hung, and for that, too, everything had to come out of Manordy and herself. Is it so surprising that I want to do what I can to repay her? When she is so wonderful, how could I go running away from her and Wyn and everything Manordy meant to them – and to me? You just don't know her, Mr Costin. She would take the heart out of her body for Wyn.'

'She's done so,' he said roughly. 'And the farm's heart. And Fred's, can't you see it? long ago.' He caught at her arm so that she had to turn and face him. 'And what about yours? Does she want that too?'

'How dare you, Mr Costin!' He saw anger and surprise flood her face, and something of confusion and shame, though whether this was shame at herself or at him he did not know. 'What a cruel thing to say! And I thought you were his friend.'

'I was and I still am.' He was pulling at her harder than he knew. 'Bronwen, Bronwen, can't you see he's past her sacrifice and yours? That he wouldn't want it anyway, that he'd be shouting to you to live your own lives and let him rest? Besides,' he said more calmly, 'there's nothing you can do any more. It ended with the *St Michael* up in the White Straits.'

'Do you tell us that after what you've seen in the barn today?'

'That!' he replied contemptuously. 'That thing she calls a shrine. Say a tomb, an open grave, instead. It's dead in there, and the pictures are dead, and they'll stay dead so long as you keep them buried out of sight and locked up with that silly black key in her silly black skirt. Nothing for sale! That's what she said so proudly. Nothing for sale for ever and ever. Poor old Wyn, who wanted his pictures to be seen and loved and argued over. I only hope she doesn't live to see them rot and drop off the walls before her.'

She shook her arm free. The silk of her sleeve, the silk of her flesh left his fingers tingling. 'You must be out of your mind to say such things. I thought this was going to be so different. Why did you have to spoil it?'

Again he saw her bosom stir like soft white birds under silk, he saw the warm red parted lips, the loose wave of her brown hair. 'You are young,' he said, feeling half-foolish as he said it. 'You are very young, Bronwen.' And because he too was young and had known much pain and unhappiness and borne them alone, she filled him with longing for many lovely and gentle things of which she stood the symbol. Anger, indignation, dismay, all left him. Pity, protectiveness, and that curious thin tang of desire took their place. 'Did I hurt you? I didn't mean to.' Only one life, he thought, for her as for me, and it hangs on a hair that the next wind can break. To think of it: Mrs Maitland filling the hollow of existence with a sacrifice long grown useless; and he, Costin, feeding his pride with bitterness. Sacrifice and bitterness: call them poison and evasion. And this warm tender girl – why didn't they all dash down the past and its burdens of denial? As though the present wasn't plenty to carry with one into the future! The platitudes he would have scowled at and ignored had they been propounded by anyone else appealed to him now as both immense and true. And surely what was so obvious to him would be obvious to her too? 'We said we'd be friends, remember? Did you mean it?' In his desire to be friendly and kind he fell headlong into folly. 'Then sell the pictures and come to the fair!'

He stretched out his hand, smiling, to take her once more by the arm. 'Don't touch me, please!' she said sharply, drawing away offended and even frightened by what she saw or imagined she saw in his eyes. 'And please stop laughing!'

'I wasn't laughing,' he protested. How ridiculous and humiliating he found it that his fine thoughts and noble sentiments should have brought him to this particular misunderstanding. They were Wyn's wife and friend and yet, he told himself with rather less than the whole truth, she was behaving suddenly like an old maid with a burglar under the bed. 'If I had been laughing, it would only have been at myself, that's all. For a minute ago I saw myself nothing more than a puppy that's had his tail stepped on and reckons to go on squealing for the rest of his life.' But this was gibberish to her and she walked on all the faster. 'Why not, Bronwen? Why won't you come with me?'

Her mouth tightened as Mrs Maitland's would have done. For one moment he saw her as the daughter of the house. 'You won't?'

All the motives which had led her to welcome his suggestion at first, the need for relief and change, the desire to please and be pleased, even the wish, so entirely innocent, to share a man's masterful yet childish company again – all these now forced her to refuse him determinedly.

'Don't let her stop you,' he warned.

'No one is stopping me.' The idea angered her as a half-truth will. 'I can see for myself how unwise it would be, that is all.'

The same rooks clambered grunting into the air from before their feet, flapped languidly off, then went on feeding.

'We were friends starting out,' he reminded her ruefully. 'What are we now?'

On these home fields strength, resolution, habit, were hers again. 'Why, friends,' she answered, with a confidence he found bright and displeasing, bred of the black-roofed home, the white-walled barn, the emblems of the mother's will. 'I hope,' she said primly, 'we shall always be friends, Mr Costin.'

'Then I mean it!' But what did he mean? That the warm, soft, tender Bronwen was no longer with him? That he had grown selfish and empty and that she could fill a void of hours? 'Come with me tonight, Bronwen.'

She was so sure of herself here at the farm that she was willing to look at him with tolerance and a little sorrow and regret. 'It's not that I mightn't want to. It's just that it's impossible, as Mrs Maitland was the first to see. Surely you can understand that, Mr Costin – you and I, his friend and wife, visiting fairs together?'

Mrs Maitland herself could not have found words of a shabbier vulgarity. 'Yes,' he agreed slowly. 'Poor old Wyn. I can see it.'

Where the three stone steps led up to the black-hasped door he halted. The repugnance he felt for Manordy would not allow him to enter the yellowed passage and the brown-plushed sunless parlour. He would have suffocated there. 'I won't come in,' he told her. Instantly she looked worried. 'But your tea!' 'I never take tea anyway,' he replied, his stomach flat with hunger. 'So I'll say good-bye, Bronwen.' He removed his cap and was aware of the theatricality of the moment.

But he was not allowed a farewell gesture or elegiac last word. The good-byes had been planned by another. Mrs Maitland had come to the door and stood above them like a grey cold cloud. She had been watching for their return, and anxiously. Costin looked at her astonished, and against his judgment was deeply moved by the change in her. It was the time of day when the first spikes of shadow were thrusting over the farm yard, stabbing at the stone steps and the black-shod tired feet that stood there. Dark lines of toil and grief showed in her face, and the hands clasped before her were worn and blackened with a thousand bitter chores. 'Why, mother,' the girl exclaimed, and ran up the steps to her, put her arm about her waist. 'You've been crying!'

Had she? Visage of grief and spirit of sacrifice though she was, to a recovering Costin she looked not without her triumph; but the stare the girl gave him was as hostile as it was reproachful. Go away, it said, go away: must you bring her still more unhappiness? The two women stood side by side, like dead-leafed autumn with the flowering spring, and he felt the overwhelming power of that unnatural alliance. 'Good-bye, Mrs Maitland. Good-bye, Bronwen.' They did not speak, but the girl's brown eyes looked down on him with what he recognized as fear and doubt as he turned and walked quickly away. He thought they would stay to watch him out of sight, but when he stopped by the prong-marks in the grass and looked around they had entered the house and were not to be seen.

He had eaten some sandwiches and was back at *The Dolphin* soon after seven o'clock. As he made for the bar-parlour door he saw Wolfe pushing his belly before him, and they went inside together. The room was stuffed with people in for a night's fun, almost half of them wives and sweethearts; the glasses on the tables, the very mirrors, rattled with their merry baffled din. No sooner were they through the door than Harris's labrador walked over to greet them. 'That beachcomber here!' grunted Wolfe, and 'On your tail,' said Harris thickly from behind them. 'What'll it be? And it had better be beer, see!' The girl he had called Sue served them disdainfully, yet with a half-way smile for Costin.

'Beauty and the Beast,' said Harris. 'Or do I mean Beauty and the Two Beasts?' He contemplated them with no apparent pleasure as they sat down opposite him. The dog was licking beer off his forefinger, curling his tongue all round it and rolling his eyes with relish. 'Fah!' said Wolfe. 'Disgusting!' 'I'd rather it was him than you any day,' said Harris loudly. Someone sniggered from the bar. 'Or you,' said Harris, looking up. There was an avenue of silence carved between them, one heard the ear-flaps dropping open, but the man addressed shrugged his round shoulders and turned to his glass and his friends. 'I've got my friends, too,' said Harris quarrelsomely. He challenged the back of the man at the bar. 'Everybody knows me. From Fishguard to Holyhead everybody knows Jack Harris. Is that right?' 'Quite right, Jack,' said the other peaceably. 'And less of your Jack! I'm Harris to you, see? *Mr* Harris.' 'Quite right, Harris. Quite right, Mr Harris.' There was some nudging and grinning in the corners. 'So long as it's understood,' said Harris, true to his catchwords and re-dipping his finger.

'Who's for Abermaid?' asked Costin, watching the anxious Sue whispering with the barman. 'You'll have it on your conscience if you make a drunkard out of a clean-living dog like that.'

To his surprise Harris emptied his glass at one pull and stood up. He could feel the relief like a hand on their backs as they went outside. Harris led the way, labrador at heel, Costin with his bag and Wolfe five yards in the rear, watching him take his corners stiffly, almost too upright. Suddenly he halted in front of a two-storied stable and loft. 'Old Wolfe's daubs,' he announced, leaning against the door-jamb. 'No light though, damn it!' He scratched with his finger-nail at the newly painted door-panels. 'Pretty good, Wolfe. P'raps this is your right line.' 'Perhaps it is,' agreed Wolfe, with a harassed, protesting glance at Costin. He added oilily: 'Some time you must let me paint your boat.' But the soft answer did not turn away wrath. 'I didn't say you were that good,' sneered Harris, and proceeded circuitously to the harbour steps.

'He'll end the day with a fight,' promised Wolfe. Costin half expected him to jack out his fat little fists and shadow-box.

'Not with me,' he said mildly. 'He's all yours, Mr Wolfe.'

Harris had disappeared down the steps in a precipitous short-heeled manner. The dog paid the iron post a penny and ran happily down after him. 'Passengers on board,' bawled Harris. 'All ports to Abermaid, Timbuctoo, and the mouths of the Morassah.'

'He'll drown you,' Wolfe prophesied, not unhopefully.

'You couldn't drown Admiral Costin,' shouted the sharp-eared Harris. 'He's born to hang, I tell you.' He touched a forelock, or where a forelock should be, as Costin stepped aboard. His red face was all grin as he lit the lanterns and cast off. 'Good night, Fatty,' he called up the steps. 'Watch out you don't overlay yourself!' Wolfe's round belly and then his offended round white face disappeared into the dusk as the boat swirled backwards into the channel and headed for the green and yellow lights marking the passage. From the water St Clair looked tired as a sigh, but somewhere beyond the village an orange light pressed upwards against cloud, and there was a bonfire leaping behind the hollow windows of the folly.

'You saw them?' asked Harris. 'Learn anything?'

'A little', he answered, 'about myself.'

He feared Harris would go on talking but at that moment they heard the toe-nails of the labrador ripping furiously at the floorboards. 'Cut it out, you big clown!' said Harris, and the dog whistled and lay down.

Daylight was almost ended. Costin sat quiet and upright, thinking of Manordy and the two women there, life in the dark low farm and death in the still white barn. The grey dusk was down there too, fingering its way through the buildings, thickening the wind-dragged tree-tops, staining the tired fields. 'Grey,' he said aloud, 'all grey.' Wyn dead a second time and sadly buried, grey land, grey home, grey mother. And the wife? White-bosomed Bronwen? As unlike the shrouded mother she seemed as April to November, juiced fruit to the dry husk, or flowers to the parched spray. And yet –

'Two on a stalk,' Harris assured him harshly. 'You mark my words, Admiral.'

Her eyes under the framing canopy of hair, her mouth and rising breast moved whitely between Costin and the bubble-flecked water. 'It's not that simple,' he said. The truth was never in one place, he knew. 'Most of all I'm sorry for them.'

'You keep your sorrow,' Harris advised him. 'You can use it yourself.'

No, thought Costin, I've done with that. Coming here has taught me that much anyhow. I'll not be a sacrifice on my own altar. The labrador's cold nose had found his hanging hand. 'Good dog,' he said, 'good Billy.'

'He's a survivor himself,' said Harris, weighing his risk. 'The only one of his litter.'

Costin heard his own laughter light and clear as a tenor bell. Harris heard it too and bent grinning to his engine. This morning, and still more this afternoon, he would have needed a fumy head before venturing half as far. By his own lights he was at the moment cold sober.

Stars were appearing where no stars had been. The weak yellow lights which were St Clair were falling behind them, and in the darkness beyond was the farm Manordy. In Manordy they must be sitting now, the wife and mother, in the brown-plushed shadowy parlour with the woollen-work horse and foal and Wyn's brilliance struggling against the grudging lamp-light. Mrs Maitland, her cracked indomitable hands never idle, would be sitting with her work-box where she had sat that afternoon, and Bronwen in his, in Costin's, chair. WE SAT DOWN, YEA, WE WEPT, WHEN WE REMEMBERED ZION.

For a while this vision hung before Costin's eyes like a dim but golden picture, but it could not sadden him. Then it faded into the dark sparkle of the night-blackened sea. Bronwen's face died last, a glow, a paleness, a blur, then nothingness. He straddled his seat, brought his back into some conformity with the mast, closed his eyes. From the stern Harris soon heard his heavy breathing and the sonorous snores of the dog and was pleased to find himself so completely his own man. Life was bother enough without the troubles of others. He settled with satisfaction to the three-hour run to Abermaid, nodded approvingly at the tarry patch on his left hand. A minute ago he had failed to distinguish it, but now – he looked over his shoulder and spat for luck into the water. At the same moment Costin roused and looked the same way. Their thought, Harris knew, was the same. Yes, the long day was over and the moon rising.

A Death on Sistersland

~

I

FOR three days and nights they had been firing gorse on the mountains north and east of the island. By daylight black oily plumes of smoke clambered then shredded in the grey upper air; at night red flame, notched like a cock's comb, burned against the dark of the hills and threw blood into the waters of the bay. Down here, in the cove, a shifting tawny light full of shadows fought against the April darkness and the tiny green stars hung between the sandstone promontories enclosing it. The boat itself was a heavy blunt shadow moving from the land. There were three people aboard. From the middle seat Mrs Yorath watched her husband's back, narrow and wary, his head tilted so that his good ear caught every sound from the shore, the fringes of his grey hair upcurled between cap and collar. His oars were raised against the sky, the boat spurted, lost way, then began to rock gently as Darran scrambled on board and into the bows, hauling the smaller ewe out of the way of his legs. Only then Yorath sat down, began to ease the boat slowly round, a man silent and lost in his triumph.

In his turn Darran from the bows was watching the woman. She was all black, the hard-worn coat over her shoulders and back, the shapeless low-crowned hat, the hair that escaped below it. But when she turned her head her cheek gleamed white; he saw her chin smooth as china, the dusky under-jaw. Without moving on his seat he extended his right hand, laid his first two fingers against her neck, and felt them imprisoned by the stealthy downward turn of her head. The suddenness of her response gave a terrifying intimacy to the caress, she felt the fingers reaching forward to her throat, but as quickly she lifted her head and turned away from him. The white of her face vanished, he saw again the fixity and drabness of her head and shoulders, and forward of her the cocked head of her husband. When? he thought, when? His hands went to the oars, gripped, grew loose, fell into his lap. And at that moment Yorath sighed reluctantly and with a slow stroke sent the boat sluggishly forward.

He had brought them away on the first wave of the falling tide, and everything else he did tonight would show the same precision. They had left the island late in the afternoon, and made their landfall off the Shearwater rock. Then with the late set of the tide they had come through the early darkness down to the cove. Here they had taken two ewes and their three lambs, and would now have the tide and the four-mile current to help them home. But nothing less than perfection should be looked for from Yorath: he had been stealing sheep all his life. He had stolen lambs as a boy, when his father had both beaten him and kept the booty. Then on his own mountain farm up north he had driven in other men's creatures from the rock grazing grounds, till the hostility of his neighbours forced him to sell and leave. Not that a charge was laid or anything ever proved. Nor was there anything proved when he was driven from his second farm in the valley above the Morwy. But one morning he was led by their bleatings to three maimed sheep in his farthest field and before the day was out their six ears with the disguised croppings had been flung on to his backyard. No neighbour complained to Yorath, nor Yorath to the police, but it was again time to be moving. So south again he shifted to the rose-coloured hills around Llanfair, from which on a clear day one can see the long arms of the bay to north and south, the glittering waterbowl of the west, and the green-topped red-rock bastion of Sistersland riding the tides. And in the end it was to Sistersland he came, as to a fortress built to defy his enemies, and from which he could from time to time descend upon their fields and stock. And from Sistersland he would never be driven as from his other farms. On Sistersland he was king. Of late with three subjects, his dog, his wife, and now this Darran.

Darran! Mrs Yorath stirred, grew restless, felt him against her, as though a more real self had left the watcher in the bows and flowed over and around her compulsively in warmth and silence. When? she thought, she too, when? Where his fingers had lain against her neck the skin glowed as from ice, and she knew briefly an intolerable desire and depression. The black water as it slid by sucked at her spirit, a gull heading inland to its nest on the marshes cried its note of desperate longing. She turned and looked at Darran, and as he came forward on the oars saw his full-lipped treacherous mouth shape the single word 'Tonight'.

'Hear anything?' asked Yorath. A spider couldn't walk the window without his knowing it.

'Nothing. It was a gull.'

'Gulls are all right,' said Yorath oracularly. 'You know where you are with gulls.'

They were outside the promontory now. Ahead of them the sea was like black glass, but to the north she had the impression of fires in its depths, their flames licking under the wave-hollows. Eastwards there was the new moon like a green-hot metal shaving soaring off the hills, but no moon-track on the water. She felt the current take them; for all her freight the boat bounded as the oar-blades split the water. She found herself breathing in rhythm with their progress, in-out, in-out, her bosom lifting and swelling, then sighing and sinking on the hiss of spray and the grunt of the row-locks. Soon Yorath shipped his oars and turned to face her: he was tough as an ash-pole and almost as springy, but he was seventy. With a fool in the boat to do the pulling he could take it easy. He groped after the lambs and ewes, too phlegmatic or too terrified to bleat from where they lay tied on the boards, satisfied himself afresh that the lambs were unmarked, gripped at a fistful of wool, laughed quietly.

'You'll be clever once too often,' said Mrs Yorath.

'You can't be,' he replied. 'At my age you'll have learned that.'

She did not understand his meaning and made a short impatient exclamation. Then: 'At your age!' she said bitterly.

'Not much I don't know,' he reminded her, with more indifference than good humour.

'For what good it's ever done you!'

'I'm middling satisfied,' he said. He stroked a lamb's back, not out of affection but with a thief's pride.

'Good thing', said Darran's rich moist voice, 'that you never fancied horses.'

'I never fancied anything', said Yorath, with a long look at his wife, 'that I didn't get.'

'Getting's one thing. Keeping's another.'

'To me the same thing,' said Yorath.

He was amused, or seemed to be amused, for a sport of nature had stamped his face with the beginning of a smile. At a first acquaintance nothing could be more attractive, or more deceptive.

It had taken Mrs Yorath a fortnight to wonder at that smile, a month to hate it, and she had been hating it now for seven years. 'We'll see,' she said, and Darran breathed heavily; 'We'll see.'

'Stop rowing,' said Yorath. Darran hesitated, then pulled his oars in. The boat was still moving, but there were heavier slappings of water against the port side. 'Keep her straighter,' said Yorath curtly. 'We'll be turning up to the island in a minute.' What he knew of tide and current was full mystery to Mrs Yorath, but in any respite from her dislike she must admit that he knew them perfectly. A lamb bleated so uncertainly that it was as though it feared to disturb the silence, and its dam gave a hoarse throbbing answer. There was a heavy splash ahead on their right. 'Seal,' said Darran. 'Seal,' repeated Yorath, with a zest of contempt. But he offered no different explanation. 'Fetch her round, will you!'

At once Mrs Yorath felt the heaviness of the boat as the current ceased to help them. Both men were pulling hard now, and above the creak of the boat she heard the hiss of her husband's breath. 'I don't know,' she said unexpectedly, 'I don't know.'

Both men, surprised, faltered in their stroke. Yorath looked quickly round at her. 'I was dreaming,' she said, 'day-dreaming. And I'm cold.'

'Not for long,' said Darran. 'Look!'

'Mind your oar,' said Yorath sharply. 'Don't you go day-dreaming too. Or I'd be better off without you.'

Better off without you. The words hung in the brain of them both, the woman who had fled her stinted, mean and godly home to marry an ageing man at Llanfair, the man who had come destitute to the island a month ago. Darran saw her as he had seen her first, in the cold sunshine of a March afternoon, the strong woman in her early thirties, with the mirthless smile, the dishevelled black hair and long, black eyes, the high cheekbones and wide sensual mouth, the milky throat and trembling breasts. And she saw him, dressed in a coarse blue-grey shirt and duffle jacket, with red neckerchief and yellow corduroy trousers, and his broken right boot. She saw the stallion strength of him, the fairground set of his shoulders, the handsome rank face. She had reached for her hair, the uplifted sleeves of her blouse falling away from the white of her underarms, her cheeks flushing at his nod and stare. 'Boss home?' he asked ambiguously, but as he asked Yorath stepped softly out of the cottage.

He had never ceased to step softly between them, and his face had never lost its mask of good humour as he did so. And probably he was amused, she concluded, using her as the carrot to draw Darran into his schemes, but careful that the donkey never got his bite. Willing that they should torment themselves with each brief and feeble caress, himself the cold master of his passions and theirs. God, she thought, I was a fool to marry an old man! In the hope of freedom and, she must confess it, the hope of inheritance, she had taken him – and all for this. Five years at Llanfair and two endless years on the island. A lifetime of waiting, and nothing to wait for.

'Not for long,' Darran had said. 'Look!'

The hammer-head of the island broke the sea's rim before them. She noticed how for all the flatness of the sea the boat was rising and dipping before a hardly visible horizon. The water cleft by the prow streamed past on either side, full now of ripples and bubbles and the thresh of spray from the oars, but fast sealed behind them. She and Darran were like that, two shifting currents met and soon to mingle, then racing madly to the whirlpool. 'Tonight,' he had whispered. 'Tonight on the island.'

'Arms gone soft on you?' asked Yorath. 'I thought you were strong.'

'Stronger than you,' Darran replied. 'You'll see.'

Yorath laughed his gently jeering laugh. 'I'm tough,' he boasted. 'Like a man of thirty. Ask the missis.'

'Old tups are always the toughest,' said Darran with a new insolence. 'Ask the butcher.'

Mrs Yorath sat tensed and silent, and against her expectation the men fell silent too. And now, with Darran's words, they were all afloat upon a second sea, carried by great tides of hate and mistrust and desire. And this second sea, like the first, was bearing them home to the island, and what it held for them.

At the same moment she saw the island's black hulk ride out at them and heard the suck and splash of waves along its base. She was astonished to find it so close, and fear stuck thin cold spears down into her throat and breast. She had the feeling that all Sistersland was afloat, that it was rising on a swell, lurching over them, that in seconds it would capsize and press them with a great roaring down through the sea to its smothering floor. 'Too close!' snarled Darran. 'Are you mad?' He pulled frantically on his left oar, trailing the right in foam-laced water. Their stern swung in under a mouldered overhang of rock, a wave swilling back fell with a heavy splash on to the terrified sheep, slipped its cold hands over Mrs Yorath's ankles.

'God in heaven!' cried Darran. But Yorath's oar reached to the rock and with a nonchalant shove he kept their stern clear. The next moment the backwash helped fling them out and away. 'Keep pulling,' he said calmly, the cliffs leaned back and she could see the stars and the sky. Soon they were rounding a rock-tooth and the landing place lay like a black hole in front of them. 'Light the lantern!' said Darran hoarsely, but Yorath only grinned back at him. 'I made a big mistake in you, Darran, I can see. The missis too.' He stood swaying easily, sculling them forward. 'It's cat whiskers you want for this job,' he told them, 'and what you haven't got, Darran.' He grunted as he shipped his oars again. 'And that's guts, my boy.' There was a faint scraping sound, the boat wobbled and was still; from the bows came the rasp of a match; she saw a brief glittering of wet rock, and then the soft effulgence of the lantern showed them the landing platform level with the gunwale, the hanging rope ladder, and Yorath's smile. The smile she knew so well. He had been showing who was boss, frightening them for fun.

'Still thinking I'll be clever once too often?' he asked his wife.

Her fingers made a swift smoothing movement over her cheeks, then past her eyes, thrusting the hair from her forehead. The ewes, as though smelling land and the grass that crowned it, baa-aaed dismally, and the furious bleating of the lambs splintered like glass on the rock. 'Give me the other lantern,' said Yorath. 'I'll send down the cradle.' He moved like a crab sideways from boat to landing ledge, lit his lantern and tugged on the rope ladder. It was Mrs Yorath's fancy that the bleached rope would rattle like bones, but he began to climb silently and with an exaggerated *élan*, as though knowing that eyes below would be watching for signs of weariness and decay. But when he called down to them from near the cliff top it was with a noticeable puffiness of breath. 'Don't sit about there,' he ordered. 'Get the sheep ashore.'

But they were no longer in the boat. Darran had jumped on to the ledge and brought Mrs Yorath alongside him, for a moment kept his arms around her and felt her lithe and cat-like body wind against his. Then 'Take me away,' she whispered. 'Back in the boat, now.' He tried to tighten his arms but she pushed him off. 'No,' she said, 'it's foolish, here. With him on the island.' 'Him!' he growled. 'What's he think he is?' He thrust his hands under the shoulders of her coat. 'I said tonight. I mean tonight.'

'What's that you are saying?' called Yorath, not because he could hear anything but cunningly, to keep them aware of him.

'A fool you'll look with your boasting,' she whispered. 'For what will he be doing all the time?' She moved back against him, and his hands moved from her shoulders to the smooth flesh of her back. 'I hate him, Jack, I hate him. Take me away, now.' Her chin was cold against his face, but her mouth sought his hot and wet. 'It'll be like it's always been,' she whispered, 'so long as he's here. If you want me, he mustn't be with us.' His fingers had driven into her back till it hurt and she again wrestled free from him. 'But if it was all talk,' she said, 'just talk.'

'Talk,' he repeated, 'I'll show him talk!' He struck his fist against the rock, turned to her scowling. 'I said tonight, didn't I?' He made a small gesture of secrecy, was opening his mouth to speak further, when: 'Look out down there,' called Yorath and the rock cradle thrashed on to the ledge. 'Give a shout when you're ready.'

Darran stepped back into the boat, swung a tied ewe on to the ledge. She bawled and struggled as he worked her into the cradle, then fell paralysedly dumb. 'Right,' he called, and the sheep, her four legs stuck ridiculously through the rope mesh, rose slowly out of the lantern light into the dark above. He pressed Mrs Yorath back to the rock face as the balancing weight came as slowly into view, stood with his hand on her neck, a smoky royalty dimming his mind. 'Get started, will you?' cried Yorath. 'Are you dead down there?' And in tones pitched to reach them as a mutter: 'Useless duffer that he is!'

'Don't notice,' said Mrs Yorath softly. 'That's his way, always. He thinks we have no spirit.'

The second ewe ascended stiff-legged to her new pasture. 'You and me, Jack, we could be so happy. We could be so happy tonight.'

She kissed the side of his face, drew his hand to her breast. 'But not with him here. So take me away now in the boat. It doesn't do to be afraid, Jack.'

He, Darran, afraid of that old tup laughing at him on top there! He stood muddled and enraged as the lambs went upwards out of sight. Some of his rage was for Mrs Yorath, to ravage and possess her, but most for her husband who stood between them and had made him look a fool all night. Lust and revenge galloped their race through his veins; he could not even see that it was not his own but Mrs Yorath's hatred which swelled and pounded within him. Who was this Yorath? To keep the woman from him? To sneer in his face? 'Old hand!' he muttered. 'We'll see, Mr Yorath.' And all the time another voice was clamouring from the back of his mind: 'Get out, Darran. What are you doing? Leave, Darran, leave the woman, leave the island. Quickly, quickly, for only seconds remain!'

'You and me,' said Mrs Yorath. Her coat had fallen open, she was between his arms, every mound and curve and hollow of her body flowed against him, her lips moved in small soft kisses over his neck and ear, draining him of will and judgment. He pressed her to him savagely; she could feel his arms and legs trembling. 'Go, Darran,' called the once clamouring voice, 'Go quickly!' But what was this? 'Yes, go. Go rape, rob, kill! Lose yourself, Darran: drown, smother, fall. There's no stopping now. Tonight, tonight, tonight.' And another voice: 'Tonight, Jack, you and me.'

Who was shouting? And who was pushing him away? 'For God's sake,' said Mrs Yorath. 'Quick!'

He stood reeling and incomplete as she stepped into the boat and sat primly on the front thwart. The rope ladder was jerking, and soon he saw Yorath's legs coming down as stiffly as the ewes' had gone up. His branded smile gave him an air of being pleased against his will. He looked jauntily enough at Darran, unwilling to betray his suspicion, but more searchingly at his straight-backed wife.

'Well?' he asked. 'What's the delay?'

'I'm afraid of the ladder,' she said. 'You know I'm afraid of the ladder.'

'And Darran?' he asked. 'Is he afraid too? Then I'll help you both up.' Something of the wryness went out of his smile, but he had been driving himself hard all day and she saw him grey with tiredness. He was short and whippy and dry, and Darran could have tossed him one-handed into the sea. 'The lantern's on the edge,' he warned. 'Mind you don't knock it off. Might brain Darran if it hit him.' He could see Darran flushed, confused, wool-browed as an ox. 'Or again it might not.'

She started to climb the ladder, her feet slipping on the rope. 'Steady the end,' said Yorath, and Darran came forward out of shadow. 'This lamp's dying,' he announced. 'Might just last you out though.' He felt sick with anger but kept most of it out of his voice. But Yorath made a point of staring him down before putting his foot into the first rung and starting to climb.

'Don't crowd me,' Darran heard Mrs Yorath call. 'Don't be more hindrance than help.'

'I'll hold on till you reach the top,' replied Yorath mildly enough. He was about six feet from the cliff edge when her hand seized the guide-rail and she stepped on to firm land.

How many times would they rack and wring their brains over those next twenty seconds? Above, below, they heard Yorath cry out – not with fright or despair, almost as if in warning, the beginning of words, the breath as though snatched from his mouth. Then a rustle, and for Darran the rushing black bird, all spread and sprawled, the smash on the ledge beside him. For Mrs Yorath the face whirling out of the lamplight, the lurch of her heart, the hands clenched in her hair.

Neither called to the other. Darran knelt alongside the broken body, coaxed the lamp to a yellow-red light. 'Who?' asked the bloody mouth, askew with ghastly jocularity. 'Someone – ' Then he was lying slack and jointless, like a straw man lolling in the last cart of harvest.

Had he lived, Darran must have howled into the night like a dog. But because he was dead and his limbs gangling he felt for him neither pity nor horror. His thoughts were on Mrs Yorath above. She, straining her ears, heard something being dragged back from the water's edge; there was a pause, then the ladder shook and tightened. Darran was climbing up to her. His head and shoulders swayed in to the light of her lantern, he came over the edge like a monster clambering out of the sea, frightening to her. And still more frightening was his silence. He put an arm over her shoulders, began to lead her away. 'Now,' he said, 'for God's sake, now!'

'What happened?'

He answered her whisper loudly, excitedly. 'You don't know? He fell, didn't he? Nothing to be done.'

'But we ought – '

'Nothing to be done, I tell you.' His arm bore down on her so heavily she thought she would sink to the ground under it. 'Now!' he said. He stumbled, she felt his feet drag, and as she turned to him he leaned with all his weight against her. 'Can't go on,' he said. 'Got to sit.' His voice had grown thick as sleep or sickness would make it. He half fell down, lay back against a low and grassy bank, and buried his face in her lap when she sat beside him. For the moment she felt utterly remote from him. From where she sat she could see the gorse fires flaring against the northern mountains; the three-night moon was green and the stars green, millions of them frosted in heaven. Invisible, unheard, the ocean flowed below, flowed in the woman too. She felt old and wise and incredibly alone. Men, all men, children and fools.

His arms were round her waist, his face pressed harder and deeper, and he groaned. She stroked his hair and twined his curls about her fingers. But the great arms were closing, they were wide steel bands about her, the stars swung down-sky as the grass-scented earth rose up to meet her head, the earth black and the stars green and this white her own body, or his, or theirs, the one. She moaned, beating at his arms, blindly enlacing him. 'Love me, love me, love me!' The world which had been vaster than mountains shrank to a man's breadth, the horizon was a ring round their heads. So violent a pulse was shaken through her blood that the earth seemed rising and falling beneath them. His brute passion spent he wondered at her fury to possess and be possessed, marvelled too to hear the rush of words from her mouth, the babble and nonsense and endearments. Her drumming heart came to frighten him, the succubus mouth, the wet black hair that clung to his eyes and lips. And yet there was no satiety for either; they were drunk on desire and the fears of the night, their terrors were a whip to their desire. Such mastering emotions had lashed them together that they lay in each other's arms as unheeding of the future as scum-drift on the lip of a weir.

They were apart. He groaned but could not have said what self-pity and disgust, what unholy joy and loathing, sounded in his throat. His face rolled sideways into the yielding grass, he flung out his arms, and his boots clashed together, heavy as a stallion's hooves. Soon Mrs Yorath sat up, watching his broad back, the sprawl of his legs. She pushed the hair off her forehead, felt the breeze chill on the hot skin there. A sudden languor flowed like oil over her limbs; she stroked her arms, palmed the smoothness of her shoulders, the dappled fleshy rib-cage. Bending her head she nodded approvingly at some self-praise of her own, her smile was brief and secretive before she drew her clothes about her, pulled the hat like a gipsy down to her ears. 'Don't sleep,' she warned, rocking his shoulder. 'It's cold. We must go.' He rested a while longer, then came to his hands and knees, grinning round at her, hollow-limbed and light-headed. 'I'm a bull,' he said, and she pulled his hair. 'Right, you're a bull,' she agreed, with a ruefulness which set them both laughing.

He had jumped up beside her. 'Home,' he said. 'Food.' His arm fell heavy as a saddle across her shoulders as they began to walk away from the cliff top, the landing ledge, and the dead Yorath. The events of the day and night were now infinitely receded, things neither done nor imagined nor heard of. There were no steps to take, no decisions to make. Sometime it would be morning: till then they would eat, go to bed, make love again, sleep and maybe dream. Some dream within the dream of living.

They were on the sandstone ridge behind the cottage, their feet feeling for the pathway down. 'Look,' he cried. 'A light in the front room!'

Her heart leapt upwards in her breast, making her sick and weak. 'It's him. It's Yorath!'

He shook his head, his fears quite different ones. 'It's not him, I tell you. He's dead. Hell,' he said, 'you ought to know.' She was frightened to find him draw away from her. 'And where's the dog?'

As he spoke they heard the first salvo of barks from inside the cottage, and a bloom of yellow light spilled outwards from the opening door. They saw a stranger, a man in a pale-coloured jacket, standing there, peering from under his hand as the dog came scampering up the path.

'What shall we say?' asked Mrs Yorath anxiously.

'Say nothing,' said Darran.

She stared at him, surprised but too weary to be anything but docile. She had reached for his arm but he was hurrying down the ridge ahead of her. At the bottom, however, he waited impatiently, and they walked together with the fawning dog into the light.

'I thought you wouldn't mind if I came inside,' said the young man by the doorway. 'My name's Rice.' He held out his hand. 'Good evening, Mrs Yorath. And you, Mr Yorath, good evening too.'

II

It was their chance to tell a story and they had missed it. To Mrs Yorath, washing teacups in the low-roofed kitchen of Mandred next morning, this still seemed as inevitable as it had been foolish. For shock and weariness, guilt and suspicion, had laid burdens too heavy on them. They had shaken hands with ridiculous formality, the young man polite and zealous as a mainland draper. A sightseer, he said. Her bruised lips and hanging hair, her stockings over her shoes – she was only too glad to get out of his sight. 'So I thought, Mr Yorath – ' She heard his eager, well-bred English voice explaining and deferring after some blank-eyed inquiry of Darran's. And at the name an exhaustion so intense descended on her that she thought she would faint.

'He's eaten all he wants,' said Darran, coming into the bedroom later. 'I said you'd been taken bad. He'll sleep in my place up in the loft.' He stood rubbing his forehead. 'I'll drop if I don't eat. What about you?'

She shook her head and he went out again. She took off her outer clothes and shoes, fell on the bed, pulled the sheet and blanket over her, turned her face to the wall, pressing at it with her open hand as though its stone was the only solid, safe thing in a world grown weltering as water. 'I can't think!' she whispered into the pillow. 'And I won't think.' The bed swayed beneath her, all Sistersland afloat on the tide, heaved up like a great liner over that small boat she lay in, surging closer, toppling – she sprang up, fingers in her mouth, hearing now the padding of the new-comer on the loft-ladder, then Darran's heavy tread over the kitchen flags.

'He's being taken off tomorrow,' he told her when next he came in. 'About four. I'll have to do some thinking.' He listened to her mutter. 'What's that? There was no need to. He's a bit of a softy, that boy.' He lay down heavily in Yorath's place. 'Wake me,' he said, 'if I'm not moving before the light.' But in minutes he had turned to her.

And now this morning he was about his business down at the landing platform. The dog was shut in the house with her, so that he might not follow. Suddenly she heard their visitor stirring overhead. It seemed to her that Darran had been gone a very long time. Could anything have happened down at the landing shelf? The thought was tormenting and foolish and she tried to repress it at once.

'Good morning, Mrs Yorath. May I come in?'

It was Rice, in his straw-coloured tweed jacket and brown corduroys. He had a round amiable face and thick glistening lenses in his glasses. 'If I might have a wash, d'you think?' He hurried to take the bowl from her hands. 'Please don't trouble. I have everything with me.'

He was hardly out of the kitchen when Darran walked in. He was wearing a clean white shirt of her husband's. He nodded in answer to her unasked question. 'Till he goes keep him away from the round pen.'

374

'Wouldn't it be better to say?'

'You're a cool one,' he said, shaking his head, puzzling her. 'Say what? We've got to think, about us and everything. At least', he said, 'I've got to think.'

'Good morning, Mr Yorath.'

Darran jerked round like a rabbit but returned Rice's greeting. How vulnerable Mrs Yorath thought him, jumping at a morning greeting. And how silly the two of them not to have told a story. Every hour it would grow harder. Him and his thinking!

Later in the morning when Rice had tagged off at Darran's heels to see something of the island she spent half her time compiling statements to account for her husband's death. These began as letters written to some understanding (yet not over-understanding) person on the mainland. 'Dear Sir,' she would see herself writing, 'I am writing to let you know of a serious accident to my husband John Yorath.' Or: 'Dear Sir, I take pen in hand to inform you that last night my husband John Yorath, late of Mandred, Sistersland, met with a fatal accident at the landing place. What happened was – ' Always at this point she paused, for indeed what had happened? And there were the newspapers, they must come into it somewhere. 'Speaking on behalf of the widow, who is prostrate, a friend (that would be Darran) said – ' But what would Darran say? He knew no more than she. Or did he? She felt a coldness brush her skin, but it was as quickly gone. She shook her black-browed head, tidied the hair fallen loose on her neck, feeling her blood stir and crawl at the memory of last night's fury and storm. It had been hard after that to do much save collapse into bed. Perhaps after all, she thought, there need be no hurry. Everything is the same whether you tell today or tomorrow. Perhaps Darran was right: they must do some thinking first, and you couldn't do that with a third moon-face lifting over your shoulder. Seeing Darran's face as she had seen it that first day, handsome, insolent, masterful, tricky – he knew his way about did Darran. Yes, she would let him have the say.

At once she felt lighter, freer. Her mood changed. She was a fiercely sensual woman who could plan pleasure ahead, and it was this that now filled her thoughts till the men returned.

Rice was loud in his praise of Mr Yorath's kindness. Mr Yorath was this and Mr Yorath was the other. 'Don't call me that,' growled Darran. Rice stood open-mouthed. 'No one calls me that,' said Darran, recovering himself. 'My name's Jack. Jack's what I like to be called.' 'That's very kind of you, Mr Yorath,' stammered Rice, and henceforth ceased to call him anything at all. With his plump, fresh face and clean linen, he was no part of their world, and his offer to help Mrs Yorath with the dinner plates did not bring him closer to it. For Mrs Yorath he had a mingled fear and admiration: the ravaged, sluttish woman he had seen the night before was an enlargement of his experience. My word, he could not help thinking, this is something to tell the fellows. And here, how queer, on this lonely Sistersland!

'It's a funny name,' he said, 'isn't it?' He looked anxiously at Darran, as though expecting a denial. 'Why did they call it Sistersland, Mrs Yorath?'

'There's a story. All lies, I expect.'

'Tell it him,' said Darran boorishly. 'Only I've heard it.'

'All right, tell it I will. But in my own time and at the right place. And those who don't want to listen', she added sharply, 'don't have to.'

But he came with them, the dog sniffing and puzzling at Yorath's boots on his feet as they walked through the tumbled boulders towards the cliff edge, and then north round the island. The first fires on the mountains had burnt themselves out, but new smoke pillars rose from far inland like signals of a destroying army. A light breeze blew out of the east, crinkling the water, and bringing with it a hardly discernible fragrance of the burning. The northern part of Sistersland was mostly precipice rising haggard from the sea and outcropping thereafter from narrow grassy strips. The rock was a dull red or greenish-grey, and in places white with bird-droppings. There were seabirds everywhere, puffins, terns and oyster-catchers, and one swift mewing flight of black-headed gulls berated the intruders. Noisiest of all were the herring gulls, wailing by land and ocean. A sheep or two with crisp new lambs browsed the springy grass but ran off at their approach. 'Eden,' said the affable Rice, 'without the serpent.' But Darran plucked his sleeve, pulled him round to follow his pointing finger. 'Watch,' he said excitedly, 'before you are too sure.'

They were in a green defile between a rock ledge and a pinnacled precipice. Darran's red finger swung in line with a bird drifting gently against the blue of the sky. 'Ask the dead 'un,' he said, his eyes brilliant and hard. The bird came lower, stooping negligently but with immense power, then soared and backed and stooped again. They could see a creamy throat and an underside ribbed with black. It was a peregrine falcon with a dead bird in its talons. A tiercel carrying to its mate. Twice it stooped over their lane, twice it called imperiously and then made height. Then they saw the she-bird flying from her nest between the pinnacles and heard her scream as she saw them. The tiercel was now high above her, his glides carrying him as though in some immense swing-boat, the she-falcon's bigger wings and lower altitude tending to dwarf and sharpen him. Again he stooped and now, by accident or design, he released his prey, the puffin's blunt head and orange legs swirling slowly in mid-air, its wings ragged in death; and triumphantly his mate swept in to meet it, struck so savagely that the feathers spurted below her, and then unpausingly swung to her station on the precipice.

'With a gun now,' said Darran. He remembered that in Rice's eyes he was a farmer and shepherd. 'Don't want her sort around, killing things.'

Mrs Yorath kicked her foot on a stone. 'And his sort?'

'No hims without hers,' said Darran.

The sun was warm between their shoulders as they climbed a rock-fall. Then the breeze struck on the left cheek, they could see the rosy hills round Llanfair, the cliffs and coves and sanded bays of the mainland, the strait a-glitter, and nearer at hand a clover-coloured rock much worn by the wind. It rose tall and fluted as a church organ, flushed as a rose-window, brooding as a tomb. 'Sistersland,' said Mrs Yorath, pointing. 'The Island of the Sisters. The Graves, they call this part.'

'I've heard it,' said Darran, with the air of one offering a witticism. 'History and stuff.'

Rice wished he would go away. The uneasiness he felt about Mrs Yorath was curiously flattering to him. It would be agreeable and exciting to have her talk to him alone. He was at that romantic and hopeful age when an older and experienced woman gave him interesting notions and at the same time his natural scruples held them decisively in check. He was glad she had left off that grotesque and squeezed-down hat; her hair lay black as nightshade against the pallid neck. As she walked before him he had seen what a strong, lithe, cat-like body she had.

Darran looked about him, his face troubled. 'Where's that dog?' He had sat down on a yellow-lichened stone but now he stood up again. 'I'll be back,' he told them. 'Or if not I'll see you at the house before you go.'

'It's the lambs,' said Mrs Yorath quickly but meaninglessly. She smiled at Rice, one side of her mouth down a little, went rambling towards the rock, the young man respectfully assiduous at her elbow. He's nice, she told herself, he's a gentleman, you can see he's been well brought up. 'Sistersland!' she said dramatically.

'Tell me, please,' he said. 'I like history.'

'I was always a great reciter back home. Oh yes, there was never a harvest festival complete without me when I was a girl. I won prizes in the eisteddfods too.' He accepted these credentials gravely. A proper gentleman, she was thinking. She felt warm and grateful towards him, and something less simple than that, a sensation tinged with contempt and envy, amusement and regard. 'It's not a long story,' she warned him, 'and who knows if it's true?' He saw her adopt the attitude of the child reciter, the fingers of the left hand held lightly in the clasp of the right, the left foot a shade advanced. Only the smile was different, with a trace of self-mockery impossible to a child. 'They say the island's right name is Sisters' Island, Mr Rice. That would be because in the old days two sisters lived here alone. Religious sisters, nuns you might say, who had taken vows never to see any man except their confessor. Nor did he come very often. But one time when he came, and they had been here then years and years it would be, a terrible thing had happened, Mr Rice.' Her eyes grew wide and mock-serious. 'One of them had had a baby. Yes! Well, that made a fine to-do, as you can imagine. They were very cruel in those days, oh, very cruel to women! There was a great court held, the bishop himself came here on a gilded boat, and all kinds of people besides, priests and lawyers and soldiers and who knows what altogether? And the executioner came in a blood-coloured boat straight after the bishop. I suppose,' she said, 'there was a rope ladder hanging there even in those days.'

Her lips stayed parted, her breast rose on a long indrawn breath. 'And then, Mrs Yorath?'

'And then they tried them. They wanted to find out which of them had had the baby, but they wouldn't tell. And they wanted to know about the father, only they wouldn't tell that either. This made the bishop very angry, they say, for he felt such a fool. And then – it's not a nice thing to say, Mr Rice, but you are a gentleman and will understand – they examined them, but that didn't help either, for the doctors said they had *both* had a baby at the same time. So what could be done? Men!' Mrs Yorath said violently. 'Men!' Her smile was a fixed but twisted thing. 'So they drowned them both in the sea north of the island, and they drowned the baby too. They put them in sacks and pushed them out of the boats with a rope tied on them, and when the sacks no longer moved and were floating just under the water they pulled them back in and hauled them up the cliffs like the carcases of ewes, and then they buried them on Sistersland.' He saw tears fill her eyes, she made a wild gesture. 'It was the law, they say. It was justice, they tell you. But what is justice? Who knows about these things? A bishop on his throne or God in the sky? Who knows best of those two what we are? And you can see it on Sistersland today. Look, Mr Rice.' She caught him by the arm, led him nearer the rock. 'Those were the graves, where the stones lie. Isn't it dreadful to think of?'

He shifted weight uncomfortably, couldn't tell how far she was sincere, how far the spectator of her own acting. The cat-like body – he had the disagreeable feeling that she saw him as a small plump mouse. And yet the tears in her eyes were real, the red in her cheeks had not been there so few minutes before.

'They say they put a curse on them, that the graves would never grow green. But someone knew a trick worth two of that, didn't he, Mr Rice? Look at the greenness now!'

He looked at the three oblongs marked off on the grass by rounded fist-size pebbles. Two large, one small. He could think of nothing to say, he was too much the victim of her and his own emotion, and unable to distinguish the true and the false in it. 'How can we know?' he asked. 'How can we know?'

There was a shout from behind them. Darran was coming through the rock-fall, the hang-face dog behind him. 'It's getting on,' he called. 'Time to be moving.' The words were more of an order than an invitation. They walked back to the cottage without much talk, Darran always increasing the pace, and Rice in embarrassed attendance on Mrs Yorath. He wanted to offer her his hand at the awkward places, but somehow she was up and over quicker than he, nor was he at all sure she would not spurn his help. He shook his head behind her, the feline gipsy that she was.

'If the boat's here at four you'd better hurry,' said Darran at the house, and when he had gone inside to collect his knapsack, 'I'm not letting any boatman ashore,' he told Mrs Yorath. 'I've pulled up the ladder.'

'We've got to tell,' she said. 'We are fools we didn't tell him last night.'

'That sissy in there?' he asked her. 'What's it to do with him?'

'The same as with everyone else. They've got to be told, haven't they?'

'It's up to you,' he told her. 'But it's tricky all right. You'd better let me think it out for you.'

'For me? What d'you want to think it out for me for? You keep your thinking for yourself, Jack Darran!'

'It's not me that needs it. So don't go talking that way.'

Rice was coming out of the house again and there was nothing she could say. 'There's one thing,' he began, 'about what I owe you.' Darran chopped his sentence short. 'Ten bob'll cover it.' Mrs Yorath felt angry and humiliated as he took out his wallet and handed Darran the note. But Yorath, she knew, would have done the same. 'I can't come with you,' Darran was explaining. 'Farmer's life, you know how it is. But Mrs Yorath will see you off all right.' Every word, every movement showed impatience to be rid of him. 'Very well, Mr Yorath.' 'And I'm not Mr Yorath!' said Darran explosively. Mrs Yorath's hand went to her mouth. 'I've told you. To my friends I'm Jack. J-a-c-k, Jack! Got it?' Rice nodded, turned his back on him, 'I'm sorry for any trouble I've been, Mrs Yorath. And you needn't come with me, thank you so much.' 'She'll come!' said Darran. 'I'd like to,' said Mrs Yorath, flashing her anger. 'It's a change for me to talk with someone nice, someone with nice manners.'

Darran went indoors without so much as a good-bye, and Rice and Mrs Yorath took the stony path up the ridge, and from there walked to the sea. He made several attempts to sound at ease, but Mrs Yorath was hot with temper at Darran's stupidity, and somewhere in her mind she knew he had said words important and menacing to her, if she could only get them clear. It was no help to have this soft-shelled Englishman at her elbow, half squiring her, half falling into rabbit holes. They were on the cliff above the landing place before she found her good humour. And then she lost it again, felt grey and apprehensive approaching the ladder, horrified to look over the side and remember the shout, the face that fled downwards out of the light, the black shadows below.

'Ahoy there!'

A half-recognized voice came sounding up the cleft, and she stood on the shallow steps cut in the cliff top, gripping the rail, erect, stiff, only her eyeballs moving down. There was a boat there, and two men in it, their jocular faces lifted to her own. She pressed her skirt in between her knees, frowning, wondering frightened. Were there marks on the rock? Could one see what had happened there? But of course, Darran had been there that morning. He was the tricky fellow for the tricky job, and would have attended to everything.

'It's four-fifteen,' called the same voice, 'and, boyo, is it costing you money?'

It was Old Vaughan and his son from Pandy, scamps both, and despite the thirty years between them more like brothers than father and son. Rice was saying the right things rightly, but she was watching the rope fall, hurrying to get him started on his descent before Old Vaughan could come swarming up. For how could she stop him if he decided to come up and see Yorath? But she was harassing herself without need. The Vaughans were joking away down below, and no hand was laid on the ladder before she drew it smartly back up to her.

'Any news on the island?'

Her heart leapt as it had leapt to see the light in Mandred last night. It was another chance to tell their story.

'Any news? I asked.'

'Might be. No, no news.'

The Vaughans were in a hurry. They were already pushing off. 'There's a small bit at home with us. Sheep-stealers down at Hendy's cove. Did you say something?'

'I said you were a dishonest lot on shore.'

Old Vaughan's hard but merry face looked up at her. 'No one on shore, my dear. The master's touch, this was. Well, when you need a friend, remember me.'

'I'd be hard put to it first!'

Rice almost fell out of the boat at Old Vaughan's rejoinder. He would have waved a farewell but Mrs Yorath had already left the cliff top. She had coiled the ladder and started for home, carrying it with her. Half-way there she met Darran. Her temper reared at the sight of him, but before she could speak: 'Guess where I found that dog?' he said. 'Smelling at the pen.' He watched her white face, gave her a knowing look. 'I'll have to move him safer. Good thing you've got me with you, eh?'

She walked on before answering. 'Tomorrow', she said then, 'I'm going on land and tell them he met with an accident.'

He nodded. 'An accident.'

'You saw it,' she said quickly. 'You saw it the same as me.'

'Did I?' He had a way of looking knowing and stupid at the same time. 'I looked up and saw him falling. But you were looked down.'

'What difference does it make where we looked from? Up, down, the story's the same.'

'That's what I say, so long as it *is* the same. But it was rotten luck,' he said, 'that sissy being there last night.'

And indeed she must admit it had been impossible for them to walk in, draggled and debauched as they were, and announce an accident to her husband. 'I looked terrible,' she said, half to herself, and he laughed boastfully. 'I said "last night", remember? All the day I was saying "Tonight".' Her eyes gleamed to think of it. 'Oh,' she cried again, 'I looked terrible!' He laughed, catching at her shoulders, pulling her round to face him. 'And now I'm saying "Now".' 'You are bending me,' she cried, 'you are hurting me!' All her doubts and fears, her memories and miseries, were swirling together like smoke from the neck of a cauldron. Then a copper flame leapt and enveloped her, burning her clear of all save her longing for this treacherous-eyed master who towered between her and the sky, beaked and keeled like the falcon, compulsive as fire. Again he marvelled at her rage to be loved, her raptness, the loud outcry as she felt herself falling, like the orange-legged bird, like the upturned face of Yorath, like the revolving world, through air and smoke and fire into the destruction that proved to be sanctuary, the death that was life.

'What can you be thinking of me?' she asked. She would not look at him, but at the short curved blades of grass, the rooty pattern of earth, the glistering snail-track over the white-veined stone. She grew animal-lazy like a dog on a summer's day blinking once, blinking twice, then closing hot eyes against the sunlight. She narrowed her eyes till the black lashes swept all gloss from the grass blades, reached for his arm and pulled it over her. She fell asleep so quietly that he did not know when.

When she awoke she was alone, but the rope ladder had been left for her to carry to Mandred. She was stiff from the hard ground, tired and chilly. The sun was at half-past six, descending into cloud that looked solid as land above the true horizon. Joy had left her, she grew heavy with foreboding. Her legs ached as she began to walk, the rope over her shoulders pressed harder than his arm as they walked homewards last night, and as her eyes met the cold western sea she had the feeling that she had ceased to live, that her body moved like a hulk in an ocean current, without wish, without volition. And the course by which she had wound to this place, this time? Childhood, girlhood, womanhood, and all the baits that coax us forward – and forward to what? The graves on Sistersland, the mean grey husband, the treacherous lover. For she did not deceive herself about Darran. The more he filled her thoughts, the closer he met her needs and desires, the more certainly he was part of that unfeeling current bearing her onward – and to what?

Her mood had lightened somewhat before she reached the house. Neither he nor the dog was there, so she went down to the cliff well for water, washed the potatoes, put them to bake in their skins. And it was only now that she made the bed, beating up the flat pillows, smoothing the unfresh sheets, picking the quilt from the floor. The loft she would attend to tomorrow.

She had fetched in and milked the cow before he returned carrying a pick and shovel. She heard their clang against the cottage wall before he entered. He nodded at her three or four times, then 'That's that,' he announced. At his heels the dog's face revealed the same ghoulish interest she had seen there the day Yorath buried a sheep dead of sickness. Later he had tried to dig it up.

'What's the matter?' he asked roughly. 'You look like you're seeing things.'

'I am,' she said, 'I am.'

'Then forget it, can't you?' He was ready to make a grievance of it. 'After all I've done for you, you could look a bit more cheerful. It isn't everybody'd have taken the trouble.'

He went on complaining as he sat to his food, and after a horrified glance at the dog she joined him, trying to say what would please him. Her will, even her temper, had deserted her. What happened, happened. What must be, would be. And everything could be put right tomorrow.

'Now,' he was saying, 'this story you want to tell. There's things to settle first. And the first thing', he went on judicially, 'is where exactly were you when it happened?'

'Happened?' she echoed. Because of the dog she had been only half listening, and she did not at first understand that he was accusing her of murder.

III

'I'll come with you,' said Old Vaughan. He leaned forward, tapping her knee under the beer-slopped table. 'I'm always the friend, and never you forget it.'

The bar parlour was full of men. They walked from counter to table chinning their brown pints or set lordly elbows on the bar and blew blue smoke into the blue air. From amidst these last Young Vaughan watched his father with much admiration and a little envy. You can't beat the old man, he thought; and said as much to the quick-nodding little drinker at his side.

'Yorath's wife, isn't she?' asked the other. 'I ought to spit in her beer.' He was the farmer from Hendy's cove.

'Not with the old man sitting there,' said Young Vaughan.

'But I ought to, I tell you!'

'And not with me standing here neither,' said Young Vaughan gently. He had been a boxer in the booths down south for five years. 'I suppose not,' said Jones thoughtfully. He nodded more slowly, like a chess player conceding the loss of his queen. 'Very well, Mr Vaughan, I'll forget it.'

'You'd need some nerve to come pushing in here,' said the broad-backed, tight-busted barmaid. 'If you had feelings.'

'The old man and me could never afford them.'

'You know who I meant. When there's a proper Ladies Only.'

'P'raps she's not a lady only,' said Young Vaughan. He winked at the V of her blouse. 'The nice ones rarely are.'

Old Vaughan let his finger rest. 'Better than waiting in the street,' he told her, 'for a bus to where was it you said?' But she had said nothing, and said nothing now. 'Anything me or the boy could do to help, we'd be very willing.'

'I don't want any help.'

'There now,' said Old Vaughan, 'and me with the mind of an angel.' His finger tapped confidentially. 'And how's life treating you these days, my dear?' His face moved closer, red and merry, notably libidinous. 'Ah, if ever I saw a tall lily grow, it's my friend Mrs Yorath, late of Llanfair.'

She hesitated between annoyance and amusement, felt her face smiling, shook her head. To the onlookers it appeared a game of spar and parry, with Old Vaughan up to his tricks again. Had Yorath been present there would have been an avoidance of him, some hostile hints, and after he left the pub high words and perhaps a blow or two in the street between him and Jones Hendy. But a woman! And the Vaughans strong for her, the old fellow pressing her to another drink, as devoted to his business as a poacher with paste in his cap. Sixty-five as near as made no difference, and strong as leather: say what you would, you had to admire him. And her, all white face and black hair: yes, you had to admire her too.

'If Yorath was here,' said the quick-nodding little drinker, 'I'd spit in *his* beer.'

'If Little Bo-Peep was here', said Young Vaughan, 'you'd twist a lamb's tail.'

'Lambs!'

The uncomfortable word, the vexed tone, carried past the chatter to the pair at the far table. A half silence fell, slurred words from dying sentences, the false brightness of new speakers intent to smother an awkwardness, one loud cracking laugh. 'He thinks he's been robbed,' said Old Vaughan tolerantly. 'They were never good counters down Hendy way.'

Hendy way was where it had started. A tang of burning in the air, the uncertain gleam in the cove, and the two men bringing the ewes and lambs to the grounded boat where she kept watch for them. She again saw the thin, tense back of her husband, felt Darran's fingers laid alongside her neck. A thousand times till then they could have avoided disaster, but from that moment it was squatting on their shoulders. Better, she thought, had we all drowned against the rock: that had been a quick and natural fear. What she felt now was horrible.

Three terrors rose up in her mind. The law, Darran, the dog. The law was the monster which had given Sistersland its name; Darran would not sacrifice a tooth to save another's soul from torture; and the dog's ghoulish mask had not been out of her thoughts all night. Not even Darran's questions had taken *him* from before her eyes.

'Where exactly were you when it happened?' He had changed his tack when it was too late. These were the questions the law might ask: you had to be prepared for them. Of course he believed her – but his shifty eyes undid his open smile. Why, where would she be now without him? 'You fool. You utter fool!' she had cried. In safety! Bored and flat and humdrum, but safe. And yet all was so simple; she could not understand how they came to be in their present plight. He had fallen – anyone could fall from a ladder. And he had been killed – anyone could be killed. Accidents were happening every minute of the day – you could read about them for hours when you collected the papers. Only a fortnight ago there had been a man of seventy who fell from a ladder, not five miles away it happened, while he was painting the rain gutter of his house. Why him and not Yorath? At least, why not Yorath too?

She smiled at Old Vaughan without seeing him, glad that his hand on her knee kept him silent and was her excuse for silence too. 'We all need a friend.' She knew the kind of friend he'd prove to be. 'Yorath's dead, you old turk, and they reckon I did it!' If she leaned forward and whispered it his hand would be whipped away as if from molten iron.

The thought of his change of face should she do this was so comical that all at once she was really smiling. It was only with difficulty that she kept from laughter. It would be wonderful to laugh – not just laugh but scream with laughter – and let everyone present into the joke, so that they might all rock and roll and yell and scream together. Old Vaughan and Young Vaughan, the thin man with the fat moustache, yes, even silly little Jones Hendy with his nodding head and lost lambs.

She shoved Old Vaughan's hand from her knee, looked down at her yellowing frail and the crammed string bag. She was unused to drink, and knew that the little she had taken had loosed her thoughts and might loosen her tongue.

'I'm going,' she said. Her voice sounded loud even to her, and there was a lifting of heads along the bar.

'Quite right, my dear,' approved Old Vaughan in a private murmur. 'Let me carry this heavy frail for you.'

'No!'

The over-resolute monosyllable reached every ear in the room.

'And why not, my dear?' asked Old Vaughan, bland, amorous, persistent as ever.

'Because I'm sick to death of old men, and I never want to see another as long as I live.'

His eyes changed and his red face went a good deal redder, but 'Very good, my dear,' he said and picked up his pint pot. 'Here's luck to the young 'uns, say I.' For the moment he had brought the laugh to his side of the table, and he held to his advantage by picking up her parcels and making a bow as he handed them to her. A minute later she was in the street.

A paved street with shops shambled down to the waterfront. On her left it began to climb a short hill, disappeared past three or four houses into hedges of blossom-sprayed blackthorn. Take that road and in ninety minutes' walking you came to Llanfair, to Yorath's old farm and her own old home. A boy and his girl were climbing the hill, their hands joined and swinging; down towards the sea there were children playing hopscotch on the buckled pavement, and beyond them an old, old woman crossing the road. She began to walk, confused and desolate, crossing the road, crossing a small bright stream by a bridge, taking the field-path south. The light was greying, near her feet she saw every blade of grass distinct from its fellow but in the distance a fine-grained haze smudged trees and fields and hillsides. Sistersland looked tall and near, its cliffs a brownish-black save for one red gleam in the north, where a thin beam of sunlight invisible from the shore touched the falcon's precipice. But even as she looked it dimmed and died. There were gulls flying out to the island; others with a sad and eager cry sought their nests on the main shore. She walked erect, her shoulders squared by the burdens which hung from her hands, her feet moving in the untiring country-woman's fashion, neither hurried nor slow. At a farm a young dog ran out at her, his head down and forward; she felt the glance of his teeth off the rushwork of the frail, but she neither shouted nor paused, and in the same swerve he had rounded her and rushed back in at the gate with pride and fear flaring from his braced bushy tail. Once only she passed anyone, a goat-faced, flat-capped fellow leaning on a stile she had to climb. He watched her with interest but did not lift a hand to help her. She was twenty yards down the path when his 'Good night missis' caught up with her. But she walked on without answering him, the path by this time a sheep-track, green and narrow. The day's heat was long past and streaks of wet showed on her dusty shoes now that she was walking on grass; once or twice fingering sensations on her cheekbones told her that moisture was in the air. Cattle breathed heavily from the neighbouring fields; they browsed with a rich and rasping succulence which reached her noisily through the dewy air. But for the weight dragging at her arms, the hot cords across her palms, she might have been walking in a dream. Confusion, loneliness, even fear, left her. Sometimes she found herself on the edge of thought, but never came to thinking. For a brief while she lived in her senses, saw, heard, smelled the fields and their creatures, felt the earth and air as they did, the rhythm of her limbs, her own weight and motion. There was a salty rime on her

lips when her tongue came out to lick them, a taste of drink
persisted at the corners of her mouth, but she did not link these
facts to her present state. There was a horse licking salt in a field
on some blue day of childhood, a forgotten coloured picture in a
shop-window of a shawl-draped woman on a high stool drinking –
what was it she was drinking? Some foreign word, yes, *amoroso*, a
brown Spanish wine. She saw these things and smiled, as a
dreaming dog sees a hare, yelps and pants but does not wake, loses
the image, knows no regret, no exultation.

A new sound was coming from her right, a soft churning near
the ear-drum. It was the sea, and suddenly the track turned
towards it, across the last unhedged field, through saucers of drab
gravel, to a beach where her feet rattled among pebbles the size of
wren's eggs. Somewhat to her left she saw the shadow of the boat,
the crimson end of Darran's cigarette. She moved through the
pebbles with long slashing strides, balancing her frail and bag,
wishing he would rise and meet her.

'You are late,' was all he said.

'I'd have been quicker if you'd met me,' she retorted. She bent
down to dip her stinging hands in the water, exclaimed at its
coldness. He was steeping the small mast, shaking out the sail.
'That old fool of a Yorath,' he said, 'what d'you think? He let me
pull my heart out last time rather than use the sail. Did it
deliberately too. Well, he deserved all he got.'

The light breeze was still blowing out of the east, but so gently
that inland one hardly noticed it. But here it cooled her forehead,
stroked at her throat, slid over wrists and forearms; Darran
pushed off with the oar, thrust a second and third time at the
shallow bottom, the sail fluttered quiet as a thrush's wing, then
filled and breasted outwards, the dead boat lived on the water, and
lightness was part of them. But not of Mrs Yorath's heart. She
closed her eyes, felt not that the wind sped them from behind but
that some mastering power drew them irresistibly forward,
something on the island itself fetching her to Sistersland and her
destiny.

Darran was speaking to her, and she made herself listen.
'Where've you been all this time?'

'Tomorrow,' she said. 'Now I'm too tired.'

Forty-eight hours ago they had come this way before. The
thought overwhelmed her, then grew unreal. She pulled her coat
tighter to her neck, pulled down the black hat.

'When I say tomorrow,' he complained, 'I get my head bitten off. But that's a woman all over.'

'A woman,' she said, 'yes, I'm a woman.'

This made him laugh out loud. With his left hand to the tiller he leaned forward, fondling her with his right. 'A woman,' he laughed, and the laugh was half a jeer, 'I'll say you're a woman.'

As he laughed she shivered. She felt herself so emptied of warmth and kindness and love that she must cry aloud. 'Be kind to me,' she said. 'Please, Jack, please be kind to me!' She blundered from her seat, the boat rocking under her. 'Hurt me, hit me if you must, only be kind to me!'

He caught at her in alarm lest she go overboard, pulled her to him with a quick change of hands on the tiller. 'Don't cry,' he said, 'there's nothing to cry about.' She pressed herself passionately against him, he felt the hot tears wetting his hand. 'If only you would be kind!'

'You are tired,' he said. 'It's been a long day.' A great unease was growing in him as she wept and lay against him. 'Look,' he said, 'we'll soon be home, we'll have tea and supper and go to bed.' She nodded, choking with grief. 'I'll make it,' he said, 'and you can go to bed at once, and I'll bring it in to you. Better than the Ritz.' He laughed, but not because he was merry. Things were happening he did not want to happen, he was deeper into things than he'd looked for, that old fool knocked off the ladder, and now this. Be kind to me! When had he been anything else? And fool she'd called him. 'You utter fool!' He didn't take that kind of talk, not from women. Besides, they were nearing the island. 'This is the tricky bit,' he said. 'Afraid I'll need both hands from here on.' She sank down, her head against his knee, sick and heavy. Briefly he stroked her shoulder, rubbed his fingers through the hair on her neck. 'Here goes,' he said, and dropped the sail. Instantly the boat slackened pace. She looked up and Sistersland gloomed over them. He began sculling the boat forward into the dark landing place, the lantern once more yellowing the rock, the ledge, the dangling skeleton of a ladder.

'Take the other lamp,' he told her. 'I'll see to everything here.' She climbed with unfeeling feet and jangling nerves, caught at the rail on top, blundered on to the cliff edge. She forced herself to look down, saw nothing to terrify her, only the orange glow of his lantern as he coaxed the boat into her tiny haven. His nailed boots scraped on rock, the ladder tightened, again his shoulders and back heaved broad as a sea-beast, and then he was with her, pulling up the ladder, flinging it round the rail, leading her away to Mandred, to food and sleep and such love as he knew and the hoped-for forgetfulness.

But at Mandred there was nightmare. She knew it at once as she smelled the emptiness of the cottage. 'I'll make the tea,' he began, but 'Where's the dog?' she asked. 'Didn't you chain him?' Her voice was so high-pitched that he whipped round at her. 'He was on the rope,' he said. 'Why?'

She caught up the lantern and ran round to the dog's kennel on the lee of the cottage. A short end of rope hung from the staple, the dog was nowhere to be seen. 'Hoy!' she heard Darran shouting, 'Hoy, Bob, Bob, Bob!' He began whistling through his fingers into the unanswering dark.

'Where?' she cried. 'Where did you put him?'

'The dog?' he asked stupidly.

'Him,' she said. '*Him!*'

'What's it matter tonight?'

'Oh great God,' she moaned. 'Great God in heaven above!'

'What's the matter?' he demanded. He held her by the shoulders, shook her roughly. 'You'll end up in the hatch the way you are carrying on.'

'The dog,' she said. 'Don't you realize what he's up to?'

He loosed her and ran into the house. When he came out he was carrying the shotgun. Cartridges spilled from his fingers as he stuffed them into his trouser pocket. 'Come on,' he ordered. 'Carry the other lantern. It was up at the Graves.'

She had known it all along, though he would not tell her. She hurried behind him, panting and sobbing for a while, and then quiet as a ghost. The deformity of the night was in everything, the blackened grass, the wavering bulk he made before her, the dismal cry of a bird in the unlighted heaven. Soon they were scrambling through the shadowed rock-fall, and she hit her hand deadeningly on a great stone there. He held his lantern high, so that the light stretched upwards into the tall and fluted memorial of the sisters, played weakly over the three pebbled oblongs, revealing the torn turf and scuffled soil of that nearest them, and for a moment the guilt and glee of the disturbed dog before he ran into the darkness. He broke open the shotgun, saw his thumb unsteady on the cartridges, and there was a whispering from Mrs Yorath behind him. He listened but there were no words, only sounds. 'Go home,' he told her. 'He'll come back, and then I'll get him.'

She went on whispering, and this frightened him more than anything else that night. The fluttering lips, the glaring eyes, the hair low on the forehead: 'Get on home,' he ordered her, as he would have ordered an animal. 'D'you want to drive yourself mad?'

'No,' she whispered, and then her voice came low and trembling. 'I *am* mad! And you are mad. We have been mad since it happened.' He meant to take hold of her, but she threw down the lantern, struck with both fists at his chest. 'You asked me,' she said, 'you pretended!' Her face was contorted with cunning and rage. 'But where were you when he fell? Tell me that,' she cried. 'You are so clever, tell me that. Where were you when he fell, Jack Darran? You fool, you no-good, you murderer you, answer me that!'

IV

The boat floated under the cliff, the five faces upturned like pink paper lanterns towards her own white one. She stood once more by the rail, the rope encumbering her feet, her black skirt pressed in between the white unstockinged legs, her arms not folded but crossed over her chest.

'These others,' said Old Vaughan, 'I can't say I blame you. But let me up just for a look.'

'I don't trust you,' she said, grinning down humourlessly.

'And me raised at the knee of a Baptist!' His voice was borne up to her, warm, indolent, suggestive and mocking. 'I see you up there,' he told her, 'as handsome as a magpie in the sunshine of May. Boss at home, did you tell us?'

'I said he was away.'

He accepted the correction lazily. 'So you did, Mrs Yorath, so you did. And it's a nice day for a sail – if only he'd taken the boat.'

'Is it any business of yours?'

'If it was, you wouldn't catch me meddling in it. No, no, it's what I told you, we all need a friend. You need a friend, and Mr Jones Hendy he also needs a friend. Now if I just came up on the island and had a quick look round, wouldn't we all be satisfied?'

'Not me,' said Jones Hendy, his face bobbing up and down. 'I'd have to come and see too.'

'Not that you don't trust the old man?' This was Young Vaughan, his bruiser's eyebrows raised warningly.

'It's her I don't trust,' said Jones loudly. 'And that sheep-stealer she calls a husband.' He appealed to the other two men in the boat. 'I don't want a lot of gab, this way and that. I want my sheep.'

They blurred their words in agreement. 'You see the problem, my dear?' called Old Vaughan.

'There are none of his sheep here,' she said angrily. 'I ought to take the law on the lot of you.'

Old Vaughan stroked his chin, nodding the while. 'Ah, you'd need a friend for that.' He sat looking in turn from the incensed Hendy farmer to the leaning-away figure of Mrs Yorath, so patently calculating his advantage that only his son stayed patient with him.

'The law,' cried Jones. 'I like your cheek!' He stood up in the boat, shook his fist at her. 'Are you going to let us up on the island?'

'Sit down,' Young Vaughan told him. He gave a tug on his coat-ends. 'Sit down, I said.'

Mrs Yorath felt a sudden reckless confidence in herself. 'No,' she shouted, 'I won't let you up on the island. We've managed to keep all vermin off so far.'

'Very proper,' said Old Vaughan. She saw him wink at her. 'But you'll have to let me up, all the same.'

'You!' she countered. 'With my husband away!'

He was pleased by this, she could tell. 'And when will he be back, my dear?'

'I'll post you a letter.'

But he was a hard man to score off. 'Don't you trouble. I'll be calling for it instead. Tomorrow.' And he added enigmatically: 'At the latest.'

All her confidence left her at these words. She thought she had won a battle, but it was only the first skirmish, and even this she was losing.

'Boss gone far?' She did not answer her tormentor, wondering how she had ever seen good nature in the loose and ageing face now quizzing her from the boat. 'Now if I was linked with a bright silver chain like yourself, you'd not find me missing by day nor firing signals of distress by night – eh, Mrs Yorath?'

At his words she was back in the doorway of Mandred, the lantern light blotching the grass, its yellow dying into the darkness above and around. She was listening with her fingers to her mouth, her lips moving, her ears aching. Her hands moved to her head, and the fingers passing over her scalp made a glassy hissing noise among the electric black hair. She desisted, listening for the quiet sounds of darkness, those stirrings and cryings that never cease in nature, and awaiting the gunshot from under the red rock which would signal her release from the worst horror of all. Her skin crept to think of the dog's grin and flashing nails, the backward spurt of turf and pebbled earth. He would be slinking now through the night, at once fearful and exultant, and irresistibly drawn to his vice and his doom. Nothing he could do would save him; his death was now as much part of him as his skin. She shivered. And nothing she could do: the tide set, the waters flowed, and on the breast of the current there were borne the chips and straws and cast feathers of humanity, their passage helpless, their destination ordained. Looking up, she was surprised to see the stars. She had filled her night with such gloom that these brisk glitterers had no place in it. The moon was thickening to the quarter, yellow and smooth as a brook-edge buttercup, but shedding little light. She swayed slowly, feeling her weight flow down the thigh and calf into her broad strong foot, then that growing light and hollow and the smooth shift of balance and power to right and left and right again. It was like standing on a ship's deck, and that ship Sistersland a-roll and corky on the waters. She could not believe that the island was a throat of rock rising from the sea bed: to her it was like a raft at moorings and dragging with the tide. Left and right, right and left: she was smiling, began to rock her head exaggeratedly, remembering the small round lead-weighted toy which stood on the ledge of her grandparents' wall-clock – a two-inch high Dutch woman, clogged, patch-skirted and shawled, and when you tapped her or poked her over with your finger, always the weight in the base rocked her safely upright. Magic it had been, and her grandfather the magician. She saw his white eyebrows, the vertical brown leathern folds of his cheeks, a kind old man he was too, she wished now that –

A double gunshot rattled out of the north, its echo thrown to and fro among the rocks, magnified five-fold by her expectant nerves. She stopped swaying and smiling, stood rigid in the doorway, clutching the jamb. It was as though a lightning flash had been thrown over the sky, and in the flash she saw the dog creep into the lantern light, his eyes white, his wet tongue hanging. She saw, too, Darran crouched beside a rock, the gun thrown forward and up, the finger squeezed backwards through the triggers, a flash and roaring and the dog crumpled on the ground. Then darkness again and silence, only the sound of Darran's nailed boots trampling their way towards Mandred.

But there was no silence. As there had been no lightning. A wild screaming of seabirds burst out of the cliff face. Their fright loaded the air with clamour. There was no rise and crescendo: the first outcry was the loudest. Then the universal panic subsided, so that Mrs Yorath heard not one compelling cry but a thousand notes of grief and misery and fear. Birds in flights and multitudes swept out from the ledges above the dark ocean; she heard wings overhead panicky as heart-beats. Loudest were the gulls, greedy even in their fear, the mewing of terns, and throaty grunts of raven and crow. Then their lament was quickly dying; the older constants of enmity and doubt asserted themselves; the puffin grew anxious about his taloned neighbour, black-backed gulls found a new note of menace in their throats, small birds dropped quietly down from the pulsing wingspreads over-near to them. The cries were now of protest and complaint, they grew thin and brief, the last rooks sounded ruminative of the night's disturbance. It was then she was Darran's lantern moving among the boulders.

She watched the lantern swing and lurch. Soon she could see Darran too, widened and wavering in its light. He came near enough to distinguish the white shell of her face in the doorway.

'You,' he said uncordially.

She stood irresolute. She had no wish to be strong and accusing. Her heart cried out for cherishing and affection, for their quarrels to be forgotten, that she might be weak and trusting and he her stay and comfort. 'It had to be done,' she said, speaking of the dog, glad to commend Darran in any way. 'I'm glad from my stomach you've done it.'

'Blast the dog!'

'It's best over and done with. He was always three-parts wild, that dog.' Her words were a proffered surrender. 'I'm glad he's dead.'

'He's not dead,' said Darran. He broke open the gun, made a show of seeing that it was unloaded. 'He was out of the light like a shadow. He knew! He was disappearing as I pulled the triggers.' He tried to sound unconcerned, but he would not meet her eye.

'But you hit him?' she pleaded. 'He can't live?'

'Missed,' he said shortly. It had been a bad sawing shot, and his ineptitude harassed him. 'I'll get him in the light, bound to. And for God's sake let's quit arguing and get to bed.'

Her day had lasted for eighteen hours, and for much of this time she had been on her feet. Her eyes could hardly force up the gritty weight of their lids. 'Shall I make tea?' he asked. Her answer was a croak. 'No. Only stay with me.' He nodded several times, put his arm round her shoulders. 'It's been a heavy day for us both.' She turned and stood upright in his arms, dull and dead; her head fell against him; if he took his arms away she would fall soundlessly into the dark of damnation that awaited her. 'I'll stay,' he told her. 'Don't worry about things. I'll be here.' She was moving forward by his strength, not her own, collapsing on to the unmade bed, turning her face to the wall, her hand to the solid stone. Sleep submerged her, her legs moved once like a drowning swimmer's, and she did not see darkness march over the lamplight, take command of the room.

That was last night. And here she stood now, shaking her head in the breeze and sunshine of the April afternoon. 'No?' asked Old Vaughan, mistaking her movement. She wondered what he had been asking while her mind roved the hours of night. 'Go on,' he coaxed, 'don't be so hard, girl. Throw us down a blade of grass to chew if you won't let us up to fetch one. You wouldn't refuse even an old ram a blade of grass, would you?' Young Vaughan and the farmer from Hendy were in the tiny haven, thrusting out the island boat. 'That's ours,' she called angrily. His genial satyr's face grinned up at her. 'Taking her in for repairs. Safety first, my dear.'

'Don't you dare,' she shouted at him. 'It's stealing to take the boat!'

'Ah,' he sympathized, 'it's a bad business, is stealing. Boats, sheep, it's cruel when it comes to that.' He poised the oar ready to shove off. 'Sure you don't want to come with us?'

'Leave the boat!' she shouted. If they lost the boat, they lost everything, were at the world's mercy. 'Please leave the boat!'

He cupped his hand round his ear. 'Can't hear you, my dear. See you tomorrow though. At the latest.'

First one boat and then the other was sliding from the landing place out to the sunny green water. For some minutes they lay there, before Young Vaughan and the farmer clambered back into their own boat and payed out the tow-rope to the smaller Sistersland craft. Then the Vaughans waved cheerfully, shouting through funnelled hands another invitation to change her mind and come with them, and the oars slid and dipped and the boats began to bob towards the mainland. Minutes later a burst of laughter came back to her off the water.

'Laugh,' she said bitterly. 'You can laugh. Men!'

But what could it matter through they had fifty boats with oar and sail and motor? Nowhere to go, no one to seek, unless the unchangeable could change, the past be shifted to the future. She stood for a time staring past the boats and the sea to the mainland. No smoke was rising there now; the fires were dead and black. She thought of Darran, and the insolent shiftless thing she had found him to be. She looked down the cliff to the landing ledge. He could have snapped her husband off the rope like an ant off a jerked string. Was that what had happened? If you thought through eternity there was no way of knowing. She pondered his charge against her, and for a moment felt no resentment, did not blame him. And then another memory from girlhood came unbidden to her mind. Her father had a black-and-white bitch which he worked to death by her eighth year. He had never given her a kind word, always the boot or the stick, and refuse to eat that made your stomach turn. And the creature doted on him and on none else. He was the god of her worship, her spirit kindled at him alone. She would leave your own caressing hand to follow his hostile heel, and with eight years of ill-treatment behind her she unquestioningly put her neck in the noose he chose to hang her with once her strength was broken past service. 'No wonder I hated him!' she whispered aloud. But the link was not with her father, but between the black-and-white bitch and herself. And Darran.

She drew no moral, pointed no lesson. Dragging the rope ladder further from the cliff edge, she set out for Mandred after one last glance at the diminishing black boats. How would Darran take this news? She would not be displeased to see more of his cock-sureness knocked out of him, and her smile was a hard one. She was not really the black-and-white bitch after all.

As she came near the cottage she heard him call to her from the stony ridge that sheltered its rear. She dropped the rope ladder inside the garden wall and walked up the earth pathway. He sat up lazily, the shotgun near his hand. 'Seen the dog?' he asked.

'I've had other things to do.' She added: 'They've taken our boat away.'

'Who?' he asked, but she made no answer, just shrugging her shoulders while he cursed the Vaughans and Jones Hendy and all other mainland names handy to his tongue. He came to realize that she was unimpressed by his outburst and ended as abruptly as he had begun. He patted the butt of the shotgun. 'I've hunted everywhere and not seen him. I thought to go up to the graves again. You coming?'

'After I've eaten.'

'I meant that,' he said hurriedly. 'It's what they say: everything's better after food.'

But there was no dog up by the sisters' graves. 'Perhaps I hit him last night? Perhaps he's gone over the cliff?'

'Have you looked?'

'I've done as much as you – '

'More,' she interrupted.

'And for God's sake, why don't you tie your hair up the same as other women?'

He had meant this to hurt. 'Because I'm myself, that's why. It seemed to do the trick with you right enough.' She went on before he could speak. 'Tramping about with a gun under your arm! Loafing about rather, home at the cottage. Are you afraid he'll bite you?'

'Afraid? Was it me screeching like a night-owl up here last night?'

'Was it me', she taunted, 'that couldn't hit a dog five yards away because my hands were all a-tremble?' She shook her fingers as though ridding them of something nasty. 'Or was it Mr Clever Darran did that?'

'Clever was I? Where would you be without me? And what thanks do I get?' She laughed contemptuously. 'You're a bitch!' he shouted. 'And you've always been one. Even with that boy the day before yesterday you couldn't keep your eyes off him.'

'He was a gentleman. He treated me like a gentleman should. Not like you.'

'A gentleman? A big sissy! And swilling beer in every pub in Pandy, while I'm wearing my behind flat down on that beach. My God, Mrs Yorath, what I've taken from you!'

'Go on,' she goaded him. 'Shout your head off if you like. There's no one to hear your rubbish. And there are things I could tell you too, only you aren't worth it and I won't bother.'

'I'll bother,' he menaced. He was beside himself with temper and swept in insults like a swallow among gnats. 'If ever I cursed a day it's the day I first met you and that grey-faced coon your husband and everything living and dead on this cursed island. How did I ever get caught up in it, that's what I ask myself?'

'There's an answer.'

'There was,' he said. 'There isn't now. I've changed.'

He had too. But how? Handsome, spry, and bright as a cockerel in his yellow corduroy trousers and blue-grey shirt, the loose scarlet knot of the neckerchief leaving his throat half-bared, the brown curls and eyes, the full dishonest mouth – how was he changed? She marked the stubble glinting on his cheeks and chin, the sullenness, yes, and the cowardice that warped his face. That was it. Yorath had seen it at once, shrewd grey rat that he was. Most of Darran's selfishness was cowardice.

'I can't think how I didn't see it at once. And ever since it's been under my eyes every day. Where was I when he fell? Protecting me, you said. Tricky, you said. In your own time, you said. And all the time terrified for your poor precious skin!' She slackened her lips in that same mirthless smile. 'Poor frightened Jack Darran! Can't you see where you've put yourself now?'

Fear, impudence and cunning showed in his face. 'Don't say things you'll be sorry for.'

'It was easy. So easy. He was old and tired after showing off all day, and he fell. And you lost your nerve because of the guilt in your heart.' It was a phrase from some childish recitation, she had struck her reciter's attitude. 'Accusing me! And look at you now. You've destroyed what could have been the truth, and what lie can go in its place? For it's got to be known, can't you see? It's got to be known?'

His eyes flicked fast as an adder's tongue. 'Least said for you the better.'

'Jack Darran,' she jeered, 'in my husband's second-best boots at that! Well, if you aren't frightened of the gun, let's go look for the dog.'

He set the shotgun against a rock, peevishly threw cartridges on to the grass. 'You can go yourself.'

She looked at the gun, took a step towards it, but stopped, all resolution draining from her. 'I couldn't do it,' she said pleadingly. 'You know that.'

At her words and action a pleased grin spread across his face. After all then, he was the boss! At once his legs were more limber, his shoulders squarer, and he shook his brown curls. 'Leave it to me,' he told her, his voice juiced with triumph. 'Leave everything to me.' He had moved from resentment to mastery, his fairground good humour was back; he was the gallant, slippery stallion of their first meeting, and she was content that this should be so. 'Me and you,' he said, 'quarrelling' – as though it were the most unnatural thing in the world. 'It's the bad nights we've had. Always we say home and supper and to bed, and always something stops it. Look at me now – I could yawn till my head cracked right off me.' But when he stooped it was as though his limbs slid in oil, he picked up the cartridges in juggling fingers. 'Let's go back,' he said. 'There's nothing that won't be better in the morning.'

No drowning swimmer fights a turning tide. Nothing cleared, nothing resolved, she walked in the crook of his arm. Her eyes were half closed and rarely lifted from the ground. When she stumbled his arm tightened and she felt herself half carried forward. It pleased him to be strong: it pleased her to be weak. The evening had closed in grey and cold: the sky masked and the sea grown metal-dull; on Sistersland the grass and rock had ceased to shine, looked tired and muted. 'The air needs wind,' he said. 'Perhaps the weather's breaking.' Did she nod? The sense of urgency left her; she let her mind grow faded and featureless as the dying day. But it could not last; she grew restive at her invalid-like progress, stiffened her shoulders, began to smile. 'God,' he said, 'you're a fine one!' 'Life's too short for misery,' she answered cryptically, pressing harder against him, turning up her face, her tongue licking over her lips so that he saw them dark and glistening. But when he bent down to her she drew her mouth aside, so that his kiss struck at her cheekbone.

'What are you thinking?'

She turned the question aside. 'You've never called me by my first name, Jack. Never once. How was that?'

'You never told it me. What is it?'

'No matter.' She laughed. 'D'you know what I'd like?' But it was almost a minute later when she answered herself. 'I'd like the fires to be burning. I'd like us to fire the gorse out here too. I'd like the whole world to be on fire and the sea red and shining like a copper kettle. Oh,' she cried, 'I'd like everything to be one big burning flame!'

'I've been thinking,' he told her. 'If I took the boat one night, with him in it, and had weights and rowed out past the shelf, it would be what you said to Old Vaughan and the rest: he'd be gone away, and no one'd know where.' At her hysterical laugh he remembered that they no longer had a boat. 'What's so funny?' he asked angrily.

She shook her head at him, grew calmer. They walked on and the cottage stood before them. 'What's that?' she cried, hand to mouth.

There was a scrambling sound, the fall of tiny stones from the ridge behind Mandred. 'The dog!' he said. 'Running for it again. You wouldn't think he'd know.'

'The guilty always know.'

They felt horror for each other load their shoulders before he pushed open the door of the cottage and she walked in before him.

'Lock the door,' she told him, turning.

'Why not leave it open? If he came back, we'd have him then.'

'Lock the door!'

With a huckster's hand he obeyed her. 'And next?'

She made a gesture of despair and abandonment and he thrust her before him into the inner room.

IV

A chilly grey light was filtering downwards as the boat neared Sistersland next morning. It was an R.A.F. wartime rescue launch bought by an ex-service Pandy sportsman, but she had been set to a modest cruising speed and made very little noise. There were five men aboard her: Senniman the owner, the two Vaughans and Jones the farmer from Hendy, and Rice. Upon Rice embarrassment, and upon Jones suspicion had a silencing effect, and little had been said by any of them as they crossed from the mainland. There were skeins of mist over the water, but the sea was an intense black blistered only, and briefly, by their bubbling wake.

As the light strengthened they were conscious of a rare silence. Soon there would be behind them roosters challenging the sun, the grunts and whistles of awakening farm yards, blinds in the houses pulled back from bedroom windows. In the village doors were opening, dogs were mouching down the street, and from stable and field the horses whinnied. And the dazed twitter of birds would be everywhere. But over the water there was nothing, and Sistersland lay in a greyness of sleep. Then, 'Whee-oo, whee-oo, whee-oo', and a gull went wailing past their heads. As though the cry were a knife the mist was sliced and shredded, a paleness shone out of the water, the cliffs of the island hardened before their eyes. It was day.

'Take her round,' said Old Vaughan. 'There's a place the other side.' He saw Senniman rub at his chin. 'You could take an aircraft-carrier there,' he added.

'Not if she was mine,' said Senniman. 'Still, I can take a baby like this one, p'raps.'

'Even if she was a submarine you could take her in,' Old Vaughan assured him. 'You could drown whales there, except on the Jaw.'

Senniman winked at the anxious Rice. 'Where whales can drown I want no swimming practice.' But he was not making an argument of it. He had spent months during the war running a motor torpedo-boat into hostile corners of the Adriatic, and he was enjoying himself. Sheep-stealers were new game for him, and that for all Old Vaughan's talk he was probably breaking the law took nothing from his pleasure. From what he could hear they had already, well, the only word for it was *stolen* the Yoraths' boat yesterday. But he approved: tactics were tactics. And by mid-morning he guessed they would be carrying off the branded ewes and lambs, operation concluded. A second time he winked at that windy-looking Rice and wondered at his glumness.

'Water,' he laughed and chanted, 'to drown a great damblasted whale!'

The Hendy farmer made a grimace of disgust. He came from another world and generation than these merrily dangerous youngsters back from the war. If the business was serious -- and what was more serious than sheep-stealing? – it should be conducted in a serious manner. You'd no more laugh and sing at a job of this kind than at the communion table. For wasn't the Lord by your elbow at both? That grey old badger Yorath would lose a claw this time; that white-faced boozing whore his wife – he'd have a word for her too. Not that a glass of beer wasn't very good in its place. Perhaps that soft-looking fellow Rice would stand them a round when they reached Pandy? Unhappily they might all be thinking the call was on him. He had his problems, had Jones Hendy, to keep him sour-faced and nodding in the bows.

'On one leg,' said Young Vaughan. 'You'll see me hopping.'

It was he who would make the climb from the root of the Jaw on to Sistersland. 'Piece of cake,' said Senniman from force of habit.

'Piece of rock cake,' the climber corrected him. 'It's like going upstairs to bed,' Old Vaughan explained. 'Once you know the way it's as easy drunk as sober. And he knows the way.'

The Jaw of Sistersland lay on the sea like a split sheep-skull, a long smooth underbone of rock crowned with mumbled tooth stumps. 'Put her alongside the second tooth,' advised Old Vaughan. 'There's six feet of water and no snags. I've seen the whole Hungarian navy anchored here.'

'Ship's insured,' said Senniman. 'Are we?'

Young Vaughan ducked his head and arm through the coil of thin rope, tightened his laces and stepped on to the Jaw. 'Like old times, Dad.' His feet went into rock-notches, sought finger-breadth holds, his arms reached and pulled, and there he was, walking upright and swift over the tooth-tops. 'No weed up there,' Old Vaughan explained. 'People don't realize. You are safer on rough rock than on a wet pavement.' But his eyes were somewhat narrowed, his lips a little bulged, as he saw his son take a long leap over a crack in the jawbone. Sombre long-necked fisher-birds splashed sullenly away from his advancing feet, there were raucous complaints from higher up the cliff, a dank heavy smell of bird-droppings and rock-pool water made Rice pull a face at Senniman. Senniman, unable to see the friendly eyes behind the thick lenses, thought him an owl of a fellow.

A second jump had now fetched Young Vaughan to the last tooth, itself a stubby buttress to the island. He went quickly up this, his toes and fingers took him sideways, and presently he was in a funnel half out of their sight. 'You could do it blindfold,' said Old Vaughan, and probably you could, for the climber was now moving steadily as a man on a ladder. 'I never knew – ' began Jones Hendy, but with 'There's plenty you don't know and never will,' Vaughan silenced him. He was helping Jones (if he *was* helping him) neither for justice nor liking; the mainsprings of his behaviour were his persistent sensuality, a desire to take the last word away from Mrs Yorath, and a slightly cruel interest in the human comedy as he saw it played by others and himself. He had seized the chance to pull the half-unwilling Rice into the expedition; it was gratifying to have a dasher like Senniman taking his orders; and Jones was the excuse for it all. Once his boy was safe on top he'd not have a grey thought: from there on, whatever happened, he'd be in his oils. Already he could see only the legs of the climber, and those from the calf down. He knew what would happen next: he would drag himself into the cleft that ran from the cliff face to the ground on top. He had himself climbed there first as a boy, and what he would never forget was how on that June morning of long ago he thrust his right hand up out of the cleft, seeking a hold for the last lift, blindly groping from cold to hot rock – and how as his fingers closed something cold slithered from under them. It was a snake, grass snake or adder he would never know, for it had slid into darkness before his heart steadied, his fingers dared to close again, and he levered his head and shoulders into the yellow sunlight. He was to tell many what had happened, enlarging on his fright, but he told no one the where of it. He nodded approval of his caution, now in the boat; there were things it paid to keep to yourself. His son's two feet had disappeared; he could smell the fusty inside of the cleft with him; when he closed his eyes he felt again that taut convulsive slipperiness under his hand. Someone else's hand now, someone else's legs, lungs, strength. Things he couldn't do, and things he could do. Now!

As clearly as if he were up there watching, he saw his son's hand grope on the rock, the fingers whiten, the boxer's face in sunshine, the shoulders and chest, the quick scramble out. He pointed silently, the conjuror with an ace up his sleeve, and within seconds Young Vaughan appeared above the cliff, waving then pointing. He would make for the landing place, and soon they would all be on Sistersland. Whereas if Old Vaughan had been vain enough to tell all, by this time there'd be a boulder sealing the cleft and the Yoraths mocking down at them.

'It's going to be a surprise,' he told them. 'I wonder if we'll find the kettle on.' He had not for one moment believed Mrs Yorath's tale of her husband's absence. He began to think out some bland, cruel sentence with which to greet them both.

'He was there all right on Tuesday?' he asked Rice.

'They were very kind to me,' Rice answered shortly. He was coming to feel wretched with hunger and sorry he had been talked into joining them, and he had scruples about gossiping behind his host's back.

'Kindest man in the county,' Vaughan agreed, with a smile for Jones's sour face. 'He'd give you the shirt off his best friend's back. For a pound, say.'

They had backed away from the Jaw, were swinging past the southern cliffs of Sistersland, the mainland full in view as they rode the shallow swell, and soon the gashes in the island's eastern flank flashed darkly past them. They all fell silent. Senniman was intent on his approach to the landing ledge and the dark little haven, but some similarity in the setting was reminding him of the raid on Vidno where he got the spent bullet in his foot. Jones brooded righteously on his lost lambs and whether Senniman would expect payment for his fuel, and who must call for drinks before they parted. Rice was growing excited to think that he would soon see Mrs Yorath again. What a woman she was! And, What a woman! was more or less the substance of Old Vaughan's thinking. He reached out and touched the rope ladder he had borrowed for the day. They were sliding gently in now, the engine sputtered and died, and rope fenders bumped softly. 'Tie her,' said Old Vaughan.

They sat waiting for Young Vaughan to appear on the cliff edge above them and send his white rope snaking down.

Some minutes earlier Mrs Yorath had gone down to the well for a bucket of clean water. The well so-called was really a spring bubbling out a few yards back from the cliff, in a rock square open to the sea. The water fell like a fine white string into a moss-green saucer, carried softly forward and dribbled almost invisibly down to the sea. She propped her white bucket to receive the flow, sat clutching her drawn-up knees till by the sound of it she knew the bucket was full; but when she stretched out her hand to lift it away she saw how a small white worm floated under its surface. With no change of expression she poured everything away, rinsed the bucket, and sat down yawning and rubbing her eyes while it refilled. Tiredness could touch her at any moment these days; there seemed deep inside her a reservoir unfilled, and sometimes she felt her body crumbling into its hollow. I didn't sleep, she thought; hardly a wink all night. But he slept – was still sleeping, or pretending to more likely.

There was a faint chugging in her ears. She shook her head, but it was growing louder, so she lifted her hair and craned forward from where she sat. At once she recognized it as the stroke of an engine, curiously in rhythm with the splashing water and the deepened throb of her heart. She rose cautiously. The boat must be almost underneath her. She crouched, then knelt, crept to the cliff edge, the damp striking through her skirt to her knees. She saw the launch, blue-grey on the grey water, the caps and rounded backs of four men. Yes, that would be Old Vaughan so beetle-like in the stern. Was that his son at the wheel? Her swift anger was succeeded by a great weariness. The boat was passing, it turned off to round the south of Sistersland, but she remained there on all fours, still as an animal and in the posture of one, her head overhanging the cliff, her hands and knees and feet growing from the ground. She saw how the hardness died out of the rock the further down it went, till before it met the water it was velvet and ruddy as a flower. To a faller it would be as a rounded cushion. Not that one would fall on rock. The cliffs here were wave-mouldered at the base, her eyes were over water; to fall would be to fall to lightlessness, through water deeper than the bay was wide. The wind rushing white past your head, the dark leap of water subsiding, then the long glide to quiet and rest and forgetfulness.

The boat was out of sight. She thrust herself back from the cliff and rising to her feet smoothed absent-mindedly at her wet skirt. The fine stream raised a lip of dark water in the middle of the bucket, from which wavelets were forced out to its rim, to topple invisibly down its chipped outside. Lifting the bucket she sent its surplus splashing out, then with her left hand wetted her dry mouth. She climbed up out of the rock-hollow and saw a man's back disappearing southwards between two boulders.

The sight was so natural and yet so impossible that for a moment again her thoughts continued along their present troubled track. But a man! Here, on the island! She stood staring at the boulders as though expecting him to reappear; then her mind filled with a picture of the boat under the cliffs, its crew waiting for this deadly visitant to stand black against the sky and fetch them up to join him. She had the animal sense of great danger drawing near; but like the braver animals she felt little fear, and like them she did not look past the next few hours. She recognized him now: it was Young Vaughan she had just seen making for the landing place. Well, his father was a fish she could play for a long time before the line broke. If Darran kept his head, and above all if he left things to her, all would yet be well. And the sooner the meeting the better.

Back at the cottage she shouted into the inner room: 'Get up. There are men on the island.' She could imagine his gape of amazement, his wonder whether he had heard aright. Soon he was in the doorway, barefooted, stuffing his shirt into his trousers. 'What? What d'you say?'

'I said you had better get dressed. There are men on the island. So don't say there can't be.'

The words had shaped in his mouth. Forbidden them, he dragged back a chair, sat slouching over the table, his wits thick with confusion. 'Who are they?' he asked at last. 'What are they here for?'

'For the sheep that were stolen from Hendy. Nothing else at all. You understand?'

'Leave it to me,' he assured her. 'Is it the police?'

'Anyone can tell you're a foreigner! What would they want poking in for? Now, listen.'

But his confidence was back inside him. The police were one thing, these country lumps another. 'It's tricky,' he said, 'but just you leave it to me.'

Tricky! It was his favourite word, and might yet be his epitaph. She considered him so long and so silently that he wanted to hector and shout at her. 'No,' she said at last, 'it is you who must leave it to me. The less you say, the better it'll be for everybody.'

He looked up aggressively. 'See here – '

'No,' she repeated, 'it's you must do the seeing. And there's not much time.' She began to talk and he perforce to listen. 'Just what I was going to say,' he told her from time to time. 'You took the words out of my mouth. And no kidding, it's tricky.' He was so affable and approving that she wondered what stupidity could be hatching under the brown curls and side-burns. 'I'll shave,' he announced at last, grandiloquently, and when next she saw him he had a clean red neckerchief at his throat and was wearing Yorath's polished market-day boots.

Her courage sank. Had she wasted her words on him? 'Keep out of sight,' she told him. 'Didn't you agree to? It's better if you don't have to be seen.'

'What's the matter with me?' he asked suspiciously. 'Have I got sheep-rot or something? Besides, I've been thinking.'

The shift in his eyes warned her that he did not trust her to put a case out of his sight and hearing. Great God, she thought then, did he really shake Yorath off the ladder? Could it be true after all? His delays, his burying him, the mystery where no mystery should exist – was that the explanation? His accusation of her, his embraces – she stared at him with such detestation, such malignancy, that he threw his fists before him, guarded his eyes. No accident at all – plain murder! And his thoughts were running the same course. You had only to see her this minute to know whether she could do it or not. Any doubt he'd ever had was lost now. Well, she could kill the old fool ten times over, but she couldn't throw the blame on him. No stoat watched a rabbit as he'd watch her from now on. After all he'd done for her, keeping his mouth shut, hiding Yorath, swallowing insults – but he was getting good and frightened. There'd be a lot of explaining to do if the wrong story came out first. Everyone to his own troubles: he had enough of his own and to spare. 'I've been thinking,' he repeated. 'And I don't like my thoughts.'

'In your boots I wouldn't neither.' He could not stop himself glancing down. 'With all you've got on your mind!'

At that moment they both heard voices. 'Keep quiet, you'd better!' she menaced, and hurried out and looked up to the ridge. Old Vaughan and his son and Jones Hendy were staring down at the cottage, with Jones's tongue a-wag at the roots. Old Vaughan at once waved his hand, his face beaming with what might have been pleasure and goodwill, and she waved briskly back. 'As fresh as the lily on its stalk,' he called to her gallantly. 'Top of the morning to you, my dear.'

He was quite ready to spend time in banter, but 'Cut the jabber,' said Jones sourly. 'We've found the sheep.'

'Then you've found what you came for,' she snapped back at him. 'So there's nothing to stop you sneaking off as quiet as you landed.'

'Not till I've had a word with that husband of yours.'

She ignored him, turned to Old Vaughan. 'He's not here. I told you so.'

'So you did, my dear. Quite right, my dear.' A minister couldn't have been more unctuous. 'And if it wasn't that we found the boat here we'd believe you.'

'That?' she asked. 'I'm surprised at you, Old Vaughan.' A smile was pulling down one corner of her mouth and he knew it was meant for him alone. 'Is there a law against having two boats on an island?'

'It's a question,' he admitted. 'And no doubt there's an answer.' He looked casually round the front of the cottage. 'Where's the dog with you? Gone with the boss, I wonder?'

Her voice stayed level, even playful. 'You want to know too much,' she chided.

'Only as a friend, my dear.'

'And I could do with a friend all right, with a sneak thief like this one on the island.' As though her attention had been unwillingly drawn to the Hendy farmer, she asked: 'And what's all this I hear about sheep – and stealing?'

Her tone combined innocence and indignation so nicely that Old Vaughan's head-shake was less by way of reproof than appreciation. 'Just a matter of a mixed mark,' he explained. 'It can happen in the best behaved flock. Only Jones here plans to take them back home with him.' He grinned at her, and still she could not determine whether he was friend or foe to her. 'But if they swim out the second time and climb the cliff, we reckon you can keep them, eh, Jones?'

'I want to see that Yorath,' he answered. 'I ought to close his eye for him.' He raised his voice and 'Oi!' he shouted towards the cottage door, 'come on out, you skulker, before we drag you out.'

'Game as a bantam,' Young Vaughan praised him. 'And very nigh as tall.'

'You shut your big mouth,' said little Jones. 'It's my sheep's gone, not yours. Come on out,' he bawled, 'and don't be wearing your wife's petticoats when you do.' He began to walk towards the doorway, but Mrs Yorath was quicker than he. 'You would, would you!' Old Vaughan watched her admiringly. What a woman! What a fury, what a flood, what a lightning-storm she'd prove. Blow, he thought, if I was thirty, even twenty, years younger, blowed if I wouldn't run off with her. He eyed her as an old dog gone soft in the tooth eyes a marrow-bone. Never too late to try. But he was laughing at himself inside.

What would happen now? Jones was hopping with rage and a sense of his ridiculousness. Why, he was hardly up to her shoulder-bone and mean-built as a squirrel. The savageness was leaving her black eyes and red mouth; she was ready to laugh at the little jumper in front of her. 'Take him away, Old Vaughan,' she cried triumphantly, 'before I do him a mischief. Him and his sheep – take them off the island, I tell you.'

'I'll do that,' Old Vaughan promised, 'but isn't it time for our cup of tea?'

'And I'm the boy to put the kettle on,' said his son, stepping briskly past the two of them. He had seen a shadow cross the window of Mandred.

'Don't you!' cried Mrs Yorath, savage again. Grinning, he dodged away from her finger-nails and was running in his doubles when Darran lounged with an affected and insolent carelessness into the doorway. Never had he looked more the bright peacock, the treading bird of spring. 'Looking for someone?' he asked.

Old Vaughan swallowed surprise and chagrin in equal doses. 'If so, we haven't found him.' He saw that he had been made to look much of a fool for the second time, and that the account of it would lose nothing in Jones Hendy's telling. Still: 'My friend Yorath not at home then?' he asked in a face-saving way.

Darran adjusted his neckerchief, looked from his questioner to Mrs Yorath. It was time to show them his mettle. 'Who's the nosy old parker?' he asked.

Old Vaughan checked his son with his arm. 'I'm middling old, and I'm middling nosy, but my name's not Parker. Though that's neither here nor there.' His nod gave best to Mrs Yorath. 'We'll be going.' But he had the usual card up his sleeve. 'Light a bonfire,' he said softly, 'when you want the boat.'

'I tell you Yorath's inside,' said the Hendy farmer excitedly. 'What are we wasting time for?'

'We'll be going,' said Vaughan for the second time. 'For any good we are doing here.'

But once more voices sounded on the ridge behind the houses, and when Darran and Mrs Yorath looked away from each other it was to see Rice and Senniman hurrying down to them. As she saw his round face and flashing lenses and his hand held out in cheerful greeting, Mrs Yorath felt the island move beneath her, lift again with the tides. Visibly she swayed forward, as she heard his voice thin and distant. 'Good morning, Mrs Yorath. It seemed a good chance to call.' But he abandoned this feeble sentence when he saw Darran in the doorway. 'Hello, Mr Yorath.'

A complete silence fell upon them all as he turned to Senniman and Old Vaughan and said : 'Mr Yorath was very kind to me when I was on the island. So was Mrs Yorath too.' He could not understand why Mrs Yorath should turn so still and pale and Yorath so red and flustered. 'So I thought,' he blundered on, 'well, you see, Mr Yorath – '

'Don't call me that,' said Darran. 'Haven't I told you?'

'Mr Yorath, eh,' said Jones Hendy. 'So it's you stole my sheep, is it? I ought to dab your eye.'

Old Vaughan looked at his antics wearily. 'You and your sheep. You've got them back, haven't you? We'll be going.'

'No,' he replied, 'I haven't got them back. There's a third ewe with her lamb somewhere.' Everyone except Senniman knew that he was lying, that he assumed there were other stolen sheep with disguised marks on Sistersland, and was determined to exact a levy. 'Round them up, the lot of them,' he called excitedly. 'Where's your dog? Fetch them in. I won't be robbed.'

'There's a dog up by the graves you showed me,' said Rice. 'He's played havoc with one of them, I'm afraid.'

He looked at Mrs Yorath and then could not look away. Her face was past whiteness; it had the hinted blueness of thin milk. Her lips were narrow and bloodless; her eyes were three-parts closed, their rounded lids purpled. He thought she could be seeing nothing, but was wrong. She was seeing the heave of the ground before her; where the air should be, between her and the grass, there was water undulating, and grinning through this water was the mask of the dog, and further back, hardly to be seen, the upturned face of her husband. Everything that was said came to her as from beyond a high and stifling wall. 'Are you ill, Mrs Yorath?' a voice was asking. 'Would you like to lie down?' That was the owl-eyed Rice: he had always treated her like a lady. 'Are you ill, Mrs Yorath?' This was a whining imitation by Jones Hendy. 'Shamming she is. Can't you see?'

'No,' she said, 'I'm not shamming. I'm not ill.'

She saw the backs of men, Old Vaughan, Young Vaughan, Senniman and Jones, walking away from her, walking up through Sistersland. Darran was with them, talking, waving his arms a lot. Where was Rice? Little blink-eyed Rice. He came trip-footing out of Mandred, fetching her a cup of cold water. 'Please drink it,' he begged her. 'You looked so white.'

She drank several sips to please him, forcing each sullen drop down her constricted throat. 'You are a good boy,' she said then. 'Whatever happens, you are a good boy.' He would prefer it had she called him a man but she was snatching at his arm, hurrying along with him after the others. He was still carrying the cup in his left hand and after some paces he threw out the water and let it dangle from his little finger. He felt the foolishness of this acutely but had a scruple about throwing another person's property away. He was hungry too and strongly affected by his closeness to Mrs Yorath. It was hard for him to realize that she thought of him, if at all, as a kind of walking stick.

They had passed the boulders, up and through the falcons' defile, and as they threaded the rock-fall there was the hammered pewter of the sea, and beyond it the rose-coloured hills which shrouded Llanfair. And glowing softly before them was the clover-hued fluted tombstone and the graves of the sisters, and nearer still the standing men and the dog rubbing against Young Vaughan's legs. 'Get out of it, you carrion!' said Young Vaughan, and bent over dusting his trousers as from something impure. The supple cat-like body wrenched free of Rice's arm; he felt denuded of warmth and weight and intimate softness as she stepped away from him, as though she were his own flesh.

'That's right,' she cried, catching at Young Vaughan's word. 'The dog's a carrion feeder. We had to bury a sheep here. Isn't that it, Jack?'

But Old Vaughan too was watching Darran. 'A sheep, you say? A sheep you stole, and it died on you, and you buried it – would that be it?'

'Might be one of mine. From the first minute I knew he was a sheep-thief,' said Jones Hendy.

'Yes, it's a sheep,' said Mrs Yorath. She found difficulty in speaking. 'I've said so. And it was ours.'

Old Vaughan had the pleased feeling of a gambler with an honest hand. There was a sheep buried there, and what surer than that it had been stolen? 'In that case,' he asked blandly, 'what are we bothering about?' He watched the smile breaking outwards through her eyes and mouth, Darran's childish elation. 'Though since we are here, and just to stop a lot of old gossip – ' He turned to Young Vaughan. 'Dig her up, son. It won't take two minutes.'

'No!'

She had almost growled the word. There was nothing of a smile on her face now. 'For my part I wouldn't bother,' said Old Vaughan. 'It's only to satisfy Jones Hendy here. Dig her up, I said.'

'No!'

Her cry was so frightful that Young Vaughan did not move to obey. 'Leave it alone,' said Senniman curtly. 'You've got your sheep, and let's get out.' He looked towards Rice, who nodded like a little white owl.

'Dig her up,' said Old Vaughan, unmoved. 'No one need stay who don't want to.'

'No!'

Old Vaughan flung his spiked stick to his son, motioned him on. 'No,' sobbed Mrs Yorath, and Senniman and Rice stopped in their going, so disproportionate and terrible was her plea. 'Oh no, no, please no!' She caught at Darran's arm, shaking him violently.

'Stop them, Jack, can't you?' But he had caught her infection of terror, his face was blurring and breaking as he saw Young Vaughan prise up a strip of turf and kick and curse at the sniffing dog.

'Don't,' he begged. 'Don't do it!'

It was as though they then all knew the truth together. Their stiffened faces, their silence, their out-turned palms, spoke their question.

'It's Yorath,' said Darran. He sat down, holding his head.

'Tie that dog,' said Young Vaughan, 'or I'll kill him!'

'An accident,' whispered Mrs Yorath. 'There was an accident. On Monday night.'

Her eyes and Darran's were on Rice. And his were on them, seeing again the couple lurching into the doorlight, the man flushed, sweaty and exhausted, the woman with her bruised mouth and half-closed eyes, the hair snaking from under the grotesque gipsy hat, the stockings draggled about her stumbling feet. It was as though their guilt still reeked from them; they saw his nostrils twitch, his throat work as though he would vomit at the memory of it.

'An accident,' she said again, weakly.

'No,' cried Darran, sick at what he had read on Rice's face. 'I don't want her telling lies. It was she did it. I did nothing!'

'No,' said Mrs Yorath, and her words could hardly be heard; 'he was the one, but he blamed me.'

The shout and the strength and the heart had gone out of her. She had known all along that it must end this way in disaster. When Yorath whirled downward off the rope she had gone whirling after him. Perhaps the fall had begun before, the day Darran came on a chance to the island, the day she married Yorath, the day she first came squalling into the light.

She closed her eyes and the island at once began to rock under her, now up, now down, rolling slowly right, then left, all Sistersland afloat on the tide. Voices spoke, Darran's full of hate and fear, frantic with explanation, Rice slowly and with self-loathing, while from his excited tone the Hendy farmer's face must be as ghoulish as the tied dog's. For a time their voices beat vainly on her ear, all babel and discord. Then she heard Old Vaughan's bass silence them, even Darran's voice cracked to an end, someone had taken her arm, and she was stumbling forward with footsteps before and behind her. She saw the ground through lids so narrowed that sometimes her lashes blackened and blinded her. Surely only minutes separated her from the time when she had stumbled this way before, borne up by Darran's arm, her mind grey as the evening? She opened her eyes. In front walked Old Vaughan and the Hendy farmer, and behind them Darran and the dog cringing on a cord. It was Young Vaughan who bore her gently but unfailingly forward, and last of all came Senniman and Rice. Rice looked ill and hung his head as she turned round. She shook off Young Vaughan's hand and walked giddily by herself till they reached Mandred. The sun was striking clear of the morning's clouds. For April it would be a hot day.

'You must come with us to Pandy,' said Old Vaughan. 'Yes, both of you.'

'Why me?' begged Darran. 'It's her you want. I did nothing.'

'Except shake him off the ladder,' said Mrs Yorath. The lie was so natural an explanation of what had happened that as she spoke she *saw* it happen. And her listeners saw it too, all save Rice, who could swear to the guilt of them both. 'And then bury him.'

'Let it wait,' said Old Vaughan.

She was without hat or coat, her feet in the black shoes were naked and white. 'I must dress,' she said, 'I must change.'

'You aren't going to a wedding,' said the Hendy farmer.

She saw Senniman clench his fist. 'Yes, you go and dress,' Old Vaughan agreed. He followed her as far as the inner door, spoke too quietly for the others to hear him. 'I'm no friend of this Darran, remember. I believe you he did it.' Then he closed the door upon her.

She was to walk to the landing place with Old Vaughan, Senniman and Rice. The others he told her would stay on at the cottage. No one had anything to say till they reached the cliff edge and there paused. 'In bad weather,' said Old Vaughan, looking down at the tied launch, 'you can go a month or six weeks and never get a boat on or off.' Senniman was scrambling down the ladder. He waved and it was Rice's turn. 'Well, my dear, are you ready?' asked Old Vaughan.

No one could know how the island had become a raft beneath her feet, and how it swayed on the water with the motion of the falcon in air. No one could know all the things present to her mind at the same time. There was Darran who would swear her life away like the cowardly fool he was, and how uselessly she had sworn his away in return; there were the sisters who had died so long ago to give the island its name; there was Yorath's face reeling out of the lamplight, and the puffin tossed in mid-air to the tiercel's mate. There was the grin of the dog, and for the first time there was Yorath the dead husband so horribly bestowed that she must scream to think of him.

As she must scream to think of Darran and the dog, the sisters and herself. Only the deep dark waters could stifle that screaming and let her forget.

To the men below, her falling body was ragged and black as a shot crow's. Breathless above, Old Vaughan heard the crunch of her bones on rock. He did not trust himself to descend the ladder till long after Senniman's gesture showed him she was dead, and even then he stood unhelping while Senniman with Rice's help carried Mrs Yorath aboard and hid her under an oilskin.

'One morning,' he mumbled at last, 'this Darran will be wishing he'd jumped with her.'

But without his son he was only half the man, and all three of them realized it together. Senniman signalled to Rice, whom he was coming to approve, and neither of them answered him. In a moment the engine roared between the cliffs, so that Mrs Yorath's oilskin leapt and trembled, and soon they were out hitting the green water hard, while the gashed red cliffs of Sistersland fell foam-sped from their stern.